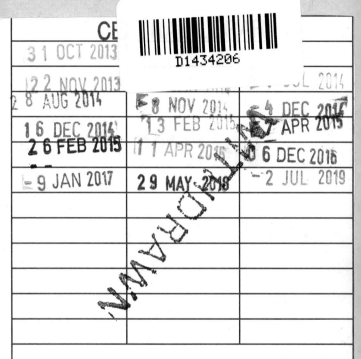

THE AGE OF ZEUS

JAMES LOVEGROVE

First published 2010 by Solaris
an imprint of Rebellion Publishing Ltd,
Riverside House, Osney Mead,
Oxford, OX1 0ES, UK

www.solarisbooks.com

ISBN: 978 1 906735 68 5

Designed & typeset by Rebellion Publishing

Printed in the UK

*This novel is dedicated to five
inspirational English teachers:
Jill Daniel, Chris Brown, Peter Holmes,
Barry Webb and Michael Gearin-Tosh.*

PROLOGUE: CORSICA

FINALLY THE MONSTER was at bay.

It had been flushed out of the forest. It had been hounded downhill, bullets thudding at its heels and smacking into the trunks of oaks and other mountain broadleafs on either side of it. It had been shepherded by gunfire into the village and driven along the streets. At last it had been corralled in a cul-de-sac with high, ancient walls on either side.

Cornered, panting, torso lathered in sweat, the monster turned.

Two of its pursuers were approaching from the open end of the cul-de-sac. Above, in the upper storeys of the stone-built houses, shutters cracked opened and villagers peered out. Their faces were fearful but hopeful. The monster had been terrorising the Corsican interior for months, killing at random. Now it was being terrorised itself. The villagers were eager to see the monster get its comeuppance. Long overdue.

But the monster was still dangerous. Just because it was trapped, that didn't mean it was helpless. It was, after all, the Minotaur – seven feet tall and 400lbs of hyperdeveloped muscle and skin-straining sinew, with the strength of several oxen. Lowering its head, the Minotaur fixed its blood-red eyes on its foes and pawed the ground with one foot. Breath rattled from its nostrils in short, thick gusts.

"Tethys, Hyperion. What is your status?"

Sam did not take her gaze off the Minotaur – specifically, not off the pair of huge horns that were now pointing towards her like ivory spears.

"Hyperion, Tethys. Mnemosyne and I are in range of target. It's about to charge."

"Do you have line of sight?"

"Roger."

"Do you have a clear shot?"

"Roger."

"Then what are you dicking about for? Take it."

Sam raised her recoilless .45mm submachine gun. It was boxy but lightweight, a skeletal weapon. Blisteringly effective nonetheless.

The Minotaur saw it, understood its purpose. It was familiar with guns. It knew what they did.

In those red eyes Sam saw the flash of comprehension, and something else. She couldn't be sure, but she thought it looked like resignation.

Which was impossible. The Minotaur was an unthinking creature, a mindless force of destruction.

There was nothing in that bull head but malevolence and the basic animal cunning needed to survive.

Or so she'd been given to believe.

The Minotaur couldn't know that it was about to die. Could it?

"Tethys?" Hyperion's voice. "Do you copy? I said take the shot."

Sam's finger curled round the trigger.

The Minotaur bent low, tensing. It would charge, for all the good that would do. These armour-clad enemies were like nothing it had come up against before. It knew it was outclassed. For the first time in its life the Minotaur was staring defeat in the eye, and defeat's shadow, death. But it would not give in meekly. That was not in the beast's nature.

"Tethys?" said Mnemosyne. She had her coilgun aimed at the monster's centre of body mass. "Sam? What are you waiting for? This is our chance."

"Tethys!" barked Hyperion over the comms net. "Why am I not hearing a kill-shot?"

The Minotaur was ready, Sam could tell by its posture. One last attack, a final act of defiance against the inevitable.

"Mnemosyne," she said, "I want to try and take it alive, if I can."

"What?" said Mnemosyne.

"*What!?*" echoed Hyperion. Sam's transponder sensor was registering his presence nearby, lower in the village, 200m southeast and closing. She had to do this before he got here. Hyperion – Ramsay – would have no qualms about making the kill. This was not any kind of retrieval op. This was supposed to be an execution.

"I'll use the stun-dusters," she said to Mnemosyne.

"You're crazy. Why?"

Sam couldn't say why. She wasn't totally sure herself. "Trust me. Please?"

Mnemosyne left a moment of silence to convey doubt. Then she said, "All right. Go on." She firmed her grip on the coilgun. "But I'm keeping this trained on it at all times."

"Cronus gave us nonlethal offensive capability for a reason," Sam said, fitting a pair of ridged metal knuckledusters onto her gauntlets.

"Let's hope the reason wasn't to kill ourselves," Mnemosyne replied.

Sam grunted. Already, a little over a month after the commencement of operations, two Titans were dead. Today at least one more could be about to join them, and this time it would be their own fault. *Her* fault, in fact.

Abruptly, the Minotaur charged.

Sam braced herself. Mnemosyne, meanwhile, stepped back and took aim.

Hyperion was yelling, "Don't be stupid. Kill-shot! Motherfucking kill-shot!"

The beast came fast – so fast – barrelling at them like a runaway goods van.

Sam knew that if she fucked this up, it was all over.

Then don't fuck it up, she told herself, and ran to meet the monster.

PART 1

THREE MONTHS EARLIER

1. THE CHICAGOAN

THERE WERE TWO of them waiting on the quay: Sam and
the man she had first encountered a couple of hours ago
on the train, the man who'd been carrying an invitation
like hers. She had spotted him in the buffet car as she
was returning to her carriage from a trip to the toilet.
He was ordering a cheese sandwich and a "club soda."
African-American. Tall. Well put together. Nice, firm
buttocks. Standing straight-spined, so much so that
everyone around him seemed to slouch by comparison.
Chicago accent? Yes, Chicago. Chewy on the syllables.
He was very handsome; in particular she'd liked his
nose. His nostrils were naturally flared, a sign of self-
assurance and the right kind of pride. And while he
waited for the woman behind the counter to fetch his
food and pour his drink, he'd taken the invitation out of
his pocket to inspect it, doubtless not for the first time.
Identical to the one Sam had in her handbag, printed

on snowdrift-smooth card in an elegant formal font, the kind of thing you might expect to receive from the host of a truly classy party. The Chicagoan had frowned at it, shaken his head, then tucked it away again. In the time he'd spent studying the invitation Sam could have gone up to him, produced her own, said something like "Snap" or "You've shown me yours, now I'll show you mine," something coy and wry like that, and introduced herself. But she hadn't. She'd just slipped past the man and gone on to her seat, and the train had continued rumbling on its way, towards the terminus from where she was to catch a taxi to the coast, to this stony little port town, this quay.

The Chicagoan was now sitting on a mooring post. He had his mackintosh collar turned up all the way to his chin and was huddled in on himself, looking miserable in the damp, bitter wind that was gusting onshore. It was a freezing early-January day. Sea and sky appeared to be in competition as to which was murkier and more tormented. Gulls plodded along the slick stones of the harbour wall, beaks to breasts, feathers ruffled.

Sam stood off at a distance from the man, sheltering in the doorway of a fish and chip shop which according to the sign hanging in its door was open but looked very firmly closed. She knew the Chicagoan had clocked her and had identified that she was there was for the same reason he was – both of them answering the same oblique, enigmatic summons. The small suitcase at her feet gave the game away. He had an item of luggage too, an overnight bag with wheels and an extendable handle. But he seemed to respect the fact that she didn't want to strike up a conversation with him, at least not just yet.

Out of the corner of her eye Sam spied a group of people approaching along the main harbourside street. More invitees? No, a young couple with two kids, one of them in a pushchair. Winter holidaymakers. The adults were bent forward against the wind, and the face of the older child, a boy of eight or nine, was one big scowl – angrily baffled as to why his parents had insisted on dragging him outside in such foul weather when he could be warm indoors with the TV and his Nintendo. The baby, by contrast, was snugly bundled up and blissfully asleep.

They passed by Sam on their way to the tip of the quay. She nodded to the parents and deliberately didn't look at either of the children. Especially not the baby. The family returned soon afterwards, and with grim jollity the father remarked to her, "Bracing!" She nodded again, and this time couldn't prevent her gaze straying to the sleeping infant.

Just a child. Just somebody else's child.

But so small. So serene in slumber. So chubbily perfect.

Sam's throat caught. Her gut knotted. She felt as if she were plummeting in an express elevator.

Her counsellor had told her there would always be moments like this. However much time went by, the feelings would never fully go away and would sometimes catch her unawares. She simply had to bear it, work through it. The moment, like all moments, would pass.

She focused on the coldness of the air, the salt tang of the wind, the rank smell of fish and cooking fat that emanated from behind her, sensations from the present, her immediate surroundings, reality, now.

The past belonged to the past.

Gradually her breathing returned to normal, the dizziness abated, her stomach unclenched. She was herself again.

A small wooden-hulled fishing smack came chugging into the harbour. It drew up alongside the quay, and the captain stepped up to the gunwales and called out, "Bleaney Island. Any here for Bleaney Island?"

Both Sam and the Chicagoan went over to the boat, and the captain helped them aboard.

"You'll be the last two then," he said. Ruddy-cheeked, bushy-sideburned, twinkly-eyed, he was the living epitome of a salty old fisherman.

"If you say so," said the Chicagoan. "How many others have there been?"

"Ten all told. Three trips I've done today, there and back. Why you couldn't all come at once I don't know. But then what do I care? I'm getting paid by the journey, and good money too!"

He started up the engine, brought the boat about, and soon they were pulling out of the harbour, onto the open sea.

Other than the wheelhouse, which had room for the captain only, there was no cover on deck. Sam sat on an upturned plastic crate while the Chicagoan stood, hands in pockets, peering ahead to the horizon. He looked at ease, comfortable despite the smack's dipping and yawing, his legs bent slightly to help him ride the swell.

Eventually he turned to Sam.

"'Bout time we met," he said. "Can't go on ignoring each other for ever." He stuck out a hand. "Rick Ramsay."

"Sam Akehurst."

They shook. His grip was tough, gnarled, tight.

"I noticed you on the train," he said.

"You did?" She couldn't mask her surprise.

"You're hard not to notice." His eye roved; returned. "When I was buying that goddamn awful sandwich made of cardboard and rubber. How do you Brits eat that stuff?"

"We don't," Sam replied. "Only tourists are daft enough to try."

Rick Ramsay grinned, dazzlingly. "Touché. That's when I spotted you, anyways. And you did your darnedest to ignore me."

"In your dreams, Casanova."

"Whatever. So what's going on? What's your take on all this?"

He didn't have to specify what he meant by *all this*.

"I have no idea," Sam said. "All I know is what it says here." She took out her invitation, which read:

MISS Samantha Akehurst,

You are hereby invited to attend a gathering which may lead to a proposition advantageous to yourself.

Your personal circumstances are known to me.

Your opportunity to seek redress has arrived.

The invitation was unsigned. A date, location and suggested travel arrangements were printed on the reverse. A cheque to cover costs – generously – had also been enclosed in the envelope.

"Yeah," said Ramsay. "Fancy, huh? I had to look up 'redress' in the dictionary. I thought maybe it had something to do with drag queens."

No, you didn't, Sam thought. *You're a damn sight smarter than you're letting on.*

"Tweaked my curiosity all the same," he went on. "I thought, if nothing else, it's an all-expenses trip to merrie olde England, why not go? Do this, then pop down to see Stonehenge and maybe pay the Queen a visit at Bucking-ham Palace."

"So you're not the sort who normally responds to anonymous, vaguely worded invitations that drop on your doormat?"

"As a rule, no. And neither, I would guess, Sam Akehurst, are you. And yet here we are. What's that say about us, I wonder."

"No life?"

Ramsay gave a husky chortle like rainwater gurgling down a downpipe. "Ain't that the truth."

2. ON BLEANEY ISLAND

BLEANEY ISLAND WAS a low-lying hump of land like the corpse of some vast, ancient leviathan, lying dead in the water. Between outcrops of bare black rock there were stretches of grass and gorse, and the remnants of dry-stone walls could be seen, still parcelling up the ground decades after the last inhabitants had left. A concrete jetty jutted out from a steep shingle beach, and a small man hunched inside a large puffy parka was waiting at the end of it to greet the boat and the new arrivals.

"Jolyon Lillicrap," he said, blinking through spectacles misted with sea spray. "Apologies for both names. Neither my fault, but each nonetheless in its own way a source of embarrassment. Captain Fuller radioed ahead to tell us you were en route. It's Rick and Samantha, right?"

"Sam," said Sam. "Nobody's ever called me Samantha apart from my parents."

The fishing smack reversed, came about and swung away in a cloud of diesel smoke, Captain Fuller bidding farewell with a double blare of his horn.

"Let's go," said Lillicrap, shivering. "It's not getting any warmer. This way. Step lively."

He trotted along the jetty onto a track that curved between two shallow folds of hill. Sam and Ramsay followed, walking fast to keep up. Lillicrap seemed a creature of nervous energy and brisk efficiency.

"Excuse me," said Sam. "Mr Lillicrap? Jolyon? Where are you taking us? Are you the one who invited us here?"

"Questions," said Lillicrap over his shoulder. "I'm not supposed to answer any questions."

"Well, I think that answers your second one," Ramsay muttered to Sam. "Monkey, not organ grinder."

The track terminated at a cave-like entrance set into the earth, braced all round by concrete and inset with heavy steel doors. As the three of them drew near, the doors rolled ponderously open, activated by a remote control from Lillicrap's pocket.

"What is this, fucking hobbit-land?" Ramsay said with a grimace. "We going to meet Gandalf?"

"Second World War bunker actually," said Lillicrap. "Bleaney Island was used as listening post, keeping an ear on German naval radio traffic and U-boat sonar pings in the North Sea. It was also going to be a last redoubt if things started to go wrong. Churchill and the rest of the war cabinet would have been spirited away here to, I don't know, make patriotic broadcasts while the Nazis hoisted the Swastika over the Houses of Parliament, something like that. The bunker was completely derelict until about seven years ago, when we started work. Don't worry, we've made it quite an agreeable place to live. Central heating, ventilation, the lot. Damp's still a problem in a few places but otherwise it's all perfectly civilised."

"Perfectly civilised," Ramsay echoed. "How come that phrase sends a chill down the back of my neck?"

"Because you're not British?" Sam offered.

"That'd do it."

The steel doors began to trundle shut behind them. Simultaneously overhead lights came on, revealing a pillared, low-ceilinged space like a storey of a parking garage. The walls were streaked with dried water stains. The floor was dotted with what looked like large wet blisters – build-ups of sediment, proto-stalagmites.

Lillicrap briskly crossed the empty area, making for the far side and a door whose locking mechanism was controlled by a handprint scanner. Sam had been beginning to wonder if perhaps she and Ramsay were the victims of some grand, elaborate hoax and there was no more to this dingy subterranean place than met the eye. The handprint scanner put paid to that. There was, self-evidently, a great deal more.

A broad corridor led them past a series of closed doors. Rock music thumped from behind one. Living quarters, she guessed. At the end lay a staircase, down which they went, Sam with a deepening sense of trepidation. What was she getting herself into? There was the feeling that she was descending into something inescapable, irrevocable. She could be about to disappear off the face of the earth. No one knew she had gone to this island. There were no witnesses to her travelling here except for Captain Fuller, and he was in the employ of whoever had organised this whole enterprise. If she vanished, who would notice? Nobody. That was the sad truth of her existence. She had no family, no close friends, not any more.

Tragic though this was, it was also perversely comforting. Whatever fate awaited her, it would affect her alone. Sam Akehurst would not be missed. Her absence would not leave a hole in anyone's life.

Rick Ramsay's presence was likewise comforting. If this situation was all some elaborate trap, a snare for the curious and unwary, she didn't think he would hesitate to fight his way out of it. And neither would she.

Lillicrap ushered them into a cramped, cluttered room that was mostly taken up by a large table. Seated around it were ten men and women, all in various stages of boredom and disaffection. Refreshments – sandwiches, pastries, dips – were heaped on the tabletop, largely untouched. Coffee and tea making facilities perched on a trolley in one corner.

"Make yourselves at home," Lillicrap said to Sam and Ramsay. "And the rest of you – it won't be much longer now, I promise."

"No worries," said a sunburned man, in a sardonic Australian drawl. "Tell your boss to take his time. I've got nothing else to do but sit around all day with my thumb up my freckle."

Lillicrap sniffed and withdrew, leaving Sam and Ramsay as the focus of ten scrutinising gazes. Sam tried a disarming smile, put on more than felt. Ramsay got a result simply by saying, "The coffee in that pot better not be the watered-down piss it looks like." Someone chuckled and the atmosphere lightened a little.

Sam sat down in the last remaining chair but one, between a sharp-nosed blonde woman and an Asian man. The latter, in almost entirely unaccented English, introduced himself as Fred Tsang. The blonde favoured Sam with nothing more than a reserved nod.

Ramsay placed a coffee in front of Sam, which she was grateful for even though she hadn't asked for it. He then took the final seat, sipped from his own cup, wrinkled his nose and confirmed aloud that it was indeed watered-down piss.

"So," he said, having drained the cup anyway, "which one of us gets murdered first?"

"You, you Yankee bastard," said the Australian cheerily.

"It's just, I'm getting a whole Agatha Christie vibe from this," Ramsay continued, pointedly disregarding the other man's comment. "Twelve folks gathered in a room together. Cut off from the mainland. Brought here by a complete stranger. Where's Miss Marple when you need her?"

"Not cut off," said a woman, another American, lighter-skinned than Ramsay, most likely mixed-race. She held up a mobile phone. "Not as long as we've got our cells."

"Reception?"

The woman checked. "Oh. Nuh-uh."

"Didn't think so, underground. Cut off, then. N'awlins?"

"Just outside. Chalmette. Chicago?"

"South Side born and raised."

"Kayla," said the woman. "Kayla Sparks."

"I'm Rick," said Ramsay. "And the lovely redhead with me is Sam. She's English, so she doesn't talk much."

"Prefers not to," said Sam.

"Same difference," said Ramsay. "But seeing as the two of us are the newcomers, and even though the rest of you have been here a whiles and probably already know a bit about one another, would you mind filling us in about yourselves? So we're up to speed? Then we can maybe figure out what the twelve of us have in common, other than being invited here, and try and make sense of this thing. How about that?"

"Did I miss the voting?" challenged the Australian. "Did you just put yourself in charge, septic?"

"No, Crocodile Dundee, I haven't put myself in charge of anything. But if you'd like me to...?"

"No way, mate. Spent thirteen years of my life taking orders. I'm done with it now."

"I doubt you ever did take orders, not really."

"Too right!"

"No, all I was doing was making a straightforward request, not a leadership bid," said Ramsay. "Like I said, to get Sam and me up to speed. Would that be OK?"

The Australian deliberated. "Can't see the harm."

"Good. Then let's start with you. Who are you and why have you come all the way from the Lucky Country to this godforsaken spot?"

3. THE BARRACUDA

DEZ "THE BARRACUDA" Barrington was his name, and the why of it was simple. He was a man with a grudge, a man seeking payback, and that was what the invitation in its ponced-up, wowsery way had promised.

"Payback for...?"

"It's not something I like to talk about."

"I'd say, 'Relax, you're among friends,'" said Ramsay, "except you're not, so I won't. I could save you the trouble of having to reveal all, though, by making an educated guess."

Barrington spread two beefy pink hands, palms up. "Go ahead, smartarse. Be my guest."

"The Olympians. Something the Olympians did to you."

The word *Olympians* sent a frisson round the table, bringing a stiffening of backs, a compressing of lips. Sam felt herself bristle along with everyone else. Couldn't help it. She couldn't hear the Olympians mentioned, couldn't read about them in a newspaper, couldn't catch a glimpse of them on television, without her whole body starting to tense up, often to the point of trembling. For her it was as much of an instinctive reaction as dread of a shark or revulsion at a snake. She was not alone in that – certainly not in this room.

"You knew already," said Barrington, both a question and an accusation.

"How?"

"I don't know, maybe you're the bloke that brought us all here. You act like you are."

"I'm as much in the dark as any of you," Ramsay said. "Just trying to fumble my way towards the light. The Olympians hurt someone you care about. Maybe did worse than hurt. Correct?"

Barrington crumpled and gave a sullen nod. "Malc. My brother. Older brother. Only member of my family worth a tinker's fart. Couldn't have been my vicious bastard of a father who got killed, could it? Couldn't have been my drunk of a mother or my slag of a sister who'll drop her grundies for every root rat that comes sniffing round. Had to be Malcolm. The only person in the world I've ever had any respect for."

"I'm sorry for your loss."

"Me bloody too, mate."

"Was it... intentional?"

"Nah, Malc just happened to be in the wrong place at the wrong time. Hercules was having one his hissy fits, storming through downtown Sydney flinging cars around and punching holes in buildings. His latest bumboy had given him the elbow, that's what

I heard; ended their affair, so off Herc the Jerk goes, taking it out on property like he does, the great arse. Malc was working on the third floor of an office block on George Street, fixing a water cooler for a legal firm. A fucking Toyota ute came flying through the window. Killed him stone dead."

Barrington's face had gone a deeper, fiercer shade of red. His voice was a balled fist.

"'Act of god,' the police report said. 'Act of bastard' more like. Still, four lawyers died too, so it wasn't a complete disaster."

Around the table there were looks of sympathy, and of empathy. Sam could feel it as strongly as Barrington did: the rage, the pain, the sense of injustice and impotence. Ramsay was a clever man, just as she'd thought. He'd immediately guessed the common denominator that tied all twelve of them together. Although, if her hunch was correct, it wasn't the *only* common denominator.

"You lost somebody too, eh?" Barrington said to Ramsay. "That's it, isn't it? That's how you knew."

"My son. Ethan. He was seven years old. He would have turned twelve next month." Ramsay's tone was matter-of-fact, and Sam wondered how hard he'd worked to be able to keep it that way while talking about this subject. "Not a day goes by that I don't think of him, wondering how he'd look now, things he'd say, what he'd be interested in. He was a great kid, handsome like his daddy, biggest brownest eyes you ever saw... and one afternoon he was at school, it was recess, he was out in the yard messing around with his pals, swapping baseball cards, talking 'bout comics, whatever, doing boy stuff – and the monster got him."

"Monster?" said Fred Tsang. "Which one?"

"The Lamia. Goddamn bloodsucking, child-murdering bitch. Ethan's elementary school was right on the shore of Lake Michigan. Lamia came out of the lake, went into the schoolyard, grabbed a kid, one kid only – mine – and picked him up and drained the life out of him, right there in front of the whole class. Threw his empty body back down like it was a Coke can and was gone, back into the water before anybody could so much as move."

"I lost a child too," said a man in his early forties with salt-and-pepper hair. A product of the English boarding school system by the look and sound of him. Imprinted with the classics, corners knocked off him on the rugby pitch, licked into shape by the headmaster's cane. "A daughter. My wife along with her. We were on holiday. Crete. Poseidon and Zeus were having a blazing row, somewhere down the coast from us. One of their spats, you know how those two are – Poseidon feeling unappreciated, his old complaint about when the gods were dividing up the earthly regions all he got was the sea and none of the land, kicking up a fuss about that and Zeus having to read the riot act, bring him back into line. Poseidon went off in a huff. Decided to end the argument with a tidal wave. I was taking a nap in the hotel at the time, blissfully unaware of what was happening just a few miles to the west. Debs – my wife – she and Megan were down on the beach. Beautiful hot day. Then suddenly this noise, this enormous roar of water. By the time I'd got to the balcony to look out, the beach was gone. Just... swept away. Sucked out to sea, leaving bare rock behind. The sand all gone, and everyone on it as well. It's Chisholm, by the way. Nigel Chisholm. I used to be a pilot. Still am, technically, though I haven't flown a plane in years."

"My husband," said the blonde woman next to Sam. Her accent was Teutonic, with that slight American lilt typical of Europeans who'd learned English via Hollywood. "Dietrich. Army officer. Killed six and a half years ago during my country's final, stupid show of defiance against the Olympians."

"The Munich Massacre," said Ramsay.

"So," she confirmed. "Nine thousand of our troops and almost as many civilians were slaughtered that day, all so that our Chancellor could pretend he had a dick bigger than my little finger. Dietrich was just one of the nine thousand. A small fraction of the total. A tiny, insignificant statistic. But he was my husband. My soulmate. My name is Kerstin, if you must know. Kerstin Harryhausen."

"You what?" exclaimed Ramsay. "You're shitting me."

"No. No shitting," said Harryhausen. "Why, is it an amusing name?"

"No, it's just, well, ironic."

"Kerstin is ironic?"

"Harryhausen. You mean you haven't heard of...?" He stopped. "Oh. I get it. You're messing with my head, aren't you?"

"I am messing with your head, Mr Ramsay," the German said, deadpan. "Of course I know the Harryhausen you speak of. The great stop-motion animator, hmm? You aren't the first to remark on it, and you surely won't be the last."

"I apologise for being so unoriginal. Moving on..." Ramsay turned to Kayla Sparks. "How about you, Miz Sparks? What's your story?"

"Grandmother," she said. "Aunt. Uncle." She fingered a tiny gold crucifix that hung on a chain around her neck. "The Hydra got them, few years back."

"And you?" Ramsay said to Fred Tsang.

"My family, most of my relatives, my friends – more or less everyone I ever knew."

"Hong Kong, yeah?"

Tsang nodded. "The Obliteration. Back near the start, when the Olympians were just beginning to exert their influence. I was out of the province on a trip to mainland China, escorting a Beijing man home, a bank robber who'd skipped bail. I should mention I was a senior inspector with the HK Police Tactical Unit. The Olympians, as you know, decided to make an example of a city, to demonstrate just what they were capable of, to show they were not to be trifled with. Hong Kong was the city they chose. And Hong Kong..."

"...is no more."

"Precisely, Mr Ramsay. Hong Kong is no more. All those houses, those skyscrapers, several million people, just so much rubble and dust. I'm one of the last few Hongkongers left."

Tsang's face appeared placid but there was no mistaking the bitter anguish in his eyes.

"I'm still kept awake at night," he said. "By guilt, mostly. I find myself wishing I had been there when it happened and had died with everyone else. To a certain extent I did die. A part of me has not been alive ever since."

A pang swelled to fill Sam's chest. Tsang had articulated something she herself had long been feeling.

"I myself did not lose any relative," said a sombre-faced man with a receding hairline. He sounded, to Sam's ears, Scandinavian. "I lost men. By which I mean troops I was responsible for. Anders Søndergaard. I was a tank commander with the Danish *Jydske Dragonregiment* – the Jutland Dragoon Regiment. My squadron was wiped out during the Battle of Sjælland, as were so many others. My own tank, a Leopard Two, was destroyed by Ares himself, with three good crewmen inside. How I survived – it was a miracle – although a miracle that left me hospitalised for six months. I still bear the marks."

He rolled up one shirtsleeve to show an arm sheathed in warped, waxy skin from wrist to elbow – scar tissue from second-degree burns.

"And believe me, that's not the worst of it," he added, re-buttoning his cuff. "To say I hate the Olympians would be an understatement. I despise them."

The admissions continued. A Cameroonian by the name of Soleil Eto'o – moon-face, tight short cornrows, her skin so black it had a bluish tinge – had watched her parents burn to death in her home village, victims of a reprisal attack by the Olympians during their efforts to stamp out the resistance movement in that country. Soleil had immediately joined the resistance herself and ever since had been helping to conduct a guerrilla campaign against the Olympians all across Africa.

A Muslim woman from Manchester, Zaina Mahmoud, had lost her two brothers while they were on *hajj* to Mecca. Several Olympians had laid into the crowd of pilgrims circling round the Kaaba, simply in order to prove that there were no deities worth worshipping but them. The irony was, neither Hamid nor Aasif, her brothers, was particularly devout. They'd just fancied making the trip and seeing what all the fuss was about.

A handsome, tough-looking Québécoise, Thérèse Hamel, had had a dear friend taken from her, the Olympians' fault of course. She didn't divulge details, but by that point didn't need to. The tales of tragedy were becoming banal; the bereavements, by accumulation, almost routine.

Of the twelve, only two remained who hadn't told their stories yet. One was Sam. The other was a pale-complexioned, ferrety-faced man who had so far shown very little in the way of emotion. He had an air about him that Sam recognised: enclosed and self-contained, as if he were someone who had learned to keep his mouth shut and his innermost thoughts private, someone who knew the value of silence. In her former life – back when she had *had* a life – she'd met countless people like this. Everything about him said to her that he had not walked the straight and narrow and had more than likely served a stretch or two at Her Majesty's pleasure.

Ramsay now addressed him. "And you, sir?"

The man glanced up, seemingly surprised, as though he'd been paying attention to none of the preceding conversation. "Me?"

"Yeah, you," said Ramsay. "How do fit in with us?"

"To be honest, I don't. 'Cause unlike you lot, I've got nothing to blub and whinge about. It was my missus they got. Ex-missus, sort of. We were separated. Separating. And I'll tell you what, they did me a favour and all. That fucking cow – she got what she deserved, and the world's better off without her."

That brought a pause to the proceedings. Eyebrows were raised. Awkward glances were exchanged across the table.

Barrington broke the silence. "I'll say this for you, mate. You speak your mind, and for a Pom that's as rare as washing. You have a name?"

"Darren."

"Darren...?"

"Darren'll do for now."

"Well, Darren'll Do For Now, put her there." Barrington held out a hand.

The other man just stared at it.

"Or don't," said Barrington, withdrawing. "See if I care."

"Eleven down, one to go," said Ramsay. "Sam. You're up."

Sam shot him a pleading look.

"Come on," he chided. "It's not so hard. You've just heard everyone. We've all been there – with the possible exception of Darren. Bring it out. Share."

"I don't –"

Sam was saved by the sound of the door opening. All heads turned as a man entered the room. He was slim, dapper, silver-haired, none too tall, with sharply pointed eyebrows and a trim goatee. He wore a tailored charcoal-grey suit, and overall had the sleek, distinguished look of somebody who possessed a great deal of money and was in no way ashamed of the fact. Wealth fitted him much like the suit, lightly and neatly.

"I do apologise for keeping you," said the man, who could only be the instigator of the invitations, the reason they were all there. "Some last-minute details that demanded my attention. I trust you've taken the opportunity to get to know one another. My name is Regis Landesman. You're wondering who I am, why I've asked you to come to this place, and what I have to offer you. In truth, what really counts is what you have to offer me. I will show you what I mean in a moment or so. But first, if you'll indulge me, I have a few words to say."

4. REGIS LANDESMAN

"DOUBTLESS," SAID REGIS Landesman, "none of you will have heard of me. That's the way I prefer it. Unlike many who have achieved a comparable level of worldly success, I shun the limelight. I have never had any interest in publicising myself. I refuse to espouse charitable causes the way others of my kind do so as to make themselves seem philanthropic or caring – a time-consuming and hypocritical exercise, if you ask me.

"I have for the majority of my fifty-odd years on this planet been a pure businessman, a capitalist of the old school, interested solely in profit, driven by the bottom line, motivated by the margin. I make no bones about it. It has served me well. I have amassed a fortune, some might say several fortunes, through a trade that most would consider abhorrent. My line of work is not for those troubled by an excess of conscience. Plainly put, I am an arms manufacturer.

My company, Daedalus Industries, has supplied everything from bullets to jet fighters, landmines to armoured personnel carriers, to any country prepared to pay for them, meaning of course every country.

"Fully one tenth of the world's existing stockpile of munitions and ordnance originated in a Daedalus-subsidiary factory. You can regard me as a merchant of death, a creator of misery, a mass murderer even. I've been called all of those things in my time, and worse. Doesn't bother me in the slightest. Somebody has to make weapons. If I didn't do it, someone else would. To me, it's that straightforward."

"Business must have dropped off lately, though," said Ramsay. "Since the Olympians came on the scene."

"Quite so, Mr Ramsay. Or may I call you Rick?"

Ramsay shrugged.

"In the past few years I've been obliged to close down nearly half of my plants," Landesman said. "Laid off many thousands of workers. There are still deals to be done these days, but far fewer than before, and often with clients of the less desirable kind. Now that every national standing army has been reduced to a rump, government contracts are less forthcoming and are hotly contested by my rivals, with the result that severe undercutting has to go on and any revenue one makes scarcely covers one's overheads. It is not a happy situation. Our share price is a shadow of its former self, and some of the wittier stockbrokers have taken to calling the company 'Dead Loss Industries.' Although you might be relieved to hear that income-wise I personally, through judicious husbanding and prudent investment, am unaffected."

"Strike me blind, are you for real?" asked Barrington. "Way you talk, it's like something out of flaming Jane Austen."

"I shall take that as a compliment, Mr Barrington."

"You can take it however you like, mate."

"I could," Landesman resumed, "resent the Olympians, the entire Pantheon as a whole, for causing the severe contraction of what was once an expansive and lucrative business empire. I should. In a sense, I do. They are the ones who, by taking it upon themselves to establish and enforce a regime of peace all across the world, have knocked the bottom out of the war market.

"But it would be churlish of me to deny that their rise to prominence has brought with it a global stability the like of which has never been known. We all must acknowledge this as a fact. Your faces disagree, but you nevertheless must concede that over the past decade and more the world has experienced no major conflicts, not one, nor any minor ones. For the first time in history there is no region where the human race is engaged in factional in-fighting, civil war, religion-based strife, a battle for resources, any kind of large-scale violence. Power blocs are no longer flexing their muscles. Terrorists are no longer targeting civilians with bombs, suicide and otherwise. Territorial tussles are a thing of the past. And who do we have to thank for that? Zeus and co. You may not like it but you know that it is so."

"But they are murderers," said Anders Søndergaard. "They have killed to further their aims, and continue to kill, recklessly, sometimes deliberately."

"Wouldn't you rather have that, the odd death here and there as the price for overall peace? Isn't that, in the broad scheme of things, a fair exchange?"

"No," said Søndergaard, and the sentiment was echoed round the table.

"But think about it," said Landesman. "The Olympians have picked off every dangerous religious-fundamentalist leader there is. They've eliminated every single tyrant and tinpot dictator, not least the ones with nuclear ambitions. Warmongers, oppressors, right-wing extremist cells, despots, jumped-up paramilitary lunatics everywhere – all gone. Assassinated. Eradicated. Only democratically elected politicians remain in power, and they're all too cowed to start any kind of trouble, knowing it would bring the wrath of the Pantheon down on their heads. They've even handed over the keys to the world's nuclear arsenals to the Olympians, so the spectre of Mutually Assured Destruction, or of even a limited nuclear skirmish, no longer hovers over us.

"And the funds originally earmarked for war budgets have been diverted to schools, hospitals, care homes, civil engineering projects, research into renewable energy, just as the greens and the peacenik brigade have been campaigning for for ages. Isn't this the kind of society we're supposed to have been working towards? The end-point of the human narrative? Every nation in harmony. Rogue states under control. Planet-wide détente. Better use of natural resources. Isn't this paradise? Utopia? We have *gods* in charge of us now. Surely that's desirable, preferable to being at the whim and mercy of mere, fallible men?"

"They ain't gods," said Sparks with a vehement nod.

"Are they not, Miss Sparks?" said Landesman. "They certainly look that way to me. The Ancient Greek pantheon, in the flesh."

"I read somewhere they're aliens," said Mahmoud.

"Do you believe that?"

"That's what some people say. Not just the barmpots, some scientists even. They've come from outer space and taken on a recognisable humanoid shape and are using their powers to save us from ourselves."

"Only they don't have powers," Harryhausen chimed in. "Just incredibly advanced technology made to look like godlike powers."

"And there's another theory," said Tsang. "It goes that the Olympians are creations of Mother Earth. They have sprung up from the collective consciousness. I can't remember it but there's a specific word for them."

"Avatars," said Chisholm.

"That's the one. Avatars of nature. You've heard that one too?"

"Oh yes," said Chisholm. "I've studied the Olympians in great depth. They've become quite a little hobby of mine. I've scoured the internet, read the books and newspaper articles, watched the documentaries. The Gaia Self-Defence Mechanism Hypothesis, that's the name for what you're talking about. Essentially, the

Olympians are the planetary ecosystem's response to our species' rapacity and destructiveness, a kind of environmental failsafe. They've manifested from the pool of our dreams, conforming to a pre-existing set of archetypes, and the purpose of their presence is to curb our violent tendencies and steer us off the path of self-annihilation that we're on." Chisholm laughed hollowly. "I think it's a load of tosh, myself. But this kind of wild supposition is only to be expected. In the absence of any hard facts about the Olympians, there'll inevitably be crackpots coming out with harebrained ideas."

"You have your own theory about them, then?" asked Barrington. "All that research you've done, you've got to."

"Sorry to disappoint, but no. Frankly I have no idea who or what they are. Nor do I think it matters. Knowing the truth of the Olympians' origins wouldn't lessen my contempt for them one little bit. Yours either, I'd imagine."

"So it seems we all hate the Olympians, Mr Landesman," said Thérèse Hamel, "apart from you. Are you here to try and convert us? Is that what all this is about? You're some kind of emissary? An evangelist? You want to help us, cure us of our loathing somehow?"

"Did I say I approved of the Olympians, Miss Hamel?"

"You appear to."

"Equally I might merely be advancing an argument, putting a positive spin on their achievements, showing how their arrival and intervention has unquestionably had some benefits. After all, their avowed intent has always been the protection and nurturing of ordinary people. Zeus himself has said so, hasn't he? On numerous occasions. I recall his speech to the United Nations, the day the Olympians first made themselves known to the world. 'We have come here, incarnate again, in order to save you from the worst among you. We are here to liberate you from fear and the shadow of war. We want nothing more than for the human race to be free to live lives of contentment and mutual prosperity.' A noble goal, without a doubt. As a mission statement, it can't be faulted."

"Oh yes it can," said Sam.

"Miss Akehurst?" Landesman raised his eyebrows, inviting her to expound.

"Well, it's self-evidently flawed," Sam said, after a moment's pause to collect her thoughts. "There's implied coercion. Between the lines, there's a threat. It's not an offer, it's an order. 'Behave, or else.' And that's how the Olympians have been ruling us: we do as they want, or suffer. And if we fail to toe the line they back up the threat with violence, or else send one of their monsters to do their dirty work for them. All of which you know perfectly well, Mr Landesman. I think you detest the Olympians as strongly as any of us, maybe more so. This grand speech of yours has simply been a way of gauging how the twelve of us feel – a test, of sorts – as well as a way of stoking us up so that we'll be all hot and bothered and keen to find out what it is you actually want from us."

Landesman smiled broadly. "Ladies and gentlemen, Miss Akehurst was until not so long ago a detective sergeant with the London Metropolitan police force, on the fast track, well on her way to becoming one of the Met's youngest ever detective inspectors, before her career was, shall we say, diverted. Clearly in the intervening period her mind has lost none of its acuity and deductive capability. She is entirely right. I have been leading you up the garden path somewhat. I have been testing you. *Brava*, Miss Akehurst. I am most impressed."

Sam could not detect even a hint of a patronising tone in Landesman's voice. To all appearances his comments were sincere, his admiration genuine.

Not that she liked flattery much, either.

"Then while I'm your star pupil, Mr Landesman," she said, "let me tell you something else I've figured out."

"Go for it," murmured Ramsay.

"We each of us have a personal reason for wanting to get back at one or more of the Pantheon. Rick spotted that almost from the off. But my feeling is there's something else, an additional criterion for us being selected by you."

"Namely?" Landesman looked very pleased with her – and with himself.

"We have training. We all do, or used to do, jobs that require giving and receiving orders, jobs that rely on discipline and a chain of command."

"Go on."

"Fred here" – she gestured at Tsang – "was a Hong Kong cop. I was a cop. I'm looking at Miss

Mahmoud over there and I'm pretty sure she is or was a cop as well."

Zaina Mahmoud's eyes widened. "How the bloomin' heck did you...?"

"Instinct. Takes one to know one. I call it copdar. And how you wear your hair, that short plait of yours, very WPC. Greater Manchester Police?"

The eyes widened still further.

"You're Mancunian." Sam shrugged. "It wasn't rocket science. Thérèse is also police. Royal Canadian Mounted, yes?"

Hamel nodded.

Sam nodded at Ramsay.

"Rick I reckon is American military. If you pushed me to narrow it down, I'd have to go with navy."

Ramsay twisted up the corner of his mouth. "US Marine Corps. Not bad."

"It's the way you stood on the boat," Sam said. "You looked at home. And the way you stand generally."

"Good to know you've been studying my physique so closely."

"As for Soleil, she told us herself she's a guerrilla fighter. Maybe you don't need formal training for that but it still means working within a hierarchy, understanding the need for a command structure. Dez, you said something about thirteen years of taking orders, or rather not taking orders. I don't think you meant waiting tables. That tattoo on your neck, poking out above your shirt collar, is another clue. Kangaroo, crown, crossed rifles... Looks like a regimental emblem to me. Australian army?"

Barrington fired off an ironic salute at her. "Infantryman, Eighth Battalion, Royal Australian Regiment. Never rose above the rank of private. Never tried to."

"Kayla, American military too?"

"Almost. National Guard."

"Thought so. That signet ring you're wearing has a military logo of some kind on it. Stars and a man carrying a musket. National Guard would have been my guess." Sam turned to Harryhausen. "Kerstin. German army, like your late husband?"

"Reservist in the *Bundeswehr*."

"Nigel, pilot. RAF?"

"Well done."

"Anders told us he was a tank commander, so that just leaves Darren. Darren... I'm going to go out on a limb and say SAS."

His jaw dropped a few millimetres, the prison-yard façade cracking ever so slightly.

"That's what you tell people, at any rate," Sam went on. First the sucker punch, now the right hook. "Truth is, you're in the Territorials. Weekend soldier. Or you *were*, 'til they had to kick you out."

Bullseye. Darren's expression soured. He fixed her with a glare of pure venom, and then the shutters came down again. His face returned to its default setting, loose indifference.

"Miss Akehurst!" Landesman exclaimed. He applauded softly. "A remarkable feat. Truly remarkable. Accurate on every count, including

Mr Pugh" – Darren – "and his somewhat less than stellar CV. Not that we hold that against him. He has qualities that could well prove useful. But really, Sam – you don't mind if it's Sam? Lillicrap tells me you prefer it to Samantha. Really, Sam, you've excelled yourself. When it came to putting together this little assemblage of ours, your name was at the top of my list. You've shown that I wasn't wrong to rate you so highly."

"I wouldn't be surprised if you spent quite a long time compiling that list," Sam said.

"Fully a year's worth of work went into it. It wasn't easy. Digging up records, going through psychological profiles, locating personnel files, some of them quite confidential. One other basic requirement for selection was a good working knowledge of English at the least, and preferably native fluency."

"Well then, I'm buggered, aren't I?" laughed Barrington. "Me and the Queen's English, we're barely on speaking terms."

"Clear lines of communication are vital for the enterprise I have planned," said Landesman. "Eventually I arrived at a long-list of just over thirty potential candidates. I winnowed it down to twelve, my ideal twelve, sent out invitations worded carefully so as to intrigue – and lo and behold all twelve of you turned up. A very gratifying result."

"So what is it?" Ramsay said. "You've got us all here, you've dropped a few teasing hints, now's the time for the big reveal, chief. We've been patient. We're ready for it. I think we deserve it."

"Yes, yes indeed," said Landesman. "Just one further moment of your time."

There were groans.

"I assure you, this is the very last thing. A question. One that begs a simple yes-or-no response. One that will determine which of you wish to proceed to the next stage and which are happy to go no further."

"Go ahead," said Ramsay. "Shoot."

"If," Landesman asked, "you had the power to kill gods – gods and monsters – would you use it?"

5. DROPOUT

THE ROOM FELL ponderingly silent.

"A show of hands will suffice," said Landesman.

"Kill gods," said Ramsay. "The Olympians."

"And their assorted monstrous hangers-on, that misbegotten menagerie of theirs – Typhon, the Minotaur, the Gorgons, all the rest."

"You can do that? You can give us that power?"

"Let's focus on the question itself for the moment, shall we?"

"No, wait, you're seriously saying you could make it so that we, the twelve of us here round this table, could hurt the Olympians?"

"Not merely hurt. Destroy."

"Impossible," said Harryhausen. "Can't be done. Whole armies have tried. Tried and failed. I know this."

"The Olympians are hard bastards," said Barrington. "Hardest of the hard. The stuff they can do..."

"I realise it seems far-fetched," said Landesman. "Let's treat this as a hypothetical, then. A thought exercise. Given sufficient means to kill an Olympian, would you? Don't tell me none of you has ever considered it. In your dreams, in your blackest, bleakest moments, you've all fantasised about it – avenging the loved ones the Olympians took from you. They've caused you such grief, such pain. It would be only natural to want to strike back at them. Of course you've also told yourselves that this is idle, wasteful speculation. Better to forget, forgive if you are able, move on with your lives. You can't exact revenge on the Pantheon in the same way that you can't exact revenge on a tornado or an earthquake. But what if you could? What if you were presented with the chance to do just that? Would you reject it or grasp it?"

"Grasp." Soleil Eto'o put up her hand. "What else have I been doing since my parents' deaths? Trying to kill Olympians whenever possible. That's what we in the resistance do. We don't succeed. With our nail bombs and our rocket-propelled grenades we try, but we don't succeed, and mostly we wind up getting ourselves killed. But if you are telling me you know of a better way, Mr Landesman, a way that might actually bring success, count me in."

"I'm a yes too," said Søndergaard, raising his hand. "At Sjælland we gave the Olympians a fight to remember. We lost. We knew going in that we would. But we showed them that Denmark wasn't going to just sit back and let the world be taken over. I'd like another chance to make that point."

"Sjælland was an empty gesture, Herr Søndergaard," Harryhausen snorted. "Were the Olympians impressed? Did they congratulate your whole country afterwards for so kindly volunteering to be crushed by them? Perhaps they were glad for the target practice."

"So you would rather we had done nothing?"

"I can't speak for Denmark, but I would rather Germany had done nothing. Then my Dietrich would still be alive. But it is my nation's curse always to follow its leaders, however misguided they are."

"So it's a *nein* from you, Frau Harryhausen?" said Landesman.

"No, not a *nein*." She raised a hand. "Unless this gesture of yours proves to be an empty one as well..."

"Trust me, it won't."

"I'm in too," said Tsang. "I'm not sure why, but I am."

Other hands followed his into the air: Sparks's, Chisholm's, Hamel's.

"That's more than half," said Landesman. "Looking good so far. Anyone else?"

Mahmoud put hers up. "Can't do any harm to find out what you're offering. I'm not promising I'm in this all the way – but I'm definitely interested."

"Good enough. Rick, what about you?"

"Either you're a deluded nutjob or a nutjob hiding one hell of an ace up your sleeve. Lucky for you, I like nutjobs." Hand up. "Former gunnery sergeant Richard Ramsay, reporting for duty."

"Mr Barrington?"

"Ah, what the hell." Up went a meaty paw. "You have the Barracuda's services. What's the pay like and will there be beer?"

"Generous, and occasionally," said Landesman. "Your salaries will be enough to leave you living in reasonable comfort for the rest of your lives without having to work again. Alcohol, on the other hand, will be in limited supply. We'll make every effort to cater to all your domestic wants and needs. Mrs Fuller, Captain Fuller's wife, makes regular trips to supermarkets on our behalf, and is happy to take orders for specific items. Booze, however, will have to be consumed in moderation, I'm afraid, and inebriation will not be tolerated at all. Rules of the house, and non-negotiable."

"Right-o. Well, that could be a deal breaker. I might have to reconsider."

"Too late now. Miss Akehurst. Sam. It goes without saying that I'd be overjoyed to have you on board. What's the verdict? Yea or nay?"

Sam felt all eyes on her. The centre of attention was not a place she liked to be. Once, in younger days, it had been. Not any more.

"I don't know."

"Please."

"You're asking me to become involved in something, something to do with the Olympians, when I've been busy doing my best to forget the Olympians even exist. You have no idea how difficult it's been for me, how hard I've struggled just to get close to being normal again. And then you come along, someone I don't know and have no great reason to trust..."

"I'll beg if I have to," Landesman said. "I'll get down on my knees and kiss the hem of your robe. Prostrate myself before you."

"Come on, Sam," said Ramsay. "The man's prepared to humiliate himself, he wants you that bad. Don't make him do it. It's not dignified. Besides, his age, he might not be able to get up again. You know how it is with old guys and their prostrates."

"I am, I'll have you know, Rick, in remarkably good shape for a man of my years," Landesman declared. "In all aspects of my physical health. But still, you're right. I do want you 'that bad,' Sam."

A couple of the others made encouraging noises: *go on, do it, say yes.*

"OK then," Sam said eventually, with a sigh, hardly believing the words were coming out of her mouth. She could always back out if she didn't like the look of what Landesman had in mind, if what he was proposing seemed too preposterous.

Landesman beamed with delight. "And that leaves Mr Pugh. Darren? Would you care to make it twelve out of twelve?"

Darren Pugh made to put his hand up, but then dropped it to the tabletop, with a smile that he might have thought was impish but looked to everyone else like a malicious leer.

"Nah," he said. "Not interested. Mainly because if ginger tits there" – he jerked a thumb at Sam – "is in, I don't want anything to do with it. And also because, you know what? This is bollocks. All of this. Heap of utter, steaming bollocks. You, Mr Landyman, Handyman, whatever your name is, you're talking shite. You can't beat the Olympians. No one can. I don't believe you've got any marvellous plan at all. You just like the idea of thinking you do, and you've roped in all these losers, got them halfway to believing your scheme, your fantasy, whatever this is, and nothing'll come of it, you mark my words. It'll all turn out to be some half-baked nonsense and the whole thing will fall apart.

"You know what you remind me of?" Pugh went on. "A posh version of those blokes you hear talking down the pub, the ones who say they know how they'd get rid of the Olympians, this is what we should do, and they've got some huge, complicated method, use poison gas or smuggle in a suitcase nuke or some such, and if only the government would listen to them then this whole thing would be sorted... But it's all just pie in the sky, just bullshitters bullshitting. And for all your money, your fancy invitations, your island and your World War Two bunker, you're no different from them."

"That's a no, then, I take it."

"Yeah, you could say it's a no. The only way you could kill the Olympians, I reckon, old man, is by boring them to death. Which, longwinded as you are, I wouldn't put past you. Other than that, though..." Pugh glanced around the table. "Good luck in your little happyland dream, all of you, and I'll keep an eye on the television for news reports about your bodies turning up charred and mangled in a field somewhere. That's assuming anything more comes from this meeting, which I seriously doubt'll happen."

He stood up, scraping back his chair.

"Now, I'd like to leave, if you wouldn't mind. I've been here long enough, and I don't enjoy being kept in places where I don't want to stay."

"I'll bet you don't," Sam muttered under her breath.

"What?" Pugh rounded on her. "What did you just say?" He took a step towards her, squaring his shoulders.

Ramsay stood up, ready to lunge.

"I asked you a question, she-pig," Pugh spat. "What did you just say?"

Sam locked gazes with him, at the same time motioning to Ramsay not to intervene. She could handle this. She'd fronted down far larger and far angrier men in the past.

"You don't like being detained against your will, Mr Pugh," she said. "That's understandable. So go. Go now. Don't make a fuss about it. No one wants any trouble."

Pugh took another step closer to her. His head was twitching. His eyes flicked to a table knife, just within his reach. Not particularly sharp, but a useable weapon all the same.

"But if you do want trouble," Sam went on, evenly, "I will give it to you. Come at me with that table knife, and I will break your wrist before you even get near me. Then I will break your elbow. Then I will break your nose. And while you're down on the floor screaming like a little girl, I will take out one of your ankles. And then I will get started on your crotch – and not in a good way. If you ever want to walk normally again, walk now, straight past me, out of that door, and don't come back. That's the one safe, sane course of action open to you right now. Try anything else, and you will regret it."

She kept her voice low, steady, to indicate that she meant every word she said. It was no bluff. She did.

Pugh weighed up his options. He could fathom only one way out of this that didn't involve losing face.

"Fuck it, you're not worth it," he growled. "Anyway, I don't hit women."

Sam wondered if Pugh's estranged wife, were she still alive, might have had something different to say about that.

"I'm off." Pugh headed for the door, skirting round the table on the opposite side from where Sam sat.

Landesman moved to intercept him. "Darren, I'm sorry it has to be this way. But, as a token of my appreciation, and by way of recompense for your time and inconvenience..."

He produced a chequebook, one of those furnished by the kind of bank that did not have high street branches, that had perhaps one premises in a Georgian townhouse in the City of London, another in Switzerland, and a third on a Caribbean island with malleable tax laws. He also produced a Mont Blanc pen. A quick scribble, a rip of perforations, and Pugh was holding a cheque for a sum whose size was sufficient to transform his normally tight-slitted mouth into a wide, gap-toothed grin.

"It was no inconvenience at all, Mr Landesman," he said, folding the cheque and tucking it into a back pocket. "For that kind of dosh, you want me to come and waste a day here again, just call, any time."

Lillicrap was waiting in the corridor outside to escort Pugh upstairs.

Landesman turned back to the remaining eleven. "No great loss," he said. His lack of disappointment seemed entirely unfeigned. "I knew he'd be fifty-fifty, and his antipathy towards Sam would have been an almost insurmountable obstacle. We're better off without him. Besides, one dropout, out of twelve, isn't bad. Now, if you'd all care to follow me, I have something to show you. The wait is over. This is where you learn that I am not, as Rick put it, a deluded nutjob, nor, in Darren Pugh's parlance, a bullshitter. I am the enabler of your vengeances and, quite possibly, the saviour of the world."

6. TITAN

THEY WERE, SAM judged, perhaps half of a mile to the east of the bunker entrance, which put them somewhere on the far side of the island, maybe even right at its opposite shore. They were in a chamber that could have comfortably housed a football pitch, with a rugged arched ceiling that had been dynamited out of the solid rock. She had the sense that the chamber was deep underground but still above sea level, the hilliness of the island affording a thick protective layer all around. Her guess would be that the far wall formed the inside of a sheer cliff. She could dimly hear waves pounding against the other side, with that heavy booming impact that suggested they were breaking against a vertical surface rather than a slanted one.

A substantial proportion of that wall was taken up by a mural, a copy of a Renaissance painting she recognised. It depicted two naked Greek gods, one young, one old, the former hacking at the latter's crotch with a scythe while various other disrobed divinities sat around looking on in postures of horror and despair. All of these huge figures had lumpen fleshy physiques, and in the background was an image of the earth enclosed in a spherical golden cage that presumably stood for the universe. Sam couldn't at that moment recall which myth the painting represented. The artist's name, likewise, escaped her. Michelangelo?

The chamber itself, however, was of lesser importance than what it contained.

It contained a handful of technicians, most dressed in casualwear, a couple in denim coveralls. They sat at flatscreen computer stations hooked up to one another by high-density cables, each with its own array of gonks, action figures, toys, pinned-up postcards and photos – geek territorial markers. The computer stations vied for floorspace with heavy-duty industrial workbenches that were littered with tools such as screwdriver sets and soldering irons.

Dominating the room were twelve pod-like units arranged in a circle, each downlit by a shaft of powerful light; and standing in these columns of illumination, held erect by mannequin-style armatures, cradled by the pods, were what appeared to be suits of armour. Utterly modern, sleekly high-tech, but still to all intents and purposes suits of armour. A medieval knight would have had no problem recognising them as such. They had helmets, breastplates, gauntlets, greaves, boots – separate sections that would have to be donned one at a time, most likely with the assistance of a latterday squire. They were coated in a matt, gunmetal grey substance which from a distance looked like paint but closer to resembled hessian.

There was also an armoury in the chamber, an array of weaponry mounted on racks and shelves, dozens upon dozens of guns, rifles, rocket launchers and the like. Enough, all told, to equip a small army, and included in it were items the like of which Sam had never seen before and whose function she couldn't identify.

The chamber was, in all, a command centre of some kind, kitted out for war. The suits of armour were the centrepiece, the thing that commanded one's attention. Certainly they were what Landesman wanted to show off.

"Ladies, gentlemen, you see before you the fruits of three years of research and development, two years of construction, and another year of rigorous, painstaking testing. The name for them is Total Immersion Tactical Armour with Nanotech. A somewhat clunky sobriquet, but we had to do it back to front, making the initial letters conform to an acronym rather than, as is more common, the acronym arising organically from the product's qualities. The acronym, of course, being TITAN – Titan."

Landesman waved a hand around him at the suits, a ringmaster flourish.

"The TITAN battlesuit is, quite simply, the ultimate in combat gear. I could waffle on for hours about the compact servomotors, the nanotech body protection, the onboard-computer-aided control system, the variable-mode head-up display, the GPS transponder triangulation, and I'd still be barely touching on what the suit is capable of. I have sunk everything into this – all my years of experience in the field of arms and armaments, all the knowledge of these outstandingly clever men and women you see at work here, the very cream of my Daedalus workforce, not to mention funds totalling nearly half a billion dollars US."

Barrington whistled through his teeth.

Ramsay said, "That's gotta put a crimp in the mortgage payments."

Landesman gave a wry look. "I am, I'll admit, a person of somewhat reduced net worth as a consequence of this project. Half the man I used to be, financially. But I wouldn't have invested so heavily in it if I didn't believe the cause was just."

"And you can always sell on the technology to someone else in the future," Harryhausen observed. "I imagine, if these suits do all you say, if they really are the ultimate in combat gear, certain nations would pay handsomely to get their hands on them. Your outlay would be well rewarded."

"There is that, too," Landesman conceded. "I already told you I am not a philanthropic man. At least not wholly. But believe me, in this instance the philanthropy comes first. The potential recouping of expenditure, with interest, is just a bonus."

Eto'o went over to inspect one of the battlesuits. Before she got there, one of the technicians in coveralls hurried into her path.

"Please don't touch," he said, the anxiety in his voice softened somewhat by an east coast Scottish lilt.

"I was only going to look. Why, is it delicate? Will it shatter like an eggshell?"

"No, of course not."

"Then what is the problem?"

"I just..."

Landesman clasped the young man's shoulder. "Jamie, it's all right. Soleil can touch it if she wants to."

"I'm sorry, sir."

"Don't be. You're only being protective. It's very admirable. Everyone, allow me to introduce you. This mother hen is Jamie McCann, our chief engineer and all-round fixer of things that need fixing."

"Hi," McCann said with a nervous bob of the head. "McCann the Manic Mechanic, that's me."

"Jamie basically built the suits from scratch with his own fair hands. They're my brainchild but it's his sweat and elbow grease that gave them shape and reality."

"Feels strange," said Eto'o, running her fingers over the battlesuit's exterior. "Rough and smooth at the same time."

"That's the nanotech you're feeling," said McCann. "Billions of wee submicroscopic bots impregnated into the outer layer of the armour's indurated polycarbonate. They're inert right now, but when activated they can do two things. One, they can colour-shift. Two, they can –"

"Jamie," said Landesman, interrupting. "Instead of telling everyone what the TITAN suits can do, why don't we go one better?"

"You mean a practical demo?" McCann looked hesitant.

"You've done a hundred of them."

"But in front of people?"

"Now's not the time for stage fright. Some of these good folk have journeyed a long way to be here today. Let's make it worth their while. We'll put a suit through its paces, so that they can get a proper idea of what they're signing up for."

7. PRACTICAL DEMO

It took McCann half an hour to get the TITAN suit on. First he had to squeeze into a one-piece Lycra bodystocking. Not very flattering as undergarments went but, he said, anything else resulted in severe chafing. Next came the battlesuit itself, piece by piece. Multiple Velcro straps had to be fastened. Wires had to be connected up. Fitting adjustments had to be made. A full preliminary diagnostics check had to be run.

Finally he was all set.

The battlesuit looked bulky but was, he assured his audience, surprisingly light. The heaviest part of it was the liquid hydrocarbon fuel cell that was attached to the back, a smoothly contoured semi-ovoid that sat between the shoulderblades and contributed no more than 15lb to the overall weight. Besides, he added, the servos compensated. Once operational, they enhanced the wearer's natural strength. By how much? The calculations weren't precise but he estimated at least threefold.

One of the other technicians, who had helped McCann into the suit, clapped him on the helmet. "You're good to go. Power up."

"Commencing power-up sequence." McCann tapped a wrist-mounted touchscreen control pad. A low whine filled the air. He lowered his helmet visor, a blister of tinted acrylic glass that covered his face down to the helmet's chin guard.

"HUD online," McCann announced, voice slightly muffled. "You won't be able to see anything as the visor is coated with a partially reflective film, like a two-way mirror. Core systems analysis readouts populating. Signal strength of wireless connection between suit and helmet CPU confirmed. Everything at nominal. The display is controlled by a voice-recognition command system, as is the suite of vision modes. There's no mic, incidentally. The helmet picks up your voice through sound sensors attuned to cranial cavity vibrations. Here we go. Visor options menu up. Available modes are night vision, thermal imaging and peripheral expansion. Thermal. There, I've just switched to thermal imaging, and you lot are now rainbow people. It's kind of like being on magic mushrooms. Not that I've done magic mushrooms lately. I mean ever. Not that I've done magic mushrooms ever. I'll stop talking now."

"No X-ray vision?" said Barrington. "Damn. I wouldn't have minded a chance to see through Sam's clothing."

"I'd pay not to see through yours, Dez," Sam retorted.

"Ouch," said Ramsay with a chuckle. "You do not cross the Akehurst."

"You do not," Sam agreed.

"Yes, ahem, anyway," said McCann. "First off, a show of strength. See that workbench over there? It's solid wood and tempered steel. How much do you reckon it weighs?"

"Shade over a coupla hundred pounds?" said Ramsay.

"Watch this."

McCann strode over to the workbench, the suit's servos whirring just audibly with every step. He moved with ease, not looking at all like someone encased in armour. With one hand he grabbed the end of the workbench and lifted. The bench came up off the floor with no apparent effort from him. He lowered it again, all four of its feet touching down with a chunky clang.

"Next, speed. How far is it to that mural would you say?"

"Hundred metres," volunteered Chisholm, "give or take."

"Anyone got a stopwatch?"

Sparks's wristwatch had a stopwatch function.

"Time me."

McCann went into a half-crouch. Sparks said go, and he launched himself forwards. His first couple of steps were slow and laboured, then all at once the suit seemed to realise what was being required of it and he accelerated to a sprint – the fastest sprint Sam had ever seen. He skidded to a halt just short of the mural, and Sparks announced, "Six point four seconds."

McCann raised both fists, as though acknowledging the cheers of an imaginary stadium crowd. "And Jamie McCann, the young contender from Kirkcaldy, takes the gold, smashing the previous world record to pieces."

"Jamie..." said Landesman, mock-reproving.

"Sorry, Mr Landesman." McCann returned at walking pace. "The suit can sustain speeds of up to forty miles per hour for six or seven minutes before the servos start to overheat, although you want to be careful because it drains the battery like you wouldn't believe. Use speed sparingly, that's the motto."

"Is that another drugs reference, Jamie?" said Sam.

"No. No! God, no. Please don't get the wrong idea. I'm not some junkie."

"Watch out, pal," said Ramsay. "Sam used to be a cop."

"I know." McCann squirmed. "I mean, I know some of you were police. I just... You can't be arrested just for saying stuff, can you?"

"Continue with the demonstration, lad," said Landesman. "You're doing fine. They're only teasing."

"Oh aye. I see."

"Show us the chameleon effect."

"Yeah. The chameleon effect. Well, it goes a bit like this. The nanobots can colour-shift to match their surroundings. It isn't quite Harry Potter's Cloak of Invisibility but it's still a hell of an effective camouflage. Here we go."

He stood against the black rock wall of the chamber. A quick prodding of his wristpad, and the surface of the suit began to darken. Soon the suit was as black as the wall, and with McCann standing stock still it was almost impossible to see him. He was a perfect silhouette.

"It can also do break-up patterns," he said, as the suit lightened again to its default-setting grey. "Jungle, desert, mountain, snow, all the basic combat camouflage designs. Urban environments are harder to deal with, but by and large buildings in localised regions conform to a standard colour, so for a Mediterranean town, for instance, you could make the setting white to match the stucco. And speaking of Mediterranean, and hot countries in general, we've fitted a microclimate conditioning subsystem which'll keep you cool in hundred-plus-degree heat and toasty warm in subzero temperatures. Basically, you'll never roast or freeze. Whatever the weather, you'll be Baby Bear's porridge – just right."

"Ah, bless," said Mahmoud.

McCann squirmed again. He was a full-grown man and clearly some kind of genius, but acted like an awkward adolescent. It was almost too easy to embarrass him. And too tempting.

"And now," said Landesman, "the *pièce de résistance*."

McCann made an imploring sound. "Do we have to?"

"I'm afraid so, Jamie."

"But it hurts."

"Oh it's not so bad. Didn't you liken it once to getting shot with a paintball?"

"Which hurts."

"Stings."

"Hurts stingingly. Oh very well then. Since you insist. You're the fella who signs the cheques, after all." McCann stationed himself at the wall again, while Landesman fetched a gun from the armoury.

"You may want to step back a little," Landesman advised the eleven. "There shouldn't be a ricochet, but just in case."

"What in the name of sweet baby Jesus's little holy halo is that?" Ramsay asked, pointing to the gun. "Never seen anything like it."

The gun was shaped like a conventional rifle but had a long, thickly cylindrical barrel and an unusually stocky body. The casing was ribbed in several places, and a lightning bolt was stencilled on a small sliding cover on one side, suggesting a battery pack was contained within.

"This," said Landesman, "is a handheld coilgun."

"A handheld what now?"

"Come, come, Mr Ramsay. Don't tell me you're unaware of your own Defence Department's current Holy Grail. A handheld coilgun. One better than a railgun – not so power intensive and producing far less excess heat. Unlike a conventional gun, a coilgun uses electromagnetic energy rather than explosive energy to launch a projectile. A series of coaxial superconductor solenoid coils switching on and off in sequence accelerate a bullet along a track until it emerges here" – Landesman tapped the end of the barrel – "at a speed of several Mach. The bullet is powderless, contained in a sabot case that separates free the moment it leaves the gun. In all, this has twice the range of the average rifle and five times the penetration and stopping power."

He smacked a magazine into place, then pulled the cocking handle, raised the coilgun to his shoulder and took aim.

"So you're going to shoot him with that sci-fi blaster of yours," said Ramsay, "at almost point-blank range."

"I am. Why ever not?"

"Shit, you can't. You just can't. Even if there's a whole bunch of Kevlar in that armour, there's still a good chance you'll –"

The report from the coilgun was a tremendous percussive *snap*. As the ringing in everyone's ears faded, all gazes turned to McCann, who had staggered when the gun went off but who remained upright and appeared unharmed. He stooped and retrieved something that lay at his feet. He held it up between thumb and forefinger for all to see. It was a bullet, blunted to a mushroom shape.

"The bots make the suit go rigid at the point of impact," McCann said, flipping up his visor. "They absorb and disperse the force of the bullet across the surrounding surface, wherever you're hit. Not pain-free," he added, with feeling, "but 'ow' is definitely preferable to, you know..." He made a gargling noise in the back of his throat, like someone fatally wounded. "And that, ladies and gentleman, concludes our demonstration of the TITAN suit. At least I hope it does, unless my boss has plans to break out the rocket launcher."

"Would you like to give it a try, Jamie?"

"Jesus no. I was only joking."

"As was I." Landesman smiled paternally at the engineer. "Off you go. You've done well. Back into your civvies."

McCann went over to the other technicians, who began helping him divest himself of the suit. Landesman, meanwhile, returned the coilgun to the armoury, then addressed his eleven recruits again.

"So you've seen the battlesuit in action. What do you think?"

"That's supposed to make us superior to the Olympians?" said Harryhausen.

"What is the single greatest disadvantage an ordinary person has against the Olympians?" Landesman asked rhetorically. "Vulnerability. The TITAN suits do away with that. They compensate for the relative physical weakness of us mere humans by giving us a sturdy, almost impregnable exoskeleton. I'm not suggesting that wearing one would allow you to go toe-to-toe with, say, Hercules, trading punches. But it would afford protection from the worst of any damage he tried to inflict, and its stealth capability would allow you to sneak up on him, and night vision would enable you to do so under cover of darkness. And you've seen the kind of cutting-edge weapons available here. I'm not offering unqualified superiority to the Pantheon. What I am offering is a significantly levelled playing field."

"But there's just eleven of us," said Barrington, "and how many of them?"

"Twelve, not counting the monsters," said Chisholm. "The standard canonical Dodekatheon. Plus Hercules and Dionysus, who are in the Kos Dodekatheon but not the canonical. Hercules, by tradition, is a demigod, but he still counts. Then there's Argus. Nobody's quite sure which he is, mainly because nobody's ever seen him – god or monster or something in between. So, depending on how you look at it, you could say there are thirteen in all, thirteen and a half, even fourteen and a half."

"And each of them, each of the main ones, is worth a regiment of soldiers at least," said Barrington. "I mean, Hamlet here fought with a whole army against just half a dozen, and look how that turned out."

Søndergaard scowled at the Australian. "Hamlet?"

"Only famous Dane I could think of, mate."

"Hans Christian Andersen? Kierkegaard? Niels Bohr? Karen Blix– ?"

"Mate, you should be grateful I've heard of any Danes at all. I'm just saying, your country's entire armed forces took on six Olympians and lost. That's however many battalions, and the eleven of us wouldn't even make a company. Sorry, Landesman, super-suits or not, the maths just doesn't add up."

"But it isn't just about the suits, Dez," Landesman said smoothly. "It'll be the tactics as well. I've a strategy mapped out that Athena herself would be proud of. A handful of Titan troops going up against the Olympians in a full-frontal assault would be, I grant you, futile. Tantamount to suicide. A series of low-key, guerrilla-style attacks, on the other hand, picking them off one by one..."

Eto'o's ears pricked up. "They wander the world," she said. "They're not always to be found on Mount Olympus. They argue among themselves too often for all of them to stay there all of the time. They're often alone."

"Precisely. And I'd be drawing particularly on your knowhow, Soleil, your experience and expertise in the field of counter-Olympian insurgency."

"I would be happy to share it."

"I'm asking," Landesman said to all eleven of them, "for six months of your lives. That's how long I envisage this taking. Six months to rid the world of the Olympian scourge. Six months to restore humanity's control of its own destiny. In the ancient myths, it was the gods who rose up against the Titans. The Titans were the children of Uranus, powerful, primeval creatures he could not control. Their name itself derives from the Greek verb *teino*, meaning 'I strain,' because according to Hesiod in his *Theogony* they 'strained in insolence.' They rampaged around, uncontrollable. Zeus was the son of one of them, Cronus. Cronus had a habit of eating his offspring, swallowing them whole so that none of them could turn on him and depose him, but Zeus managed to escape that fate. He forced Cronus to vomit up his fellow gods, then enlisted their aid in attacking him. So began the Titanomachy, the War of the Titans. Sorry, am I boring you, Dez?"

"No, mate, don't mind me. You carry on. I always yawn when I'm fascinated."

"That war lasted ten years. Eventually the immortals overthrew the Titans and took their place as rulers of the world. The Titans were imprisoned in the bowels of the earth, and Zeus – well, he castrated his father."

"Is that what's going on in that charming picture over there?" said Ramsay, indicating the mural. "Is that Zeus with that – that Batman scythe?" The blade of the scythe was black and curiously batwing-shaped. If Batman ever had need of a pre-technological farming implement, it would surely look like the one in the painting.

"Ah, no," said Landesman. "There is no famous image of the castration of Cronus, unfortunately, so what you're looking at is a reproduction of Vasari's fresco *The Castration Of Uranus*. It's Cronus who's doing the testicular lopping off there and *his* father, Uranus, who's the poor fellow being deprived of his assets. In that respect Zeus, when he chose to remove Cronus's testicles, was simply following on in a patrilinear tradition. Apparently a lot of that sort of thing went on between the gods and their daddies. It's a recurring motif."

"Paging Dr Freud," said Hamel.

"Indeed," said Landesman.

"Don't tell me," said Ramsay. "There's some kinda code hidden in the picture, right? Some historical message that reveals the secret of the Olympians. Dan Brown's working on the novel even as we speak."

"I'm afraid the answer's no, although it's an ingenious guess. There's no code, no secret message. The painting is just a painting, albeit a splendid and rather beautiful one. Oh, and by the way, the blade of the scythe looks like that because it's supposed to be made of knapped flint. Most pre-Bronze Age tools used flint, Vasari's point being that the myth is ancient, even by classical standards."

"So what's the mural up there for?" Sam asked. "If it's to cheer up the workplace, you'd probably have been better off with a picture of Daniel Craig or a kitten in a tree instead."

"I had it painted there as a – you could say as a source of inspiration," replied Landesman. "A reminder of gods' natures. Their cruelty, their vindictiveness. What I'm actually intending to do, with the help of you people, is invert the Titan story. An act of symmetry. I'm proposing Titanomachy II, an uprising of Titans against the gods, or whatever the Olympians actually are. And just as Zeus and his Olympian cohorts succeeded in defeating the Titans, I fully anticipate that events in the real world will mirror myth – you, *my* Titans, will defeat the Olympians. If, that is, you're willing. Are you? Now that you've some idea of the resources you'll have at your disposal, the level of logistical and technological support I'll be able to provide, are you up for this? Half a year to eliminate the entire Pantheon and lay to rest the ghosts that haunt you. Come on, what do you say?"

Nothing.

"Tell you what," Landesman continued, unfazed, "I'll give you a week to decide. You start training with the battlesuits tomorrow, testing out some of the weaponry as well."

"Tomorrow?" said Ramsay. "Isn't that kinda soon? Some of us have lives, you know. We can't drop everything and start working for you, just like that."

"Is that so, Mr Ramsay? I daresay you, for one, could put everything on hold, close down your life, with just a couple of phone calls. I daresay all of you could. You've all come here with few burdens and even fewer emotional ties. That was intentional on my part. Be honest. Whatever you have at home, how hard will it be to leave behind? Even just for a week. And if after that week any of you come to the conclusion that this isn't for you, fine, you may depart without a stain on your reputation and with head held high. You won't be leaving me short-handed. I have reserve candidates. How about that? A fair deal, I'd have thought."

8. PAIRING OFF

BY HER SECOND day trialling the TITAN suit, Sam was half convinced she would quit once the week was out. By her third day, she was fully convinced.

She couldn't seem to get the knack of using the suit. She felt as if she were fighting it rather than wearing it. The servos made her limbs want to do things she didn't want them to. When she raised an arm, the suit tried to get her to loft it into the air. When she put a foot forward to walk, the suit urged her to leap. She spent a great deal of time tottering, almost falling over, and falling over, like a novice ice skater or a little girl trying on mummy's high heels. Out of the others, only Mahmoud was having similar problems. The rest got to grips with the suits relatively easily, and Sam watched with envy as they strolled around, performed feats of strength like the one McCann had shown them, and even learned how to sprint.

The training took place almost entirely in the car-park-like area that formed the entrance hall to the bunker. It was open-plan and spacious enough to allow the recruits to move around without, on the whole, bumping into one another – although collisions did occur and Sam was the cause of more than her fair share of them. The lights could be doused, too, to create total darkness so that the night vision mode on the visors could be brought into play. Again, Sam found the ghostly green imaging difficult to get accustomed to. It was like wading through some blurry monochrome dreamscape, where anything that moved left a phosphorescent trail. Even more confusing, though, was the peripheral vision expansion mode, which stretched her field of view sideways in either direction like some kind of warped wraparound Cinemascope. Objects and people loomed from the left and right, baffling her sense of spatial awareness which was telling her they weren't where her eyes were reporting them to be. Yet further colliding went on whenever she activated the option.

McCann kept telling her she would adapt to the suit. It would just take time. "It's like a sports car," he said. "Most folk think you can just climb in one and race off. They've no idea that in most of your modern sports models the gearstick is two paddle shifters on either side of the steering column, and that the steering wheel is super sensitive, the accelerator too, and that sometimes the accelerator pedal's in the middle, not on the right. First time out everyone nearly always stalls or just misses having a crash. You have to relearn how to drive. And it's the same here. Think of the TITAN suit as a Lamborghini Murciélago and yourself as, I dunno, a Volkswagen Golf. Forget everything your body knows about walking and so on. The suit'll teach you a new way. Listen to it. Feel it. Trust it to do what it's meant to, and soon enough you'll find it becoming second nature."

She attempted to follow this advice, and blundered headlong into the nearest support pillar.

McCann helped her to her feet.

"Aye, well," he said, "maybe it's going to take you a wee bit longer than 'soon enough.' But you'll get there, Sam."

"You're talking to a woman who failed her driving test three times," Sam said. "But thanks for the vote of confidence."

The eleven recruits ate meals together in the room with the table where they'd first met. The cuisine was good. Landesman did not scrimp on the small luxuries like that. A professional chef rustled up fine fodder from the supplies that Captain Fuller ferried over every other day.

The recruits also bunked together, in pairs, in rooms that boasted clean, simple décor, neither Spartan nor flowery, and lacked only one thing: a view. The communal washing facilities were decent. There was a well-equipped recreation room with a pool table and a plasma-screen TV. There was a library. There was even a laundry. Lillicrap had undersold things somewhat to Sam and Ramsay, or perhaps had been deliberately lowering their expectations. His "perfectly civilised" had implied basic functionality, but the bunker on Bleaney Island was actually quite a pleasant place to be, the absence of natural daylight notwithstanding. Sam had stayed at worse hotels.

Her roommate was Mahmoud, and the two of them quickly formed a bond, partly because of their background in the police but mostly because they shared the honour of being the least accomplished with the battlesuits. Each evening at bedtime they would go over the disasters of that day and compare fresh aches and blisters. Mahmoud remarked that the two of them would be completely covered in bruises if it wasn't for the suits' impact-absorbing abilities. Sam, in turn, lamented the sad irony that an invention designed to put her on a par with gods was making her feel more of a clumsy mortal than ever. She didn't confess that she doubted she was going to stay beyond the end of the week, but she had a feeling Mahmoud knew and was thinking much the same.

They found another point of similarity in the fact that they were both bereft of immediate family. Sam was an only child whose parents had both passed away while she was in her late teens, her father of a massive coronary, her mother of complications from the type 1 diabetes that had dogged her all her life. At the end of a torturous period of hospitals, hospices and funeral parlours Sam was left with the freehold on a house on Kensal Rise, enough in the way of inherited savings to last her through university, and an abiding sense of the fragility and unfairness of life. Mahmoud's parents hadn't survived the deaths of her two brothers. Her father's despair had driven him to seek consolation in his religion, but neither the Qur'an nor frequent visits to the mosque and long talks with the imam had provided him with the answers he wanted. So he had turned to another common source of consolation, alcohol, and it, at least, had ended his torment – by killing him. A fatality on the M602 near Salford. A lone driver, late at night, in a head-on collision with the central reservation. Straight through the windscreen. Not wearing his seatbelt. DUI, judging by the shards of broken bottle and the reek of whisky all over the upholstery. No other vehicle involved. Mahmoud had been on duty that night, and a colleague, having identified the victim by means of his wallet and recognising the name, had called her to the scene. She wished he hadn't.

"What was lying across the bonnet of that car wasn't my dad," she told Sam. "It didn't even look like a person, not any more."

The fatal pulmonary embolism Mahmoud's mother had suffered in her sleep a week later came as a direct consequence of the crash. The doctors had said it was merely a tragic coincidence, there was no medical correlation between the two events, it was something that had just been waiting to happen. A blood clot had been there all along, they said, lurking in her mother's artery, waiting for its moment to break free and make its catastrophic journey to her lungs. But Mahmoud knew better.

"No boyfriend, no husband," Mahmoud said. "Friends don't come to see me. I scared them all away. I'm on a permanent sabbatical from the force. You could say I'm unattached."

"Snap," Sam replied. "But we're not just unattached. We're totally detached. And I don't think we're alone in that here. Remember what Landesman said? 'Few burdens and even fewer emotional ties.' That's another reason why he wanted us, why he chose us."

The other recruits paired off too. Hamel and Eto'o were often to be found in each other's company, speaking French, the first language for both of them. Harryhausen and Sparks established a rapport, united not least by the aplomb with which they took to using the suits. They were by far the most proficient and the most at-ease in the armour. Tsang and Chisholm seemed a mismatched duo but had in common the fact that they were by some margin the most cultured of the group, Tsang having received his higher education at one of Hong Kong's most prestigious and expensive private academies. Søndergaard and Barrington made for an even odder couple – the slim, reserved Scandinavian and the burly, coarse Antipodean – and their bickering became a fixture of bunker life, whether it was Søndergaard nagging Barrington over his habit of farting malodorously at all times of day and night, or Barrington having a go at Søndergaard for his fastidiousness when it came to room tidying and bed making. The mutual antagonism seemed real enough. It was just possible, however, that it masked a growing, grudging friendship.

That left Ramsay, who had a room to himself and who, when it was pointed out to him how lucky he was not to have to share accommodation, said, "Yeah, but think about it. I'd have had to double up with that asshole Pugh. So it's only fair I get to sleep on my own, on account of the possibility of how bad it might have been." Which as an argument had no logic to it whatsoever but was still somehow perversely persuasive.

Ramsay did his utmost to encourage Sam to keep trying with the suit. By the end of the fifth day he could see how frustrated she was. He invited her to come outside with him, take a walk round the island, explore. The night was cloudless, the moon full and the stars bright, so that everything was bathed in a pristine, icy brilliance. The mainland twinkled in the distance. They tramped along the shoreline, over pebble beach and smooth rocks, their breaths coming out in wispy white curls. Their journey took them past the locations of a number of security cameras, part of a host of such devices mounted round the island perimeter, all facing outward and mostly camouflaged or hidden, disguised to merge with the landscape. Landesman had said these were a precaution against an Olympian attack, which he considered highly improbable. The cameras fed to a computer equipped with facial recognition software that had the features of all of the Pantheon on its database. Only an Olympian appearing on the island would trip the bunker alarms, no one else.

Soon the ground sloped up and Ramsay and Sam were trekking across a field of tussocky, ankle-deep grass. This took them to Bleaney's southernmost tip, where a high promontory afforded a panoramic view of a sea like a glittering plain of black diamonds.

"Don't give up, girl," Ramsay said, as they stood there gazing out.

"Don't call me 'girl,'" Sam replied. "Unless you'd like me to start calling you 'boy.'"

"There are several reasons why I wouldn't want that," Ramsay said. "But I take the point. Don't give up, *Sam*."

"I can't see why I should carry on. I'm rubbish at this. Landesman wants a squad of crack troops, not crap troops. The way I am in that suit, I'd only be a liability."

"Landesman wants you to be a part of this more than anyone. Don't do yourself down. Just keep at it, and meantime cut yourself a little slack."

"But this is so typical of me. I was always the one at school who'd have to have the quadratic equation explained to me one more time, always the one the teachers would single out to make sure I'd completely understood the reproductive cycle of the frog or how an oxbow lake is formed or whatever. The slow one. If I'd got it, that meant everyone else in the class had."

"What I've seen, you're the smartest among us."

"Which might be taken as an indictment of the rest of you."

Ramsay snorted.

"I'm thorough, that's my thing," Sam said. "I'm good with details – assessing them, sifting through them, arriving at a conclusion. I don't get there fast but I do get there in the end."

"Then that'll be the case here, won't it? You'll need a little longer than the rest of us, but once you catch up there'll be no stopping you."

"You believe that?"

"You just told me that's how you are, so of course I believe it."

Had there been less of a moon, more darkness for concealment, Sam would have smiled.

"You were on your way to becoming a top cop, weren't you?" Ramsay continued. "That's proof of how able you are. The only person who's stopping you right now, Sam, is Sam. You just need to have faith in yourself. Be a bit more confident."

"Like you, you mean?"

"Hell yeah."

"Where's the line between confident and cocksure?"

"No idea, but if I cross it, I'll let you know."

Ramsay gave that gurgling-downpipe chortle of his. It was becoming the thing that Sam most liked about him, after his perma-flared nostrils. It was an ungraceful sound but so full of authentic amusement that you couldn't help but warm to it.

Hot on the heels of that thought came another: the memory of a man who had loved to laugh and whose laugh she had loved. And with that Sam felt a familiar brittleness inside, a sense of breaking, as a structure built to contain grief suddenly gave in to its own frailty – yet again – unable to support the weight of anything much that came to rest on it, any emotion, whether it be sadness or joy, regret or hope.

"Sam? You OK?"

"Hmm? Yes."

"You went quiet there."

"Getting chilly. I should have worn something warmer. Can we go back in?"

Halfway back to the bunker, Ramsay said, "That business between Landesman and Pugh. What's your take on what happened?"

"What do you mean?"

"It's been bugging me. When Landesman paid Pugh off – I don't know how much it was but I glimpsed a fair few zeroes on that cheque – but when he did that, didn't the whole thing strike you as kinda, well, staged?"

"You're saying Pugh was a ringer? Landesman planted him in that room?"

"Yeah."

"Why?"

"I was hoping you might be able to tell me."

"It all looked pretty above board to me. Pugh's a waster, a liar, a crook. He realised he didn't want to be there after all, and Landesman realised he didn't want him there. The cheque was compensation but also to buy silence. Just in case."

"You reckon? You don't reckon Landesman hired Pugh to play the part of a screwup so that it'd help the rest of us pull together – make us feel better about ourselves and about the idea of enlisting with him. You want to unite people, give them someone they can all look down on."

Sam shrugged. "It's possible, I suppose. Landesman is devious, no doubt about it. But I don't think he's that devious, not in that way. And I don't think Pugh was acting."

"Still, Pugh could have been chosen because it was more'n likely he'd do what he did. That's why Landesman was so calm about losing him. Pugh was meant to drop out. He was never going to be one of the twelve."

"Landesman was calm because, like he said himself, he has reserve candidates."

"I still think there's something else going on there."

"Me too. But I don't believe Landesman set Pugh up as a patsy. That isn't my reading of it at all."

They were approaching the bunker entrance.

"So you're going to stick with us?" Ramsay said.

"For another couple of days."

"And then?"

"We'll see."

"It would be..." Ramsay, uncharacteristically, fumbled for words. "It would be a great shame not to have you on the team, Sam."

"We're a team? Already?"

"We're getting there. And in my not so humble opinion, Landesman is onto something with this project of his. Maybe the bunch of us stand a cat's chance in hell of getting rid of the Olympians. Maybe the whole thing's pure craziness. But I'm itching to give it a shot, you know? And I'd feel a whole lot more certain of success if I knew you were coming along for the ride."

"No pressure then."

He chortled, as she'd expected he would – hoped he would. "None whatsoever!"

9. BOLDER AND BOULDER

RAMSAY WAS RIGHT. They *were* becoming a team.

Sam saw it the following day, as they took the TITAN suits outside to practise in the open air. A morning mist shrouded the island, ideal conditions for trying out the thermal imaging. Through her visor, person-shaped agglomerations of lurid colour roved through a whiteout world. She watched them mingle and interact, each indistinguishable from the other, her colleagues, and in their comings together and their gesturings and their mirrorings of movement she saw how comfortable they now were in one another's company. She heard it in the comms link chatter too – banter passing to and fro, sometimes a massed cry of "Shut up!" in response to an especially crude remark from Barrington, and plenty of bullish talk about the Pantheon, belittling references to their powers and prowess. Within the group a clear sense of purpose was coalescing. The battlesuits were all they were cracked up to be and more, and the promise of vengeance was looking like one that Landesman could make good on. After only a handful of days the recruits were lining up in the same direction, like fish in a strong current. Even Mahmoud had overcome her initial awkwardness with her suit and was bounding around like the rest of them, exulting in the sensation of power lent her by this ultra high-tech carapace and joining happily in with the deity-dissing. She was in with the gang. Only Sam remained the outsider, and she couldn't figure out why.

Unless Ramsay was right on another count: the thing that was holding her back was herself.

Did she really want to topple the Olympians? Did she hate them that much? Was hatred a solid enough motivation for putting herself on the front line of a conflict with them?

She tried looking at it another way. Would the world be a better place if the Olympians were removed from it?

Landesman, on that first day, had advanced all the arguments in the Olympians' favour, the lines of reasoning that many a politician and Pantheonic apologist had used to justify kowtowing to them. No question, people were no longer being killed in their thousands, no longer butchering one another in the name of God, politics and profit. The disease of war, which had for centuries had never failed to infect some region of the planet, had been cured. Nowhere was armed conflict a daily fact of life now. Nations coexisted. Rival countries glowered at each other across their borders and exchanged occasional disgruntled verbal salvoes, but the rhetoric was always muted, never reaching a level of bellicosity that would draw the Olympians' attention and arouse their disapproval. The world sat like schoolchildren in the presence of a strict teacher, bolt upright, hands on desks, facing forwards, with nary a paper dart or an ink pellet sailing through the air.

But it was a classroom with bloodstains on the walls, and the hush that filled it buzzed with fear and horror.

And if you complained –

If you protested –

And people did –

If you did have the temerity to do that –

The hubris –

Then the wrath of gods would be visited upon you.

As, for instance, in Hyde Park, July 25th, two and a half years ago.

When Apollo and Artemis descended on a milling, militant crowd, and chants turned to screams, and placards and banners carrying messages such as "Down With The Olympians" and "Ban The Pantheon" and "No To Divine Terror" became spattered to illegibility with gore.

Sam had not been there.

But *he* had.

And *he* had died.

And with his death something inside Sam had died as well, and that was no mere figure of speech.

Hatred? Did she still feel that for the Olympians?

Not to the extent that she used to. For months after the events at Hyde Park, hatred had burned fiercely inside her, and its heat had made her feel alive, had maybe even kept her alive. But eventually like any fire it had subsided. She couldn't sustain it. Her heart ran out of fuel for it.

The embers still smouldered, however. And Landesman's Titan project was a breeze blowing across them, fanning them back to life.

Right, Sam told herself, *if you really want to do this, do it*.

She recalled McCann telling her to listen to the battlesuit, trust it.

There was a boulder in front of her, a hunk of black granite firmly embedded in the ground. The other recruits were all some distance off. The mist gave her cover. Nobody would see her fail, if she failed.

The boulder was clearly heavier than anything she could normally lift. Even the strongest man alive would have struggled with it, most likely in vain, with nothing to show for his efforts apart from maybe a hernia or some kind of prolapse.

Sam squatted down. She clamped her gauntleted hands on either side of the boulder. She concentrated on being in the battlesuit, being at one with the battlesuit, working in tandem with it. So far, so good. Before now, the mere act of grabbing the boulder would have been beyond her. The manoeuvre would have gone awry somehow. Either she wouldn't have been able to control the positioning of her hands or she'd have misgauged the squat and ended up flat on her bum or her back.

Heartened, she heaved.

Next thing she knew, she was standing upright, no boulder in her hands.

"Shit."

She looked down. Odd. No boulder on the ground either, just a depression, a patch of bare soil where it had once sat.

So where – ?

She looked up.

The boulder was falling. Fast.

She sprang backwards out of its path of descent.

The boulder thudded to earth at almost the exact same instant she did.

She sat up with her legs akimbo, propped on her elbows, dazed. *What just happened?*

Except, she knew what had just happened.

How high had she hurled the boulder? Fifteen, maybe twenty metres straight up, she estimated.

How far had she leapt? Ten metres, thereabouts, in a single bound.

Sam thought about it for a moment.

Then she broke into a giggle. She listened to herself. Actual giggling. *Tee-hee-hee.*

This TITAN suit.

Oh, all of a sudden she was starting to like this TITAN suit.

10. BREAKTHROUGH

FROM THEN ON, she had no trouble. Her learning curve was steep but, by virtue of having taken so long a run-up at it, she ascended smoothly and rapidly. By noon, as the mist began to thin, Sam was utterly at home in the battlesuit. She understood at last the exhilaration all the others were feeling in theirs. The suit took her and improved her, enhanced her. Made her a better her. A her that could heft impossible weights, run at impossible speeds, see in impossible wavelengths and ranges, even hear at impossible distances, not only through the comms link but via directional aural amplification scanners that made the cry of a herring gull half a kilometre away sound as though the bird was perched on her shoulder.

The basic functions of the suit soon seemed old hat. Sam wanted to try something else. She wanted to challenge it and herself.

She squared up to one of the remnants of drystone wall that criss-crossed the island. She hadn't yet seen any of the others attempt what she was intending to do, but given what she understood of the TITAN suit's operation, there was no reason why this shouldn't work.

She drew back an arm at waist height and punched the wall.

Punched straight through it, knocking a cavity in the top couple of runs of stone.

Didn't feel a thing.

Repeated the action.

In no time she had flattened an entire section of the wall, strewing stones and fragments of stone in a wide arc on the other side as though she were some kind of human wrecking ball.

And someone was applauding.

It was Landesman, standing nearby, Lillicrap beside him, in scarves and overcoats.

"Great stuff, Sam," Landesman said. "A fine piece of demolition. And deduction. I was wondering if, when, one of you would make that intuitive leap. No surprises, you were the one."

"The nanobot coating isn't purely defensive."

"Indeed. Its ability to absorb and deflect force can be turned to offensive purposes. Had it not been there, and you had punched the wall as you just did with the assistance of the servos, your hand would now be a mess of shattered bone and pulped muscle. Instead of which, thanks to the nanobots, you can hit with impunity, and with considerable power."

"Any other features of the suit you haven't told us about?"

"Probably," Landesman replied with a grin. "But

discovery is all part of the fun, isn't it? Nobody buys a computer and reads the manual from cover to cover. The best way to find out what a complex machine can do is by putting it through its paces and experimenting."

Lillicrap gave a polite, meaningful cough. "Mr Landesman?" he said, with a glance at his watch.

"Yes, yes, Jolyon, I know."

"Nagging's what you pay me for, sir."

"And you earn every penny. Sam, I'm afraid I must ask you and your colleagues to head inside now. The mist is lifting, and you know what that means."

"Sunshine?"

"Come, come, Sam. Argus? Satellites?"

"Oh. Ah."

"Yes. We run a software program that plots the course of every known manmade object in earth orbit. It's alerted us that a US military Key Hole optical reconnaissance satellite is due to pass overhead within the next few minutes. Discretion is necessarily one of our watchwords at Bleaney Island. Last thing we want is the Hundred-Eyed One spotting what we're up to. Crimps in plans don't come much more serious than that."

"Then we'd better get under cover," Sam said. She relayed the message over the comms link, and the eleven recruits converged on the bunker entrance.

Ramsay flipped up his visor. "What's this I see? Can it be Sam Akehurst? Miss I'm Never Going To Get The Hang Of This Shit? Look at you now, strolling along all smug and ooh-la-la. I'm guessing someone's made a breakthrough."

"That she has," said Landesman.

"Good news," said Ramsay. "So, you on-side now? You with the program?"

Sam shook her head noncommittally.

"Come on. The ten of us here, I think it's safe to say we're all of a like mind. Isn't that so, guys? We want to keep at this. We want to keep working with the suits and get our hands on some of that ordnance as well and pull together as a unit and then, when we're ready, go out and kick some Olympian butt. Yeah?"

The others voiced their assent.

Ramsay fixed Sam with his gaze. "We want to be Titans," the Chicagoan said. "We want to put the smackdown on those sick, self-righteous sons of bitches, and get ourselves a little payback into the bargain. Any way you slice it, it's a worthy cause. But – and I'm speaking for all of us here, and I'm not afraid to admit that we have been discussing you behind your back, Sam – we're keen for you to come to the party as well. In fact, not just come, but we're kinda hoping you might agree to be the hostess."

"I'm sorry?"

"Dumb analogy. Didn't work. What I mean is, how about you running the show? Being the top dog. *El jefe*. The big kahuna. Numero uno. I'm going to have to spell it out, aren't I? Our leader."

Sam recoiled. "No. Oh, no, absolutely not. Me? Lead? No. I'm not the right material. Far from it."

"I'd beg to differ."

Lillicrap started making desperate ushering motions. "We really don't have time for this.

Everyone, please, into the bunker. Now. You can carry on your conversation in there."

"Nope," said Ramsay, not moving. "This brother's not going anywhere. Not 'til Sam says yes."

"Me either," said Mahmoud.

"Likewise," said Hamel.

The rest agreed.

Lillicrap threw a pained glance upwards. The mist had almost completely gone. The air was getting clearer by the second, the blue of the sky less pale, the cold sunlight stronger.

Landesman, for his part, appeared highly intrigued by this turn of events, and not a little gratified.

"What's it gonna be, Sam?" said Ramsay. "What's the answer?"

"It's going to be thanks but no thanks. Why not you, Rick? You should be in charge. Everyone pays attention to what you say. They're doing it right now."

"One, I'm a grunt, a jarhead, a born footsoldier. And two, I'm just a loudmouth. Folk may listen to me but they don't respect me."

"Too bloody right they don't," said Barrington.

"You, Sam, are respected," Ramsay said. "I know this. Granted, it's early days for all of us. We've only just begun. But if we don't get the top slot filled now, we maybe never will."

"I don't want the job."

"Want it or not, you're the only one suitable."

"I implore you..." Lillicrap said. He was hopping from foot to foot like a child with a full bladder.

Sam looked at the ten faces before her. They were firm-set, adamant, unanimous. How had this come about? Until today she'd been the least competent among them, unlikely to last. Not only that but she had minimal experience of giving orders. As a detective sergeant her role had been to follow her DI's lead and do much of his legwork for him. The rank carried authority but mainly that of someone else, in her case Inspector Dai Prothero. Uniformed officers had done as she asked but really only out of courtesy, deference to the man under whose aegis she sheltered. DI "Do Or Dai" Prothero had been a grave, commanding presence. A guv'nor. A natural boss. And thanks to him, Sam had realised she was not. It was a skill she hadn't yet developed and had been hoping to learn from him by example.

And here, now, was this thing, zooming in at her utterly out of the blue, this weird mutiny-in-reverse, where ten people were united, militantly refusing to budge, their complaint not that someone had misgoverned them but that someone was reluctant to govern them.

What could she do? She could, under the circumstances, only give in.

"All right," she said. "Under protest, and on condition that if it turns out that I don't meet up to expectations I can step down any time – I'll do it."

Lillicrap puffed out his cheeks in relief, and the Titans let out cheers.

"Good choice," Ramsay muttered to Sam as they went into the bunker.

"Was it?" she replied brusquely. "Was it even a choice?"

11. SUPERIOR FUCKED-UP-NESS

DAYS PASSED, MERGING into one another, and became weeks, which also merged into one another. The majority of the training was conducted underground, and was rigorous and intensive, so that come evening the Titans were so exhausted, it was all they could do just to eat supper and crawl into bed. Lights out, lights on, and then another few hours of suit practice and weapons drill, and then to bed once more, over and over, *ad infinitum*. Sessions in the upper world, the land above, were infrequent. Not only were reconnaissance satellites an issue but there was always the possibility of, as Landesman put it, "eyeball observation" – people on a passing yacht or the crew of a trawler or freighter catching sight of men and women roving across the rugged slopes of Bleaney Island in bizarre armour.

There were the locals to consider as well. People on

the mainland were aware that something out of the ordinary was going on over on Bleaney. A few years back they'd seen construction crews travelling back and forth to the island from the harbour, plus heavy equipment getting transported across. Rumour was that the old bunker had been converted into some kind of top-secret government research facility where they were investigating alternative fuels, cold fusion, something along those lines. Lillicrap primed Captain Fuller with a flow of titbits of information that supported this rumour, without ever revealing any of the truth to him, and the captain of course was only too happy to spread the insider knowledge around after a pint or three down at the pub. It wouldn't do, therefore, for the battlesuits to be glimpsed in action, which would be just conceivable for someone on the mainland with a decent telescope, and it certainly wouldn't do for the noise of weapons fire to be overheard, particularly as sound carried a long way across open water.

Sam found this largely subterranean existence, this involuntary hibernation in a manmade cave, hard to cope with. She pined for daylight, vistas, fresh air. Any chance she could get, she sneaked up out of the bunker, just to be able to spend a few minutes on the beach watching the breakers pounce on the shingles, smelling the brine, and examining the detritus washed up on the foreshore – tangles of kelp, empty crab shells, plastic bottles and six-pack holders and scraps of fishing net. Even at night-time, even in rain, it was good to get outdoors. It was a relief to be away, however briefly, from battlesuits and guns and scrutiny.

Scrutiny, because her fellow Titans were looking at her, judging her every word and deed, trying to gauge how well she wore the mantle of leadership and whether in electing her they had chosen wisely. She didn't know what they wanted from her, so she behaved as she thought a leader should, offering commendation and condemnation wherever either seemed due and otherwise remaining aloof. It put a strain on her relations with Mahmoud, their friendship settling into a more formal mode, still cordial but no longer quite as warm.

With Ramsay, things were somewhat stickier.

He came up to her one evening at the end of training. Sam was sitting on the floor, having just divested herself of her suit. She wanted to get up and go and hit the showers but she was worn out from the day's efforts and her muscles, for now, refused to do anything but lie inert and ache.

She was in her oh-so-flattering Lycra bodystocking, and so was he. They both looked ridiculous and Ramsay knew it. That, most likely, was why he had chosen this moment to approach her.

"So, you and me," he said, "are we cool?"

She didn't turn to look at him. "What do you think?"

"Wild guess: you're still mad at me."

"No shit, Sherlock."

"I appreciate I blindsided you with the whole leader thing. Maybe I could have handled it a bit better."

"Or not done it at all."

If Ramsay had been waiting for an invitation to join her on the floor, she didn't offer one. He went down on his haunches next to her anyway. "You've got to understand, Sam, it was the right time. The matter needed to be raised. And you really shouldn't hold it against me. I was only a spokesman, saying what we'd all agreed on."

"Why me?"

"Well, that's the million-dollar question, ain't it?" He blew out air. "Why you? Apart from your brains. And everything else."

"But I have no combat experience. I've been in the odd brawl, had to subdue the odd villain, but that's it as far as fighting goes. You've been in war zones, seen actual action. So have Anders and Soleil and Nigel and Dez. You know what's involved, what to expect. When we're out in the field, I could be hopeless. I might not have a clue what to do."

"It isn't about combat experience," Ramsay said. "It's about taking charge. Responding decisively to events. Keeping a cool head under pressure."

"And if I cock it up royally and wind up getting everybody killed?"

"Then we'll all be dead and in no position to care. But you see, Sam, there's another reason why we want you as boss."

"Because no one else would do it?"

"No." A short burst of downpipe gurgle. "Well, yeah, maybe a little. But the truth is, what folks are looking for in a leader is somebody who's like them, only more so. Somebody who represents what they are in its purest form. We, us Titans, we're all... we're all broken. We're broken people. Life's picked us up in its jaws and given us a long hard shake and dumped us back down again all busted up and twisted. We've all been changed by something the Olympians did, and we can never go back to being who we were before. We've lost something. And you..."

"I'm the worst of the lot. The most broken. The most changed. The one who's lost the most."

"You won't even tell us what happened to you. You can't even bring yourself to talk about it, that's how deeply it's affected you. We all can sense how hurt you are inside, how damaged."

"So let me get this straight. I got voted in on the grounds of being the most fucked up? That's my main qualification?"

"Bingo." A grim grin. "Screwy, ain't it? But that's how it works. That's what gives you authority over us. Your superior fucked-up-ness. We've all of us got an axe to grind with the Olympians but the one you're carrying over your shoulder is way the biggest."

Sam thought for a moment.

"Rick?"

"Yeah?"

"Piss off and leave me alone. That's a direct order from your commanding officer."

Ramsay rolled it around inside his head for a few seconds. Then – saying, "Yes, ma'am," gravely, without a trace of humour or irony – he hauled himself to his feet and left.

Sam put her face in her hands.

No crying, though. These days, Sam Akehurst did not cry. Not ever. Her tear ducts were bone-dry.

12. POSEIDON PASSING

It HAD BEEN trailed on the BBC and the cable news channels for days. Poseidon was making a state visit – paying a courtesy call on the new Prime Minister, who had been swept to power last autumn on the strength of a platform of policies that included pensioning off a third of the nation's already substantially depleted armed forces, siphoning yet more tax revenue away from defence and towards education and social welfare, and decommissioning the very last of Britain's nuclear submarines. Five months after taking office, Catesby Bartlett was still enjoying a huge groundswell of public support, his approval ratings hovering around the 70% mark, a level unprecedented in modern political history. To his critics Bartlett was an Olympianite of the worst, most craven kind, and it was certainly true that he made no secret of his admiration for the Olympians and all that they had wrought, even if he had been known to cavil over some of their methods.

His ovine devotion to the Pantheon had prompted a political sketch writer to dub him *Baa*tlett, and the sobriquet had stuck. But his victory in the polls had proved, if nothing else, that he was a man in tune with the mood of the electorate, even though his party had scraped in with only a tiny majority.

"I'm not blind," Bartlett had told reporters outside Number 10, shortly after his swearing-in. "I realise there are things the Olympians have done that are, y'know, not quite the done thing. I wouldn't for a moment condone, say, the Obliteration, or the regime change they carried out in certain countries. I mean, human rights, you know what I'm saying? Due process of law – I'm all in favour of that as well. As an ex-barrister, why wouldn't I be? But on balance, weighing up the pros and cons, you've got to hand it to the Pantheon. They made some tough choices. They took the bull by the horns and did what needed to be done. They took responsibility for humanity's security, because they had the power to. Full credit to them for that. So let's accept the status quo, shall we? Let's be pragmatic. Let's live in the world as it now is, not as some people might wish it to be. That's my take on the situation. Thank you."

For Poseidon to come by, for him to agree to make a personal appearance at Westminster and thereby put the Pantheonic seal on Bartlett's premiership, was a terrific coup for the Prime Minister. He was playing it down, though, modest as ever.

"Look at me," he said in a TV interview on the eve of the great event, "I'm just an ordinary chap, and tomorrow I'm going to step forward and shake the hand of the god of the oceans himself. Poseidon the Wide-Ruling, the Securer, the Cleaver Of The Rock. I'm as thrilled at the prospect as anyone would be. It's like meeting a superstar, one of the all-time greats. Elvis, or Frank Sinatra."

"A junkie and a gangster," Barrington muttered at the screen. He and a handful of other Titans were watching the interview in the rec room. "That'd be about bloody right."

"Both dead, though," Søndergaard pointed out.

"There is that," said Barrington.

"What I want most to come from this meeting," Bartlett went on, "is for people to see – not just here in the UK but around the world – that we can get along with the Olympians. We don't have to fear them. All we have to do is give them our complete co-operation, and they'll leave us be."

"Co-operation," said Harryhausen. "From his lips it sounds like another word for cowardice."

"That," said Bartlett, "is the Catesby Bartlett philosophy."

"Beware the politician who starts referring to himself in the third person," said Ramsay.

Sam felt obscurely embarrassed at Bartlett's performance and the reaction it was provoking from the non-Britons in the room. She didn't, as a British citizen, like being associated with Bartlett. She didn't want to be tarred with the same brush. He wasn't speaking for her, he didn't represent her, and she didn't want anyone to think he did.

For reassurance that she wasn't alone in this, she

looked to her only compatriot present, Chisholm. He was staring fixedly at the television, his jaw clenched hard, the tendon below his ear taut and twitching. Irked by Bartlett too? No, the source of his tension wasn't, she realised, the Prime Minister. His jaw began clenching even more tightly as some library footage was aired showing Poseidon sailing majestically across the sea, riding the crest of an immense wave. Tomorrow the Olympian would be making a complete circuit of the British Isles, a kind of lap of honour before sweeping up the Thames into London for his rendezvous with the PM at Parliament. A map appeared onscreen, tracing the route of his circumnavigation and marking out the best vantage points along the coastline from which to see him go by. He would, it turned out, be passing Bleaney Island sometime around 3pm.

And so, sometime around 3pm, the Titans assembled on the island's highest hilltop, armed with binoculars – and not in their battlesuits, naturally – to observe the godly transit. This was Landesman's idea. "Know your enemy," was his reasoning. "Take the opportunity to see him in the flesh when you can." He himself was out there, as were Lillicrap, McCann, and all the technicians. There was only one absentee.

"Any of you guys seen Nigel?" Sparks wondered.

"He said he preferred to stay below," Tsang replied. "He has no wish to be here."

"Why not?"

"His family, as you may remember. It was Poseidon who..." The rest was left unsaid.

"Oh. Oh yeah."

Poseidon came into sight somewhat later than scheduled. His progress was attended by a swarm of news helicopters, flying flat out to keep up with him. Through her binoculars Sam beheld a powerful, muscular physique that was running to flab, like a retired wrestler's. Long aquamarine hair and a long aquamarine beard flowed backwards from his face. A necklace of clamshells nestled on his hairy chest, while shiny fish-scale longjohns clad his lower half. He brandished his trident in one hand like a royal sceptre. His feet were lost in the foam of the wave that was supporting him and bearing him along. The wave was four or five metres high at its peak, and cut a white chevron half a mile wide across the sea's surface.

"Look at that," McCann said. "How does he do that?"

"You mean you don't know?" said a colleague of his, Rajesh Patanjali, responsible for all things IT at Bleaney. "Didn't you read the *New Scientist* special on the Olympians?"

"Must've missed that one. I prefer my magazines to have pictures of nudie girls and articles about the Grand Prix in them. So what's the trick? Magic?"

Patanjali rolled his eyes, as though it was his greatest burden in life to have to be confronted with such childishness on a daily basis. "Aquakinesis. Poseidon manipulates water with his mind. Water or any other liquid. He can control it down the molecular level. Shape it, congeal it, turn it to vapour – I've seen him on TV doing all of those."

"Turn a man's blood to mud in his veins," said

Eto'o. "I've seen him do that. And not on TV."

"A very dangerous creature," said Landesman. "Perhaps second only to Zeus in terms of threat level. We shan't be tackling him 'til we've a few lesser Olympians under our belt first."

"You're wrong there, Mr Landesman," said a voice from behind.

Everyone spun round to see Chisholm marching up to the hilltop from the direction of the bunker entrance. On his face was a look of implacable determination – and in his arms was a rocket launcher from the armoury.

"We're tackling him right now."

Cresting the hill, Chisholm swung the rocket launcher up onto his shoulder and put an eye to the sight.

"Round's already in. Laser-guided high-ex. I'm blowing the bastard out of the water."

"No!" Landesman barked. "I forbid it. Put that thing down, Nigel. This instant. You are not going to do this."

"Looks like I am, actually," said Chisholm.

"Shoot, and you jeopardise this entire operation."

"Not if I don't miss."

"Even if you don't. Attack Poseidon, and whether you kill him or not the Olympians will retaliate. They'll come down on us like a ton of bricks."

"Don't care. This is for Debs and Megan." Chisholm depressed the launch lever and curled his finger round the trigger.

Sam stepped in front of him.

"Mr Landesman's right, Nigel," she said. "Put the launcher down."

"Out of my way."

"No."

Chisholm moved to one side, re-sighting on Poseidon. Sam sidestepped too, keeping her face level with the launcher's front opening.

"Get out of the bloody way," Chisholm growled.

"Or what?" said Sam. She kept her voice gentle but firm, as you did when talking to the deranged and the weapon-wielding. "You'll shoot me instead?"

"He'll be out of range in a couple of seconds. I need to do this. Move, Sam. Please."

"You'll get your chance, Nigel. But when the time's right. Not now."

"Sam..." The launcher trembled in Chisholm's grasp. She saw a tear roll down his cheek.

"Just wait. Poseidon is yours, I promise. You'll have first crack at him. But you need to be patient. Stow the launcher. There are cameras in those helicopters. If anyone zooms in you, we're sunk."

She laid a hand on the launcher and slowly pushed it down, getting no resistance from Chisholm. It was a relief not to be staring into that lethal hollow any more.

"Fuck," Chisholm breathed. His eyes were glassy, his expression one of crumpled, abject misery. "All right, you win. God, I was so furious, and there he is, parading by, arrogant as you please, and I... I just..." He shook his head like a man emerging from a trance. "I've made an utter tit of myself, haven't I?"

"Not at all."

"What was I thinking?"

"You were thinking about your wife and daughter. You were remembering them and how much you loved them. And there isn't one of us here who wouldn't at least have been tempted to do what you did, in your shoes."

"Rocket probably wouldn't even have got him. He'd have seen it coming and thrown up a wall of water to protect himself."

"And then would have conjured up a massive tsunami to swamp the entire island and drown the lot of us," Sam said. "Your motives were noble, Nigel. Your strategy, on the other hand..."

"...was atrocious. Mr Landesman – everyone –"

Chisholm found he couldn't look any of the assembled company in the eye. He couldn't even finish the sentence. Letting the launcher drop to the ground, he turned and walked off, shoulders slumped in shame.

Poseidon by now was a dwindling speck on the horizon, the helicopters too, the ruckus of their rotors reduced to a faint locust whirr.

Landesman came over to Sam. "Adroitly handled," he said. "Well done."

All of the Titans present were of the same opinion. They didn't have to say anything; Sam could see it in their faces. Ramsay gave her the merest ghost of a nod, and that seemed to sum it up. If any of them had been harbouring reservations about her, they weren't now. Like it or not – and for Sam it was still the latter – she was team leader. This incident had been her unofficial anointing. There could be no going back.

13. MISTAKES

CHISHOLM WANTED TO quit after that. "Damn near scuppered your ship," he said to Landesman, "before she'd even set out on her maiden voyage." He had his bag packed and was preparing to leave.

Landesman, however, over several balloons of Chivas Regal and a couple of plump Cohiba cigars, convinced him to unpack his bag and stay.

"I'm all for giving a fellow a second chance," Landesman told Sam privately in his office later. One of the bunker's larger rooms, the office was decked out like a clubland snug, with thick Axminster on the floor, oak panelling and reproduction Old Masters on the walls, and shelfloads of gilt-titled antique books. A sleek Apple PowerBook was its sole concession to the 21st century.

"But what if he does it again?" Sam said. "Goes off the rails at a crucial moment?"

"He won't. Man's learned his lesson."

"I'm not so sure. I don't know if I can trust him now."

"Nigel Chisholm was a captain in the RAF's Number 32 Squadron," Landesman said. "Meaning, among other things, he's piloted Tristars with members of government and the royal family on board. They don't let just anyone fly VIPs of that calibre around the world."

"That was then. Nigel's not the person he used to be. None of us is."

"Even so, it was an aberration, Sam. It won't happen again."

"I have responsibility for this team. I need to know that –"

"Sam, Sam," Landesman interrupted, wafting a hand. "Nigel will be fine, I guarantee it. He's got something out of his system, and he's duly embarrassed about what he did and is busy eating more humble pie than is good for the digestion. He won't be any more trouble. In fact, I suspect that from now on he'll be eager to prove just what an asset he can be."

"That might not be such a good thing, either. Someone who's trying too hard is as much of a loose cannon as someone who's unreliable. But" – she let out a theatrical sigh – "I can see I don't have any choice in this."

"As it happens, you don't," Landesman said genially. "That we're discussing the matter at all should be taken as a mark of the high esteem in which I hold you. Now, if there's anything else...?"

Sam knew that she had just, ever so politely, been dismissed. As she rose from her chair, her eye fell on a photograph sitting on Landesman's desk in a silver frame. It was a studio portrait of a woman and a small boy, taken some thirty years ago to judge by the woman's clothes and hairstyle. She was sharply, aristocratically beautiful, with eyes that were strikingly large, dark and limpid. The boy was cute and had the same eyes, but his blazed with an extraordinarily intense and challenging light, as if everything, even posing for a photo, was a source of great puzzlement and irritation to him. He was, she guessed, three, four years old. Maybe the photographer had caught him on a bad day.

"Your wife and son?" she asked.

Landesman nodded. "Arianna. Alexander."

Something about the way he said it prompted her next question. "Are they...?"

Her implication was clear. Were they dead? Had they been killed by Olympians? If so, it would explain a lot.

Landesman certainly understood what she was getting at. He shook his head.

"Arianna," he said, following a long intake of breath, "died shortly after that picture was taken, long before the Olympians were around. Natural causes. An unusually aggressive form of lymphatic cancer, and all the money in the world couldn't save her – it could only make her descent a little slower and her landing a little softer than it might otherwise have been. As for Xander, he's still with us, though not with *me*. By which I mean, he and I aren't in touch any more. We were always combative during his childhood, and had a terrible falling-out when he was in his early twenties. I'd tried my best to raise him on my own, using as little hired help as possible, but it wasn't easy. I was a busy man, not often home. He needed a stability in his life that I couldn't give him, so it was inevitable, I suppose, that we should come to a parting of the ways. I wish it hadn't been quite so terminal, though. I don't think he could forgive me for not having been a good enough father."

"I'm sorry."

"Thank you, but I'm reconciled to it. Some mistakes cannot be rectified. They can only be lived with, or erased."

"As in forgotten."

"Perhaps," said Landesman.

As Sam turned to go, Landesman said, "Our pasts shape us, Sam. None of us is the person he or she used to be, it's true, but what we are still contains a great proportion of what we once were. Nothing, not even suffering the worst kind of tragedy, alters us completely. At core, we are set in stone."

For some time afterward Sam debated whether he'd been referring to Chisholm, to her, or to himself. It very possibly could have been all three.

14. CALLSIGNS

THE TRAINING CONTINUED. The Titans familiarised themselves with all the weapons on offer, not just the conventional ones – the guns, the grenades, the rocket launchers – but the more unusual items such as the knuckledusters that packed a stunning million-volt punch and the semiautomatic pistol with hinged barrel and videocamera sight that could shoot round corners.

They practised manoeuvres as well, learning from Ramsay and Barrington about flanking crossfire, cover formation, shooting lines and the like. For those among them with no military background it was a crash course in the basics of armed combat, courtesy of two drill sergeants with very different teaching styles. Surprisingly it was the Australian who was the more even-tempered of the two, the one who would dismiss errors with a shrug and a "never mind, try again" attitude. The Chicagoan was less forgiving, quicker to scold. He might pepper his instruction with wisecracks, but he took the role of tutor very seriously. "This shit," he said, "if you don't get it right, you could get yourself killed. Worse, you could get the guy next to you killed." And if Ramsay was harsh with all of his pupils, there was none he was harsher with than Sam. His feeling seemed to be that, as leader, she could least afford to get things wrong – although in Sam's view there was more than a little bit of petty revenge going on. He was still smarting from her *Piss off and leave me alone* remark a while back. Not a man who took rejection well, obviously.

And then, come early March, they were ready.

They knew it, without having to be told. They were now moving in synch with one another, each instinctively understanding what his or her place was in any given manoeuvre. All of them were able to handle the weapons comfortably, although each had developed his or her own preference for and aptitude with a particular one. They had discovered that sense of quiet, deep-seated joy that comes from being part of a cohesive unit, the satisfaction that a wolf might feel in the sinuous ebb and flow of a pack on the hunt. They weren't perfect. Now and then one or other of them could still slip up. Nor were all the interpersonal relationships within the group in harmony. Barrington and Søndergaard continued their two-way sniping, which would sometimes escalate into out-and-out insults; Sparks and Hamel had started to get on each other's nerves, for reasons no one, perhaps not even they, could quite fathom; Chisholm had become ostracised since the rocket launcher incident (which he had self-deprecatingly dubbed his "Poseidon Misadventure"), although he was doing his utmost to ingratiate himself back into the group; and Sam and Ramsay remained on frosty terms, the initial affection each had felt for the other in the early weeks having now become submerged, leaving no trace of itself on the surface.

Nevertheless, they were ready. They were beginning to get impatient, wanting to know from Landesman when they were going to hit the Olympians, pestering him to be allowed to put theory into practice. If that wasn't a sign that they were ready, then nothing was.

And then one morning they arrived in the command centre to find that their battlesuits now sported names. Each of the Titans had adopted a particular suit as his or her own. The straps were permanently adjusted to fit just so, the visor display configured how each of them wanted it, and in the case of southpaw Barrington the control pad had been transferred to his right wrist. A few of them had even added customising details, having asked Patanjali to reprogram the nanobots to form particular patterns or images when the suits were in their default colour setting. Eto'o, for instance, had the green, red and yellow stripes and yellow star of the Cameroonian flag on one shoulder of her suit, Hamel had a rainbow on one shoulder of hers, Barrington had facsimile beer labels on his helmet, and Tsang's breastplate was ornamented with the symbol of the Obliteration – the letters HK surrounded by a black border.

Every suit now had a single word on the front as well, just above the heart: the name of one of the mythical Titans.

"Phoebe," said Harryhausen, reading hers.

"Rhea," said Hamel.

"Oceanus," said Chisholm.

"Hyperion," said Ramsay. "I like how it sounds. Hyperion. Yeah, I'm cool with that."

"Yer wot?" said Mahmoud, frowning at hers. "Mnemo... Memonsy... Flipping 'eck, I can't hardly read it, let alone pronounce it. Mnemosyne. Is that right? I think that's right."

"Iapetus," said Barrington. "Just what in flaming fuck is a Iapetus? Can anyone tell me?"

Tsang was Crius, Søndergaard Coeus, Sparks Theia, Eto'o Themis.

Sam approached her suit.

Tethys.

She spoke the name aloud, trying it on for size.

"I am Tethys."

It felt strange, to be rechristened in this way, without consultation, without anyone asking whether she wanted it or not. Strange but also intriguing, as though she was being invited to exchange one identity for another.

"Your callsigns," Landesman said. "Out in the field, this is how you will refer to one another and address one another. You are Titans. From now on, once you don your suits, that is what you become. Titans. Theocides. God killers. Today is your final day of training. As of tomorrow, you are on active duty. Our campaign begins."

"What about that other suit?" Ramsay asked, pointing. "'Cronus' over there. Still haven't got someone to wear that. You had trouble finding your twelfth guy, Landesman?"

"The position will be filled, don't you worry," said Landesman. "All in due course."

Putting on the suit, this time, felt ceremonial. As Sam fastened each section into place, she was conscious of taking on a role. Encasing herself in armour was, perversely, like shedding a skin, sloughing off a dry, worn-out old self to become someone gleaming and new.

I am Tethys, a Titan.

It surprised her how much that suddenly seemed to mean. And she could see it in the others' faces, the same sense of shock, the same joyous realisation.

We are Titans.

We are here to kill gods.

15. BLUE EROS MYTHOPORN

LANDESMAN ANNOUNCED THAT their first target was going to be the Cyclops.

"A giant, yes," he said, "quite strong, very violent, but its great advantage, from our point of view, is that it's none too bright. Positively stupid, in fact."

The monster had turned up recently in Wales, where anti-Olympian sentiment was rife. The Welsh National Assembly, and in particular its Plaid Cymru members, had taken a vociferous stance against Catesby Bartlett, mocking him for his views and calling him the worst and most misguided appeaser since Neville Chamberlain. The people of Wales were broadly behind their government in this, and hence the Olympians had dispatched the Cyclops to that country so as to re-establish a sense of the proper order of things. The monster had wrought havoc in various suburbs of Cardiff and Swansea, and had since then retired to the rugged climes of Snowdonia, where it had taken up residence in a nice cosy cave from which it ventured out from time to time to catch a sheep for its supper.

The proprietors of businesses in and around the area that relied on tourism for their livelihood saw a sudden, steep drop in income and were incensed, and even more so were the local hill farmers whose livestock was being depleted. They lobbied their leaders to take action. The National Assembly, however, was in a chastened and somewhat less gung-ho frame of mind than before. They had, after all, just seen Wales's two main cities sustain considerable damage at the Cyclops's hands, with attendant loss of life (although, blessedly, the fatality figures were in the low teens). If the monocular beast wished to hole up for the time being in a remote rural spot, well away from major population centres, then let it. For an absence of human casualties, the loss of a few sheep was a small price to pay.

"I'm sending a group of you to Snowdonia," Landesman informed his Titans. "Three of you should do it, I think. The objective is simple: kill the Cyclops. Make it look like an accident if you can. That way, we'll lessen the likelihood of Olympian reprisals against Wales."

"And if it's not possible to make it look like an accident?" said Harryhausen.

"The Olympians aren't any too fond of the Cyclops. It's a messy and malodorous thing. I doubt they'll miss it, and if they do want to hold the Welsh to account for its death, the punishment will be a token gesture at best. That's why I've chosen it as the object of our opening salvo in Titanomachy II – that and the fact that Wales is a convenient hop, skip and a jump away."

The chosen three were Ramsay, Eto'o and Tsang.

"Not me?" said Sam.

"A leader," said Landesman, "need not always lead from the front. And on a first operation like this, I'd rather not risk losing you. Not that I believe the op to be an especially dangerous one. I'd just like to keep you in reserve for now."

Landesman owned a private jet, a Gulfstream G550, which was kept at an aerodrome on the mainland, five miles inland from the coast, and which sported the Daedalus Industries logo, the letter "D" sprouting a pair of wings, on its tailfin. Piloting it was a man called Gray whose demeanour was so dour and imperturbable he might as well have had NO QUESTIONS ASKED tattooed across his forehead. His co-pilot and navigator, Greene, was much the same. The plane took the three Titans – Hyperion, Themis and Crius – plus two technicians and several flightcases full of equipment to Caernarfon airport, from where they travelled by rented van to Snowdonia.

The command centre at Bleaney, meanwhile, was abuzz with activity. The flatscreens were set up to display images streamed in realtime from the Titans' helmet visors. The visors doubled as integrated digital lenses. What the Titans saw, those back at base saw too.

Everyone clustered around the screens as the operation got under way. It was night, and the three Titans were moving in on the Cyclops's lair from the reconnaissance positions they had been holding all day, on a ridge overlooking the rockface into which the cave was set. Hyperion took point. Themis and Crius followed, the rear corners of a triangle. A topographical map of the region showed them as three red dots moving across the contour lines, the suits' GPS transponders pinpointing their locations to within one metre.

Sam concentrated on the trio of night-vision visor-cam images. Rugged, grainy green landscape juddered and jerked. Now and then an armoured figure would come into view, ghosting in and out of a fellow Titan's sightline. Comms chatter was at a minimum, although the mics picked up the sound of three sets of breathing, rapid with nervousness.

"How are we getting this?" Sam asked Landesman. "Via satellite?"

"Correct," came the reply. "And I know what your next question is going to be, and for the answer I shall refer you to Mr Patanjali here."

"The signals we're receiving are bounced across a number of civil telecommunications satellites before reaching us," Patanjali explained to Sam, "making both their points of origin and their point of receipt less easy to trace. But our main protection against Argus noticing what we're up to is that the signals are buried inside another signal, like parasites inside a host. Basically they're wearing a disguise. There's a primary transmission, which is tricked out to resemble a cable channel feed – to all intents and purposes *is* a cable channel feed. Embedded within that are secondary transmissions, ours, encrypted so that without the correct decoder they register as just static and white noise. Secret services have taken to using a similar method to send messages, stuff they don't want the Pantheon to find out about."

"Doesn't always work," said Sam.

"Agreed, but it does more often than it doesn't. Argus is fallible. He can't monitor and analyse every single scrap of data traffic that's out there. At any given moment there's trillions of bytes of information zipping around between mobiles, computers, TV and radio stations and so on, and he's just one person. Or god, or whatever, but still just one person. He's almost omnipresent in the electronic noösphere – almost, but not quite. Law of averages, some of it's got to slip past him, and it's likelier to do so if it's masquerading as something else. Especially if, as in this instance, the something else is as distracting as..."

He tapped a keyboard.

"This."

An image appeared on one screen in an inset window: a pair of naked men contorted together, writhing and moaning passionately.

Laughter, and one or two appalled gasps, echoed through the chamber.

"Is that...?" said Sam.

"It is," said Patanjali, "Mythoporn."

The two men were styled in the manner of Ancient Greek heroes. Their hair was curled and entwined with laurel wreaths, and their pumped-up physiques glistened with oil. The backdrop to their lubricious thrusting, tugging and tonguing was a set of cheap polystyrene Ionic columns, a badly painted diorama of an Arcadian glade, and a few olive trees. The musical soundtrack that played insistently in the background consisted of lyre, flute, cithara and cymbal twanging and clashing in time to a cheesy disco beat.

"We've set up a fake subscription channel called Blue Eros," Patanjali went on. "Beaming nothing but twenty-four-hour mythoporn to the world. This little man-on-man extravaganza is called... erm..." He turned to McCann. "Blue Eros was your idea, Jamie. What's this one?"

"*Jason And The Arse-onauts*," said McCann, adding, with a blush, "I think. Or it could be *The Labias Of Hercules*. No, wait, that's not a gay one, that's transsexual. Maybe *Homo's Odd-ass-ey*? I honestly can't remember."

"Strewth!" exclaimed Barrington. "Doesn't matter what it's called. Just switch it off. I don't want to watch a pair of Vegemite drillers doing the dirty with each other. It's downright disgusting."

"Although you wouldn't mind watching a pair of *women* 'doing the dirty with each other,' I bet," said Hamel.

"Course not. That's a whole different thing. Sheilas going at it together – it's only natural, and a thing of great beauty. And I think you'd agree with me on that, Thérèse." Barrington gave a leery grin. "If I'm not mistaken."

Hamel said nothing, although her usually tight-pursed lips did seem to twitch at the corners.

Patanjali clicked off the inset image. "Hopefully Argus won't look twice at Blue Eros, and if he does, hopefully all the hardcore shaggery will be so diverting he won't suspect there's anything else lurking beneath."

"It's not known what Argus's sexual proclivities are, or if he even has any," said McCann, "but we've programmed Blue Eros with a wide mix of genres – straight, gay, lesbian, orgy, S and M, gender bender, bestiality even – so that either he'll find something we show so fascinating that that's all he notices or, like Dez over there, so repellent that he can't bear to look. Win-win for us."

"You can both feel justly proud of yourselves, gentlemen," said Landesman, "but for now I think we should focus our attention on the matter at hand."

The three Titans had got to within 100 metres of the cave. On the screens there were now three slightly different views of the same steep-sided opening, a crooked black fissure in the rockface like an inverted lightning strike, with an apron of scree at its base.

Ramsay's voice came over the speakers. "Base, this is Hyperion. We are in contact range of objective. Target has not re-emerged since we saw him enter this afternoon with a fresh kill. Target assumed to be sleeping off his meal. Please confirm that we are go for next stage. Repeat, please confirm we are go."

Landesman bent to the microphone in front of him. "That's affirmative, Hyperion. Proceed to next stage. You might want to make sure first that target *is* asleep."

"Understood, base."

"And Titans? Best of luck."

"Luck is for the ill-prepared," said Hyperion. "That's a Schwarzenegger quote, by the way. 'Course, it happens to be from *Junior*, so I don't think it really counts. Crius?"

Crius's visor-cam image panned left, centring on Ramsay/Hyperion. Hyperion hand-signalled, touching the side of his head then pointing to the cave.

Tsang/Crius stole up to the cave entrance. His head-up display registered a maximising of aural scanner input gain, and the speakers relayed speleological sounds: the drip-drip-drip of water, the drift of breezes in a confined space, the hissing echo of depth and hollowness. In the midst of it all, clearly discernible, was a noise like a sheet of canvas being slowly and repeatedly ripped in two, little by little.

"That's..." said Sam. "That's snoring."

"Certainly sounds like it," said Landesman.

"Base, Crius. Are you getting this?"

"We are, Crius," said Landesman. "Target does appear to be deep in the arms of Morpheus. Hyperion, Themis, move up to Crius's position. Start laying the charges."

"Roger that," said Hyperion.

Off-mic, Landesman said, "We're clear for all surveillance satellites, aren't we?"

"We have an Indian RISAT-2 synthetic aperture radar spy satellite currently mid-Atlantic," replied one of the technicians, "and an Israeli Ofek-7 infrared job just south of Iceland. Nothing's scheduled to pass directly over north Wales 'til just after 10pm, and nothing to our knowledge has been retasked or repositioned in the last couple of hours. We have a clear sixty-minute window."

"Excellent."

Just inside the cavemouth, Eto'o/Themis got busy inserting charges into clefts in the walls. She wasn't using ordinary explosive material but a substance of Landesman's devising, a chlorofluorocarbon refrigerant derivative which he'd dubbed "frostique." Normally of a tacky, putty-like consistency, frostique underwent spectacular molecular alteration when subjected to an electric current. The charge reduced its core temperature to absolute zero and the frostique in turn flash-froze everything it was in contact with. Whatever it touched, up to a radius of 5 metres, became brittle and would break up into fragments. For covert work like this, frostique was ideal, in as much as it was remarkably effective but left little evidence of itself behind other than a few minute battery-powered blasting triggers that could easily be overlooked by anyone scouring the rubble for clues.

The plan was to set off a quickfire chain of discharges that would bring the entire cave crashing down in on itself. Themis chose the sites for the wads of frostique with precision, inserting and priming the radio-controlled blasting triggers carefully. As she moved deeper into the cave, the atmosphere in mission control became quieter and more tense. Sam had to force herself to unclench her hands; she was digging her fingernails into her palms so hard it hurt. Hyperion and Crius, weapons drawn, covered Themis's every step.

"Boy, this place stinks," said Hyperion, and about 50 metres into the cave the source of the stench became apparent. There was a litter of bones on the floor, interspersed with ragged scraps of fleece and hunks of rotting offal. Sheep skulls leered up with hollow eye sockets and inane death grins.

The three Titans continued on. The scanner-enhanced snoring grew louder and more vibrant. Somewhere in the darkness up ahead a five-metre-tall monster slumbered on a full belly, blissfully unaware that its remaining lifespan could be measured in minutes. These rumbling stentorian inhalations were its few final breaths.

"Done," said Themis softly, as she finished setting the last charge.

"Then let's get the hot holy fuck out of here," said Hyperion.

They trod warily back towards the cave entrance, stepping over or skirting round the carcasses of the Cyclops's prey. A sliver of night appeared ahead, glimmering bright green against the darker greenness of the cave interior.

"Almost there," said Hyperion. "Themis, you all set to remote-detonate?"

Themis raised her left arm to check her wristpad. "One touch, and adieu Cyclops."

"Soon as we're a dozen paces clear of the cave, bring the house down. Don't wait for instructions, just do it."

"Roger."

In mission control the tension began to ease. Things were looking good. A minute from now, perhaps less, the Cyclops was going to be buried beneath thousands of tons of rock. Mission accomplished.

Then Sam said, "Do you hear that?"

"Hear what?" said Landesman.

"Exactly. The snoring's stopped."

Everyone listened.

Barrington said, "Oh shit."

Landesman grabbed the mic. "Titans, base. Target is awake. Repeat, target is awake. Go. Get out. Run. Now!"

Immediately, the three screen images started to shudder and veer crazily as the Titans launched into sprint mode.

At the same time the speakers were filled with a terrible roaring.

16. THE CYCLOPS

Hyperion and Crius reached the cavemouth first, hurtling down the short scree slope and out onto the rock-strewn grass beyond. Themis was close behind, but suddenly the image from her visor whirled upwards, then stuttered and was almost lost in a blizzard of interference. When the image resumed clarity, it showed the apex of the cave roof.

"Themis," said Landesman. "Themis. Come in. Do you read me? Themis!"

"She tripped over," Sam said. "She's lying on the floor. Probably hit her head as she fell."

"Themis!" Landesman said again.

There was a groan, then Eto's voice replied, thickly, "I read you."

"Get up, Themis. You have to move."

"Sure. Yes. *D'accord.*"

The image swung from side to side.

"My chin hurts," Themis said. "And my suit... I think... a malfunction. Legs heavy."

"Servo might've been knocked out of commission," said McCann.

"That can happen?" said Hamel.

"It's not supposed to, but aye, it can. That or a connection's come loose somewhere."

"You can still walk," Landesman said into the mic. "It'll feel ungainly but you have to. Hyperion? Crius? Themis's down."

"Copy that, base," said Hyperion. "We know. We're on our way back for her."

Themis was staggering to her feet. Something loomed in the green haze of her vision. Sam glimpsed a vast hairy hand tipped with nails that looked like talons, a barrel chest covered in dark stains that could only be patches of dried blood, and then a face – a lantern jaw, a mouth lined with tent-peg teeth, a crop of shaggy, matted hair, and an eye. A single, central eye the size of a tennis ball. Narrowed in confusion, then widening in comprehension, then narrowing again as it fixed Themis with a look of hungry malevolence.

The hand reached for Themis. She screamed.

Crius was first back into the cave. His visor-cam showed the Cyclops hoisting Themis off the floor by the head, bearing her entire weight with just one arm. Nearly three times as tall as her, the monster's head brushed the ceiling of the cave. Themis latched onto the Cyclops's wrist with both hands to support herself and take the pressure off the join between her neck and skull. She kicked out. The Cyclops extended its arm to full length, putting its body out of range of her feet.

Crius opened fire, strafing the monster with assault rifle fire. Ricochet sparks dazzled emerald-bright off the walls. Hyperion arrived and joined in with a semiautomatic pistol. The Cyclops recoiled, letting out a howl of affront.

"What are they doing?" McCann cried. "Mr Landesman, what are they doing?"

"Obviously they're trying to scare that thing into dropping Themis," said Landesman. "At the very least wing him. With luck, kill him. Why?"

"They might hit her."

"So? She's in her battlesuit."

"But the suit's integrity has been compromised," said McCann. "There's every chance she's not bulletproof any more."

Landesman swore under his breath. Into the mic he said, "Hyperion, Crius, hold your fire."

"What the – ?" said Hyperion. "Say again, base."

"Hold your fire. Themis is vulnerable."

"Shit. You're kidding. What the hell else are we supposed to do, then?"

"Charge him. Use stun-dusters on him."

But it was too late. The Cyclops had tightened its grip on Themis. Her helmet started to crack and crumple in its hand. Over the comms link came the desperate gasps and grunts of someone whose abject helplessness was almost as agonising to her as the sensation of her own skull being slowly crushed. The creaking of bone under pressure was all too crisply relayed back to base by the helmet's inbuilt sound sensors.

As Hyperion and Crius stowed their weapons and prepared for a close-up assault, all at once Themis stopped struggling. She let go of the monster's wrist and made a very deliberate show of raising her left arm and moving her right hand towards it.

Landesman understood. White-faced, grim-lipped, he said, "Hyperion, Crius, fall back."

"What?" said Hyperion. "No way."

"Themis is going to detonate."

"We can get to him before –"

"There isn't time. *Fall back*."

Sam commandeered the mic. "Hyperion, Crius, do it. Themis has made her decision."

Themis's right index finger was poised over her wristpad. She managed to choke out a few words. "This is good," she said. "I am happy with this."

"Go!" Sam shouted at Hyperion and Crius. "Move or die!"

"Aw fuck," said Hyperion, and he and his fellow Titan turned and fled.

The Cyclops raised Themis's face level with its own. A gaping mouth filled the screen, each tooth like an elephant tusk. The look in the monster's eye was now one of curiosity. What was this little human female up to? She wasn't dead yet, so why had she stopped writhing in distress?

Themis – Eto'o – spat out a curse at the monster in French. Then she said, "*Maman, papa, je viens pour vous voir de nouveau...*"

Hyperion turned back to look at the cave just as the dozen or so frostique charges went off in swift succession. There was a ripple of reports from within, like the sound of ice cubes cracking but magnified a thousandfold, and then the entire cavemouth seemed to implode, sucking shut and taking a section of the rockface with it. The *boom* was tremendous, overloading the speakers. At the same instant, Themis's visor-cam image went blank.

Hyperion and Crius, and all at mission control, were left staring at a shattered, sagging indentation in the rockface, from which a thick swirl of dust, like a soul released from a body, billowed up and dispersed into the starry sky.

17. THE PROTHERO STARE

"JUST WHAT THE fuck happened last night?"

This was Ramsay, to McCann, early the next morning, minutes after he set foot back on Bleaney Island. He had McCann backed up against a wall in the command centre, with a forearm pressed to the engineer's epiglottis and a section of his shirtfront bunched around the other hand. McCann looked terrified, as well he might be. The Chicagoan's expression was pure murderous rage. Others – technicians, Titans, Sam – looked on, startled. It had happened so quickly. Ramsay had marched in and grabbed hold of McCann before most of them knew he was even in the room.

"I don't know!" McCann gasped. "Some kind of breakdown in Soleil's suit."

"I thought the damn things were supposed to be indestructible."

"I never said that. Clearly there's a design flaw. Maybe

the servomotor housings need to be hardened, or, or... I just don't know. If I had the suit I could examine it, run some tests..."

"Well, you can't," Ramsay snarled, "on account of it's buried under half a hillside in the middle of goddamn Wales, along with Soleil. And I'm holding you personally responsible."

"It wasn't my fault," McCann protested.

"Oh yeah?" Ramsay drew him away from the wall and slammed him back into it hard enough to wind him. "You built the fuckers. Whose else fault can it be?"

"Rick."

"Sam, back off."

Sam placed a hand on Ramsay's shoulder. "That's enough. We get it. You're upset. But so's Jamie. So are all of us."

Ramsay peered at her hand as though it was dog dirt. Sam, taking the hint, withdrew it.

"Upset?" he said. "Let me tell you, the last thing I am is upset. I'm mad as hell, is what I am. I just lost a man. I was unit leader on that op, and I lost a man, which I wouldn't have if Scotty here had done his job properly."

He thrust McCann against the wall a third time, forearm pushing upwards on the engineer's trachea so that McCann was forced to go on tiptoes to avoid strangulation.

"Taking it out on Jamie isn't going to help anyone," Sam said.

"Oh no?" Ramsay retorted. "'Cause it's sure as hell making *me* feel better."

"It won't bring Soleil back, it won't undo what's done. Rick, what happened in that cave was an accident. You know that."

"Do I?"

"Deep down you do. Soleil tripped, and something in her battlesuit took a knock and broke. If any good is to come of this, it's the fact that now we know there's a potential problem with all the suits that we didn't know was there before. Something Jamie can look into and put right. Right, Jamie?"

Avidly McCann nodded.

"Oh, that's twisted fucking logic," said Ramsay. "A Titan died – on our first fucking outing, what's more – but hey, it's OK, look on the bright side, at least it's shown us that we're all going to have to twinkletoe around like ballerinas from now on if we don't want to get ourselves killed."

"You eliminated the Cyclops. The op was a success."

"Whoopee-fucking-doo. Medals all round."

Letting go of McCann with a snort of disgust, Ramsay swung away from him. The engineer sank to the floor, limp with relief.

"You know, I'm thinking maybe that Pugh guy was right after all," Ramsay said to Sam, to everyone. "This *is* bullshit. Those suits are deathtraps. Landesman's plan sucks. This whole crusade against the Pantheon is a waste of time. It's bullshit, and I'm not sure I wanna be a part of it any more."

And with that, he stormed out.

Technician looked at technician. Titan looked at Titan. Unease was in everybody's eyes.

Sam wished Landesman was there to make some rallying speech and raise people's spirits. He, however, was taking Eto'o's death particularly hard. Immediately after her act of supreme self-sacrifice, he had sequestered himself away in his office, and was refusing to open the door to anyone or even answer anyone's knock.

In his absence, the role of morale booster fell on Sam.

"Jamie," she said to McCann.

"Aye?" said the engineer, getting to his feet, looking ruffled and still very alarmed.

"You can figure out what went wrong with Soleil's suit, can't you?"

"I hope so. Without the suit itself –"

"Wrong answer. Not 'I hope so.' That's not good enough. You *will*. You'll work day and night, you won't stop, you won't rest and neither will any of your colleagues until the fault is found and rectified. Do you understand?"

"Yes."

"I want your word on it. I am not kidding around here. I want you to promise me that you'll give it your all."

McCann was all seriousness. "I will, I promise. Of course I will."

"Good. Because otherwise I will be unhappy. Rick just now, being unhappy? That, believe me, is nothing compared to me being unhappy. That was *happy* compared to me being unhappy."

She then gave McCann a stare that she'd seen Inspector Prothero give on a number of occasions, most memorably to a constable who'd managed to contaminate a crime scene by opening several drawers without first taking the basic precaution of putting on latex gloves. It was a look that combined equal parts disdain, derision and annoyance, with a pinch of world-weary resignation thrown in for good measure, and it invariably left the recipient feeling as low as it was humanly possible to feel while at the same time determined to improve and do better next time. Sam knew this because she herself had had the look directed against her once. Once had been enough.

She must have emulated her DI and mentor pretty well, because McCann withered visibly before her, seeming almost to shrink, to become physically the small boy that he was inside. Moments later he was scurrying around marshalling the other technicians, getting them to pull battlesuits off their stands and onto workbenches, starting to dismantle them, generally whipping up a frenzy of keen investigative fervour.

Sam knew she had bullied the poor kid. Equally, it had got results, and her fellow Titans appeared reassured. Something was being seen to be done. If McCann could prevent the suits from ever going wrong in that way again, then Eto'o would not have died in vain.

Later, Hamel drew Sam aside for a private word, and confirmed that her handling of the situation had been spot-on.

"You did well," she said. "I am going to miss Soleil, very much. But I'm glad to know that hers won't have been a wasted death."

"Thérèse, do you mind if I ask? Were you and Soleil... you know?"

"Sam. You can say it. Were we lovers?"

"Yes."

"No." Hamel lofted her shoulders slightly, disappointed but philosophical. "No. Soleil was not the way I am. However, I liked her a great deal. She reminded me very much of my partner."

"The partner you mentioned, the one the Olympians killed."

"Yes. Mélanie. They looked nothing alike. Mélanie was Caucasian, for one thing. But they both had this straightforwardness about them, this pragmatism, so admirable. Also, with Soleil I was able to speak French, and that was nice. It's tiring to speak a second language all day, and the French was a reminder of home, you know? Like putting on a pair of old slippers."

"You could speak French with me if you like," Sam said, "as long as you don't mind limiting it to GCSE level. *Comment est votre baguette, monsieur boulanger?*"

Hamel pulled a face. "Your accent is horrible, and your grammar not much better."

"But apart from that..."

"Also, it sounded like you were asking the baker how his penis is, which I don't think was your intention at all."

"Ah. Best we stick to English, then."

"Yes, I think that would be a good idea. Sam?"

"Yes?"

"Deaths were inevitable, of course," Hamel said. "We must accept that. You must most of all."

"I know, I know. Just, why so early on? On our very first outing? It doesn't bode well for the future."

"Don't be discouraged. Feel sad, yes, but stay strong. That's my advice. As leader, you must feel hurt by each casualty as much as anyone, perhaps more than anyone, but must show it less than anyone."

"A tall order."

"Then be tall."

"I'm five foot six in my socks."

"Then wear high heels."

"I would," Sam said, "if I could only find a pair that go with a battlesuit."

"Curse those men," said Hamel, "for making battlesuits that are so hard to accessorise with. Why couldn't Landesman have spent a bit more money and brought in Ralph Lauren to help with the design?"

"He just wasn't thinking, was he?"

They laughed, and the laughter felt good. It warded off the sense of despair that was gnawing at Sam, the fear that the task Landesman had set them was of Herculean proportions – perhaps Sisyphean proportions – too great for them to accomplish, futile, unfulfillable. After all, the Cyclops was supposed to have been a relatively easy takedown, entry-level stuff. One of the least feared of the Olympians' monsters, a moronic brute of a creature – and yet killing him exacted a heavy price. If for each monster scalp the Titans claimed one of their number had to die, that was a rate of attrition they simply couldn't sustain. There'd be none of them left when the time came to confront the Olympians themselves.

"One thing I am sure of," Sam said. "From now on, no op takes place that I don't go on. I'm not staying behind the lines like some First World War general. I'm not prepared to sit back and watch while others go out and risk their lives. I want to lead from the front. If I'm there in the thick of things, then maybe I can prevent any further mishaps. At the very least I'll be in a position to try and do something, rather than just looking on helplessly."

"As I recall, you were hardly 'looking on helplessly' last night," Hamel said. "You were very proactive. But still, I take your point, and I respect it. Do you know what my therapist would say about you? He'd say you have 'control issues.'"

"I think your therapist probably has no idea what it's like to make life-or-death decisions or be responsible for other people's physical safety."

"True. To be honest, I'm not sure why I used to go to see him so regularly. He always seemed to me an overpaid fool with too many degrees and too little life experience. He was supposed to be helping me get over Mélanie's death, but again and again the conversation would come round to me being a lesbian."

"He was too fascinated by that?"

"Much too. But here's a funny thing. I haven't felt the need for therapy since coming to this island – haven't felt that need, that compulsion to talk to someone about how I'm feeling. It's like, this, what we're doing, this is a kind of therapy in itself. Do you not agree?"

Sam pondered. "I have a purpose again. I don't have that sense of being adrift in my own life any more. You could be right. Or maybe it's just that I don't have as much time on my hands as I used to. Before, I'd sit at home for days on end, obsessing about myself and my misery. Haven't had a spare moment to do that here."

"Revenge as the cure for bereavement?" wondered Hamel.

"Perhaps," said Sam.

Or perhaps not.

Perhaps there was only one true cure for bereavement – the one Eto'o had found in the course of exacting revenge.

18. STRATOSPHERICALLY REMOTE

NINE DAYS LATER, Landesman's Gulfstream was flying west at a mean speed of 500 knots towards one of the small commercial airports in the environs of Miami.

On board were Sam, Hamel, Sparks and Barrington, plus McCann and another two technicians. Three hours into the trip, Barrington was stretched out fast asleep on the plush sofa in the plane's cabin, Hamel was plugged into her iPod nodding along to Patsy Cline and k.d. lang, Sparks was watching a Pixar movie on a portable DVD player, and Sam was listening to McCann explain the necessary alterations he had made to the battlesuits.

"I've got to say," the engineer said, "it's something that never occurred to me, and I'm a great hairy numpty for not thinking of it. Any complex system that's run by microprocessor, you need redundancy. You have to have backup in the event something goes wrong with the main CPU. I just felt, with the suits being so impact-resistant and all, that'd never be a problem. The CPU couldn't get damaged, so why install an auxiliary one in case it did? All that'd mean was extra weight, extra wiring, extra hassle."

McCann had been hangdog – more accurately, hangpuppy – these past few days, once he'd realised the mistake he had made in the suit's design. A number of times Sam had had to tell him he wasn't to blame, it was a simple oversight, he shouldn't beat himself up so about it, even Einstein had his off-days. She couldn't quite console him, however, nor did she have the strength to, not really. She had her own burdens. He couldn't expect her to carry his as well.

"Took us ages to pin down why Soleil's leg servos failed," he went on. "We broke those suits down to the smallest wee parts, and when that didn't turn up anything we put them back together and started banging them about every which way. We reckoned you lot had given them such a pounding during training, if that hadn't found a chink in the armour then nothing would. Thanks to you they'd been tested almost to destruction and passed. But it still seemed worth a try. Trouble is, what none of you had done was whack your head hard enough against the ground to jangle the onboard computer."

"Silly us."

"Aye, well, it was a thousand-to-one thing, Soleil falling just how she did, catching her helmet against a rock just so, at just the right angle and with just the right amount of force to scramble the hardware.

That's what paralysed the servos. In all fairness, most of the suit continued to work fine. I mean, it could have been much worse, the whole damn thing could have gone down..."

He flicked a hand as though to drive off a persistent gnat.

"No, that doesn't make up for it. I bollocksed up. That's what it comes down to. I bollocksed up, and someone died because of that."

His voice faltered, tightening, threatening to become a sob. Sam reached out and clasped his arm. She felt like a priest offering absolution, except instead of a confessional they were in a luxury jet cruising at 40,000 feet.

"Soleil died because of the Cyclops," she said, "not because of you. She chose to go out the way she did, and under the circumstances it was the only thing she could do, and the best thing. I know how Rick keeps grumbling, but never mind him. The problem with her suit was a contributing factor but it was far from being the sole cause."

McCann wiped his eyes and sniffed. "It's sorted now, though, I swear. All the suits have been fitted with an auxiliary CPU that'll kick in a millisecond after the main CPU registers any kind of runtime error. The auxiliary'll offer support in the affected areas or else take over altogether if the main CPU's fritzed beyond redemption. It's installed just beneath the power pack, well out of harm's way. The odds against both computers getting knocked out of commission – well, they've got to be stratospherically remote, haven't they?"

"You tell me."

"Aye," the engineer said, confirming it in his own mind. "Stratospherically remote."

The plane darted onwards across the broad blue glitter of the Atlantic. A couple of hundred miles off the coast of Florida it hit clouds and some severe turbulence. The co-pilot, Greene, suggested over the intercom that everyone might like to fasten their seatbelts, and for quarter of an hour the Gulfstream bucked and jolted in the grip of elemental forces, as though the sky were a fractious child and the plane were the sky's plaything. Across the cabin from Sam, Sparks sat hunched in her seat, clutching the gold crucifix at her neck and murmuring a prayer. As the turbulence subsided and the flight smoothed, Sam leaned over and said, "He was listening."

"He always does," Sparks replied matter-of-factly. "My aunt and uncle were churchgoing folk and they raised me right. They taught me to fear God and trust in Him, and so far He ain't steered me wrong."

"You were brought up by your aunt and uncle? What about your parents?"

"Nobody knows nothing about my daddy 'cept he was white, and my mom was a no-account who left soon after I was born and never came back. My aunt and uncle, them and my grandmother, they were all the family I ever had, all I ever needed. They've gone to their reward now, of course, but I still have Jesus. A shoulder to cry on, a friend to rely on, Jesus sees me through everything. He's the one who guided Mr Landesman's hand in choosing me to become a

Titan, and He saw to it that Mr Landesman selected me for this mission."

To Sam's knowledge, Landesman hadn't needed supervision from on high when it came to deciding which Titan went up against which particular monster or Olympian. "My policy," he had told her yesterday, "is that each of you gets to confront whoever – or, as the case may be, whatever – was responsible for the deaths of your loved ones. It's only right and fair. Sparks lost relatives to the Hydra, ergo she is a shoo-in for tomorrow's op."

Landesman had recovered most of the pep and vigour that had gone out of him in the wake of the Snowdonia débâcle. He'd been encouraged by the fact that the Olympians had chosen not to visit retaliation on Wales in response to the Cyclops's fatal entombing. A day earlier a terse video statement had been sent to every TV station on earth and also disseminated across the internet, showing Zeus making a statement on that very topic.

"It has come to our attention," he declared, "that the being whom you and we know as the Cyclops has perished as a result of a cave-in in north Wales. Our understanding is that the event was pure accident, due most likely to local tectonic instability. We will not make efforts to recover the body. We mourn his loss, and salute a fallen comrade."

That was all, a handful of sentences couched in Zeus's usual orotund tones, delivered to camera with blazing eyes and furrowed brow. If the king of the Pantheon suspected foul play in connection with the Cyclops's demise, it showed in neither his face nor his words. Landesman, certainly, was convinced the Olympians were ignorant of the truth behind the apparent misfortune.

"We pulled it off," he had said, with quiet vindication. "I'd've preferred to have done it without losing anyone, but still – we pulled it off."

Sparks, watching Sam's face, noted scepticism there. Sam was trying hard to hide it but couldn't quite manage to.

"You ain't a believer," she said. "That's OK. Can't all of us be believers, though the Lord'd like it that way. He lets some folk think they can do without faith, 'til they realise they can't. It's all part of His plan, sister. All part of His plan. You'll get there in the end."

"Maybe," Sam said. "It's possible, I suppose."

"You're a good person, no doubt about it. There's some among our number who's not deserving of His grace and mercy, but you ain't one of them. Your heart is true, and you're doing the Lord's work, whether you realise it or not. We all are."

"We are?"

"Sure we are!" Sparks said, wide-eyed, as though it was the most obvious thing in the world. "Them Olympians go around calling themselves gods. That is an offence in His eyes. No one can call themself that but Him. So somebody taking those guys out, knocking 'em off their perch? That's His work all right. And now through His infinite wisdom He's given me the chance to slay the evil beast that took my Nanna and my Aunt Celeste and my Uncle Hubert. An eye for an eye. I bless Him for that, and I bless His agent on earth Mr Landesman too, and I relish the thought of being the one to rid the world of that thing."

Sam couldn't not ask. "Some among us who don't deserve God's grace and mercy? Anyone specifically?"

"I won't name names," Sparks said in low, conspiratorial tones, "but... you know." She cast a glance over her shoulder, towards the rear of the cabin.

Sam immediately looked at Barrington, who had contrived to remain asleep despite the bout of turbulence.

"Dez is a bit rough round the edges, I grant you," she said, dropping her voice to match the other woman's. "Not the most enlightened of human beings. And his sense of humour is, let's say, an acquired taste. But basically he's sound."

"Oh no, not him," Sparks said, now whispering. "Her. The sinner."

Sam transferred her gaze to Hamel, who was staring out of a porthole, still in thrall to her music.

"Oh," she said.

"'If there is a man who lies with a male as those who lie with a woman, both of them have committed a detestable act; they shall surely be put to death. Their bloodguiltness is upon them.' Leviticus. Applies to the ladies as well." Sparks mimed a shudder. "She's an abomination. Makes my skin crawl just being in the same room as her."

"She's – she's a good person too."

"That's as may be, but she has chosen a lifestyle that is sick and unclean and will damn her soul to hell for all eternity."

"But she's one of us, doing God's work with us. Surely that, well, redeems her?"

"Afraid not." Sparks's dark eyes were as hard as coal. "'Less she renounces her deviant ways, whatever deeds she's done in life won't save her from His judgement. Oh, don't worry. I can tell what you're thinking. I'll work alongside her, I'll be her comrade-in-arms, I'll have her back, you needn't have any doubts on that score. Just don't ask me to be her friend, OK?"

"OK." Sam looked back at Hamel, who caught her eye briefly then returned her attention to the view outside. Sam wondered whether the Canadian had overheard anything Sparks had just said. Likely not. The music was still hissing in Hamel's earbuds, and Sparks had done her best to be discreet. All the same, it was conceivable that the odd word might have leaked through, enough to enlighten Hamel as to her fellow Titan's true feelings about her. Perhaps she knew anyway. Neither woman much cared for the other. There'd been mutual antipathy there almost from the start. Maybe Hamel had sensed Sparks's disapproval and divined the reason behind it without having to be told.

Sam shunted it to the back of her mind. It wasn't a problem – wouldn't be as long as it didn't interfere with the op.

"Commencing our descent now," co-pilot Greene announced. "We should be landing in –"

The rest was drowned out by a fart from Barrington that was so raucous and percussive he startled himself awake with it.

"Strewth!" he cried, sitting up and glancing worriedly out of a porthole. "Was that a bird strike? Are we about to crash?"

"We," said Sam, with a pained expression, fanning her face, "should be so lucky."

19. THE EVERGLADES

KNEE-DEEP IN SWAMP and spatterdock lilies, they moved in a staggered line, weapons at the ready. The air wasn't much less foetid and soupy than the water they were wading through. Warbling birdcalls echoed through the tree canopy overhead. Flying insects whined about their faces and stung the few portions of exposed skin available. Spanish moss dangled from the boughs of overhanging oaks and mangroves, brushing their helmets like dry, insubstantial fingers. Forest-pattern camouflage turned each Titan into walking vegetation, human-shaped embodiments of their surroundings. They trod like ghosts, dark dazzle green through dark dazzle green, and the Everglades spread around them, mile upon mile upon mile of it, steaming and overgrown and silty, neither earth nor sea but the worst possible merging of the two elements: unsolid, humid, a vast rotting floorboard of a place.

This had been the home of the Hydra for going on four years now. Originally the monster had been deployed by the Olympians in southern Texas as part of their strategy for dealing with an armed insurrection that was going on there, in and around Houston. Once that was successfully quelled, and the ringleaders treated to a public execution, the Olympians had left the Hydra behind, a kind of memento, a token to remind those rednecks not to get too uppity again, and also something for them to focus on so that further rebellion would be far from their thoughts. A large, multi-headed reptilian creature roaming the countryside, attacking ranches and homesteads and killing cattle and even the odd human was, after all, quite a demand on people's attention, and quite a drain on the state's appetite for violent confrontation.

Soon, however, the Hydra had decided it found the arid Texan climate uncongenial and it had gravitated east towards the Mississippi Delta, a habitat moister and muddier and much more to the monster's liking. For a time it had wallowed contentedly in the New Orleans region, prowling the bayous and lurking in the levees. It was during that period that Kayla Sparks's relatives had had the bad luck to run into it late one night while driving home from dinner at a seafood restaurant in Port Sulphur. Their bellies full of crawfish soup and soft-shell crab, they'd run into the Hydra on a lonely northbound stretch of Highway 23. Or actually, *not* run into. Sparks's Uncle Hubert had swerved his Ford Taurus off the road in order to avoid a head-on collision with the monster, and the car had ploughed nose-first down a steep bank into a gully.

Had Hubert, his wife and her mother died instantly in the crash, that would have been a mercy. But seatbelts and airbags preserved all three of them from fatal injury and reserved all three of them for a far worse fate. The Hydra descended the bank to the wrecked vehicle and proceeded to devour the dazed occupants more or less simultaneously, reaching in through the smashed-out windows with separate heads, hauling the family members out and tearing them apart. Louisiana PD had pieced the sequence of events together from the available evidence: skidmarks, Hydra spoor – oh, and the appalling bloody carnage of human remains that surrounded the Taurus for several yards in every direction.

Subsequently the Hydra had resumed its journey eastward and southward, passing down Florida's Gulf Coast to settle eventually in the Everglades, which were now a domain it had almost exclusively to itself. Since its arrival, most of the human residents in the southern portion of the state had moved out, leading to, among other things, a grievous property slump, with multimillion-dollar beachfront mansions now going for a song. Other victims of the Hydra's presence were the plethora of local theme parks – for all that they boasted newly erected 20-foot-tall steel security fences and watchtowers with manned machine-gun posts – and, indeed, the Florida tourism industry in general, those airboat rides and those tours of Hemingway's house looking increasingly unattractive to overseas visitors and Americans alike. Only the state's substantial population of retirees, because they were either too old or too ornery to care, were unwilling to be intimidated by having the Hydra on their doorsteps. They, therefore, had become the monster's principal quarry, its primary source of nutrition, a tastier and easier-to-catch morsel, softer in every sense, than its *secondary* source of nutrition, alligators. Every so often the Hydra would steal into the grounds of a rest home or gated community, using canals as its means of access, pluck some unwary Grey Panther or Silver Surfer from a sun lounger or wheelchair, and drag its screaming pension-age prey back into the water.

"It's quicker'n cancer," commented one octogenarian Floridian, when asked by a TV reporter why she continued to live where she did after having watched two of her closest friends succumb to Hydra attack on separate occasions. "You get to my age, you begin to think it's better to go fast, and while you've still got most of your inner organs and all of your marbles. Hydra wants to take me, like it did my gal pals Annie-May and Elvira? I say bring it on. Hope the damn thing chokes on my hip replacement."

As for the Olympians, they appeared oblivious to the fact that the Hydra was at large, bringing impoverishment and euthanasia to the Sunshine State. Hermes could have come any time to retrieve it. He, along with Hera, who had power over the monsters, could have whisked the Hydra back to its pen on Mount Olympus, had Zeus instructed them to do so. Zeus, however, was not bothered, it would seem. Either he'd forgotten the Hydra was still out there, or else, perhaps, he simply had it in for America's Deep South.

The last confirmed sighting of the Hydra had been at a location just north of the Tamiami Canal, not far from the city of Copeland. That was just over a week ago, when an intrepid – some would say foolhardy – wildlife documentary film crew looking for footage of the creature had got exactly what they were after. Unfortunately their encounter with it had been a little more up-close and personal than they might have liked, and only one of them had emerged unscathed. The other two had been savaged to pieces and partially eaten, their deaths recorded for posterity on hi-def video by the surviving member, who was traumatised by the event but not so traumatised that he hadn't managed to auction the tape to the highest-bidding TV network for a seven-figure sum.

Landesman had made the Titans watch the gruesome video clip prior to embarking on the op.

"That is what you'll be facing," he had said after they'd sat through it a harrowing three times. "Be under no illusion: the Hydra is a hellish lethal beast. Hard to kill, too. It's capable of regenerating lost or damaged tissue almost instantly. No one's sure how. Some biologists have posited that it has huge quantities of self-organising blastema cells, which give it an exaggerated form of the ability of many reptiles and amphibians to re-grow lost legs or tails. Or it could, of course, be a magical creature of myth, and therefore has abilities that are beyond the powers of rational empiricism to account for."

"It *can* be killed, though," Sparks had said.

"Oh yes," Landesman had replied. "I believe it can."

A few hours since venturing into the Everglades, the four Titans had seen a couple of alligators but nothing larger or more alarming than that. The 'gators had slithered away at their approach, seeking refuge in underbrush or deep water, and Barrington had remarked disparagingly about how small they were "compared to the crocs back home." Their snaggletooth grins were unnerving, though, and Sam was glad to be kitted out in armour that they hadn't a hope of biting through. She was gladder still of the substantial firepower that she and her cohorts were carrying.

Near midday, she called a rest stop. The Titans clambered out of the swamp onto the shady, dry elevation of a tree island, and broke out energy bars and bottled water. Removing her helmet, Sam felt the stagnant, damp Everglades air close in around her head, unbearably clammy, like being swaddled in a hot wet towel.

"Now I really appreciate these suits' microclimates," she said. "We'd be roasting alive otherwise."

Barrington concurred. "I'm as chilly as a brew in an eski."

"If you'll excuse me," said Sparks, standing, "I need a comfort break. This may take some time."

"Five minutes, no more," Sam said.

"I'll need that long just to get my drawers down. These darn suits, they ain't toilet-friendly, you knowum saying?"

"Ten minutes, then. We need to get moving again soon."

Sparks disappeared into a dense thicket of saw palmetto.

The time ticked by. Hamel occupied herself by checking her weapon, a lightweight, self-contained flamethrower fuelled by capsules of liquid hydrazine. Sam did likewise with her recoilless submachine gun. Not long ago Landesman had enthused to her about the beauty of the gun's design. It was constructed so as to direct the force of the recoil downwards, rather than into your shoulder. Where a .45-calibre weapon typically had a kick like a mule, and you had muzzle climb to contend with, this one fired straight and true with scarcely a twitch in your hands, while still spitting out the rounds at a rate of over 4,000 per minute on full-auto. To Sam it looked like a gun that had been stripped down to its bare essentials, flensed, inelegant. She couldn't deny, though, that it was a joy to fire. There was something almost obscene in the way it could rip apart paper targets and yet, to the wielder, it might as well have been a water pistol for all the handling trouble it gave.

"Sam?" said Barrington. "Base is calling in. They want a sitrep."

"Not Sam. Tethys," Sam said as she slid her helmet back on. She was reminding herself about her callsign as much as Barrington. "Base, this is Tethys. We're just taking a breather."

"I know," said Landesman, five time zones and several thousand miles away. "I can see. But why has Theia gone offline?"

"Theia's answering the call of nature. I imagine she wants some privacy."

"I don't like being incommunicado with a Titan in the field."

"Her ten minutes are nearly up. I'll go and see what's keeping her."

Sam pushed her way into the palmetto thicket, shoving aside the long spiky leaves. There was no sign of Sparks – Theia. She forged further in. How deep into the thicket had Theia gone? How much privacy did a girl need? There was shy and then there was ridiculously bashful.

An unsettling feeling came over Sam. How still everything suddenly seemed. Not just still. Silent. The birdcalls were absent. Minutes earlier there had been a cacophony of cuckoo hoots and stork squawks and the up-down trills of mockingbirds. Now nothing. Even the incessant insect hum sounded subdued.

She knew then, without knowing quite how she knew, that the Hydra was nearby.

She lowered her gun from port-arms to ready.

Had it got Theia? Snatched her from the thicket?

There was no sign of a struggle, as far as she could see. The palmetto leaves and the ground underfoot appeared undisturbed, unbroken. But the Hydra was a cunning creature. It hunted alligators, after all, and they were no easy prey. Elderly humans were one thing, but it took stealth and guile to stalk and catch an alligator. The monster might well have sneaked up on Theia and grabbed her without a sound, too quickly for her to put up a fight.

Sam reached the outer edge of the thicket, where it gave onto open ground – a narrow mud beach that sloped down into the swamp water.

Here she found Sparks/Theia, who was in a squatting position with her back to Sam, bodystocking bunched around her ankles to expose the pear-shape of her bare buttocks. Portions of her battlesuit lay near her, neatly stacked on a scrubby patch of grass. Her rifle was with them, just out of her reach.

Theia was staring straight ahead. Her entire body was trembling, gripped with dread, and a stream of faeces was squirting out of her and plopping onto the mud between her feet.

Understandably – because in front of her, rearing out of the water, was the Hydra.

It was like some hideous huge sea anemone. The nine necks that sprouted frond-fashion from its body waved sinuously, balletically alongside one another, sometimes entwining, sometimes vying for position, dripping swamp water as they writhed. Each was capped with a serpentine head into which were set bulbous pus-yellow eyes that glowed with venomous greed. The body itself, mostly submerged, was reminiscent of a lizard's, sheathed in fleshy grey-green scales, with a ridge of finny dorsal spines.

Glaring down at Theia, paralysed and shitting herself with terror, the Hydra opened all nine of its mouths at once and let out a multiplicity of sibilant hisses. Fangs were revealed – nine sets of them, more fangs than Sam could count or wanted to count, and even the smallest longer than her little finger.

For a second – a single, endless-seeming second – Sam just wanted to scream and run away. Never mind that she had watched film of this monster, that she already knew what it looked like, knew what to expect. Seeing a video clip was nothing compared with coming face-to-face with the actual thing. The documentarians' onscreen deaths were preparation but not inoculation. Every bit of her squirmed in primal, atavistic disgust.

Then the reek of the Hydra's breath hit her. It was quite the most repulsive thing she had ever smelled – worse, far worse, than the smell she had once been greeted by on entering a flat in a tower block in Stoke Newington, where she and Prothero had been called after the discovery was made of the three-day-old corpse of a Nigerian people-trafficker. She had puked then, and thought subsequently that this death stench was the most unpleasant olfactory assault her nose had ever suffered and would ever have to suffer. She'd been wrong. She felt beyond nauseated now, sickened to the core of her being. The smell of the Hydra's breath was the smell of decay and slime and marshes and bloat magnified a hundredfold, something dredged up from the bottom of the most stinking, disease-ridden cesspool imaginable, something that would make flies caper in the air with glee before the noxiousness of it sent them spiralling to the ground stone-cold dead.

But it had one benefit. It was so shockingly repugnant, that smell, that it roused her from her fear-struck stupor. It galvanised her into action.

If only to get rid of it, purge the smell from the vicinity, Sam raised her gun and fired. Bullets raked the Hydra's flank. A chain of holes erupted in the monster's scaly hide, spurting blood. Meanwhile, dimly, she could hear Landesman ordering Iapetus and Rhea to go to her assistance.

The Hydra roared in pain, all nine heads abruptly switching their attention from Theia to Sam, which had in part been her intention. The creature launched itself up the beach towards her, and even as it came Sam could see the bullet holes healing, flesh puckering shut as though being sealed from within with putty.

She loosed off another volley of shots, aiming this time at one of the heads. Fragments of skull and gobbets of brain flew away, and the Hydra howled and recoiled. Its other eight heads swivelled to inspect the damaged one. Though Sam had blown it half off, the head rapidly regenerated itself. With astonishing speed the plates of the skull re-grew, knitted together and were patched over with fresh skin. A new eye appeared, popping up to fill a socket that had been hollowed out by the gunfire. It all happened as if in a piece of time-lapse film – from ruin to repair in a matter of seconds – until once more the monster had nine identical intact heads.

It lunged at Sam again with all nine mouths gaping wide, claws propelling it up the beach, gouging furrows in the mud. In her ear Landesman was urging her to stay calm. "Take another head off," he said. "Drive it back. The others are on their way." More faintly she could hear Ramsay, further from the mic at mission control, giving much the same advice.

Sam did as bidden, strafing the frontmost head and all but severing it below the jaw. Immediately another of the Hydra's heads finished the job for her, chewing the loosely dangling head free so that it fell to the ground. This left the way clear for a new head to sprout up from the stump of the neck, flesh and bone swelling and taking shape like a cunningly wrought balloon.

Sam barely paused to register this small miracle. She removed another head. That too was swiftly replaced, as was a third. The Hydra found these decapitations agonising, but each succeeded only in stalling it briefly. It kept on coming up the beach, growing angrier with every step, keener than ever to reach the human who was tormenting it in this way and rend her limb from limb.

Then the gun ran dry. Sam ejected the magazine and groped for a fresh one, and the Hydra, spying an opening, charged at her with redoubled ferocity.

It was mere feet away, and Sam was still trying to slot the new magazine into place, when, to her left, a shotgun blast boomed. The Hydra, struck in the belly, staggered sideways. A Titan appeared from the palmetto thicket. The transponder sensor display in Sam's visor informed her this was Iapetus, although she knew anyway. Not only was Barrington fond of pump-action shotguns, but he was also yelling at the top of his lungs, hurling every insult he could think of at the Hydra, most of them relating to sexual organs, illegitimacy and, in true Ocker tradition, species of native Australian wildlife. "Gift from the Barracuda!" he cried as he unloaded three more cartridges into the monster, hacking fist-sized craters out of it. The wounds of course soon filled themselves in, but they diverted the Hydra from Sam long enough to allow her to reload, and then she joined in the assault again.

All at once the Hydra was looking less enraged, more beleaguered. Its necks thrashed this way and that as it tried to respond to being besieged on two fronts at once. Sam sprayed away with her submachine gun while Iapetus gave the monster buckshot hell. The pair of them were far from repelling the Hydra, let alone killing it, but they were holding it at bay if nothing else.

"Rhea?" Sam said into the comms. "Where the hell are you, Rhea?"

Her gun ran dry again. Iapetus gave her covering fire while she smacked a full magazine into place, and just as she did so, Rhea came into view immediately to her left.

"Finally," Sam said. "Ready?"

"Ready," said Rhea. She sparked her flamethrower into life with its magnesium igniter. A finger of fire rippled out from the nozzle. "Let's do it."

Briskly Sam deprived the Hydra of another of its heads, then Rhea stepped up and subjected the neck stump to a concentrated jet of fire. Meat crackled and sizzled, and eight Hydra mouths simultaneously let out eight piercing shrieks.

The two Titans repeated the process again, and again. Hydra heads thudded into the beach mud. The severed ends of Hydra necks became ovals of charred, blistered flesh and bone. The odour of cooking reptile filled the air, oddly pleasant, certainly when compared with the smell of the Hydra itself.

"It's working," Rhea said, slapping a fresh capsule of hydrazine into the flamethrower's reservoir breech. "Landesman was right."

Landesman had theorised that the Hydra would have a much harder time repairing burns than any other kind of injury. "It was Hercules's method, in the myths," he had said. "Behead, then burn."

The cauterised stumps did start to re-grow new heads, but at a greatly retarded rate. The burnt tissue had to be sloughed off first before the proto-head could bubble up and take shape. Now Tethys and Rhea were in a race against the clock. They needed to destroy all nine heads before any of them could renew itself completely. Entirely headless, the monster would surely not survive.

Landesman had made Tethys and Rhea spend a whole afternoon rehearsing this move back at Bleaney. Iapetus was contributing now by taking potshots at the gradually emerging new heads, blowing them to smithereens while they were still just glistening, formless bulges.

All the same it required concentration and nerve to keep the production-line decapitation and cauterisation going, especially as the Hydra was rearing up and all of its necks, beheaded and otherwise, were thrashing to and fro, presenting a set of confusing and highly unstable targets. The monster stood its ground, at least. It seemed fully aware that these humans had discovered a vulnerability which they were exploiting without mercy, but it was either too enraged or too stubborn to think of retreating. Perhaps it simply couldn't believe that after all these years spent at the top of the food chain, during which time it had got used to humans being slow-moving and almost willing prey, it could ever be defeated. It continued to hiss and snap viciously at the Titans even as they whittled its headcount down to three, then two.

At last only a single head remained. Its features had a look of distress and resignation about them, and the baleful yellow glare in that final remaining pair of eyes was suddenly dulled. The Hydra knew the game was up. As if in pique, it swung away from Tethys and Rhea, turning its attention back to the human it had first spotted, the one it had been on the verge of attacking before another of them had so rudely interrupted. If it must die, the Hydra wasn't going to without taking one of these infernal creatures with it, the one it perceived as the weakest.

Theia, however, was on her feet. She had only a few pieces of her armour on. She was, in fact, mostly naked. But clasped in her right hand was a combat knife with a ten-inch blade, and as the Hydra lowered its head towards her, teeth glinting avariciously, Theia said, "This is for Nanna," and she plunged the knife into the monster's throat. "This is for Hubert and Celeste," she said, twisting the knife once back and forth, its tantalum-carbide-coated titanium blade widening the jagged slash she had created. Blood gushed over her arm, sluicing out from both the wound and the Hydra's open maw. "And this," she said, "is for me." She jerked the knife upwards, parting two vertebrae.

The head lolled sideways on the neck. A flap of

skin held it on for a few seconds, but the weight was too much for it and it stretched and tore, and the head landed with a thump at Theia's feet.

Nine truncated necks suddenly went limp, and the Hydra swayed for a moment, then slumped heavily into the mud. Its body convulsed, a shudder ran along the necks, and then it lay still.

"Step aside," Rhea told Theia, and Theia numbly obeyed, and Rhea set about incinerating the Hydra, scorching the carcass until her last flamethrower capsule was used up.

Barrington, thumbing his visor up, surveyed the smoking, blackened mound of ex-monster.

"Now that," he said, "is one hell of a barbie."

20. CHAMPAGNE

DURING THE FLIGHT home, a couple of bottles of Krug were broached and everyone partook except Barrington, who had beer instead – "Aussie champagne" – and Sparks, who didn't drink.

"And even if I did," she said to Sam, "I ain't in the mood."

Sparks felt ashamed, that much Sam knew. The Hydra had caught her with her pants down (in more ways than one) which was bad enough, but then there'd been further humiliation to follow. First, Sam had had to send Barrington off. He, not famous for his sense of propriety, had been openly leering at the half-dressed Sparks. Then Hamel had gone over to the Louisianan, offering to help clean her up and get her back into her battlesuit, only to be rudely rebuffed.

"Don't you come near me, woman," Sparks had snapped. "Don't you touch me with your filthy hands."

Sam had volunteered instead, and Hamel was now pretending to be indifferent about the incident, but her chagrin showed. She wouldn't even look at Sparks.

Celebrating hardest on the plane was McCann, who soon became flush-faced and unsteady on his legs.

"No cockups," he said to Sam, leaning too close, breathing winey breath in her face. "Clean bill of health for the TITAN suits. Who's the greatest engineer in the whole world? Only me!"

When they got back to Bleaney Island there was more Krug to be had, and more celebrating, and although Sam felt leaden-headed from jetlag she couldn't not join in. The mood was boisterous and relieved, and in the midst of it all Landesman stood up to make a short speech, the gist of which was: this was the first Titan op that could be considered a truly unqualified success, congratulations were in order, but no time for resting on laurels, onward and upward from here.

He concluded by saying, "Even now, back in the Everglades, I imagine alligators are busy disposing of the Hydra's mortal remains. I envisage them tearing the carcass to pieces and squabbling over the scraps. Perhaps, if alligators can think at all, they're thinking what an unexpected boon this is. A gift from the gods, one might even say. And perhaps also, somewhere in the dim recesses of their brains, they're feeling a satisfaction far deeper than the mere quenching of physical appetite. The tyrant who was slaughtering their kind is dead. The upstart, usurping emperor of their domain has been deposed. Their home is theirs again. They are free to enjoy it as before, to roam uncontested and unmolested. They are the rulers once more."

"It's a metaphor," Ramsay murmured to Sam out of the side of his mouth, "in case you didn't realise."

Sam laughed, until she remembered she was still pissed off at Ramsay. Then, thanks no doubt to all the pricey bubbly, she forgot why she was pissed off at Ramsay, and resumed laughing.

"That's more like it," the Chicagoan said. "You did a good job back there, Sam, you know. You don't want or need my endorsement but I'm giving it to you anyway 'cause that's how conceited a motherfucker I am. You dealt with everything like a pro – way better than I could have. You knocked it out of the park. You played a blinder."

"Picking up some of the local parlance there, Rick."

"Hey, lie down with dogs, you get up with fleas."

"I just think it's nice some of our Britishness is rubbing off on you. You could do with a bit of polish," Sam said.

"Any Britishness I'm getting off you guys mostly comes from the techs, and I don't think 'polish' applies there. Still, I reckon I've absorbed enough to be able to pass for a native." He adopted the most appalling English accent Sam had ever heard. "'Ey, luv, fetch moy a cuppa, woodjer? I'm roit gaspin,' I am."

"Please," she said. "Please stop."

"Leave it aht, you muppet."

She mimed being on the phone. "Hello, Dick van Dyke? You can relax. We've found someone worse."

"Blimey, worra load of bonkers bollocks yer spoutin.'"

"That's enough, Rick. Seriously. If you carry on, I will have to kill you."

"Cheers, ta."

"There is an arsenal of weapons not far from where we're standing. Don't believe that I am not willing to use one of them on you. For everyone's sake."

"Yeah, mate, wha'ever, know wha' ah mean?"

"Stop!" Sam cried, and the loud, mock-desperate plea happened to fall into a lull in the general conversation, so that everyone turned to see where it had come from and what had given rise to it.

Ramsay downpipe-gurgled. Sam sniggered. Conversation resumed.

"I knew it," Ramsay said.

"Knew what?"

"Knew you couldn't stay mad at me for ever."

"And I knew," Sam retorted, "that you couldn't stay mad at yourself for ever."

"Heh. Touché. So where do we go from here?"

"Me personally, to bed. I'm absolutely knackered."

"That an invitation?"

"Only an idiot would mistake it for one."

Ramsay made a goofy face. "I can be an idiot."

"As we know only too well. Goodnight, Rick."

"Goodnight, Sam. Sleep well."

And she did. Better than she'd done in ages.

21. OPERATION: THREE LIONS

A DAY PASSED, two days, three, and nothing from the Pantheon, not a word about the Hydra, no official statement, not a peep.

"They haven't noticed," said Landesman. "They don't care enough about the Hydra to be bothered to check up on it, so they've no clue it's dead and probably won't have for weeks. Just as I'd hoped. A lot of the time they treat their monsters as fire-and-forget missiles. Launch them, let them cause havoc, recall them maybe later, if at all, but maybe not. Hera has her favourites, that much we know. The Lamia, the Gorgons, Typhon. The slightly more sentient ones. Cerberus too. Any of those she'd miss if they were absent for too long. But the rest are, I think it's safe to say, regarded as expendable."

"And it's those ones we're going to continue going after?" said Sam. The two of them were in

Landesman's office, an informal strategy meeting. "The expendable monsters."

"For the time being," Landesman said with a nod.

"But if they're unlikely to be missed..."

"...then what's the point? Why waste our time on them? The point, Sam, is that we can't afford to tip our hand just yet. Lower-profile targets first. Once we begin eliminating creatures from the menagerie that the Olympians actually have the time of day for, we run the risk of drawing their fire and our operations become exponentially more hazardous. I'd like to postpone that moment for as long as possible. Moreover the Titans need the practice, the battlefield experience, which the lesser monsters amply provide."

"Agreed. I just –"

"Keen to go after bigger game, eh? Already? Sam, Sam, patience. One victory does not a campaign make. Little by little we'll do this. It's the only way."

"Did you ever consider, when you were planning all this, an all-out assault?" she asked. "Mass-produce the battlesuits, assemble an army and go at the Olympians that way?"

"Besiege Olympus? Attack them in their mountain stronghold? The thought did occur, once, briefly, before I dismissed it out of hand. For a start, it's been tried, hasn't it? Remember the Raffles Syndicate and their paratroopers? What a botch job that was. But also, and more to the point, for me it isn't viable financially. Or logistically, for that matter. A few hundred troops, a regiment's worth – how would

I recruit that many? Train, equip, supply, support, house that many warm bodies, all on my own? Not to mention the cost of constructing that many suits."

"Make it an international effort. Get governments covertly involved."

Landesman managed to smile and sneer at once. "Our beloved leaders, you mean? Pusillanimous nitwits like Catesby *Baa*tlett? Engage their help? What do you think are the chances of *that* happening? And how far do you think I'd get, trying to get a bunch of politicians on my side? Since when do politicians ever agree on anything? No, Sam, almost from the outset I understood that, if this was to have any hope of success, I had to think small. Trust me, for a man as ambitious as myself, accustomed to thinking big, big, big, that was a very hard adjustment to make. But also, there was the appeal of making this a project that accorded with classical precedence, which meant keeping the numbers low – to twelve, precisely. Once I'd hit on using the mythical Titans as my template, any other approach seemed clumsy and inelegant. How better to fight the Olympians than with a group inspired by figures from the selfsame mythology? How more apt? I just couldn't help myself.

"As a boy, you see, I loved books about the Ancient Greek gods and heroes. Still do. Hawthorne's *Tanglewood Tales*, Robert Graves, Mary Renault, Leon Garfield's *The God Beneath The Sea* – all terrific stuff. Homer as well, naturally, and Ovid, Aesop, Hesiod, Pindar, Apollonius Rhodius. And later the playwrights, Aeschylus, Euripides, that dirty-minded bugger Aristophanes. Even inane American superhero comics that used characters and motifs from the myths. Those old Technicolor movies too, with the gladiators and the rubbery-looking monsters. I devoured them all. There was such a grandeur about the stories, along with a sense that anything could happen and would.

"And the way the gods behaved – just like human beings but with the bonus of power and immortality. They had unfettered freedom to do as they pleased, which was thrilling to me as an only child growing up in a strict Jewish household and as a boy who knew from a very early age that he was a budding tycoon, destined to earn several fortunes, a Croesus or a Midas in the making. I instilled in my son the same love of classical lore. It was the one thing Xander and I both enjoyed doing together, poring over those old stories. The one thing that truly bound us. He'd badger me to read to him about the adventures of Theseus, Perseus, Hercules, Jason, whoever, any and all of them, and I did, when I could, when I had the time..."

His gaze strayed wistfully to the framed photo on the desk – the beautiful and soon-to-be-dead mother and the four-year-old Alexander already looking aggrieved, as if he knew what lay around the corner, knew that in a few short months he was going to be semi-orphaned, the parent he could count on the most was going to be torn away from him.

"And I didn't often have the time, or thought I didn't. And maybe Xander was only pretending to love those stories simply because he knew how much I loved them and it was a way of getting my undivided attention." Landesman's eyes darkened, and for a moment he looked much older than his fifty-odd years.

"The Olympians must seem like, well, like sacrilege to you then," Sam said.

"Oh yes. Oh yes. Absolutely. In fact I'd go further and say 'blasphemy.' Whoever – whatever – they are, they're corrupted versions of those wonderful, wayward beings that the poets sang about and the priests worshipped and sacrificed to and celebrated in their Mysteries. They're a travesty of the true Hellenic pantheon, that bizarre dysfunctional family with all their feuds and fancies and foibles."

"And you've come up with a way of turning the tables on them that also restores what you cherish so much about the myths."

"Yes, correct. So perceptive. In that respect alone, Titanomachy II is personal to me. In that respect and..."

"And...?" said Sam.

Landesman didn't finish the sentence, peremptorily starting a new one instead. "So we continue as we are, for now. We stay on the course as it is set. I have our next three monsters lined up. This is going to be an exhausting few days for you, Sam. The scheduling is tight. But since you insist on participating in every op, it's your own fault. You're going to be on your knees by the end, probably, but you'll only have yourself to blame."

"I'm my own worst enemy, Mr Landesman."

"Fortunately for us you're also the Olympians.'"
Landesman handed her a sheet of paper. "Here's
your itinerary. I'm calling this job Operation: Three
Lions. You'll see why. Phoebe, Coeus, Oceanus,
Mnemosyne and Hyperion will be travelling with
you. Feel free to use whichever of them you want on
each phase of the op, in whatever permutation you
see fit. If all goes well, you should be back within the
week – and all will, I have no doubt, go well."

22. THE GRIFFIN

THE GRIFFIN WAS loose in Kashmir, prowling that mountainous zone of contention between India and Pakistan. The Olympians had stationed it there to serve as a warning to the subcontinent's two great feuding powers: *we are keeping an eye on you*. The huge lion/eagle hybrid flew among the peaks of the Himalayas and the Karakoram Range, and every so often, when it was hungry, swooped into the nearest valley community and made off with a calf, a goat or, very occasionally, a small child. Inhabitants on both sides of the line of control could have importuned their nations' rulers to do something about the monster, but never bothered. It wasn't that they were fatalistic. It was just that they knew nothing would come of any efforts made in that direction. The governments in New Delhi and Islamabad, although they could agree on little else, were of one mind when it came to the Olympians: *Don't rock the boat*. Thus the Griffin was free to roam and raid and kill with impunity, like some deranged policeman, unconstrained by law. Once, a posse of villagers from the Indian-administered part of the region banded together and went after it, armed with rifles. They were never seen again.

The Griffin was known to have several nests in the area, all of them high up above the snowline. Anyone with any sense shunned the locations of these nests. They were places of ill omen.

On a particular day in March, however, a goatherd from a village near the Burzil Pass, in the Pakistani Northern Areas, was searching for a kid which had gone astray from the flock. He had a feeling that the quest would be fruitless. The Griffin had been sighted not far from that spot only yesterday, and the kid was doubtless even now being digested in the beast's stomach. The goatherd went looking anyway, because he was young and dutiful and it was his father's flock and he wanted to be able to tell the old man, who was sick at home with a fever, that he had at least tried to find the lost animal.

And wonder of wonders, he did. The bleating baby goat came trotting into view along a narrow, stony path that led up to a rocky overhang where the Griffin liked to roost when it was in the vicinity. The kid was covered in blood and seemed distressed, but a quick examination showed that it was unhurt. The goatherd thanked God for this small blessing. Curiosity then impelled him to venture a short way further up the path. If the blood was not the kid's own, where could it have possibly come from?

The goatherd, whose name was Asif Abbasi, got to within 500 metres of the overhang. He was trembling, praying to Allah the Compassionate, Allah the Merciful, with every breath. He unslung the telescopic rifle gunsight that hung around his neck on a piece of string. It had been a gift from his uncle in Karachi, a spice merchant who also ran a lucrative sideline in military-surplus goods. The cash-strapped Pakistani army was unburdening itself of as much equipment as it could spare, in order to make ends meet and keep going. Asif put the gunsight to his eye and zeroed in on the Griffin's nest. The monster was certainly there, but it was not moving. It lay on its side, and Asif knew with sudden, startling certainty that it was dead. He crept a little closer and focused the gunsight again on the monster. The Griffin's wings were spread out flat on the ground. There was a huge hole in its tawny-furred belly. Spilled blue and purple entrails steamed in the high-altitude air.

Asif raced home, breathless, to spread the news. No one in his village believed him at first. Asif had a reputation as something of a fantasist. So adamant was he that he wasn't making things up, however, that at last a deputation of headmen went out to check on his story. They returned grim-faced.

The village went into panic. The Griffin was slain, and none of them had done it but the Olympians would nevertheless assume they were to blame.

Vengeance would be swift and terrible. The villagers resolved to keep the monster's death a secret.

But the truth would leak out eventually. Truth always did.

Meanwhile the Blue Eros channel was broadcasting a movie about a horny teenager who repeatedly had sex with his middle-aged but still very beddable mother. It was called *Oedipussy*.

23. THE SPHINX

FUNDAMENTALIST TERRORIST FACTIONS in the Middle East had been having a frustrating time of it lately. Every way they turned, their plans were being curtailed and derailed. No longer were they able to recruit fresh young converts at the mosques and madrasas, for fear of the Olympians finding out. Hardline preachers could not publicly condemn Western imperialism, call for *jihad*, or instigate a *fatwa*, for much the same reason. The dream of obtaining a nuclear warhead from some rogue state and detonating it on Israeli soil or mainland America was now further than ever from being realised. Even simple suicide bombings had become trickier to organise and pull off successfully. The Olympians invariably seemed to know when one was imminent and would arrive and neutralise the would-be martyr before he'd had a chance to press the trigger. Hermes could move faster than thought, and the suicide bomber, rather than sending himself to paradise and everyone around him to hell in a single fiery burst, would instead wind up lying in the dirt, watching blood pump from the severed stump of his arm while his hand rested a couple of metres away, still clutching a disconnected detonator. Death would come to him eventually, but the beat of its black wings was slow and heavy with failure, and the seventy-two virgins waiting patiently to greet him in the afterlife would just have to bestow the flowers of their womanhood on some other holy warrior who'd made a better job of his self-immolation.

The terrorists had been driven underground, deep underground, and were fissured, split into tiny discrete cells that had scant contact with one another, since all phone and email communication was now in effect bugged. Argus had wiretapped the planet. Still the terrorists persisted with their plans as best they could. The hope of establishing a worldwide caliphate was not abandoned. One day the one true religion would rule all, and any unbelievers would be put to the sword. The infidel Pantheon might have the advantage for now, but this state of affairs would not last indefinitely.

For the past month terror cells in Syria had been suffering particularly harsh harassment, not directly at the hands of the Olympians themselves but courtesy of one of their monsters, the Sphinx. The creature was an abomination, a fusion of lion, bird and woman that was unclean to behold, not least because it went around flagrantly displaying its naked female torso and its uncovered female head – an offence to the eyes of the Almighty in so many ways.

The Sphinx haunted crossroads and narrow passes where men walked, and anyone it waylaid, it posed questions to. Its mythical forebear was famous for setting riddles and killing those who answered them incorrectly. This Sphinx, however, merely requested information, in a strange, etiolated yet hideously compelling voice. It asked for the whereabouts of terrorists. It asked if you knew of anyone who was plotting, or who knew someone who was plotting, any kind of religiously motivated attack or atrocity.

And always, when you replied, you told it the truth. You found yourself forced to. It was impossible not to comply with the Sphinx's interrogation. Something in its tone seemed to wheedle facts out of you, however desperately you tried to keep them buried. Many said the Sphinx's voice reminded them of their mother's – was in fact a perfect simulacrum of their mother's – and who could lie to their mother? Its face, too, had something universally maternal about it, making your recall something you'd forgotten, how beautiful your mother had looked when, as an infant, you lay gazing up at her while she cradled you in her arms or tucked you up in bed. Never mind the lion body or the pair of immense wings that wafted softly in the air as the Sphinx spoke. Never mind the flawless, globular breasts. It was the face and the voice that captivated you and that wormed secrets out of you far more efficient and effectively than any truth serum or torture, and afterwards left you feeling weirdly better about yourself, as if a great weight had been lifted from your shoulders. Unless you happened to be a fundamentalist terrorist, in which case you would confess as much to the Sphinx and it would, having gleaned all further useful data out of you, lift a great weight from your shoulders in another way, by lopping off your head with a single savage swipe of its forepaw.

The Sphinx either relayed any useful titbits it garnered to the Olympians, and they would act appropriately, or else, if the mood took it, it would respond of its own accord. If, say, it had just learned the location of a terrorist hideout, it would fly there and slaughter everyone it found. It seldom encountered resistance. With a few well-chosen words the Sphinx calmed and entranced its opponents, before proceeding to annihilate them at its leisure.

Then one day, abruptly, the Sphinx was gone. Syria – all Syria, not just its extremists – breathed a sigh of relief. The general consensus was that the monster had completed its tour of duty in the region and been recalled to Olympus, although this was more hope than belief. Rooting out terrorism was a neverending task, like rooting out weeds in a garden.

Few made the connection between the Sphinx's sudden departure and the discovery of a heap of mashed, mutilated animal body-parts not far from the highway running between An-Nabk and Damascus. The remains were stumbled upon by a group of schoolchildren, who assumed this gory, flyblown abattoir scene was what was left after jackals had brought down a couple of camels. A vet summoned by police concurred. He made a witness statement to that effect. Camels. Definitely. Without a shadow of a doubt.

The vet said this because he was frightened to say what he really thought. The consequences would be too dire. He saw to it that the "camels" were buried at the site, and told no one, not even his wife, that there had been bird feathers amid the mammalian mess, along with portions of anatomy that looked, to his untrained eye, human.

Among the adult entertainments on offer from Blue Eros on the day of the Sphinx's disappearance was a retelling of the affair between Dido, queen of Carthage, and Aeneas, peregrine survivor of the sack of Troy. The original elegiac narrative of passionate but destiny-doomed love had been spiced up – and perhaps, who knows, improved – by the inclusion of sex toys and sodomy. The film's title? *Dildo And Anus.*

24. THE CHIMERA

From time to time Russia still glowered at her neighbours, those pilot-fish states that had formerly swum alongside the great Soviet shark but now insisted on going their own separate ways. Russia seemed to yearn for their company, missing them, missing the old days. She felt naked without them, stripped of the veil of respectability these coerced allies had given to her plans for expansion and eventual world domination. She wanted them back, though knowing there wasn't a hope in hell of getting what she wanted.

The Chimera stalked Russia's western frontier, zigzagging along the overlap between her and eastern Europe, through Baltic buffer nations such as Latvia, Belarus and the Ukraine. It was, by some degree, the bizarrest of all the Olympian monsters, being composed of the fore part of a lion, the middle part of a goat, and the hind part of a large snake. How these three disparate portions coexisted was mystery and miracle. That the Chimera could walk at all, given the contrast between its powerful leonine forelegs and its spindly caprine rearlegs, was amazing in itself. Yet it moved with a surprising supple grace, its thick scaly tail lending support and stability. It was, in fact, a fearsome hunter, combining the lion's stalking skills with the goat's surefootedness, all aided and abetted by an inbuilt serpentine cunning. Somebody had once filmed a cameraphone clip of the Chimera pouncing on and killing a Shetland pony – a multimillion-view hit when uploaded onto YouTube. The little horse could be seen running as fast as its stumpy legs could carry it, but it never stood a chance.

Although the Chimera's stamping grounds ranged far and wide, it frequently returned to the same place, the rural south-east corner of Estonia, not far from Lake Peipsi, the fourth largest freshwater lake on the continent. There was a reason for this, albeit one not widely known. A local dairy-farming family, the Lepiks, had taken to feeding it. Some years back the patriarch of the family, Joosep, had lost several head of cattle to the monster, good livestock getting massacred day after day for a week. Fed up of this, and noting that the Chimera never ate more than a quarter of the meat from each of its kills, Joosep had reasoned that it didn't need much to fill its belly, which was, after all, goat-sized. Why not, then, donate a segment of meat at a time, to prevent entire cows being superfluously destroyed?

On a tree stump, the remnants of a once-towering pine, Joosep had laid out a haunch of beef for the Chimera. The monster had taken it and devoured it, bones and all, and the next night had returned for more.

So a pattern had begun. Whenever the Chimera paid a visit, the Lepiks would lay out meat for it every evening until at last it went away again. This had become something of a ritual, a means of propitiating the beast and sparing the family and the herd from its depredations. A single cow, in managed portions, could last ten days. That meant nine other cows saved, a good trade-off. Of course, had Joosep Lepik not started feeding the Chimera in the first place, the monster might not have kept coming back. But it was too late to remedy that now. Besides, Joosep had a developed a strange affection for the Chimera, a grudging admiration. He liked to watch from the safety of a nearby timber barn as the monster approached the tree stump and retrieved the offering set out there. It was a thrill, of course, to observe this extraordinary misfit creature in the flesh, at such close range.

But there was more to it than that. While a young man, barely in his twenties, Joosep had had an accident with a tractor, a Soviet-built Kharkov T-25, a bloody-minded brute of a machine that never seemed to work and only ever caused trouble on the rare occasions it did work. He'd climbed out of the tractor cab to adjust the plough at the rear, leaving the engine idling in neutral. The gear lever had slipped and the tractor had lurched into reverse before stalling. It hadn't travelled far, just a couple of metres, or particularly fast, but it had moved with enough speed and force for the plough to knock Joosep down and shear his left leg off at the thigh. Though now fitted with a false leg, Joosep walked with barely a limp. He prided himself on the fact that nobody could tell from appearances that he was minus a limb. And so he felt a kinship with the Chimera, which looked as if it should be crippled even though it was not. The monster had become a magical touchstone for him. On some basic level he identified with it. Getting run over by that tractor had nearly killed him. He shouldn't be alive, let alone ambulatory. The same applied to the Chimera.

One night in late March, Joosep was in his usual spot in the barn, up in the hayloft, peeping out through a knothole in a wall plank at the tree stump some forty paces away. A fresh, juicy rack of ribs rested there, slowly contributing to the patina of bloodstains that coated the stump's upper surface. The moon was high and full. It was a bright, not too cold night. The hour was almost ten. The Chimera should have been here by now. Shortly after sunset was its customary time for turning up for its free dinner. Where had it got to?

Joosep wondered, with a pang, if the Chimera had moved on again, early. Each of its visits lasted a fortnight or so. So far, this time, it had been here for only a handful of days. Well, it was a free agent. It came and went as it pleased. If it had left the area, it would be back again soon enough.

Joosep was thinking about wending his way back to the farmhouse when he glimpsed a flash of light in the hills that overlooked the Lepik family property. Further flashes followed, up there in the woods, accompanied by a series of faint but distinct *pops* that could only be gunfire. Joosep couldn't help himself. He left the barn, heading out for a closer look.

He was less than a kilometre from the woods when he saw the Chimera suddenly come bounding out into the open. It hurtled across a pasture, and it looked to Joosep – although he found this hard to believe – that the monster was in a state of alarm. It was fleeing for its life. But from what?

Phantoms.

That was what Joosep thought as he saw a quartet of figures emerge from among the trees, giving chase to the Chimera. They seemed to be people but he couldn't be sure because, somehow, he could barely make them out. Though his eyesight was good and the moonlight strong, their outlines seemed to ripple and waver, now there, now not. He saw them by the shadows they cast more than anything. And they were moving so fast, *too* fast, surely, to be people. Nothing human could run at such speeds. Hermes could, but then was he human?

The four flitting figures caught up with the Chimera, and within seconds the monster was being subjected to sustained bursts of gunfire that pinned it to the ground and made its body twitch and stutter all over. The coup de grâce was delivered by something which Joosep presumed was a shoulder-mounted rocket launcher. All at once there was an almighty, dazzling explosion that seemed to light up the entire landscape, and as the echoes of its roar caromed away through the hills and the glowing afterimage faded from Joosep's vision, he perceived that the Chimera was no more. Where the monster had been crouching there was now a smoking crater in the earth, dotted with flickers of flame. Never again would this fantastic beast lope down to the Lepik homestead to seize its gladly given sacrifice off the tree-stump altar.

The four phantoms set off back up the hillside, melting into the woods, and Joosep watched them go. He couldn't imagine who – what – these people were. They might not even be people. In a world where the Ancient Greek Pantheon walked, real and alive, anything was possible. What he did grasp was that something major was afoot. Death had been brought to an Olympian monster. That was not some casual, random act. That was the deliberate breaking of a taboo, and tantamount to a declaration of war.

Wearily, feeling all of a sudden very old and very lame, Joosep turned and limped off homeward, into the dark.

That same night, among the bill of mythopornographic delights being offered by Blue Eros to its subscribers was a cinematic masterpiece detailing a young girl's initiation into the world of mixed-sex threesomes, set against the backdrop of the Trojan War. *Troilists And Cressida*.

25. MAN-LION DREAM

SAM SLEPT FOR almost a full twenty-four hours. She was dimly aware of Mahmoud entering and leaving their room every so often, for all that Mahmoud was as surreptitious as she could be. Otherwise, she was dead to the world.

Dreams came thick and fast, and lions featured in many of them. Dead lions, for the most part. Whole prides of them, slaughtered, eviscerated, bullet-riddled, their corpses strewn across mountainsides and deserts and strange dark forested landscapes. Sometimes the lions morphed into monsters such as the three Sam had recently helped kill, things that had lionlike attributes but were amalgams of other beasts as well. One of these started speaking to her as it lay, sprawled in a stew of its own blood and internal organs, dying.

"It hurts," groaned the creature, which had distinctly human facial features. "Why have you done this to me? What did I ever do to you?"

Sam's dream self could come up with no good answer to that. Rationally, she knew that the monster had to die, just as all the Olympian monsters did. Landesman's plan demanded it. The world was crying out for it.

Emotionally, a justification was harder to find.

"I'm sorry," she said, conscious how pathetic this sounded.

The man-lion shook its mane. "'Sorry' really won't do. Where is this all going, Sam? Have you even thought about that? Say you wipe out all us monsters, and the Olympians too. Unlikely, but not beyond the realms of possibility. What then? What happens after?"

"I feel better."

"You're sure? And will the *world* feel better? Years of pent-up aggression. The dozens of simmering conflicts the Olympians have been keeping a lid on. All that anger held in check. Ancient hatchets buried but not forgotten. All of it comes exploding out at once. Remember the Balkans after *perestroika*? Now imagine the same but on a worldwide scale. Humankind will tear itself apart."

"Or we'll all heave a sigh of relief and get back to the business of being ourselves again."

"And being yourselves, was that really so great?" the man-lion asked, its voice seeming to grow stronger even as its life ebbed away. "What was so fantastic about a world where men like Regis Landesman, purveyor of instruments of death, could flourish? Remember what you used to see day in, day out at work, Sam

– the degradation, the crime, the mindless brutality. Lives ruined at a single stroke. That was your job, cleaning up the mess left behind by people who were at best thoughtless, at worst evil incarnate. You know better than most the corruption that lurks beneath the surface film of everyday life, and how thin and fragile that surface film is. The husbands who just suddenly snap and turn into wife beaters, wife killers even. The lunatics who listen when God tells them to go out with that Stanley knife and use it on whoever looks at them with the Devil's eyes. The junkies who rob pensioners' savings tins then take a shit on their living-room rugs for good measure. The whores so worn out and numb inside that they think getting beaten black and blue by their pimps is proof of affection. *That's* what you want to go back to? *That's* a status quo worth restoring?"

"There's still crime, even under the Pantheon."

"Nowhere near as much as there used to be."

"Crime is the shadow of freedom."

"That's what Ade used to say, isn't it? That was his personal favourite little Christmas cracker motto."

"Don't you mention his name. Don't you dare."

"You raised the subject. You quoted him. Very liberal for a copper, was Ade, wasn't he? Always could see the other guy's point of view. Always tried to understand the crims' mentality. That's probably why he was destined to stay a uniform for ever. Didn't have the detachment, the inner steel. Not like you."

"Ade was a good man."

"Of course, of course." For a being that was on the brink of death, and sinking fast, the man-lion seemed to have a lot to say still and plenty of breath to say it with. "And that's why you loved him. Deep down, though, you always felt he was a bit of a sap. How did he do it? How did he survive day after day on the beat, being abused and derided, having teenagers spit and jeer and call him '*cunt*stable,' and not get ground down by it, not become bitter and cold? How did his heart continue to remain open and honest and fair? Because he lacked guts, that's why."

"It isn't weakness, staying uncynical."

"Oh but I think you think it is, Sam. Wasn't it because Ade was so wide-eyed and eager to help that he got himself killed? That's the truth of it, no? If he hadn't volunteered with the Police Support Unit, hadn't trained for crowd control, hadn't been at Hyde Park that day, hadn't dashed in to save a life when Apollo and Artemis arrived and everything went to hell..."

"Shut up." Sam realised she had a submachine gun in her hands.

"Shut me up," the man-lion replied.

So she did, pouring bullets into the expiring monster's face until it had no face left.

"There, that's you put out of your misery," she said as the gunsmoke cleared, "and mine."

That could well have been the last of the dreams that came to her during her long sleep. If there were subsequent ones, she didn't remember them on waking. She crawled stiffly out of her bunk and went to make herself coffee in the dining area. Then she went in search of company. The subterranean complex seemed quiet. Far quieter than usual.

Emptier, too. Eventually she found people down in the command centre. Everyone, in fact, was there, gathered around one of the screens.

"Ah, she is risen!" Landesman declared. "Come on over and join us, Sam. You're just in time. The Olympians are about to make a statement. I believe our moment has come. The proverbial feline has exited the proverbial flexible receptacle. The Olympians have realised somebody is tweaking their noses and they can't ignore it any longer."

Onscreen, a BBC newscaster was filling airtime while below her a "breaking news" strapline scrolled from right to left promising that an important announcement from Mount Olympus was imminent.

"We're expecting the live feed to begin any minute now," she said. "To repeat, in case you've just tuned in: the Olympians are shortly to broadcast a message to the world. We don't know yet what they have to tell us. All we know is it's a top-priority simulcast that's being beamed to every single known national network and news channel. Here in the studio with me is our Pantheonic Affairs correspondent Tom Marsters. Tom. Any clue what Zeus and the rest are likely to say?"

"None at all, Julia," the correspondent replied. "This has all come rather as a shock. Normally we're given at least a day's advance notice if Zeus has something he wants to share with the world, and more often than not we have some idea what topic he intends to cover. It's either obvious or guessable. In this instance, we've had no prior warning, we only knew an hour ago that something was in the offing, and that itself is fairly unprecedented and not insignificant, I'd say."

"And is it also not insignificant that all of the Olympians are going to be there when Zeus makes this statement? In the past it's been just him in front of the camera, perhaps with Hera beside him, but this time, as I understand it, if the information we've received is correct, the entire Pantheon will be on hand."

"It's definitely not insignificant, Julia. I believe the last time something like this happened, it was in the wake of the Obliteration, and that's going back a few years. Then, I think, it was as much a show of solidarity as anything, a case of putting on a unified front. All of the Olympians took part in the Obliteration, and all of them were keen to go on TV and show they had no regrets about it. So yes, we can only assume this is a broadcast on the same level of momentousness as that one. What's unclear is what has prompted it. So far as we're aware, the Olympians haven't carried out any major police actions recently. There've been no protests to quell, no conflicts to curb. The world's been rather quiet of late. This is all so unexpected."

"There have been rumours, though, haven't there?" said the newscaster. "Unconfirmed reports about missing and dead monsters."

"There have," the correspondent said cautiously, "although it's important to stress that they *are* just rumours, they *are* unconfirmed."

"The Griffin killed in Kashmir. The Chimera in Estonia. No attacks on people by the Hydra for over two weeks, and no fresh sightings of it either."

"All highly disturbing, I agree. But let's not jump to conclusions, Julia."

"In the light of that, the Cyclops's death is starting to look a little suspicious too, don't you think?"

"As I said, let's not jump to conclusions. If something *is* happening, if somebody is really going around bagging Olympian monsters, then it's very serious stuff indeed. But let's wait and see, shall we? It could turn out to be –"

"Sorry, Tom, have to interrupt you there." The newscaster was pressing a finger to her in-ear talkback monitor. "I'm getting word... yes... I'm being told the statement is just about to begin, so we're going to go straight over to that. This is coming live from Mount Olympus."

The image cut to the Olympians' stronghold. The fourteen gods were assembled on the steps of the central temple at their mountaintop home. Behind them, fluted Doric columns supported a portico on which, just visible, was a frieze of the Olympians' faces. Those faces, sculpted in marble, were smiling, benevolent, just a touch smug. The Olympians' actual faces were anything but.

Zeus was foregrounded. Flanking him were his wife Hera and son Hermes, the one matronly, the other leanly muscled. Behind them stood two more of Zeus's offspring, the half-siblings Ares – copper armour, tree-branch arms folded in front of his tree-trunk torso, double-headed battleaxe sheathed in his belt – and statuesque Athena, her martial helmet raised high on her forehead. Beside them were a further pair of his offspring, the twins Apollo and Artemis, he with his golden bow slung crosswise over his torso, she leaning on her silver hunting spear. They were joined by Hercules, Zeus's illegitimate son, posing with his knuckles on hips, looking beetle-browed and surly and ever so slightly camp, as only Hercules could. Forming the third row were an ill-assorted bunch: proud Poseidon, shy Demeter, ruddy-cheeked Dionysus, and sullen, sallow-faced Hades. Aphrodite – pale, slender, inordinately beautiful – stood at the rear, along with her husband Hephaestus, a stunted dwarf of a man who held onto her shoulder for support. His left leg was a twisted, crippled thing encased in a brace and an orthopaedic shoe.

All fourteen members of the Pantheon stared straight into the camera, and the anger radiating off them, even off loving Aphrodite, was palpable.

They remained like this for several seconds, stern parents letting their children know the severity of the trouble they were in.

Then white-bearded, dark-eyed Zeus – Zeus the Wide-Seeing, Zeus the Master Of The Bright Lightning – spoke.

"Mortals," he said, "how dare you. How *dare* you! Such great things we have done on your behalf, and all we have asked in return is for you to stay peaceable and abide by our governance. It seems, however, that even that is too much for some among you."

A pause, then he continued: "It has come to our attention that a number of our beasts – those custodians of your wellbeing, guardians of your good conscience – have been foully and cruelly slain. I refer to the Sphinx, the Griffin, the Chimera and the Hydra. It is our belief, moreover, that the supposed accident which took the life of the Cyclops was not, in fact, an accident at all. These five deaths having occurred within the space of a single month leads us to one conclusion and one only. There is a concerted effort being undertaken to kill our loyal creatures. We are facing a co-ordinated series of attacks by persons unknown. A conspiracy has been hatched."

"And here was I thinking Landesman was long-winded," muttered Barrington. "This fella could teach you a thing or two, Regis."

Landesman shot him a sharp look.

"This cannot stand," said Zeus, his voice lowering to a menacing rumble. "This *will* not stand. Harming innocent beasts who are simply doing the tasks they have been instructed to do is a craven act. Only a coward would kill the watchman's dog but not the watchman. If you wish to attack Olympians, then by all means attack us. See how far it gets you. To go after our vassals achieves nothing... other than arousing our ire."

Hera, at his side, nodded in vehement agreement. She, keeper of the monsters, was doubtless feeling a sharper grief than any of her fellow Olympians. Her eyes gleamed with imperious indignation.

"We do not know who you are, you butchers, you murderers," Zeus said, "but rest assured, we will find out, and once we know your names and where you live, we will come for you and we will pinch you out like match flames. In the meantime, you must learn that your actions have consequences, if not immediately for you then for others. A show of our displeasure is in order. World, prepare yourself. See, once again, what it means to incur the wrath of your divine guardians."

Zeus directed a grave, searching stare into the camera. Blue-white light crackled in his eyes.

Then the transmission from Olympus ended, the screen went blank, and a moment later the BBC studio reappeared. The newscaster and the Pantheonic Affairs correspondent were looking at each other with expressions that were, frankly, alarmed.

"Well, that's... That's certainly..." said the newscaster, and groped for a description.

"A worrisome turn of events," the correspondent said. "Zeus sounding there like he means business."

The newscaster collected herself. "What, in your view, will the 'consequences' he just mentioned be, Tom?"

"No idea, Julia. But I expect it won't be long before we find out, and I, for one, am not looking forward to it."

"Oh God."

"Indeed. Oh God."

26. REPERCUSSIONS

LANDESMAN ORDERED THE screen switched off. A hubbub broke out among the Titans and the technicians, a dozen voices speaking at once. Landesman requested, and got, silence.

"Let's just take a moment, shall we?" he said. "Think things through calmly and rationally. We knew something like this was going to happen. It was inevitable. There was no way the Olympians weren't going to react once they twigged what we're up to. All we can hope for is that the fallout is relatively mild."

"People are going to die," said Søndergaard.

"We don't know that yet," said Landesman. "We'll have to wait and see."

"I signed up to stop the Olympians," said Tsang. "I didn't sign up to provoke them into attacking civilians."

"What did you *think* they were going to do, Fred?" Landesman asked with some asperity. "Sit back and take it? What have they ever done when they've felt threatened? Lashed out. It's their way. We need to be grown-up about this. We need to accept that there will, alas, be unavoidable by-products of our campaign. There will be – that ugly euphemism – collateral damage. It simply can't be helped. Sam, you'll back me up here, won't you?"

"I hate it," Sam said. "I'm sure you hate it too, Mr Landesman. We all do. But..." She couldn't see a way around it. Landesman was right. The Olympians were bound to strike back. That had been their policy from the very start: let no insult or protest go unpunished. "We are at war now. We started it. The Olympians are taking it to the next level. How could they not? And it will keep on escalating if we carry on, that's obvious. So what do we do? Do we stop? We could, and then whatever repercussions the Olympians have in mind right now will be the end of it. War over. Titanomachy II dribbles to a halt. I don't know about any of you but that seems pretty ignominious to me. It'd make everything we've done so far a waste. Soleil's death – pointless.

"The alternative is to forge on in the full and frank knowledge that non-combatants are going to suffer. We have to weigh that against what we're hoping to accomplish. Is it worth it? Is it a good trade-off? I don't know. I'd like to think so. I don't have much stomach for watching the Olympians penalise others for what we've done, but equally, every death they cause in our name, every life they take as retribution, is one more reason to keep fighting against them, one further incentive to topple the bastards. That's the only consolation I can see, but I think it counts for something."

A "Hear! Hear!" came from Ramsay, and was echoed by Mahmoud, Barrington and Chisholm. If the others were less convinced by her argument, none of them showed it.

"Well said, Sam," said Landesman. "Couldn't have put it better myself."

After that it was simply a question of waiting – waiting to find out what the Olympians were going to do and how bad it was going to be. Landesman had BBC News put back up on the screen, along with a number of rolling-news channels including CNN, Al-Jazeera and the Nippon News Network in inset windows. Zeus's message was being played and replayed across the world, translated or subtitled in every known language, spreading to the farthest corners of the globe, reaching places where it was midnight or later and few were awake to hear and heed. Landesman viewed it over and over, scowling hard. To Sam it seemed as though he was scrutinising the speech, analysing Zeus's every word, every nuance, in the hope of gleaning some insight from it, some clue as to what the Pantheon had in mind.

Perhaps, she thought, it would be only a lenient rebuke, a token gesture, a slap on the wrist. Some destruction of property, a handful of deaths, no more.

She didn't really believe that, though. If she knew anything about the Olympians, it was that they rarely did things by halves.

27. LOST LANDMARKS

It began in Paris.

A breezy spring morning in the City of Light. Tourists milled beneath the Eiffel Tower, queuing for tickets to travel up in the lifts or posing for photographs with the mighty metal structure behind them. The first hint any of them had that something was awry was a deep, resonant groan like the creak of some immense door easing open on rusty hinges. All looked up. Those standing at a distance, those perhaps peering through camera viewfinders, got the clearest impression of what was going on. The upper section of the Tower had begun to tilt. No, not tilt. To *bend*. It was angling away from true, bowing to one side like the head of a wilting flower, hundreds of tons of iron girder unstraightening, the tower's outline starting to describe a shallow and then a not so shallow arc. Thin screams issued from up in its framework, and on the ground. People started running – and, from the top of the structure, falling. One moment you were admiring the panorama of the French capital from the summit of its tallest edifice. The next, the floor was tipping beneath you and you had lost your footing and gone sliding over the safety railings. Some in the tower, though, did not plunge to their deaths. They were trapped between the shifting, twisting girders and crushed. A few were killed by two-inch rivets that popped out from their sockets with the force of bullets.

When the Eiffel Tower finally stopped moving, it was bent double, apex pointing downwards, the tip of the radio transmitter antenna that crowned it now almost touching the ground. Its sweeping uprightness had become an inverted U. What had once been a thrusting erection now drooped in impotence, beyond resurrection, and for several nights running many a Frenchman would find, to his intense dismay, that he was unable to perform satisfactorily for his wife, or for that matter his mistress, and even though he would know where the blame lay, it was still no great comfort.

But, for now, all that mattered was the tragedy of dozens of tourist corpses strewn below the disfigured Tower or stuck within its iron innards like flies in a spider web.

Hephaestus was responsible. Hephaestus the stunted, lame blacksmith, telekinetic manipulator of all things metal. From his position in the Parc du Champs de Mars, south of the Tower, he took a moment to survey his handiwork, and was pleased with what he had wrought; more accurately, unwrought. Then Hermes arrived to whisk him home.

A couple of hours later, visitors to the Mount Rushmore National Memorial were appalled to see Ares and Hercules setting about the carved presidential faces with their fists and feet. First to go was Abraham Lincoln. Roosevelt followed, then Jefferson, and finally Washington. Each solemn granite visage cracked and crumbled from the forehead downward, slumping away in fragments. God and demigod abseiled down the faces on ropes, pounding and stamping until the sculptures were destroyed. A handful of tourists and one tour guide didn't get clear in time and were engulfed by tumbling rubble. Ares and Hercules laughed heartily, schoolboys taking part in an enormous prank.

At roughly the same time, almost 1,400 miles away, over on the western seaboard of the United States, a wave of gigantic proportions arose in the Pacific and came sweeping into San Francisco Bay. In the space of a minute it grew from nothing to a height of nearly 500 feet. Calm wine-dark sea became a towering, foam-capped wedge of water that swallowed ferries, fishing vessels, police boats and pleasure cruisers whole and rolled onward looking for more. Eventually this super-tsunami collided with the Golden Gate Bridge with an impact as forceful and as deafening as an atomic bomb. The bridge didn't stand a chance, and neither did the occupants of the vehicles that were driving across it at the time. Three-foot-thick steel bracing cables snapped like baling twine. The twin stanchions buckled and toppled from their concrete bases. The entire structure was shunted sideways, snapping free of its anchor points at either end. Parts of the bridge slammed onto Alcatraz Island, whole sections of roadway embedding themselves in the empty prison buildings. Other parts fetched up further inland, borne on the ebb of the super-tsunami to places like Oakland, San Rafael and Fremont. The wave even carried on down as far as San Jose, its last eddies struck with enough power still in them to capsize boats in the marinas in San Mateo and overturn planes on the runway at Moffett Federal Airfield. All of the Bay's coastal areas were ravaged. The eventual death toll reached the mid three figures.

Poseidon, however, had quit the scene long before the wave he had conjured up was spent. Hermes came to collect him, appearing at his side as if from nowhere and spiriting them both back to Mount Olympus.

The sun was setting over Rome as Dionysus and Hades arrived there. It was the time of *passeggio*, when Romans put on their very best clothes and went promenading. To anyone but an Italian it looked like pointless milling about, a continual round of ambling in one direction then doubling back and ambling the other way, pausing now and then to kiss and greet and chat. To the participants, however, it was a dignified social gavotte. The younger ones flirted and gabbled, the older ones ate *gelati* and exchanged news and views.

Today there was much to talk about: the Olympians, their monsters, the recent events in

France and America. The usually ebullient evening atmosphere was subdued, and there were fewer people out and about than was customary in such clement weather, but the general feeling in the city was that life must go on as normal. Besides, what had happened elsewhere couldn't happen here, could it? Not in Rome.

But it could, of course, and did. No sooner had Dionysus strode into the Piazza Santa Maria in the Trastevere district than he set to work. With one hand aloft and splayed, he spread his influence among the unsuspecting crowds. It radiated out from him, a powerful sense of intoxication, a surge of heady glee expanding in a circle of which he was the centre point. People began to giggle. Then, quickly, the euphoria turned to rowdiness. Everybody staggered around, bumping into one another. Tempers flared. Fights erupted. Soon the entire square was filled with Romans in their designer finery punching, kicking, biting, headbutting, clawing at one another. Blood flowed. Eyeballs were gouged. Dislodged teeth flew. Bones snapped. Here and there arose the sound of hysterical laughter, as well as hoots like the cries of mad gibbons. Civilised citizens were transformed into a vicious, howling, mauling rabble. It was quite a decline and fall.

Then came Hades's turn. In another part of Rome, the area around the Trevi Fountain, he removed the black leather gloves that were his constant item of apparel and began to touch people. A finger to someone's cheek, a tap on the side of the head, that was all it took. A moment of skin-to-skin contact, and the person fell down stone dead. Hades glided from victim to victim, repeatedly performing this lethal laying on of hands, so that there were a score of corpses on the ground before it became widely apparent what he was up to. A woman screamed as her husband, for no apparent reason, suddenly collapsed beside her. The scream intensified as the woman saw and recognised Hades, and then it was cut short as the Olympian stroked her bare forearm and she too keeled over, as lifeless as the statues of tritons and horses that presided over the fountain which she and her beloved had just, moments earlier, been admiring.

There was panic, Romans and tourists fleeing in every direction, trying to escape from Hades. He merely smiled a lipless smile and continued to touch anyone who strayed within his reach. The terror of the crowd was disorderly, confused. Some who thought they were running away from the Olympian were actually running towards him. Hades accounted for a further seventeen lives before the area was entirely vacated and it was just him alone, standing among thirty-odd sprawled bodies, some of them floating in the waters of the fountain. His cadaverous yellowy face was lit up with a gleam of intense satisfaction as he slipped his gloves back on.

Meanwhile, on the other side of the planet, the sun was rising over the Sydney Opera House, lending the white sails of that building a glowing pink blush. Rosy-fingered dawn didn't last long, however. The sun had barely cracked the horizon when clouds started to amass, dark as ink blots in the sky, all but extinguishing the nascent daylight. Growls of thunder pealed overhead. No rain came, but a cold wind hissed along the esplanade that stood between the Opera House and the waters of Sydney Harbour. Early-morning joggers turned their heads in alarm. Businesspeople taking the scenic route to their offices, hoping to get a head start on the day's work, anxiously bent forward and quickened their pace.

Zeus was there, in the shadow of the building. The thunderclouds were his, and so was the lightning that now flickered within them. His to command. He raised both arms and called the lightning down. It zigzagged onto the opera house's roofs. It jagged from the bases of the clouds in blinding white jolts. It struck and struck again, and concrete exploded, the roofs shattered, the roofs caved in like eggshells. Zeus stood, legs apart, and directed the lightning bolts like a conductor conducting a symphony. He orchestrated the building's destruction with dramatic gesticulations and lofty shakes of the head and a look on his face of stern-eyed rapture. To reduce a marvellous specimen of modernist architecture, fourteen years in construction, to a heap of rubble and dust took him a little under five minutes. Some passers-by suffered in the process, either getting hit by falling debris or else fried by wayward lightning bolts. Their deaths were unintentional but hardly a source of regret. These things happened.

And with that, it was over. There were no further demonstrations of power. A number of the world's great landmarks were gone – besmirched, ruined – along with several hundred human beings. That was the extent of the Olympians' revenge for a handful of dead monsters.

"It could have been worse," Landesman remarked, and he wasn't being callous or flippant. It could have been far worse. One might even argue that the Pantheon had let the world off lightly. Given what it was in their capacity to do, they had acted with something approaching restraint. They had vented their anger on symbols, emblems of human aspiration and achievement, more than on actual humans.

A shroud of guilt hung over Bleaney Island nonetheless. For a day or so, nobody could quite meet anybody else's eye. Conversations were curt and choppy. People retreated to their rooms; sedated themselves with television and booze. Sam could see it in faces, almost hear the sound of it – consciences being wrestled with. An inner struggle grinding away. *Are these losses acceptable? Should we carry on? Do we have the right to?*

She herself could see no solution other than to press ahead. Giving up now would mean the Olympians had got their way, yet again, and surely the whole aim of Titanomachy II was to prevent that.

She went to find Landesman. He wasn't in his office, but Lillicrap was next door in *his* office, a smaller and much less plushly furnished space than his boss's.

"Be with you in a moment," Lillicrap said, holding up a finger. He scowled at the laptop that sat on the steel-frame desk in front of him. "Just going over some figures."

Finally he sat back, sighing. "Mr Landesman's personal accounts. We're coming to the end of the tax year. It's a nightmare keeping it all straight. So many different holdings in so many different places."

"You're his bookkeeper as well as his personal assistant?"

"I'm Mr Landesman's everything, Miss Akehurst. PA, secretary, general factotum, chief cook and bottle washer. And now aide de camp. Been with him for more than twenty-five years. Quarter of a century! Right from the inception of Daedalus Industries, almost, when I was a graduate fresh out of university, the ink still wet on my diploma."

"Congratulations on your silver wedding anniversary."

"Thank you," Lillicrap replied, his tone no less droll than hers. "I think it's safe to say my employer couldn't ever manage without me. I know the man better than anyone. I'm indispensible to him. Which is why this whole business here..."

Sam's antennae twitched. "What? What about it?"

"Well, I'm going to be candid, Miss Akehurst – the Titan project, it's been an obsession for Mr Landesman, it's consumed his life for the best part of a decade, and it's also consumed a great deal of his finances."

"He told us that. Half a billion. Half his worldly wealth."

"He was being somewhat economical with the truth there. Which is about the only area where he's being economical." Lillicrap took off his spectacles and polished the lenses on one shirttail. His eyes, exposed, looked small and lost. "Mr Landesman... What I'm about to tell you goes no further than this room, of course."

"Of course."

Lillicrap replaced his spectacles on his nose, adjusting them until they were immaculately balanced. "Mr Landesman has all but bankrupted himself pursuing this dream of his, this vendetta against the Olympians. I've warned him countless times to be more cautious, less spendthrift. These account spreadsheets I've been preparing for him – they make for grim reading. Will he listen to me, though? Will he hell. Deaf to all my protests. I find it... I find it distressing to see such prosperity, such affluence, being recklessly squandered. It hurts me. It causes me physical pain."

"Mr Landesman doesn't look at it as squandering," Sam pointed out. "And it is his money. He can do with it as he likes."

"Granted. All these years, though, I've served as his conscience, the little warning voice that tells him if he's gone too far or if he's in danger of doing so, and always he's paid attention to me and valued my judgement. My advice has got him out of more than a couple of nasty scrapes, believe you me, and steered him clear of numerous others. Until now. Now he simply won't be told. Won't be swayed. And it makes me feel like I'm nothing to him any more. Just another one of his employees."

Sam didn't know whether to laugh at Lillicrap or pity him. The man clearly loved Landesman. It wasn't some mere romantic attachment, it was a sincere Platonic love buried at a level so deep that not even he himself was aware of it. He adored his boss as a dog adores its master. The master in this case, unfortunately, did not reciprocate. Doubtless Landesman considered Lillicrap nothing more than a useful functionary. He had no idea of the slavish devotion he inspired in his assistant.

"You said 'vendetta' just now," Sam said, wanting to change the subject, and also curious about the choice of word.

"Did I?"

"Did you mean that? This war against the Olympians is somehow personal for Mr Landesman?"

"No. No, you must have misinterpreted. If that's what I said, it's not what I meant."

"Oh. OK."

"Anyway," Lillicrap said, resuming his usual brisk and businesslike demeanour, "you didn't come to speak to me, I'm sure, and you certainly didn't expect to have to stand there and listen to me witter on about my problems. You want to know where our fearless leader is. Last time I saw him, he was in the command centre. Try there."

Sam did, and found Landesman, alone, standing before the huge mural with his hands clasped together behind his back. He looked as if he'd been in this pose a while. The gods on the wall, each at least 15 feet tall, loomed over him, dwarfing him.

"Sam," he said, then turned back and resumed his study of the picture. Sam waited. Eventually, after a minute or two of contemplative silence, he spoke again. "What's remarkable about this painting, I find, what's so psychologically intriguing, and why it never fails to fascinate me, is the way Vasari and his collaborator Cristofano Gherardi have managed to make the act of castration seem painless, functional, almost desirable even. There's no blood, for one thing. Not a drop of it in sight. But look at Uranus, too. There he is with the tip of a scythe buried in his crotch, and no trace of anguish on his face, no hint of distress, only a kind of dull, bovine bewilderment. He's supine, hands on the ground beside him, hardly resisting as Cronus digs the blade in. He's looking up at his son more with resignation than anything. It's as if he's at least a half-willing participant in his own unmanning. The other gods are distraught but Uranus himself is just taking it, as if it's unavoidable, just something that needs to be done."

"Why isn't he fighting back?"

"Well now, that's the question, isn't it? Maybe all sons emasculate their fathers, maybe that's the point Vasari is making. When, as a father, you bring a son into the world, what you're in effect doing, consciously or not, is acknowledging that your days of usefulness and productivity are numbered. You've sired your replacement, the boy who is going to grow up into the man who will usurp your position in the world. You raise him, nurture him, teach him, knowing all along that once he reaches adulthood you yourself are going to be superseded, rendered surplus to requirements – your vitality, your vigour as a man, no longer called for. To put it bluntly, every son cuts his dad's balls off sooner or later. Not always knowingly, and certainly not literally, not like Cronus there, or like Zeus later on. But every son does, and every father is more or less complicit in the deed. That's what Vasari is getting at, I believe. That's why Uranus is so passive. Myths are metaphors, and Vasari has chosen to interpret this one in that way. The next generation..."

He shook his head.

"Well, enough of that," he said. "You came to ask if you Titans can resume operations."

"Yes."

"I've been leaving you lot be, giving you some breathing space so that you can make the necessary inner adjustments. I thought a couple of days would be enough, and it seems it is. Back into action, Sam? Eager for more? But of course, of course. Still plenty of monsters left on the hit-list, not to mention the Olympians themselves. Do you really think everyone's ready?"

"I do."

"And you." He looked at her levelly. "Are you ready?"

She met and matched his gaze. "I am."

"The Sphinx. It was a humanoid creature. You were there at the kill. Did that trouble you?"

"It was humanoid, but still a monster. I didn't find that a problem. Not too much. Besides, Rick did most of the work."

"Rick is experienced in that field," Landesman said. "And I believe he saw in it something of his own personal bête noire, the Lamia, another monster with female-human attributes. Hence it was little trouble for him, pulling the trigger on the Sphinx. It was a dry run, you might say, for his upcoming appointment with the murderer of his son. He's a soldier. In his eyes one can see the look of a man who has come to an accommodation with the act of discriminate killing. And in yours, I can see it too, now. It's there. Faint, but there, discernible. You understand the demands that are being placed on you, the sacrifices you're having to make. You know what all this is doing to you. You realise how it's going to change you irrevocably."

"If it doesn't finish me off altogether."

"Quite. Death: the most irrevocable change of all." Landesman leaned back. "Very well, let's get to it then. No need to ask me twice. Back in the saddle and on with the hunt!"

28. MONSTERCIDE

MOVE FAST, HIT hard, get out quick.

That was the Titans' mantra for the next phase of the campaign. Each act of monstercide had to be conducted at optimum speed. There was no room for lingering and no margin for error. The Olympians were on the alert now. Every attack could bring them running and therefore had to be as swift and clandestine as it was in the Titans' power to make it.

Tellingly, all but one of the monsters still roved freely. The exception was Cerberus, Hera's pet, her triple-headed lapdog, who seldom left her side. The rest continued to skulk or rampage in set areas as before, unchecked, unabated. Zeus had not summoned them to the safety of Mount Olympus.

That, according to Landesman, revealed two things about their adversaries' frame of mind. One: the Olympians were positive that their recent retaliation would have the desired effect. Two: the Olympians were overconfident, indeed complacent. Both of these were flaws to be taken advantage of.

The Gulfstream covered huge distances, circumnavigating the globe. Ramsay joked that he wished he was collecting air miles. He'd have a free trip to the Bahamas by the end of all this jetsetting.

Chisholm spelled Gray and Greene in the cockpit every now and then, so as to give the pilots a break. "Don't worry," he announced over the intercom the first time he took the controls. "I've chauffeured princes and presidents around the world. You're in safe hands. Now, would someone mind looking after my guide dog for a while?"

Other than him and Ramsay, the team the Titans were fielding this time around consisted of Sam, Mahmoud, Harryhausen, and Hamel.

In Japan, Sirens were at large. Successive Japanese prime ministers had been voicing opinions that were openly contrary to Pantheonic *diktat*. Successive Japanese prime ministers had been assassinated by the Olympians for voicing such opinions. Successive candidates for the post of Japanese prime minister had been voted in precisely because they promised to voice the same opinions as their predecessors. To be elected to the highest office in the National Diet these days was tantamount to signing your own death warrant.

Still, there was no shortage of applicants. It was the collective will of the nation, apparently, that its supreme leader, its spokesperson on the world stage, should verbally bait the Olympians, however dire the consequences for him or her. Every three months or so there was yet another state funeral followed by yet another general election. A part, now, of the swearing-in of a new prime minister involved the formal donning of a Rising Sun bandanna, kamikaze-pilot-fashion, and a vow to give one's life for one's country – less an oath, more a promise. It would have been farcical, almost, if it hadn't been done with such utter solemnity and sincerity.

The Sirens had been stationed in Japan much in the manner of an occupying force, there to dampen the country's ardour for self-sacrificial political insubordination. In that regard, though, the Olympians had miscalculated somewhat. The Sirens were a gaggle of gorgeous, partially feathered women who sang songs of such unspeakable loveliness that anyone who heard them was driven to commit an act of fatal self-harm. Any *man*, that is. Their song had no effect on women. Oestrogen or the absence of a Y-chromosome – biologists could not make up their minds which it was – rendered the fairer sex immune. To female ears, the Sirens' voices were just so much warble and twitter. To male ears, by contrast, they were an irresistible lure, and the message that permeated each note and phrase of their song was doom. Cut your wrists, overdose on prescription tranquillisers, take poison, hang yourself from a tree, put a gun in your mouth – the choices were many, the outcome always the same.

The Sirens were, in other words, suicide-manufacturing machines. This, for many a Japanese male, many a young one in particular, made them an attractive proposition, something to seek out rather than steer clear of. The monsters drew two specific types of man to them – the melancholic type who saw glory in the idea of terminating his own life under the influence of a thing of great beauty, and the patriotic type who wished to demonstrate his complete self-effacing love of country without having to go through the rigmarole of taking part in electoral processes and rising to the top position and dying then.

Song aside, the Sirens were pretty much defenceless, birds of prey who were also sitting ducks. The Titans tackled them in the old capital, Kyoto, low-lying city of temples and shrines, where a number of municipal parks had become designated Siren zones, places to visit only if you were keen to hear the Sirens sing for the first and last time. The city council had started charging admission to the parks, in the region of ¥200,000 per head, to cover the cost of removal of people's mortal remains. Someone, after all, had to pay for the women-only clean-up crews who went in twice daily, morning and evening, to zip corpses into bodybags and cart them out on stretchers.

Under cover of darkness, a women-only clean-up crew of a different kind stole into all the Siren parks one after another in swift succession. With external audio gain on their helmets turned down to zero and thumping heavy metal piped over the comms link for good measure – just in case – Tethys, Mnemosyne, Phoebe and Rhea carried out a series of surgical strikes. Muzzle suppressors were used to minimise gun noise. The night was long and harrowing. Had the Sirens not had downy feathers for hair, and a glossy pinnate covering on their arms and backs, it would have been very difficult, if not downright impossible, to kill them in cold blood like this. Up until now the monsters had been mostly animalistic and, more to the point, monstrous. The Sirens were, in essence, women. Killing them was, in essence, murder. And they were, of course, utterly ravishing to look at, these *hara kiri* canaries. Where their close kin the Harpies were demonic in appearance, these were angelic. Asleep, nesting in the bough of a tree or in a self-made bower amid some deftly trimmed ornamental shrubbery, they seemed innocuous and exquisitely fragile, something that should be cared for and protected, not ruthlessly exterminated.

Sam managed to overcome her qualms. Given that she had helped take out the Sphinx, the Sirens' vaguely human aspect cut no ice with her. She knew what had to be done, and did it, and once she'd set the example, shown the other three the way, they found it easy enough to copy her. Each Siren perished in silence, unawares. By the time it came to despatch the last of them, all four Titans were hardened to the task and it felt much like wringing the neck of a chicken or putting down an enraged swan. A distasteful but necessary deed. How many deaths had the Sirens been responsible for? The total ran into the hundreds. This, then, was a reasonable and justifiable reckoning.

The Gulfstream departed from Kansai International Airport in Osaka that same night, before the sun was up and well before the Sirens' bodies were discovered by suicide-seekers who had travelled far, some of them the length of the Japanese archipelago, had coughed up their park entrance fees, and were disappointed to have their plans for self-annihilation thwarted. (Kyoto city council did, incidentally, reimburse the ¥200,000 entrance fees, but only to the suicide-seekers who didn't, for form's sake, go ahead and take their own lives regardless.)

The incumbent prime minister, Sayu Urasawa, went on national TV that very day to announce, with great pride, that the Sirens were no more. "We have been rid of a scourge in our midst," she crowed. "Death has been brought to the death-bringers. Down with the Olympians!" The inevitable upshot of this was that, within an hour, Urasawa herself was dead. Hermes teleported into a cabinet meeting at her official residence, the Kantei, teleported out again with Urasawa in his clutches, reappeared at the pinnacle of the Tokyo Tower, shoved the prime minister off, and was gone again before the screaming Urasawa had even hit the pavement a thousand feet below.

29. THE GORGONS

THE GULFSTREAM FLEW south-west to the Malay Peninsula, passing Hong Kong en route.

What was left of Hong Kong.

The Titans gazed out at the remnants of the city from the plane's starboard portholes. A few skeletal skyscrapers still stood, canted at angles like gravestones in an untended cemetery. The coastline was pitted with craters, many of them awash with seawater like small lagoons. Wrecked jumbo jets lay sprawled across the runways of the reclaimed-land airport. Houses high in the hills were hollow, roofless shells, overrun with vines and creepers.

Here and there could be seen pockets of makeshift habitation – tents set up on streets in the central business district, clusters of junks and sampans moored in Victoria Harbour, shanty towns along the waterfront. Cooking fires sent up thin trails of smoke between the devastated buildings. Many survivors of the Obliteration still could not bear to leave Hong Kong – it would seem like abandoning the corpse of a loved one – and a number of non-residents had moved there, coming from as nearby as Kowloon and as far away as America, in a gesture of protest against the city's destroyers. Some had even set themselves the task of burying the dead, a huge undertaking. Mass ossuaries had been established in the basements of banks and financial services corporations. Vaults that had once been crammed with wealth and treasure were now gradually being filled with millions of sun-bleached bones.

"Glad Fred's not with us," Ramsay said sombrely, as the shattered, humiliated city receded into the distance. "Imagine that was Chicago... Nah, doesn't bear thinking about."

They landed at Singapore, at a freight airport where, in sweltering equatorial heat, the techs unloaded the TITAN suits and weapons into the back of a waiting hire truck. It had become a routine procedure by now. The battlesuits and weapons were brought out in locked steel flightcases embossed with the Daedalus Industries logo. Permits were checked by officials. Import duties were paid on the "product" contained in the flightcases. Bribes were also paid where required, and they almost always were required. That way, airport officials were disincentivised from opening the flightcases to make sure what was stated on the computer docket – components for keeping missile defence systems in basic working order – matched what actually lay inside. Then began the road journey to the site of enemy engagement.

In Singapore itself, a strict nighttime curfew was in effect. This was because, after dark, the entire island city-state belonged to the Gorgons. Every evening at sundown the trio of snake-haired creatures would emerge from their lair, a pit they had dug for themselves at the Botanic Gardens on Tanglin Road, and wander the streets in a group, communicating with one another by means of hisses, their forked tongues flickering. Singaporeans lived in terror of them. Blinds were kept tightly drawn between dusk and daybreak, and only a fool would venture outdoors during that time. One look from a Gorgon, one moment's exposure to those slitted serpentine eyes, and...

Well, the evidence of what would happen was all around, plain to see. On pavements, in parks, street corners, temple steps, everywhere – the statues. Statues of people, some cowering or shying away, others with their arms extended imploringly, still others frozen in the act of fleeing, looking over their shoulders. The statues appeared to be made of stone but in fact were composed of a carbon compound that had the ashy, powdery texture of pumice. Samples tested by scientists had shown that this substance was living tissue after it had been scorched by a sudden, massive burst of heat from the inside out, desiccated and hardened to a rocklike texture. The statues were the mortal remains of those who had been baked on the spot, instantaneously cooked somehow by a Gorgon's stare. To the locals they had become objects of superstition and dread. Living Singaporeans refused to touch them or, for that matter, move them or dispose of them. They simply walked around them, eyes averted, and hoped they themselves wouldn't share the same fate.

Singapore's crime, for which the Gorgons were the punishment, was that it had been the venue for a failed attempt to overthrow the Olympians. A group of businesspeople, principally weapons manufacturers and oil sheiks, had got together, united by their disgust at the steep decline in profits that had come about as a result of Olympian policies on defence spending and renewable energy sources. This, the so-called Raffles Syndicate – named not after the fictional gentleman thief, as some literary-minded wags liked to suggest, but after the sumptuous colonial-era hotel where their conspiratorial meetings took place – had provided funding for a battalion of international paratrooper mercenaries to launch a direct assault on Mount Olympus.

The raid had been well-intentioned, but doomed to disaster. In all, it had lasted a little under half an hour, from the moment the first mercenary had his heart clawed out in midair by a shrieking Harpy to the moment the final remaining mercenary died on the ground, choking on the spear which Artemis had plunged through his neck; and not once during that half an hour had the Olympians' stronghold been in danger of being breached. Nor had any Olympian suffered any injury beyond the odd bullet wound, which was well within the powers of their resident healer, Demeter, to cure.

The members of the Raffles Syndicate had all, naturally, been tracked down and executed in various messy ways, and the Gorgons had ever since been teaching Singapore, and the world, a lesson – the lesson being it wasn't just wrong to plot against the Pantheon, it was wrong even to harbour those who would plot against the Pantheon.

Nightfall. Six Titans fanned out through the Downtown Core, Singapore's oldest urbanised area and one of the Gorgons' preferred haunts. They moved in pairs along the deserted streets, Tethys with Mnemosyne, Phoebe with Rhea, Hyperion with Oceanus. The city's nocturnal stillness, combined with its immaculate cleanliness, was more than a little eerie. The place seemed more museum, or mausoleum, than municipality. It felt like a specimen of the modern world that had been isolated and preserved for future generations to admire. Adding to this impression were the statues, rough-featured but in all-too-real poses of horror and fear, caught in the pure amber glow of the streetlights. What a contrast they made with the statue of the city's founder Sir Stamford Raffles who stood on the east of the Singapore River, polymarble arms folded, looking out with monumental pride over all he surveyed.

"Base – Tethys," Sam said, after the Titans had spent an hour quartering the Downtown Core, without sign of the Gorgons. "No luck so far. Suggest we widen our sweep."

"Roger that," Landesman replied. Satellite bounce lent a faint echo to his voice. "Remember, if you spot one of them, for God's sake get away as fast as you can and take cover. Unlike the mythical Gorgons these ones don't need eye-to-eye contact. They just need to be able to see you."

"And then they roast you," said Hyperion. "Does anyone else think that's just plain wack? These bitches being able to flash-fry you just by looking at you?"

"I've known a couple of ladies in my time who could do that," Oceanus chipped in.

Mnemosyne groaned. "And we're sharing open comms with a pair of Neanderthals."

"Ah, you've just never been around real men before," said Hyperion.

"Oh, that's right. Silly me. I should be grateful to be in the company of such prime specimens of macho manhood. In fact, just talking to you, hearing your butch voices, it's made me come in my trolleys."

"Do any of you people even speak English?" Hyperion said. "I mean, 'trolleys'? What the hell does – ?"

"Titans," Landesman cut in tersely, "need I remind you that the Gorgons appear to exhibit an advanced and refined form of pyrokinesis. They can superheat any object to a core temperature of two thousand degrees Fahrenheit or higher, as long as they have direct line of sight of it. I'd suggest, therefore, that you concentrate all your energies on looking for them, because if they see you first..."

"Understood, base," said Sam. "Get that, everyone? Let's stow the banter and stay focused."

"Snakes for hair, too," Hyperion muttered. "Not enough that they're three crazed Martha Stewarts who want to make biscuits out of you, but they gotta have snakes for hair as well."

"Hyperion."

"Stowing the banter, ma'am. Banter stowed."

On they strode through the silent, pristine city, past malls where no night watchmen patrolled any more, past terraced shophouses whose window displays weren't lit up because there was no point (nobody was about, out of hours, to stop and glance in), past a hospital whose emergency department was closed (woe betide you if you were taken ill at night in Singapore these days), and along tree-lined avenues such as Orchard Road where nothing stirred but the occasional gutter-hugging rat and the palm and angsana fronds simmering gently in the hot night breeze. Another hour elapsed. A bead of sweat trickled down Sam's back and she commanded the battlesuit to lower its inner temperature by a couple of degrees. Her visor HUD pinpointed the other five Titans' relative locations: Mnemosyne within 5 metres of her, Hyperion and Oceanus a couple of hundred metres north-east, Phoebe and Rhea roughly quarter of a kilometre due east. Each was represented by a dot of light, with a callsign marker attached and a cluster of characters displaying ever-shifting values of distance, vector and relative direction. It gave her a weird, heady sense of connectedness to see this data hovering in front of the streetscape before her, to know precisely where her fellow team-members were even when they were out of sight. It was a kind of technology-enabled omniscience. The battlesuits lent their wearers the abilities of gods. The Titans had yet to discover, though, whether the suits made them the equals of gods.

That will come, she thought. This systematic, methodical killing of monsters was the warm-up to the main event, like the preliminary heats of a race that led to the finals. Useful practice for the Titans but also, according to Landesman, tactically important. The Olympians were now aware that somebody was coming for them. Arrogance and bluster would remain their outward response. Inwardly, however, might they not be feeling a certain amount of anxiety right now? The first prickings of doubt? Watching the ranks of their monsters getting whittled down, they might well have a sense that their position was being undermined, like people on a dais feeling the support struts beneath them being pulled away one by one. The Olympians' sturdy Olympus redoubt, that Acropolis-like structure with its palisades and battlements and its squadron of guardian Harpies, might be impregnable, but not so their hearts. Even the Olympians weren't immune to fear. This programme of monstercide was a propaganda tool as much as anything. For that reason alone, it was vital that the Titans continue to pursue it. Fear among the Pantheon could lead to discord, discord to disunity, disunity to a reduction in effectiveness. Which, as Landesman said, could only be a good thing.

"All Titans – Hyperion. I have visual. Repeat, I have visual."

The urgency in his tone sparked a jolt of adrenaline inside Sam.

"Hyperion, get to cover," she said. "You too, Oceanus."

"Copy that," said Hyperion. "Already on it."

"You're sure it's them?" said Phoebe.

"Three women with wavy snaky hair strolling along the road like they own the place? I'd say it's a pretty fair guess."

"Hyperion, Oceanus, when you're safe, hold position," said Sam. "All Titans, converge. Prepare to deploy Perseus guns. Phoebe, Rhea, I have you at half a klick south and east of Hyperion and Oceanus. Proceed on a north-westerly heading. If we're lucky, this is a pincer movement waiting to happen."

"Roger that, Tethys."

Sam started to run, Mnemosyne close at her heels. The pace of her pounding feet vibrated her vision, blurring things at the periphery. The visor readout clocked her speed at a little over 30 mph.

Exceeding thirty in a built-up area, she thought. *That's a fine and penalty points.*

Gunfire stuttered, close by. Sam and Mnemosyne turned a corner and skidded to a halt. Hyperion and Oceanus were a few metres ahead, hunkered behind a parked car. Hyperion was at the engine end of the car, his Perseus gun protruding round the front bumper, cracking off round after round. Distantly, Sam could see three figures silhouetted in the roadway. They were running fast towards the car, down on all fours like lizards, hissing and shrieking to one another as they went.

Grabbing Mnemosyne, she ducked back around the corner. Then she unlocked her Perseus gun, swivelled the hinged barrel to the left at a 60° angle, and poked it out into the street. The digital camera mounted on the business end of the barrel relayed an image to a small LCD screen near the trigger guard. A target sight was superimposed on the image.

Hyperion was still firing, but appeared not to have scored a hit yet. The Gorgons were still coming, enraged, scurrying along with their hair erect and wildly writhing.

Sam took aim, centring the target sight on the frontmost of the creatures. Her first two shots with the semiautomatic pistol missed. The third struck the Gorgon in the shoulder. The monster sprawled onto its belly, screaming in pain. The other two hurried to their sister's aid.

Oceanus laid the barrel of his Perseus gun flat across the car's bonnet and loosed off a couple of rounds. The bullets ricocheted off tarmac. At the same moment the two uninjured Gorgons reared up. Both stared hard at the parked car, bending their heads purposefully.

"Hyperion, Oceanus," Sam said, "you need to move your backsides. Now!"

Both Titans hurled themselves clear of the car, and a split-second later the combined gazes of the two Gorgons ignited the fuel tank and the car exploded, bucking into the air atop a roiling cushion of flame. Hyperion and Oceanus hustled across the pavement to the shelter of a shop doorway, even as the burning vehicle crashed back down to earth on its side, shedding pieces of itself in all directions.

The Gorgons skirted around the fiery wreckage. All three of them were on their feet, upright this time. The one Sam had shot was clutching its shoulder but still eager, it seemed, for battle. They closed in on Hyperion and Oceanus, who were pinned down in the shop doorway, unable to break cover for fear of exposing themselves.

"Tethys, this is Rhea. We are in position."

Sam's visor display placed Phoebe and Rhea on the opposite side of the street, in the mouth of an alleyway. *Gotcha*. She gave them the command to fire at will. Shots rippled towards the Gorgons. Sam and Mnemosyne, the one kneeling, the other standing, let rip from their own hiding place. The Gorgons were caught in a withering diagonal crossfire. On the screen of her Perseus gun Sam saw the monsters, flickeringly sidelit by the flames from the car, swivelling in all directions, trying to see where the bullets were coming from, where their attackers were, but unable to. Their voices rose in a howl, a wavering ululation of outrage and frustration. Then one of the Gorgons went down, as though poleaxed, raging one moment, spreadeagled and motionless the next. Another of them took a bullet to the head. Gobbets of brain and fragments of snake hair flew. No sooner had this one hit the ground than the third fell too.

"Cease fire," Sam announced.

In the silence that followed, the guns' reports could be heard echoing all across the city, pealing between buildings. Closer to, the only sounds were the crackle and pop of the burning car, the twanging of heat-warped metal.

"All Titans sound off," Sam said. "Are you OK?"

Five affirmatives.

"Though for a moment there..." said Hyperion, his voice raspy with emotion. "Ladies, Oceanus and I owe you big-time."

"Let's go and take a look," Sam said. "Confirm the kills. Then we get ourselves the hell out of here."

They congregated around the three bodies. Each Gorgon had a glossy scaly hide and each was identical to its sisters in every respect except colouring – one was greenish, one greyish, one brownish. All three lay still, apart from the slender little snakes which sprouted from their scalps in thick profusion. These were twitching in their death throes. Now and then their tiny mouths gaped in spasms of soundless, shuddering, fang-baring agony.

"Jeez-us," breathed Hyperion. "Those are about three of the most hideous things I've ever clapped eyes on."

"Shouldn't be allowed to exist," agreed Rhea.

"Abominations," Phoebe added, her German accent tripping slightly over the word.

"Well, they're dead now," said Oceanus, "and good sodding riddance, I say."

Sam peered down at the monsters, and for some reason the man-lion from her dream flitted into her thoughts.

"What *are* they?" she wondered aloud. "Where did they come from? I don't believe they're supernatural beings. Did someone make them? Were they people once?"

"Does it matter?" said Hyperion.

"Quite," said Oceanus. "They're killable. That's all we need to know."

"But they're intelligent," said Sam. "They're more than just animals. And that –"

She was cut short by an abrupt loud yelp from Hyperion. "Whoa! Its eyes are open! Motherfucker's still alive!"

One of the Gorgons, the greyish one, was staring up at the surrounding Titans. Its lips parted in a snarl. Its eyes blazed with hatred.

Sam was closest to it. She knew she had just a matter of heartbeats in which to act. She didn't go for her gun. Her response was instinctual, visceral, a convulsion of disgust. She raised a leg and brought her foot down on the Gorgon's face, stamping with servomotor-augmented strength. Her boot went straight through the monster's head, crushing the midsection of it flat as easily as if she had been stamping on a watermelon. Blood spurted everywhere. The *crunch* was horrendous but also, at some deep, primal gut level, exhilarating.

"Well," said Hyperion, scanning the mess Sam had made. He took off a gauntlet and wiped blood drips from his visor. "Yeah. Motherfucker *was* still alive. But I think it's safe to say, not any more."

30. BRUGES

Then came Bruges.

And the Titans' second casualty.

The elegant little Belgian city had endured a French attempt at annexation in the 14th century and, more recently, Nazi occupation, as well as lengthy periods of impoverishment when the canals that connected it to the coast silted up, meaning the arteries which carried its lifeblood, commerce, were blocked. It had survived all these hardships with its medieval architecture more or less intact and its air of resilience undiminished. Bruges sat in the midst of farmed flatlands like a well-preserved lesson in the art of quietly getting on with business and hoping for a brighter tomorrow.

Except... the good burghers of Bruges had slipped up lately. They'd forgotten their history – neglected the tradition of passive, sedate stoicism that had served them so well in the past. The city had become the hub of a youth movement that was prevalent throughout Europe and particularly in the Benelux: the Agonides, the Children of Struggle.

They were teenagers, mostly, who had grown up knowing little other than the Pantheonic rule and who chafed under the yoke of this unasked-for, quasi-divine governance. They were rebels, as passionate in their beliefs as only young people could be. They refused to accede to the Olympians' authority. They would not bend the knee the way all the older folks seemed to, especially the ones in positions of political power. They took it upon themselves to resist by mocking and denouncing the so-called gods at every turn.

They'd become famous – notorious – for their art stunts, graffiti sloganeering, and internet pranks such as a Trojan horse virus, called the "Trojan Horse," which embedded a subroutine in operating systems so that whenever the name or image of an Olympian appeared onscreen, a tiny wooden horse would pop up and disgorge a band of even tinier animated hoplites armed with mops and brushes who would set about scrubbing the word or picture out of existence. Millions of PCs and Macs were infected worldwide before All-Moderator Argus managed to expunge the virus from the Web. The Agonides were also responsible for a number of skilfully organised flashmob events that saw dozens of random strangers flock to some open public space and allow themselves to be arranged, through a cunning piece of mobile-phone GPS trickery, into a pattern that could be best seen by nearby surveillance cameras. They'd remain in place for as long as it took to guarantee the pattern had been recorded on CCTV, but no more than 30 seconds, before dispersing. On one occasion a reasonable likeness of Zeus's face was formed, showing the king of the Pantheon with eyes crossed and tongue sticking out. On another, a hundred or so bodies aligned to spell out the words FUCK THE GODS. Most often, though, the flashmobs adopted the official symbol of the Agonides, a circle representing the letter O – for Olympian – surrounded by a larger circle with a line slashing across it diagonally.

The movement had arisen in the genteel backstreets of Bruges. That was where its spiritual heart lay. Accordingly, Bruges was where the Olympians had chosen to site one of their vilest monsters. If the presence of the Lamia in their midst couldn't deter the Agonides from their adolescent shenanigans, then nothing could.

The Lamia was a vampiric thing, half woman, half snake, that seemed quite at home among the towering spires and torpid canals of the town. Night and day it swam and lolled in the water, lurking under bridges or crawling onto jetties to bask in the sun. Its preferred prey was small children, and as a consequence there were no small children to be found anywhere in Bruges. Everyone under the age of twelve had been evacuated into the surrounding countryside or found temporary lodgings in Brussels and Ghent. The Lamia was partial to the odd adult as well, but its attacks on mature victims were seldom fatal, whereas its attacks on minors almost always were. It was a question of blood volume. The Lamia sucked three or four pints at a single sitting, never any more. Most adults could survive that level of blood loss and the attendant shock, just, if given immediate medical treatment and an on-the-spot transfusion. Small children could not.

The inhabitants of Bruges tried to go about their daily lives as normal, acting as if the Lamia wasn't there. It wasn't easy, though. They could feel their city slowly dying around them. The empty playgrounds, the lack of high-pitched voices yelling, the toy shops, kindergartens and primary schools that had "Closed Until Further Notice" signs in the window – nobody had realised, until they were gone, quite how much children added to a community and quite how great a void was left by their absence. Without them, there was no tangible evidence of a future, no visible sense of continuum. There were just glum parents, missing their offspring terribly, and the elderly, feeling the cold wind of mortality more keenly than ever.

Also, tourists had stopped coming. Bruges's principal source of income these days were the visitors who were drawn in their droves to the "Venice of the north" thanks to its art treasures and its stately basilicas with their Gothic and neo-Gothic stylings. But the Lamia had put paid to that. Now the horse-drawn carriages stood idle in the Markt, the cobbles of the Burg were untroubled by the soles of sightseeing and coach-party crowds, and open-topped tour boats sat at their moorings with tarpaulins stretched over them and green slime accumulating on their hulls.

Then, one spring night, a rare event. A group of outsiders did arrive in town, unbeknownst to the residents. Although they had come to explore the place and their visit would ultimately be beneficial to the Brugesian economy, they were hardly tourists. Their reason for being there was, as one of them put it, to "find that motherfucking leech and blow it to bits."

Ramsay uttered these words in the back of the van as McCann drove him, Sam and Chisholm into the town. The Chicagoan's sense of humour had been on the wane since they'd left Singapore, and now his face was nothing but a mask of resolute, implacable hatred. His moment had come. Once more he reasserted that nobody else, *nobody*, would deliver the killing blow tonight. Nobody but him.

"I said it on the plane, I'll say it one more time. The bloodsucker is mine. I'm staking my claim. I've waited five goddamn years for this. You two are welcome to come with. I'll appreciate your support. But so help me, if either of you gets in my way when we have the thing cornered, you better damn well get out of it, or else. It's me and the Lamia, OK? For my little boy's sake. For Ethan. Me and that monster. To the death."

Sam said nothing, just nodded to show that she understood; Chisholm likewise.

McCann parked in a leafy residential square, and the Titans put their helmets on and powered up. Tethys, Hyperion and Oceanus exited from the back doors, and the hunt for the Lamia began.

Much like Singapore, Bruges was deserted after dark, the streets abandoned by its inhabitants, indoors seeming altogether a safer and more sensible place to be. The belfry of the Belfort-Hallen rang out every fifteen minutes, its carillon playing tunes to parcel out the hours, but it seemed nobody was out and about to hear, other than the three Titans.

"I know that one," Oceanus remarked, as the bells tolled half past midnight. "Bugger me, it's 'Danny Boy.'" He joined in. "'The pipes, the pipes are ca-all-ling.'"

"Hey," said Hyperion. "Zip it."

"Only having a bit of a singalong."

"Well, don't."

Oceanus bristled. "Now hold on a moment. Who are you to –"

Behind Hyperion's back, Sam made an air-patting gesture. *Leave it.*

Oceanus jutted his jaw, but relented.

They traversed several low bridges, weapons trained on the canals below. The water was mirror-motionless, black as oil. Mist drifted up from it in thready swirls.

"Come on out, Lamia," Hyperion muttered. "Show your face. I got something for you."

The "something" was the rocket launcher that he carried slung over his back, a Daedalus special, short enough that the user could flip it forward, slot the rocket in, and assume firing position in one easy manoeuvre. Its effectiveness in the field had been proved twice, first against the Sphinx, then against the Chimera. The projectiles' thermobaric warheads, designed to stop armoured vehicles and penetrate masonry, made mincemeat of monsters. Overkill? Hyperion would argue that under these circumstances there was no such thing.

"Movement," said Oceanus.

"Where?" said Hyperion.

"Your eleven."

"Got it."

The Titans had just crossed yet another bridge, having performed almost a complete circuit of the central part of the city. On the corner of a narrow street up ahead, Sam could see what looked like an arm – waving? Reaching up? She could also, now, detect an intermittent hissing noise.

Hyperion swung the launcher, already loaded, onto his shoulder and advanced. Back at Bleaney, Landesman advised caution. Sam followed Hyperion, machine gun at the ready. She kept to his left side, steering well clear of the launcher's rear end. Thanks to her battlesuit the backblast wouldn't kill her but it would certainly knock her off her feet.

The hissing continued, reminding Sam of the sound the Gorgons had made. Perhaps they and the Lamia were related, members of the same composite woman/snake species. But the Lamia was a stealth predator. Its *modus operandi* was to creep up on its prey and latch on, injecting them with a venom that served as a muscle relaxant before it took its fill of their blood. Why would it be making any noise? Why alert anyone to its presence in this way?

Hyperion rounded the corner, adopting a feet-spread firing stance.

"Ah shit," he said. Angry, disappointed. "One of *them*."

Sam joined him, and found a scared teenage boy cowering before him. The teenager's face was covered with a balaclava, and in his hand was an aerosol can. On the wall beside him, part of the façade of a chocolate shop, were two freshly painted concentric O's. He hadn't yet managed to add the diagonal line that would complete the Agonides symbol.

"Please, don't shoot!" the teenager begged. "I am good kid. No threat. Just doing my thing."

"I'm not going to shoot," Hyperion assured him. "What do you mean, your thing?"

"I must paint ten of these, ten logos around the city, then I am able to join Agonides as full member. It's my – I'm not sure of the word." The teenager's English carried a Flemish accent, not dissimilar to a Netherlands accent. *Word* came out *voord*.

"Initiation."

"Yes! Initiation."

"It's dangerous out here at night," Sam said.

"True," said the teenager, "but in daytime police would try to stop me. At night, no police."

"You'd rather risk death than being arrested."

He shrugged. "What we do – it is worth dying for." Through the balaclava eyeholes Sam saw his gaze turn inquisitive. "But who are you people? Not army. Not proper army."

"We're no one," said Hyperion. "Ghosts. We don't exist. Got that? Now run home and forget you ever saw us."

"Ghosts..." A light of comprehension dawned in the teenager's eyes. "I know! I know it! You are them!" he exclaimed. "The ones. The monster killers. That is right, no? The ones who do the Griffin, the Sphinx... The Sirens also, I think. It is on the news today. And now the Lamia. You're here to kill her too."

"It," Hyperion corrected him. "Kill it. Now what part of 'run home' did I not say clearly enough for you to understand, son?"

"Please, I must shake your hands. You are heroes to us. We Agonides, we are talking about you the whole time. We love you. Many people love you. You are big buzz online. Go to the chat rooms, the forums, you'll see. Our leaders do not like you. They say you are bad. You are too much making waves. But the people, they know you are doing good thing. And the Olympians next? First the monsters, then the assholes who say they are gods but are not? That is the plan?"

"I'm not going to tell you," said Hyperion. "And I'm not going to be shaking any hands either. Just scram, kid. I mean it."

The teenager produced a mobile phone from his back pocket. "A picture. So I can post it online and show everyone who you are. Proof that you exist. The world needs to see you."

"For God's sake don't let him," said Landesman.

"Gimme that." Hyperion reached for the phone.

"Um, Tethys, Hyperion..." came Oceanus's voice, quaverily over the comms. "Help."

They turned.

"I'm sorry," Oceanus croaked. "Came up from behind. Didn't see."

The Lamia had him. A glistening trail of canal water led from the parapet of the bridge to where the monster now was, draped around Oceanus. Its snakelike lower half enveloped him to the waist like the coils of some immense boa constrictor. Its womanlike upper half clutched his torso, pinning his arms to his sides in a muscular embrace. He was helpless. The Lamia had torn off the rubberised gorget which protected his neck. Now its mouth was latched onto his exposed throat, and its venom was already taking effect. Oceanus writhed feebly in its clutches but, even with the added strength from his battlesuit, his efforts were in vain. The Lamia's head bobbed slightly as it drank deeply from his jugular.

Without hesitating, Hyperion sighted the rocket launcher on the monster.

"Hyperion!" Sam snapped. "What the hell are you doing?"

"What needs to be done," Hyperion said, off-comms. Launch lever down. Finger on trigger. "He's as good as dead already."

"No he is not." Sam raised her submachine gun. "Back off and leave this to me."

"The Lamia's mine, Tethys. You can't have it."

"That isn't your decision to make," Sam replied. "And besides, I don't recall asking your permission."

She darted towards the Lamia. Hyperion was yelling at her, pleading with her – she ignored him. The situation being what it was, his choice of weapon had put him out of the running.

"Hey!" she shouted at the monster. "Hey! Over here! Look at me!"

The Lamia broke off from its feasting and looked up. Its mouth was round and fringed with needle teeth like a lamprey's. Gore trickled from the puckered, sphincter-like orifice, dribbling down the monster's chin onto its bare flaccid breasts. Orange-irised eyes fixed Sam with a look of gluttonous glee. Oceanus now hung slack in the Lamia's clutches. His jaw drooped and his head was starting to loll.

Sam drew a bead on the Lamia's face and fired. Quicker than she'd anticipated, however, the monster swivelled. The shot ricocheted off Oceanus's shoulder, zinging into the stonework of the bridge. Next moment, the Lamia relaxed its hold on Oceanus, loosening its coils, but not completely, and not for long, only for the couple of seconds it took the monster to slither to the bridge parapet and over the side. It dived headlong into the canal, taking its victim with it.

Sam was at the parapet before the Lamia was even fully submerged. The canal was shallow, no more than a couple of metres deep. She switched to thermal imaging. Within the water a dim red blob appeared, roughly the shape of Oceanus and the Lamia entwined. Sam fired and fired again. The Lamia flexed its tail and lanced off through the water, dragging Oceanus along. A turbulent wake swelled up from below.

Then a rocket pierced the surface of the canal, its small splash followed swiftly by a tremendous subaquatic detonation that flared white in Sam's visor and raised a ten-metre-diameter blister of water. Hyperion reloaded and fired the launcher again. A second blister of water overwrote the tumultuous ripples left by the first.

"I got it," Hyperion breathed. "Tell me I got it."

The canal churned, waves slapping and slopping against its embankments. Gradually the tortured water subsided to calmness. Moments passed. Then, with a slow, sinister grace, two bodies broke the surface. They bobbed up side by side like a pair of synchronised swimmers, Oceanus face down, the Lamia rolling over onto its back, its thick tail uncoiling. Outwardly both looked more or less intact. The blasts hadn't killed them directly, the hydrostatic pressure had.

"Ah goddammit." Hyperion sounded sick and weary all of a sudden, drained of all energy. "Shit."

"Yes," said Sam. "Quite. Shit."

"I didn't... I mean, he was a goner the moment –"

"Save it for later. Police'll be here soon. Those bangs will have woken up half of Belgium. Let's get down there and retrieve Oceanus's body, then scarper."

"Sam, I –"

"*Later*. And if you ever call me anything but Tethys again while we're on an op, I will smack you in the mouth. The way I'm feeling right now, I've a good mind to smack you in the mouth anyway, so don't give me an excuse."

"Do as she says, Hyperion," said Landesman, "and make it quick. We can't leave Oceanus. We need him home – him and his suit. We can't leave any trace of ourselves behind."

On a nearby jetty Sam found a boathook which she used to draw Oceanus over. His head-up display was still lit; the suit was still functioning, even though its wearer was not. She left Hyperion to haul the body out of the water and sling it over his shoulder. As he did so, she spared a glance for the Lamia, which floated serenely, eyes open but unseeing, lamprey mouth agape. In spite of herself, Sam thought that the monster looked at peace.

Oceanus's death had been a mercy killing. She was angry about it but deep down she knew Hyperion had done the kindest possible thing, if not necessarily for the noblest possible motive. Slow drowning versus instant oblivion? No contest.

But the Lamia's death – it occurred to her that that might be regarded as a mercy killing too. An end to a repugnant, unnatural existence.

God help her, was she actually starting to feel pity for these creatures?

The siren of an emergency services vehicle skirled in the distance. Hyperion bounded up the jetty steps and started running towards where the van was parked, accelerating to his top speed, barely impeded by the bulk of Oceanus. Sam followed suit.

31. THE AGONIDES CLIP

Nigel Chisholm was laid to rest at Bleaney. His grave was dug on a windswept slope looking out to sea. His headstone was a cairn which Sam and Mahmoud built painstakingly and to which Landesman and all of the Titans ceremonially added a small rock on top, a way of paying their respects. There was no funeral service as such, just this silent piling-on of rocks followed by a few minutes of sombre reflection. Each Titan was acutely aware that he or she, too, might one day be killed in action. Chisholm's death brought home that fact even more forcefully than Eto'o's had. Each foresaw the possibility of being interred next to him on this very stretch of hillside and of the single burial site soon becoming a cemetery, the number of graves increasing as the number of mourners dwindled. Here, in that six-foot-long rectangle of spaded-over turf, that waist-high stack of small black stones, was irrefutable evidence of the risks they faced and the extreme price they might have to pay. It would be fair to state that the Titans' thoughts were more on themselves, that blustery April morning, than on their fallen comrade. But then, wasn't that often so with funerals? *There but for the grace of God go I.* Or rather, in this instance, *of gods.*

Tsang delivered a brief, muted elegy. He said he'd been glad to have Nigel Chisholm as a colleague and as a friend. Then, to round off the proceedings, Sparks led everyone in a prayer. She extemporised much in the manner of the Baptist preachers whose services she regularly attended back in New Orleans, stitching gilded strands of scripture into the plain cloth of more colloquial phrasing. Her loud "aymen" at the end was echoed by the others with degrees of enthusiasm ranging from sheepish to none at all. Only Ramsay put any real effort into it, almost as if he had something to prove.

Ramsay had been testy and on edge since coming back from Bruges. He wasn't a man who often felt the need to defend anything he did or answer for his actions to anyone but himself. He was anticipating criticism, though, and so was ready to meet even a hint of it with a counterblast of self-justification.

"You'd have fired too," had been his refrain whenever anyone even looked like mentioning Chisholm. "The Lamia was going to get away. Nigel didn't have a hope of surviving. I weighed it up and I made a call and I can live with that call and if I can then so the hell can you."

For Sam the problem was not so much that Ramsay had sent rockets into the canal but that he'd been willing to send them at the Lamia moments earlier, while the monster was still on the bridge, mouth fastened to Chisholm's neck. He had held off from pulling the trigger, but he'd wanted to, and probably would have if she hadn't stopped him.

She'd challenged him on this during the van ride out of Bruges, and Ramsay's answer had been: "Nigel's suit would have protected him. Ain't that right, McCann? A TITAN suit can withstand an indirect hit from a rocket, yeah?"

"Uhh... maybe," McCann had replied, his tone implying *But I wouldn't bet on it.*

"It would have," Ramsay had said, staring down at his gauntleted hands. "It would."

Will I be like that? Sam had asked herself, looking across at the Chicagoan from the other side of the van's rear cab. Chisholm's body lay between them, rocking with the van's motion, lent a jerky semblance of life by every bump and pothole in the road. *Will I be the same as Rick when I come up against Apollo and Artemis? When I'm facing them, will nothing matter except my revenge, not even the safety of others?*

She couldn't know, she supposed, until the actual moment arrived.

Ramsay's behaviour in Bruges wasn't, at any rate, of primary importance just then, and even the shock of Chisholm's death took a backseat when it emerged that phone footage had been recorded of the Titans' attack on the Lamia and uploaded onto the internet. The

Agonides wannabe in Bruges had filmed everything that had occurred from Sam closing in on the monster to Ramsay lobbing rockets into the canal. Ramsay hadn't had a chance to confiscate his phone, and the teenager had fled the scene while Ramsay and Sam were preoccupied with fishing Chisholm's body out of the canal, and now the clip was all over the Web. It was a worldwide sensation, pinging to and fro across the globe as an email attachment, copies of it cropping up on countless blogs, homepages and networking sites, link leading to link. It proliferated so far, so fast, that by the time Argus became aware of its existence and set about the business of suppressing and erasing, he was too late. The clip was digital ivy, and for every tendril that the Hundred-Eyed One pruned another three sprang up elsewhere. There was hardly a crevice of the internet it didn't take root in, hardly a website that didn't give it a purchase to affix itself to.

The footage itself wasn't much to look at – less than a minute's worth of shaky, murky playback. All the figures in it were fuzzed at the edges, their outlines dissolving into a haze of blocky pixels as they moved. At times the low ambient light rendered the four participants little more than indistinct grey silhouettes. Nonetheless the muzzle flash from Sam's gun and the backblast from Ramsay's rocket launcher were spectacularly bright and dramatic, white rips in the darkness, and, for all the blurriness, it was obvious what was going on. It was obvious, too, that the three military-looking individuals in the clip were not conventional soldiers. The Agonides' own website, where, naturally, the footage first appeared, made this point in the accompanying commentary.

"They have no insignia," someone had written, in excitable and somewhat stilted English. "They belonging to no country. Their battle armour is like nothing anyone has seen before. Who are this people? We donot know. But they are kiiling Olympian monsters and so we salute them and are offering them our every support. GO, STRANGERS! THE WORLD IS WITH YOU!! FIGHT THE GOOD FIGHT!!!"

"It's an unmitigated disaster," said Lillicrap. He, Landesman and Sam were in the command centre, channel-hopping. The international news networks had picked up on the phone clip and were airing it over and over again for the benefit of, presumably, the last half-dozen people left on the planet who'd failed to catch it online.

"Is it?" said Landesman.

"Isn't it?" came the plaintive reply, Lillicrap no longer sure of his opinions, no longer sure if he even had opinions of any value still.

"I admit that I'd have preferred not to go public quite so soon," said his boss. "A little longer in the shadows would have been no bad thing. But this was inevitably going to happen. The Titans were inevitably going to be spotted and, yes, filmed by somebody. And now that it's happened, we should be thanking our lucky stars that, one, you can't see anyone's face, so we've managed to keep our anonymity from being compromised; and, two, the footage makes it abundantly clear what the Titans are about. Agreed, Sam?"

"It doesn't leave much room for doubt as to who the good guys and the bad guys are," Sam said. "You've got the Lamia biting Nigel's neck. You've got us – well, me – trying to save Nigel. You've got Rick taking no prisoners once the Lamia's in the water. To the average punter we look compassionate but seriously hardcore. I think that sends out the right message. We were fortunate, too, that the Agonides got the footage up first, them being naturally inclined to be sympathetic to our cause. They put the most positive spin on it that we could hope for, and that may well have influenced how others feel about it. First impressions count."

"Although not everyone, it seems, is happy." Landesman toggled the screens to show a broadcast of live proceedings from the House of Commons. "Bartlett's in the middle of making a statement to Parliament. Look at his face. No prizes for guessing what tack he's taking."

"...inexcusable and unforgivable," the prime minister rumbled. The Honourable Members around him nodded and lowed like cattle at milking time. "The Olympians have done nothing to provoke these fiendish, murderous attacks on their prodigies, Mr Speaker, nothing to invite such wilful, premeditated acts of slaughter. Nothing whatsoever."

"Did he just say 'fiendish'?" said Sam.

"It's 'prodigies' I'm having difficulty with," said Landesman. "I daresay someone on his speechwriting team was handed a thesaurus and charged with finding the most euphemistic synonym for 'monster.'"

"These people, whoever they may be," Bartlett continued, "may think of themselves as agitators. Liberators. Freedom fighters. But let me tell you this." He thumped the despatch box with a statesmanlike fist. "They do not fight for *my* freedom, nor for the freedom of the Great British public."

This elicited plenty of "Hear! Hear!"-ing from his cabinet and backbenchers, and from across the floor as well.

"Great British public," Landesman echoed. "Words that always get a cheer in the Commons, regardless of what's actually being said. It's a political Pavlovian bell, and my, how it makes the dogs salivate!"

"No," said Bartlett, "what they are, Mr Speaker, what they so abundantly and incontrovertibly are, are terrorists."

Landesman heaved a theatrical sigh. "And there it is. The T-word. I knew it was coming. Didn't I say, Jolyon? Didn't I predict it?"

"You did, Mr Landesman."

"The minute we emerged into the limelight, some political stooge or other would get up on his hind legs and call us terrorists. I knew it would happen. And I'd have laid good money on it being Capitulating Catesby, too. We should have had a wager, Jolyon."

"I would have been foolish to take on that wager, sir, knowing I would surely lose. Rashly dispensing money is not something I'm too fond of."

"Yes, yes, no need to remind me. King of the purse strings. Master of the budget. We all know how diligent you are at your job."

"Or try to be. When I get the chance."

"It wasn't a complai– Oh, now hold on. What's this?" Landesman flipped to a different channel, an inset picture expanding to fill the entire screen. It was an American local news affiliate, and the words "Live From New York" were emblazoned across the top. Reasonably steady handheld camerawork showed a brawny, thickset figure staggering along a Manhattan street. The time was approaching noon, EST, and the person onscreen looked horribly drunk. He pinballed from lamppost to shopfront to parked car.

Which would have been unremarkable, perhaps, were it not for the fact that the figure was clad in a loincloth and a lion-skin cloak and that each time he collided with something it bent or broke. Behind him he had left a trail of damage – shattered plate-glass windows, tilted streetlights, splintered tree trunks, deeply dented car wings. Burglar alarms were whooping. Car alarms were wailing. Manhattanites could be seen peering out from office windows above or looking nervously on from the opposite side of the road.

"Hercules," Sam said, and sure enough, it *was* the ultra-strong Olympian, and the only conclusion to be drawn from his behaviour was that he'd just come from enjoying ample hospitality at some downtown bar, probably one of his favourite Chelsea or Greenwich Village hangouts.

A reporter, off-camera, was providing a breathless, blow-by-blow commentary.

"So, yeah, Hercules has been on the rampage for maybe half an hour now," he said, "and we have these amazing scenes of carnage that we're sending you, I mean look at him, he's out of control, totally blotto, got to be, and you can probably hear him, the guy's shouting, through it's impossible to make out what he's actually saying, it's all just kind of a incoherent howl, but – holy cow! Did you see that?" To the cameraman: "Did you get that, Chuck? Hercules just, just, he just walked into a mailbox, and he seemed to hurt himself, stub his toe maybe, and so he just kicked the thing, kicked it clean across the street, and now it's, well, it's embedded I guess is the word, embedded in the side of that building over there, jeez, that was some kick, dude should think of trying out for the NFL, 'cause that mailbox is well and truly stuck in the wall of that building, like a dart in a dartboard, and now – whoa! Somebody's SUV is taking a pasting. Zoom in on that, Chuck. Got it? Herc is really not pleased with that car, he's real ticked off with it, maybe he doesn't like four-by-fours, you know, gas guzzlers, maybe there's some kind of eco thing going on here..."

Hercules was, indeed, hitting the SUV with everything he had, and the chunky oversized car was rapidly getting beaten out of shape. Segments of bodywork flew off. The radiator grille fell. The headlamps popped out and dangled on their wires like enucleated eyeballs still attached to their optic nerves. Finally, with a grunt, Hercules clean-and-jerked the SUV off the ground and tossed it into the air. It came down in the centre of the road on its roof and lay there, crumpled, leaking oil and water.

That was when Hercules noticed the cameraman and the reporter. He came straight over, cloak billowing out behind him. His face was flushed, his eyes bloodshot and swimmy. He reached for the camera. The cameraman shied away, the image veering shakily to one side.

"Give me that," the Olympian growled. "Give me that fucking – that fucking thing, fucker."

"Hey, I'm filming here," the cameraman said. "I'm allowed to film. This is a public space."

"Give!" Hercules made another lunge for the camera, missing, his outstretched arm blurring from right to left.

"Chuck, give it to him," hissed the reporter.

"Freedom of the press," said the cameraman. The man behind the lens was, it seemed, braver than the man who usually stood in front. "In this country we have something called the Constitution. We have rights. We're allowed to shoot whatever we –"

Hercules's third attempt to grab the camera was successful. The onscreen image swerved in all directions, now showing a section of kerb, now the sky, now someone's sneakers, before finally settling on an extreme close-up of the Olympian's own face. Every pore in his skin was visible. The pockmarks on his nose looked like lunar craters.

"Rights?" he boomed, so loud that it overloaded the microphone and his voice crackled with distortion. "Hey! People out there! You hear this man? You think you have rights? Don't make me laugh. What about my right to walk down a street without some moron poking a camera at me? Huh? What about that? What about my right to let off steam and have a few drinks and chat up some nice piece of *eromenos* without some dick of a paparazzi intruding?"

"*Eromenos*?" said Sam.

"Boy lover," said Landesman.

"I'm not paparazzi," the reporter protested. "I'm an accredited journalist with –"

"Shut up, you cheap-suited media monkey," Hercules snapped. Spittle flecked the lens. "I'm talking here. Didn't your mother ever teach you to keep quiet and listen when your betters are talking? Now, where was I? Oh yes. Rights. Understand this, people of America and the rest of the world. You have no rights. Not while we're in charge. You used to have some, maybe, a few, in the early days after we took over. We started out treating you with respect – as much as we felt you deserved. We hoped you'd be wise enough, mature enough, to gladly and meekly accept what we were offering. But *no-o-o*, you objected, you resisted, you fought back, and that was when you forfeited your rights, any rights you thought you had. And now you're doing it once again, resisting. We thought you'd settled down but you haven't. You've started being treacherous, treasonous little savages again, and that means as far as we're concerned the gloves are off and the only right you have left now – hah, right, left, ha ha – the only right you have left is to bow your heads and do whatever the fuck we tell you to. Case in point: these two bottom-feeders."

He swung the camera round to show the reporter, whose suit *was* a cheap designer knockoff, and the cameraman, scruffily but more honestly dressed in jeans, windcheater and Phillies cap. Both of them were very scared, but the cameraman was doing the better job of hiding it. He fixed Hercules with a hard stare.

"See them?" the Olympian sneered. "These cogs in the media machine. They work for... Which channel do you work for?"

The reporter told him.

"Well," said Hercules, "I have a message for your employers, and for everyone watching. And it's this: do not harass us, do not question us, do not cast us in a bad light, do not challenge us – in short, do not fuck with us. Because *this* is what happens to those who do."

The image juddered wildly, as though an earthquake had just struck. It broke up into green and white squares, then stuttered, blinking in and out of blackness. This was soundtracked by yells of pain, and thumps, and then some ghastly wet crunching noises.

Finally normal transmission resumed. The camera had been set down on the ground, on its side. There was a spidery pattern of cracks across the lens. There were spatters of red on the lens as well. And lying within shot, slumped on the now-vertical sidewalk as though leaning against a wall, were the reporter and the cameraman. They were recognisable by their clothes only. Where they had once had heads, now they had collapsed, vaguely head-shaped messes. Their hair was matted with blood and dribbles of brain matter. Shards of skull poked out here and there. The slap-slap sound of Hercules's sandalled footfalls could be heard, diminishing in volume. Far off, a woman started screaming.

Then, thankfully, someone back at the studio had the presence of mind to cut the live feed.

Landesman, Lillicrap and Sam were silent. Stunned. Sickened.

"My God," Landesman said at last. "That was... My God. Truly horrible. But looking on the bright side – and there is one, and we must look on it – Hercules's timing can't be faulted. What a godsend, no pun intended. He's just handed us a propaganda coup. Our second today. First the Agonides clip, now this. Nobody, seeing what we've just seen, can have any uncertainty any more that what the Titans are doing is right, that we're on the side of the angels. If anybody was hesitant about backing us before, they won't be now."

"Popularity is all well and fine," said Sam. "I'd rather have the public on my side than against me. But it's hardly going to help us win the war, is it?"

"We'll see, Sam," said Landesman. "If things continue to go as I hope they do... well, you never know. Public support might just make all the difference."

32. THE MINOTAUR

THE RESISTENZA CONTRU-DIU Corsu, to be honest, did very little actual resisting but talked a good fight and had made enough of a nuisance of itself to warrant the Olympians' interest and earn their antipathy.

That was principally on the strength of two incidents. The first took place during a diplomatic visit by Aphrodite to the island's capital Ajaccio, when the goddess of love came under fire from an RCDC member with an antiquated Kalashnikov. The sniper's accuracy was hampered by three things: the age of his rifle, the half bottle of cognac he had downed beforehand in order to steady his nerves, and the fact that, in his crosshairs, Aphrodite looked so lusciously, delectably beautiful that it seemed to him almost a crime to damage such magnificent female physical perfection in any way. All these factors conspired to make him miss her by a mile and instead wing his country's president and gravely wound the regional *préfet*, both of whom were sharing a podium with the Olympian as they bestowed on her the freedom of the island and a civic medal or some such meaningless official trinket.

Immediately, Aphrodite spoke over the PA system, calling for calm and asking the would-be assassin to step forward and show himself. This the man did, because there were few who could resist the call of Aphrodite's voice or the love that she exuded. He left his rooftop vantage point and walked through the crowd of startled onlookers to the podium, where he knelt submissively before the Olympian, telling her over and over how much he loved her and how sorry he was for trying to kill her. Aphrodite then invited the people from the crowd to come up and hit him. One by one they complied, gladly, with beatific smiles and any hard objects that came to hand. It took them half an hour to beat the man to death, and he relished every minute of his slow capital punishment with a smile no less beatific.

On the other occasion, Apollo dropped by with a view to hunting the indigenous Corsican red deer, an endangered species which he took closer to the brink of extinction by shooting great numbers of them in the Parc Naturel Régional with his bow and arrows. The RCDC, discovering a streak of conservationist concern within themselves that they'd never known they had, waxed indignant. To protect the poor deer they laced the nature reserve with tripwires attached to grenades which were in turn attached to tree trunks. Apollo, however, was too sharp-sighted to fail to spot the tripwires, and decided to make a sport of splitting them from a range of 100 metres or more and detonating the grenades. A couple of the red deer also sprang the traps, inadvertently, which somewhat undercut the whole purpose of laying them in the first place. So much for the RCDC's new-found green credentials. So much, too, for a number of RCDC members. Apollo elected to remain a little longer in Corsica and to hunt much more interesting game. His tally, by the end of his stay, stood at 52 deer, 9 men, 2 women, and one child. Of the twelve humans he bagged, seven definitely belonged to the RCDC, three were suspected of belonging, one had strong ties to the resistance, and one, the child, was simply an innocent bystander who happened to stray into the path of an arrow. Apollo claimed he deeply regretted the death of the last, although he added, with some pride at his own prowess, that his shaft passed clean through the little girl's head, from ear to ear, and continued onward to kill its intended target. A shot in a million, and a quick, instant death that had barely left a mark on the kid. To look at her, lying on the ground, you'd have thought she had just fallen asleep.

There were demonstrations, of course. Protest marches on the streets of Ajaccio, Bastia, Corte and other major towns. The girl, Ghjuvanna Venturini, became a martyr, her death leading countless hitherto unaligned Corsicans to rally to the RCDC's cause.

The Olympians' solution was the typical one: send in a monster. The Minotaur was relieved of its duties in Crete, where it had been busy stamping down on unrest in the aftermath of the tidal wave – the wave which took the lives of Deborah and Megan Chisholm among many others. The Cretans' anger had more or less run its course, so Hermes took the man-bull from its spiritual homeland and transported it northwest across the Mediterranean to the birthplace of Napoleon Bonaparte where, for almost a year now, it had been carrying out a similar function as it had on Crete. The mountains that occupied most of Corsica's interior were where the RCDC could be found. Heavily forested on their lower slopes, dotted with nigh-on inaccessible villages, riddled with clefts and caves and secret valleys, the mountains were a great place to hide. Through them wound a labyrinth of goat paths and narrow rocky defiles, the solution of which, if it had one, was known only to the locals.

The Minotaur, however, if legend was to be believed, had form when it came to things labyrinthine. No maze fazed it. It stomped along the mountain passes, trekking from village to village, and anyone who challenged it, anyone who got in its way, anyone who so much as looked at it funny, it attacked. No warning, no hesitation, the Minotaur just put its head down and charged. Few could outrun it. Fewer still could survive being tossed or gored by its horns.

Once or twice an RCDC member might manage to get off a lucky shot at the beast before, inevitably, becoming its next victim. Bullets, however, barely pierced the man-bull's thick black hide, and the sting of their impact was an irritant rather than a deterrent. A surefire way to get the Minotaur angry at you was to take a potshot at it.

Landesman told the Titans that this should be borne in mind when it came to killing the monster.

"Nothing short of a rocket or a coilgun is going to put the thing down," he said. "Lesser weapons will simply annoy it and draw its attention. You'd be waving a – No, I shan't say it. Too trite."

"A red rag to a bull?" said Barrington.

"I was so trying to avoid the simile."

"You want the obvious said, Landy old mate, you can always rely on me."

"I know, Dez. I know."

That was during the pre-op briefing. Now, two days later, five Titans were in the field – Tethys, Mnemosyne, Hyperion, Iapetus, Crius – and they had just spent a hot, dusty, and ultimately fruitless nine hours combing the area where the Minotaur had most recently been sighted. They'd found tracks that could only be Minotaur tracks, the imprints of bare human feet far larger than any normal human feet, but the monster itself had proved scarce.

Base camp was a half-dozen tents clustered around a van. Divested of their suits, the Titans gathered wood for a fire, and for their supper Tsang barbecued chicken breasts coated in a marinade that he had prepared specially for this cookout, a sticky, sinfully sweet concoction akin to toffee.

"An old family recipe," he said. "The trick is to boil the soy sauce down to the consistency of tar, then add the chilli, ginger and the other spices and ladle honey on like there's no tomorrow."

"Eat enough of it and there *will* be no tomorrow," said Mahmoud through a mouthful. "I can feel my arteries furring up."

"You won't be having second helpings then?"

She held out her plate. "I never said that, duck."

Soon everyone had retired to their tents, the two techs included. Only Sam and Ramsay remained up.

"Not sleepy?" he asked her.

"Tired but wired," she replied. She stared into the dark, insect-throbbing landscape around them. The scent of heather was strong on the breeze. "The Minotaur's out there somewhere. Not far. And I don't have my suit on, and, to be blunt, I feel naked without it."

"And here's where I don't make some wisecrack about you being naked."

"Absolutely you don't."

"'Cause it wouldn't be right because you hate me. Again."

"No, it wouldn't be right because it would be inappropriate. If you said that kind of thing in any normal workplace, they'd have you up before a disciplinary tribunal and off on a sexual harassment awareness course before you even knew what hit you."

"So you *don't* hate me," said Ramsay. "Is that what I can take away from this?"

"Rick, frankly I'm not sure how I feel about you," Sam said. "Let's turn it around. How do you feel about you right now?"

"Honestly?"

She twitched her shoulders – *what else?*

Ramsay gazed into the fire for a time. "Honestly, what I feel is... empty. I feel I've done it now, I've killed the thing that killed my son, but all that's left me with is this sense of: is that it? Now what? I was expecting to have this great swelling in my chest of triumph, satisfaction, completion..."

"Closure?"

"Oh yeah."

"You Americans are big on your closure."

"We are. And it ain't there, or maybe it is but it doesn't feel like I was hoping. It doesn't feel solid. There's no 'Oh, OK, so that's that chapter done with, let's turn the page and start the next.' Ethan's still dead. Ain't nothing going to change that. Ain't nothing going to bring my little boy back. The Lamia being dead as well kinda balances up the scales but somehow not all the way, not even near. I'm glad it's dead, but mainly I'm glad because that's a whole bunch of other kids who won't be sucked dry by it now, a whole bunch of other parents who won't have the light taken out of their world like I did. So that's something. But it's not everything."

"Ethan's mother. I don't even know her name."

"LaVonne."

"Is she around any more?"

"Why d'you ask?"

"You just never mention her, that's all."

Ramsay shook his head a fraction, just enough to convey regret, regret of the mildest kind. "We'd already split up by the time Ethan was two. LaVonne didn't make a good military wife. Didn't like it when I was off on tours of duty. Didn't like being on her own and me being away for long periods and in danger. Wasn't what she'd married me for, she said. That stopped after the Olympians came. President Mayhew, as it then was, called the troops back home once she realised the Olympians weren't going to let us keep on with our police actions in the 'Istans. Most sensible thing that woman did. Lost her any chance of re-election, of course. She said she was a realist, the other party called her a coward and un-American, although the guy who got in and replaced her hasn't been any more proactive or 'American' than she was, has he? Stavropoulos has even hinted he thinks the Olympians might be actual gods, which gives you some idea where he's coming from. Plays up his Greek ethnicity like anything, that man. Says belief in the Pantheon is in his blood.

"Anyways, Mizz Mayhew got me home permanently, is my point, and then I got laid off in the personnel cuts that followed. Half pension, not enough to live on, so I found myself a job as mall security, would you believe, and I thought that'd make LaVonne happy, me in a safe job, clocking on and off like a regular Joe commuter, only it was too late for us by then, unfortunately. There hadn't been enough of a marriage to start with, and it turned out that Vonnie didn't like living with me there every day any more than she'd liked me being off in some desert hellhole for months at a stretch. We were bickering like crazy, and then Ethan came along and I thought he'd be the saving of us. But all he was, poor kid, was the final straw – a baby on top of all the other frustrations in LaVonne's life. So she bailed. Just packed a bag one day and went. I got sole custody, and Vonnie became visitation-rights mom, only she hardly ever exercised those rights.

"We didn't see or speak to each other much, and then after Ethan was gone, we didn't have a reason to see or speak to each other at all any more. She moved back to be with her folks in Gary, Indiana, where, far as I know, she still is. Short question, long answer. How about you, while we're on this subject? No other half? No, of course not. Would you be here if there was? But were you ever married?"

"No. I was... not quite engaged. My partner and I lived together. We'd talked about marrying. We were definitely going to. It just didn't have a chance to happen."

Ramsay waited. Sam didn't offer anything further.

"That's all I'm going to get, isn't it?" he said drily. "All anyone's going to get out of you, Sam. You know something? This enigmatic schtick, this whole keeping-it-all-to-yourself thing – I tell you, it's getting real old. What you don't appear to realise is that, whatever you're holding inside you, not talking about it doesn't make you heroic, it just makes you seem..."

"Seem...?"

"Like not a normal person. Normal people talk about stuff. Normal people open up."

"Just because I don't yammer on all the time about –"

"No." Ramsay stopped her with a jabbing index finger. "It ain't yammering. It's being human. It's accepting that bad things have happened, not trying to act as if they never did. It's being the same as everyone else, not imagining you've somehow had it worse than everyone else and that that somehow makes you superior in some way, privileged 'cause life took a bigger shit on you than it does on most folk and it's beyond your ability to express how much you've been hurt. Hell, we all get shit on, and us Titans got shit on particularly heavily, but I don't believe your pain is worse than the pain I've suffered or Fred has suffered or Dez has suffered or any of us has suffered, and I dare you to prove otherwise."

"You're trying to piss me off, aren't you?"

"Figure I've got nothing to lose."

"Goad me and I'll lose my temper and drop my guard and blurt everything out?"

"That's the general idea."

"And then what? I'll feel better? I went to a counsellor twice a week for nearly a year, Rick. I talked and talked with him. And after a hundred hours of that I didn't feel one ounce better. What makes you think it'll be any different, talking to you?"

"Because, Sam Akehurst," Ramsay said, chidingly, "I'm your friend."

"Oh, right. And maybe you're hoping I'll confess all and then fall sobbing into your arms and you can comfort me and next thing you know, hey presto, we're shagging like rabbits."

"Yeah, that's always been my technique with women. I only sleep with the crying ones. Distraught's such a goddamn turn-on. Those puffy eyes, that runny nose..."

"Ha!" said Sam. It was both a laugh and a victory cry. "Watch this, then. No tears. Dry-eyed, Sam Akehurst delves deep and comes up with the goods. This is what happened. You want to know? I'll give it to you in two sentences. My boyfriend was killed at Hyde Park, July 25th, coming up for three years ago now. I was pregnant with his baby and I miscarried. There." She looked at him, hard. "What do you think? How does that rate on the 'life shit' scale? I'm thinking it's a good nine, maybe even a ten. You would probably downgrade it, though. Not as bad as Fred, who lost everybody he knew. Not as bad as Nigel, who was actually married and whose daughter was, you know, a child and not just a foetus, which gets him extra points. But better at least than Kerstin – husband but no child. And way better than Anders, because it wasn't even relatives of his who died, just comrades, fellow soldiers."

Her voice was a low growl. She could hear the throb of resentment in it, resentment that was simply pain that had taken a wrong turn.

"You just don't get it, do you, Rick? You can't compare tragedies like they're scores on Top Trumps cards. Everyone feels grief in their own way. What I lost was... was everything. Everything. Ade getting killed, the baby – it destroyed me. It was apocalypse. Does it matter to me how well or badly I got off next to other people? No. All I care about is me, what happened to me and how huge it was, how unbearable."

"Ade. His name was Ade," Ramsay said gently.

"Adrian Walters." Sam couldn't recall the last time she'd spoken his name aloud and in full like that. It felt strange, like trying on a pair of old boots from the back of the cupboard that were once comfy and snug but had stiffened with disuse. "Constable Adrian Walters."

"Cop, like you."

She nodded. Damn him, how was he managing to get this stuff out of her? More to the point – why was she letting him?

"Uniform," she said. "Beat copper. The best kind of beat copper. He enjoyed it. He actually enjoyed getting out there, being on the street, being visible, high-profile, wearing the tit-shaped helmet, trying to make a difference in the community he served."

"Nice guy."

"Through and through. Too nice, I sometimes thought. We girls aren't supposed to fall for the good boys. We're supposed to like a bit of grit in our oyster. That's how you get a pearl, after all. But after the crap and slog of work I liked coming home to a stable, dependable, reliable man. Ade wasn't dynamic in any way. He was my antidote to the poison of the world, and not only that but he could understand what I went through on a day-to-day basis, because he went through something similar, so we were on a par in that respect. Only, he always dealt with it better because he was just... better. A better person than me. Sometimes I'd have it up to here with all the sleaze and the wrongness that I had to deal with, and I'd start bitching and whining, and he'd talk me down, all quiet and calm. And – and he always brought me tea in bed in the mornings. Every morning, without fail. Even if our shifts were different and I had to get up at sparrow-fart and he didn't, he always made sure he was awake and could bring me my cup of Earl Grey, milk, one sugar. Such a small thing, but it meant so much."

"Was he looking forward to being a dad? Sounds like he'd have made a good father."

"He never knew. I didn't get the chance to tell him. I planned to. In fact, the day he – the day he was killed, I was going to tell him that evening. I was only a couple of months into the pregnancy. I was sure I was pregnant, I just hadn't been sure enough yet. But that evening, I had it all worked out. I was going to make Ade dinner. He usually made the dinner, so he'd have realised something was up when he came home to me burning saucepans."

"You can't cook."

"I can cook like elephants can tap-dance," Sam said. "But it's the thought that counts. I was going to put something charred and inedible in front of him, uncap a bottle of his favourite lager, and then, when he was good and intrigued, I was going to break the news."

"How do you think he would have reacted?"

"Ade? Over the moon. He'd have grabbed me, squeezed me tight, then let go because he was scared that squeezing me tight might harm the baby somehow. He always wanted kids. He was dying to be a dad. Dying." She laughed hollowly. "I know that that's how it would have gone. I've played the scene out so many times in my head. I can see him running round and round the kitchen, whooping like a loon, then getting on the phone to his parents in New Zealand – they'd emigrated. Never mind that it'd be about five in the morning there. He wouldn't be able to wait to ring them. But instead, I was the one who had to ring them and wake them up. With something very different to say. That was after a friend had called and asked if I'd heard."

"Heard...?"

"About the protest. About Apollo and Artemis. About the stampede they'd caused. I was aware Ade was helping police the march, but I couldn't imagine anything bad was going to happen, certainly not to him. As a rule, the Olympians don't go for cops, do they? We're all on the same side, allegedly. We all belong to the forces of law and order. So I assumed even if the Olympians decided the protest shouldn't be allowed to continue, Ade would be OK. All the police there would be. But what I hadn't factored in was Ade being Ade. One of his fellow PSU officers, the friend, guy called Trev, he phoned me from the scene. There was chaos, I could hear it in the background. Shouting. Screaming. Ambulance sirens. And Trev told me Ade was dead. Just like that. Came right out and said it, his voice quivering: 'Ade's dead.' I said I didn't believe it, and Trev said he didn't believe it either but it was true. He'd watched it with his own eyes, he'd held the body, attempted mouth-to-mouth, for all the good it had done. The rally'd been completely peaceful, he said, up to the moment the

Olympians appeared. He and Ade and a couple of hundred others were waiting in vans along Exhibition Road, togged up in their Code Two gear, shields but no sticks, just in case trouble started. Hermes teleported the twins into the park, everything went to hell, the Code One regulars radioed for assistance, and the boys rushed out there to help sort out the mess. That was Ade's thing, why he sidelined with the Police Support Unit, because he believed wholeheartedly in the public's right to peaceful protest and he saw the job of the PSU as helping to facilitate that and keep the protestors safe."

"Didn't work out so well for himself, though."

"There was a kid. This girl, twelve, thirteen, something like that. She was in the Serpentine River in the middle of Hyde Park. It's called a river but it's actually a lake. Lots of people were in the water, desperate to get away, trying to swim to the other side. Apollo and Artemis were just laying into the crowd indiscriminately, Apollo shooting his arrows, Artemis lashing out with her spear. I saw a video of it on TV some time later, and they were wolves among sheep, foxes in the henhouse. Slaughtering. Just... slaughtering. But anyway, the girl, she'd waded into the Serpentine, waist-deep, and she got knocked over by someone shoving past her. She tried to get up but other people kept jumping in, trampling her, pushing her under the surface. Soon as Ade saw, he went to help. Didn't think twice, according to Trev. Battled through the crowd to the bank, dived in, got to the girl, pulled her up from the water, shielded her from the stampede with his own body, started trying to help her back to dry land.

"But he was so concerned about her, he wasn't looking out for himself. Got knocked over by someone, and then people were trampling *him*, pushing *him* under. Blind panic. They didn't even see him there. All they wanted to do was get out of the Olympians' way. Ade thrashed around. Never a strong swimmer at the best of times, and his Code Two kit didn't help. Cotton overalls impregnated with flame retardant, leg guards, thigh guards, arm guards, Alt-Berg Peacekeeper boots – all waterlogged and heavy, weighing him down. He tried again and again to get up, get air, and couldn't... and then he couldn't even try. They drowned him. People. The same civilians he'd dedicated his life to looking after and protecting. Drowned him. The girl, far as I know, managed to get away. She was OK. She lived. So that's something, I suppose. It wasn't a completely pointless death."

"You felt numb then, didn't you?" said Ramsay. "That's how I felt when I got the call from Ethan's principal. 'Mr Ramsay? Steadman Block here. I have something to tell you.' First I was like, 'Oh no, what's Ethan done? Flunked a math test?' But Block asked me if I was sitting down, and that's when I knew something bad was coming. And as I listened to what he had to say, I could feel a part of me shutting down. I could feel myself just sort of locking into autopilot. A robot took over and started doing everything for me, acting like me, saying everything I needed to, and I was happy to let it. Kinda like being in the battlesuit. Safe, shielded. I was inside me, far away, deep in this shell that looked and sounded exactly like I did, could pass for me but wasn't, not really. I stayed there for quite a few weeks."

"Yeah, that was it. Me too. Only it was longer than a few weeks. A lot longer. Sometimes, in fact..."

"Sometimes you feel like you haven't altogether come out of it."

Sam picked up a branch and tossed it on the fire. Sparks danced up from the crackling flames, twinkling then gone like fairies when people stopped believing in them.

"Or ever will," she said. "The miscarriage came the next day. I was in hospital, rather conveniently. In the morgue, ID-ing Ade's body. Suddenly there was this... Well, I'll spare you the gory details."

"I thank you for that."

"Gory is the word, though. The strange thing was, I wasn't surprised. It just seemed natural. I remember thinking, *Yes, of course. Ade isn't here any more. Why would his child want to stick around either?* And then later, much later, I came to the conclusion that it was my fault. I'd been dreading motherhood, I can't deny it. I could see how it was going to mess with my career. Terribly. I'd had this whole path mapped out for myself – DI by thirty, Chief Constable by forty – maybe an unrealisable dream, but I was well on my way there, and having a baby was going to derail the Sam Akehurst ambition express, perhaps for good, so afterwards I had myself believing that I'd somehow willed the foetus to abort itself."

"Whereas in fact it was down to shock and stress, you know that."

"Cognitively I know that. No one can make themselves miscarry just by wishing for it. But you start falling prey to all sorts of strange ideas when you're traumatised, when your whole world has been shaken to pieces. I'd been in that state before, after my parents died, only not as bad. That was the past being taken away from me, which is sort of what's supposed to happen. This was the future being taken away, which isn't. My mind wasn't right. It kept insisting I'd jettisoned the baby on purpose, so I could be free to carry on clambering up the career ladder. The irony is, by that stage I didn't have much of a career left. I was on disability leave, on account of I was a basket case, half an inch away from a total nervous breakdown, or maybe half an inch into one, and it really didn't look as if I'd be coming back from it to any kind of meaningful employment. Even if I did eventually rejoin the Met, I knew they'd have had me on permanent desk duty somewhere in Traffic or Fraud for the rest of my time. I'd be no good to my guv'nor, my DI, any more. Prothero said he'd have me back soon as I was ready, but I knew he was only saying that to make me feel better, and he knew I knew. The whole detective thing was over for me. Dead and buried. So that was why it didn't seem to matter if one day *I* was over as well. Dead and buried as well. And that was when I started thinking about killing myself."

"Ah." Ramsay's mouth downturned at the corners. "Well now. You can stop there if you like. You don't have to go on."

"No, you asked for it, you wanted it, you're getting the lot, all of it. I drove down to Beachy Head a couple of times. That's a cliff on the south coast of England. It's a beauty spot and also where dozens of people a year throw themselves off. Don't ask me if the two things are connected. I stood there looking out to sea, but I couldn't quite do it, couldn't quite step over the little barrier and then take the next step, right off the edge. So that was a washout, but I had pills at home. Sleeping tablets. I was needing them at the time, and one night I laid out ten of them in a row on my bedside table instead of the usual one, and I placed them all in the palm of my hand, and I even got as far as tipping them into my mouth. But I spat them out. I didn't fancy just falling asleep and not waking up. I wanted to feel my death. I wanted to experience it. So then, the final time, there was a hot bath and the blade from Ade's razor. Ade liked a proper blade. Not one of those clip-in multi-head ones with bits of wire across them for extra safety – a proper old-fashioned thin bendy metal blade with two cutting edges. I lay in the bath and I held the blade at the crook of my elbow. You have to slice down along the inside of the forearm, open up as much of the length of the ulnar artery as you can. I'd seen the body of a young woman who'd topped herself like that, done it the way it should be done. She was anorexic, a heroin addict, in an abusive relationship, and she'd 'ridden the Gillette train out of the station,' as Prothero said. I couldn't understand at the time why she'd done it. Her life was shit, yes, but I thought she'd just been a coward. Why didn't she ditch the bastard of a boyfriend, get into a rehab program and just try and sort herself out? Make an effort, the stupid, self-pitying cow. But I got it later. When I was on the brink of killing myself in the exact same way, I understood. It was the only form of control she had left over her life, the only decision she could still make that would have any effect. Everything else had got the better of her. This was the one way she could still score a victory. Self-pity didn't come into it. It was all about recovering some small shred of dignity while she still could."

"Slashing your wrists in a bath ain't dignified."

"But when you're in that particular mindset, it is. And there's also an element of 'There. See? See how truly miserable I am?' You're leaving your body as a message to the world: life hurts, it hurts too much to bear, this is the only sane solution."

"But actually the sane solution isn't to end it all, it's to go on living," said Ramsay. "Stand up and say 'fuck you' to the pain and bludgeon on."

"I realised that. At the very last moment. Look." She rolled up her sleeve and showed him the inside of her left elbow. "You can just see it. There. Tiny little scar. That's how far I got with the razor blade. Less than a centimetre. It stung like fuck, and I just couldn't continue. That pain was sharper, more real, than the other kind of pain, and it brought me to my senses.

The way out, I realised, was worse than the situation. The cure was worse than the disease. It seems trite, looking back, but it honestly was a revelation. I was clearly not suffering as badly as I thought I'd been, if I could be deterred by a little bit of 'ouch' and a trickle of blood. That put things into perspective. I didn't climb out of that bath any happier than when I'd got in, but I did climb out knowing I'd troughed, I'd found rock bottom, and the only way from there was up."

"Wanna know something?" Ramsay said. "Something I've never, ever told anyone else?"

"OK."

"I tried it too. Suicide. Just me, the bathroom mirror, and my Marine-issue pistol. After Ethan, every morning for about a month I'd stand at the sink and look at myself and put the barrel of a MEU(SOC) .45 in my mouth and almost nearly pull the trigger. Morning after morning. After a while, the taste of gunmetal and grease got so familiar, I couldn't get rid of it. There on my tongue the whole time. Everything I ate or drank seemed to have the tang of it. In the end, it started to make me feel sick. That was why I stopped wanting to blow my brains out, after a month of repeatedly trying to summon up the guts to and failing: I hated eating a breakfast that tasted of sidearm. It was a small thing, a stupid reason for going on living, but sometimes a stupid reason is enough, especially when the alternative is nothing. At least it's a *reason*."

"You chose to live because you like your food, is that what you're telling me?"

"I like my meals to taste like a meal should, hell yeah."

Sam couldn't keep a straight face, and didn't think she was meant to. "That is so a Rick Ramsay thing to do, go off the idea of suicide for your stomach's sake."

"Hey, never underestimate the power of the stomach. Or the tastebuds."

Their laughter dwindled into silence. The fire embered, the cicadas shook their maracas.

"See?" Ramsay said. "You've talked, and it hasn't made your head fall off or anything."

"And you haven't hit on me, either."

"So the worst didn't happen."

"Halleluiah."

Some time later, she stood up. "I'm going to turn in."

"I'm going to stay here a little longer. It's a nice night. The stars are pretty."

She touched his shoulder. "Thanks, Rick."

"All part of the service, ma'am."

She knew then that, at some point, she was going to sleep with this man.

But not tonight. That would be like giving the dog a treat as a reward for having nipped her finger.

33. HAUT-PIETRA

ANOTHER DAY WAS spent looking, in vain, for the Minotaur. The monster was proving more elusive than any they'd hunted so far.

A third day passed, with a similar lack of results, and at the end of it, as the Titans were trudging back to camp, Hyperion said, "Base, we're wasting time here. Time and power cells. The forests round here are as dense as Daffy Duck, and the damn monster seems to know how to make itself scarce if it wants to. Is there any way you guys can help?"

"How do you mean?" said Landesman.

"You've got computer geeks there. Couldn't you get them to, I don't know, take over a spy satellite and try and pinpoint the Minotaur from space by its heat signature or some such?"

"Speaking as one of those computer geeks," said Patanjali, "I have mad skills, but I'm still not that good. No way could I infiltrate anybody's defence surveillance system without Argus noticing and tracing the hack back to here."

"Sorry, Hyperion," said Landesman, "but you're just going to have to keep doing it the hard way."

"All right then, how about this? In the Gulf, when our side needed to track down a bunch of insurgents, often as not we'd draft in some local help. Nobody knows the lay of the land better than the folks who live there. And there's guys here who'd be willing, I reckon, to work with us."

"You're suggesting we contact the Resistenza?"

"Contact 'em, draft 'em in. That way we could double, maybe even triple the number of pairs of eyes we've got on the ground. And it's not as if we're needing to keep ourselves so much of a secret now, not since Bruges."

"I'm with Hyperion," said Crius. "I can't see the harm in bringing the RCDC in on this."

"If you want my opinion, not that anyone does," said Iapetus, "it's got to beat fossicking through this fucking bush all day long."

"Tethys?" said Landesman.

"I've got nothing against the idea, in principle," Sam said. "We just have to be careful. We give our presence away to the wrong person, a Pantheonic sympathiser, say, or just someone with a computer who thinks it'd be cool to tell the world that those monster hunters from Bruges are here, and we're screwed. The Olympians'll come down on this island like a ton of bricks, with us right underneath. And while I'm not scared of facing them, I want it to be on our terms, when we're the ones with the element of surprise, not them."

"Let me think about it," said Landesman. "I'll get back to you with an answer as soon as I can."

An hour later, he did.

"Right, I've done some homework. There's a town roughly twenty miles from your current position. Haut-Pietra. It's reputed to be a hotbed of RCDC activity. Go there in civvies and see if you can't rustle up interest among the indigenes. But, as Tethys said, be sure you choose people you think can be trusted."

Haut-Pietra perched on a hilltop. Its focus, and highest point, was a church, with a hundred or so houses shelving away around it on all sides, many looking as though they were clinging onto the steep slopes for dear life. Vineyards and groves of fig and mulberry lined the one and only approach road. So did a parade of telegraph poles, to each of which someone had tacked a photocopied sheet of A4 showing the face of the little girl killed by Apollo, Ghjuvanna Venturini, with the slogan "*Giammai dimenticà!*" – "Never forget!."

The town square, in the lee of the church, was dusty and shaded by a couple of plane trees. A game of pétanque was under way in the middle of it, while outside two cafés, at opposite corners of the square, townspeople sat at tin tables and imbibed aperitifs along with the cooling evening air.

Sam and Ramsay had come alone. There was no point in all the Titans turning up mob-handed. Two of them could nose out the RCDC as effectively as five, without arousing as much curiosity.

They drew stares nonetheless.

"It's you," Ramsay told Sam as they took a seat at one of the cafés, the Bar Galetti. "Everyone's dark and Italian-looking. They can't have seen many pale redheads before."

"Oh yeah? And how many black men do you think drop by every day?"

"Well, if it is me they're so fascinated by, it's only because they ain't ever laid eyes on a brother this handsome. Or else they're mistaking me for Denzel Washington. I often get taken for Denzel, and him for me."

For all the interest the other patrons of the café were showing in them, it took a while to attract the waiter's attention. He spoke to them in Corsu, confident they wouldn't have a clue what he was saying. Sam responded in her best GCSE French, and the waiter, evidently a proud nationalist, pretended this was a language unknown to him. In the end, however, he took pity and grudgingly acknowledged her order of "*un vin maison et une bière*" with a curt "*d'accord.*"

When he returned with the drinks, Sam tipped him generously. Then, as there was nothing to be lost by taking the direct approach, she asked him if he knew of anyone in the Resistenza Contru-Diu Corsu.

Silence fell over the café, a hush so complete that the metallic click of the pétanque balls out in the square sounded like planets colliding.

"Uh oh, tumbleweed moment," Ramsay murmured.

The waiter shrugged, circling a finger at his ear as if he'd misheard or else had not recognised those particular words with his oh-so-severely limited French.

Sam shrugged too, as if it was of no consequence; her enquiry had been a casual one, nothing more.

Conversation slowly resumed in the café like a flock of birds settling after a gunshot. Moments later it scattered to the winds again as a round-bodied, bullet-headed little man emerged from the café interior. He made straight for Sam and Ramsay, moving unhurriedly but with a dead-eyed purposefulness. Sam could sense Ramsay tensing up beside her, ready to meet violence with reciprocal or, if need be, greater force.

"Wait," she hissed out of the side of her mouth. "I think we've flushed out our RCDC member already."

The man halted at their table and said, in guttural English, "Please finish your drinks and leave."

"Of course," Sam said. "But first, we'd like to talk to you. In private."

"Drink," said the man, "then go."

"I believe you are an important person here. You have an enemy on this island. I believe you, or people you know, would like to remove that enemy. We do too." She felt safe saying this. She doubted any of the Corsicans within earshot knew English as well as this man did, if at all. The exchange, in that sense, was already a private one.

The man's eyes were coal. "Enemy? Corsicans have no enemies. We have been invaded by Greeks, Romans, *Genovese*, French. They are all gone. Only Corsicans are here now."

"Bull." Sam was unable to resist the pun. "We have experience in dealing with the kind of enemy I'm referring to. We want to make you an offer. We want to join forces with you. Do you understand what I'm saying? Do you know who we are?"

The man gave a slow nod, and something occurred briefly with his lips, a twitch that could have been a smile had the stony seriousness of his face allowed it. He appraised Sam and Ramsay for a moment or two longer, then beckoned them with a flick of his fingers. "Come this way."

In a back room that was part office and part stock-room, he introduced himself as Paulu Galetti, the café's owner, and confirmed that he did belong to the RCDC. He was, in fact, commandant of the Haut-Pietra arm of the Resistenza and a member of the movement's supreme body, its five-man ruling committee.

"And you," he said, "you are the ones in Brussels, and in Singapore, and in Syria." It wasn't a huge room, but Galetti had a presence that seemed to fill it – though perhaps that was just his abysmal underarm odour.

"We get around," said Ramsay.

"You are brave. To kill the monsters. To make the Olympians angry. Very brave. Crazy also. The Olympians will tear you to confetti if they get their hands on you."

"Don't we know it."

"They might try," Sam said. "And they might just be in for a surprise. But let's not worry about that now. Our aim, for now, is to deal with the

Minotaur, Mr Galetti. We have the means. We have the weapons. What we don't have is the manpower. Put simply, we've been looking and we can't find the monster. And we were thinking the Resistenza might be able to help out with that."

"Might be keen to, too," Ramsay added.

Galetti canted his head to one side. "Hmm. Interesting. I am tempted. The Minotaur has been a curse on Corsica for so long. But if we help you, and you kill it, what then? Maybe the Olympians get angry with *us*. Maybe they do to Corsica the same as to San Francisco and Paris, but worse. When they finish with us, there could be no Corsica left."

"Would they, though?" Sam said. "After all, when I last looked, Bruges was still standing. It hasn't been attacked. Neither has Singapore or any of those other places we hit."

"True," said Galetti. "But who is to say they won't change their tactics, if they decide to set an example again?"

"It's a possibility, I agree. But Mr Galetti, your Resistenza hasn't been afraid to shoot at the Minotaur. I don't think you are afraid of the Olympians either. You said it yourself. Corsica has been conquered time after time, but still remains the home of Corsicans."

"You appeal to my patriotism."

"Of course."

"And to my male pride. If I refuse to help you, it will look as if I'm a coward. You seem wise to the nature of the Corsican man."

Or just men, Sam thought.

Galetti grinned. A sudden softening of those impenetrably hard features of his, as startling and remarkable as a thaw in permafrost. An upper premolar was missing, but that didn't lessen the effect.

"The offer is appealing," he said, leaning towards Sam in a way which implied that part of its appeal lay with her. "The RCDC will be only too glad to join you. You have my assurance of twenty men, perhaps more."

"Twenty would be plenty."

"It will be a pleasure working with you, Miss...?"

"Tethys. It's best if you know me only as Tethys. And this is Hyperion."

Galetti took the callsigns in his stride. "Miss Tethys, Mr Hyperion, together we are going to do a great thing."

Seemingly from nowhere he rustled up a bottle of myrtle liquor and three shot glasses.

"A drink to celebrate? Seal the deal?"

The liquor was both sickeningly sweet and chokingly raw, fiery enough to seal a weld, not just a deal. Potent too. Even though Sam and Ramsay both stopped after three glasses, they left the Bar Galetti extremely drunk.

Drunk enough to find themselves sharing a tent later.

And a sleeping bag.

And each other.

But not so drunk that they regretted it afterwards.

34. LAKESIDE ENCOUNTER

Sam uncoupled her helmet from her gorget and took it off. Then she knelt down by the lake's edge and splashed a handful of water onto her face. The water was alpine-cold, icily invigorating. She scooped up some more to dampen her head with. Suit microclimate notwithstanding, it got hot inside the helmet and her scalp itched with sweat. Having long hair didn't help. The other female Titans had taken to cutting theirs short – Hamel's was so close-cropped now it was more pelt than hair – but Sam had always liked the feel of her own locks brushing her shoulders. Always liked how long hair looked on her, too. Vain, but there you go. Ade had dubbed her his "Pre-Raphaelite angel" and she wasn't sure he'd known precisely what he was talking about – she herself thought that, being auburn, she was more a "Titian" than anything – but he'd meant it as the highest of compliments and he would usually say it while stroking her head lovingly, in a voice husky with postcoital contentment, and the aftermath of a bout of vigorous sex was not the moment to start challenging a man on his grasp of art history terminology.

The lake was near the top of the tree line, a slender finger of water whose surface mirrored the oaks and pines around it and the snowy peaks above. On the advice of the Resistenza, the Titans were venturing up into the mountains in their search for the Minotaur. Galetti had said the monster often retreated to the higher altitudes between attacks. Why? How should he know? To get away from people, was his guess. People seemed to plague it as much as it plagued them. Maybe even monsters needed to be on their own from time to time.

The op, in its present incarnation, was pure reconnaissance. The Titans and twenty-plus RCDC members were combing the area singly, spaced out at one-kilometre intervals in order to cover as much ground as possible. Once the Minotaur was located, all forces would reconvene and an attempt would be made to herd the beast downhill. So far the Corsicans had been diligent collaborators and Sam had had little reason to worry about them. They were a taciturn lot, surly their default setting, all of them fond of a cigarette and a good throaty expectoration and all of them sporting a motley selection of bad heavy metal band T-shirts and even worse moustaches. But their hatred of the Minotaur was palpable, as was their enthralment with the Titans and their battlesuits. Furthermore, Galetti appeared to have them fully under his control and would keep them honest, and his obvious infatuation with Sam herself would, she thought, keep *him* honest.

She drenched her head a final time, then settled back against a rock, lifted her face to the sun, and closed her eyes. Just a few moments' rest. She deserved it. Needed it, too. Last night had been her and Ramsay's second night together. Sober this time, they had been less rushed, nowhere near as frantic as before. They had taken longer, savouring the intimacy, and it had been good. Very good. And afterwards Sam had returned to her tent, because they were agreed that no one should know, they were going to be professional about this; and she'd lain in the chilly cocoon of her own sleeping bag, awake into the small hours, wondering why she felt so guilty. Was it because she felt she was betraying Ade? But how could you betray a lover who'd been dead nearly three years? He was a memory, that was all, and you couldn't cheat on a memory. Unless the memory was as vivid as hers was of Ade. Then perhaps you could.

The solution had come to her at three in the morning, just as she was lapsing into an uneasy sleep.

You have to start forgetting about him.

With the sun making dazzle-patterns behind her eyelids and her skin warming as the water evaporated, she pondered this. Forgetting about Ade – it seemed like another kind of betrayal. Realistically, though, how long could she keep on mourning him and missing him? Hadn't she done so enough?

Besides, Ramsay was no Ade. He was about as far from Ade as you could get. Where Ade had been thoughtful and consistently self-effacing, Ramsay was impulsive and at times insufferably smug. So it wasn't as if she could be said to be replacing Ade with another version of him, upgrading to Ade 2.0, as it were. Perhaps that was Ramsay's great attraction to her, that he wasn't a substitute or a surrogate, he was something else. Perhaps she liked him, and had chosen to sleep with him, because he was far outside her zone of –

A sound.

A heavy footfall.

And then... a snort of breath?

Sam's eyes snapped open.

Across the lake, some 20 metres further along its opposite bank, the Minotaur stepped out from the forest.

Sam found that all at once she couldn't inhale. Her heart seemed to be obstructing her windpipe.

The Minotaur didn't look in her direction. It didn't appear to realise she was there... yet. It halted beside the lake, then squatted on its massive haunches, reached down with cupped hands, lifted water to its bovine maw and lapped with a long, slurping, bright pink tongue.

The breeze changed direction slightly, and Sam, downwind, caught a whiff of a powerful musk coming from the creature. She couldn't help noticing, too, even as she stared in horror, that the Minotaur was prodigiously well-endowed. What looked like a black butternut squash and a pair of oranges in a black sac hung between its legs.

The Minotaur drank for several minutes, using its hands as a bowl, till its thirst was slaked. Then it gave a deep, satisfied grunt and shook its head so that droplets flew from its floppy lips and whiskery chin.

By that point Sam had recovered her wits. Her right hand was edging towards her submachine gun while her left was busy stealthily unclipping a grenade from her hip. She had no wish to tackle the Minotaur on her own, but if she had to, she had to. Everything depended on what the Minotaur itself did next.

Behind her a bird shot abruptly from the treetops with a raucous clapping of wings. The Minotaur started in surprise. It swivelled its head, scanning the other side of the lake. Its gaze roved to and fro. Sam froze. Those eyes – black pupils swimming in pools of red –swept straight over her, twice, without stopping. Had it seen her? Sam hoped not, and the hope became a conviction. A thought had occurred to her. Cattle had poor vision. Ade's father, a large-animal vet, had told her that. Cattle were near-sighted, with a huge blindspot for middle-distance objects dead ahead. That was why you approached a bull slowly and from an angle, so as not to startle it. And maybe a man-bull's vision wasn't much better.

The monster bowed its head, seeming to have found nothing to trouble it. Keeping stock-still, Sam watched as it began peering intently into the lake.

She couldn't fathom what it was so fascinated by all at once. A fish? Then the penny dropped.

The Minotaur was studying its own reflection.

It tilted its head to one side then the other. One hand probed its massive horns then the contours of its heavy overhanging brow, as though these things were unfamiliar and felt wrong. The Minotaur was inspecting its features in the manner of Narcissus – but unlike Narcissus it did not like what it saw.

The monster let out a profound, dolorous bellow. Then it began pounding the water, fists scattering its reflection into a million ripples and then scattering those ripples. Finally it collapsed into a sitting position on the bank, now beating rocks rather than the lake. Its torso swayed and its mouth gaped in a soundless lament.

It knows, Sam thought, with an inward gasp. *It knows it's a monster.*

Her astonishment rapidly gave way to something akin to pity. Somehow this creature, this hideous half-breed thing, was aware of its own unnaturalness. It couldn't bear to look at itself. It didn't want to be what it was. Trapped inside it was some dim spark of a sentience that was more than animal – that was, could only be, human.

Unconsciously, Sam let go of grenade and gun.

At last the Minotaur clambered to its feet and stalked off into the trees, head hanging low.

Sam slipped her helmet on.

"All Titans, this, uh, this is Tethys reporting it. I have a sighting. Repeat, I have a confirmed sighting of the target."

"You OK, Tethys? You don't sound right."

"I'm fine, Hyperion. Absolutely fine. Relay the message to Galetti on the RCDC's shortwave frequency, then let's make for the rendezvous point."

She was already thinking the unthinkable, trying to work out how she could take the Minotaur alive.

It was madness.

That didn't mean it was wrong, though.

35. CUL-DE-SAC

THE RESISTENZA MEMBERS did their bit, descending in a sweeping arc from behind the Minotaur, driving it downslope with small arms fire. There were too many of them for it to pick one to charge at. Whenever it turned menacingly on any of its pursuers, bullets would spray at it from another direction and, confused, maddened, the monster would recoil and lumber away to escape the stinging barrage.

The Corsicans yelped with glee and pressed the Minotaur harder. They had it on the run. But success made them bold, and boldness made them reckless. One of them dared himself to go right up to the beast, puffing out his chest and singing a folk tune about foxes and wolves that was an uncomplimentary allegory of French colonialism. The Minotaur rounded on him with a startling turn of speed, impaling him in the belly then flipping him high into the air. Entrails uncoiled as the Corsican spun skyward. He landed on rocks with an immense splash of blood, bursting like a bag of water.

From then on, everyone was a bit more cautious. But the herding continued.

A village below was the designated kill zone. It nestled at one end of a steep-sided valley, in a natural bottleneck. The residents had been instructed to stay indoors and were heeding the warning. Iapetus and Hyperion were stationed at the village's two main entry points, waiting for the monster to appear. The other three Titans were strategically positioned in the streets.

The boom of a shotgun announced that the Minotaur had arrived.

"Buckshot up the clacker. Don't much like that, do you, you flaming mongrel," said Iapetus. "Crius, it's coming your way."

"Roger that." Moments later there was the chunky staccato of an assault rifle on triple-burst setting. "Tethys, Mnemosyne, it's heading straight for you now."

"Roger, Crius," said Sam. "We're cloaked and ready." She looked over at Mnemosyne, whose battlesuit was brick-red like the wall she was standing against. Mnemosyne had the coilgun. To her fell responsibility for delivering the fatal shot.

"I'm scared as all buggery," Mnemosyne said off-comms.

"Don't be," Sam said. "You can do this. Just stay calm. Wait for me to give you the OK."

The Minotaur lurched into view. It lumbered up the road towards them, glistening with sweat, eyes panic-wild. It passed straight between the two

Titans, seeing neither, and ran headlong into the cul-de-sac whose mouth they were flanking. Only at the last moment, as the end of the cul-de-sac loomed before it, did the Minotaur realise it had blundered into a blind alley. It turned in order to retrace its steps, and that was when two human figures seemed to manifest in front of it from nowhere. Magically, they detached themselves from the walls on either side, blocking its route to freedom.

The idea was that Sam would pin the monster down with suppressing fire from her submachine gun so as to allow Mnemosyne to line up a clean, surgical takedown shot. Landesman was confident the coilgun's superior velocity would be able to put a bullet through the Minotaur's hide where other, lesser guns could not.

But Sam, of course, was brewing another plan. When she saw the look of resignation in the Minotaur's eyes, that clinched it for her. Ignoring the protestations of Hyperion from afar, she had Mnemosyne temporarily stand down, then fitted on and activated a pair of stun-dusters. Fists crackling with voltage, she ran to meet the charging Minotaur head-on.

Don't fuck it up.

Her weight was no match for the monster's but her momentum was. The two of them collided halfway along the cul-de-sac, and even through the suit Sam felt the jarring impact. But the Minotaur was the one who was shunted backwards, not her, and Sam felt a surge of something like hilarity bubble up in her as she pushed the monster bodily along the road, less than a hundred pounds of woman successfully manhandling a creature more than four times bulkier. She rammed the Minotaur against the wall at the end, brickwork cracking, mortar dust puffing.

Voices were yelling in her ear – Landesman's, Hyperion's, McCann's, even Lillicrap's. Everyone wanted to know what the hell she thought she was up to. Loud as all the shouting was, however, the pounding of her blood was louder.

The Minotaur bellowed. Its musk smell was almost overpoweringly rank. Sam grappled with the monster, pushing it against the wall, using every ounce of suit-enhanced strength to keep it in place. The Minotaur butted her, its horns clattering on her helmet. She ducked her head and, one-armed, punched the monster in the gut. Electricity sparked from the stun-duster and the Minotaur let out a roar of pain. She punched again, and the beast convulsed from head to toe.

But it didn't fall and it didn't stop struggling either. And then a kick from a powerful leg booted Sam in the midriff and sent her hurtling through space. She crashed into an iron gate; through the gate into a small courtyard; across the courtyard into a wooden bench, which was smashed to kindling. Immediately she was back on her feet, thanking her stars that the courtyard was empty – no one there to be injured by a flying Titan. A second later the enraged Minotaur burst in through the gateway. Sam went for it, taking it down with a waist-high rugby tackle. Monster and Titan went tumbling to the ground. There was grappling, jockeying for advantage. A table overturned. An earthenware urn full of herbs broke. Sam, almost to her surprise, found she had managed to gain the upper hand. Servos whirring, she levered herself on top of the Minotaur, straddling it. Three quick punches to its face depleted all the charge from her right stun-duster. The monster groaned. Blood-red eyes rolled in their sockets. She gave it a further couple of punches with her left stun-duster. The creature's skull was as sturdy as steel but the blows, and the million-volt jolts that came with them, took their toll. Sam clambered off its chest. The Minotaur made a feeble, flailing attempt to get up, but the best it could manage was propping itself on one elbow. Then it slumped back onto the courtyard flagstones, head sagging, tongue lolling out.

Panting hard, Sam knelt beside it. Eyes shut. Breathing slow. The monster was out cold. Neutralised. But alive.

Mnemosyne appeared in the gateway. She peeked in, coilgun at the ready.

"Bloomin' 'eck," she said. "You did it."

Sam nodded.

"So now what?"

"Yeah, now what?" Hyperion demanded, over Mnemosyne's shoulder. He barged past her into the courtyard. "What the fuck kind of stunt was that you just pulled?" He nudged the insensible Minotaur with one toecap. "It ain't even dead. What the hell are we supposed to do now? Sell it to a museum? Put it in a petting zoo? Huh?"

"Take it home," Sam replied simply.

"Yeah, right. Take it home. Are you nuts?"

At Bleaney, Landesman echoed the sentiment. "Tethys, have you quite taken leave of your senses? Bring the Minotaur here? How? More to the point, why?"

"I don't expect you to understand, any of you," Sam said. "But the Minotaur isn't just a monster. I don't think any of the monsters are just monsters, at least not the part-human ones. I think they're more than that. I think, buried in them, there's something else – a personality, a person even. I think they can be reasoned with, engaged with, won over. I think they could even be reformed and turned into useful assets. And I'd like to prove that with the Minotaur. At any rate I'd like to be able to try."

"Base, give the word and I'll bust a rocket in this thing's ass," said Hyperion. "Turn it into ground beef."

"Don't you dare, Hyperion," Sam said. "Don't even think about it. I just risked my neck to take it alive. I've earned the right to do what I want with it."

"Right, schmight. Base? Overrule her. We can't just turn Bleaney into a goddamn monster sanctuary."

Silence from Landesman.

"Base?"

"I'm thinking, Hyperion."

"You can't seriously be... Ah, c'mon! No way!"

"Very well, Tethys," Landesman said finally. "You get your wish. We'll make preparations this end. How you get the Minotaur here is up to you."

"I'll find a way."

"I'm sure you will. This is, it goes without saying, sheer insanity. But you've laid out a decent enough argument, and if there's even a slim possibility of what you're proposing working, then it's worth a shot. Let's just hope that my faith in your powers of logic and reasoning isn't, in this instance, misplaced."

Sam didn't say anything, but she herself was hoping much the same.

36. CRONUS

Deep in Bleaney Island lay a bomb shelter where Churchill and his cabinet were to have taken refuge should the worst have happened and the Luftwaffe were to have launched Heinkels from a commandeered RAF base to put paid to this last outpost of British governance. The shelter boasted cross-braced blast doors and extra-thick reinforced concrete walls and ceiling. Until now, Landesman's Titan project had been using it for storing superfluous materials – discarded TITAN suit and weapon prototypes, offcuts from the suit production process, industrial machinery that wasn't needed for the time being, lathes and such – so that it was essentially a huge dustbin, or the Bleaney equivalent of a domestic attic, a place where all the clutter and clobber accumulated over the years fetched up.

Cleared out and spring-cleaned, it now became a Minotaur pen.

The monster was brought over from Corsica under tarpaulin wraps, heavily sedated on horse tranquillisers which Sam had sourced through Galetti. He and all the RCDC members were pleased to have played a crucial role in the Minotaur's capture, even if some of them were a little surprised that the outcome of the hunt had been so bloodless. Hoping for the satisfaction of a kill, they were happy nonetheless to settle for the monster's removal from their homeland.

"The Resistenza owes you," Galetti said as he enfolded Sam in a crushing farewell embrace. His underarm odour was as potent as the Minotaur's musk, and somehow less tolerable. "Naturally, if asked, we shall take the lion's share of the credit. How could we not? We are Corsicans. No one fights our battles for us. But if you need us at any time, we will be there. We do not forget a debt."

The liquid ketamine he obtained for her had to administered orally, seeing as no hypodermic could pierce the Minotaur's hide. Sam tipped phials of it repeatedly down the monster's throat all the way to Bleaney. She had no idea what a safe dosage was, but she erred on the side of caution. Better a Minotaur dead from an overdose than one that sprang unexpectedly to life in the back of the van, or in the Gulfstream somewhere over the Channel, or in Captain Fuller's boat halfway across the strait to the island.

She allowed herself to relax only when the doped, still unconscious Minotaur was safely stowed in the bomb shelter and the blast doors were firmly shut.

Then she went to find Ramsay, who was in his room, towelling himself off after a shower.

"I have a bone to pick with you," she began.

But before she could get any further, he halted her in her tracks with a simple, humble "sorry."

"I was a jerk, Sam," he went on. "I was out of line. I should never have questioned your actions in front of everybody. That was uncool. Want to know why I did? 'Cause you'd just scared the bejeezus out of me. Going up against that thing hand-to-hand – that was ten kinds of foolish. I thought you were dead for sure. That was why I was so pissed at you. I couldn't help myself. When I'm scared, I get mad. It won't happen again."

"You can't worry about me," she said. "You mustn't. I'm a big girl. I can take care of myself. If you start getting all protective, especially when we're on an op, it won't help anyone and could compromise the mission. We agreed, remember? Professional. We compartmentalise. When we're alone, just the two of us, we can be ourselves, but when we're working, I'm Tethys, you're Hyperion, we're Titans, and you don't fret over me and you certainly don't countermand me. Otherwise this – us – what we are in private – will have to end. Are we straight on that?"

"We are. Office romances, huh?"

"Quite. Having said all which, thanks for apologising. I know that's something you don't often do."

"Hey!... No, you're right. I don't."

"So now... You're still looking a bit damp in places. Don't suppose there's anything I can do to help? Any hard-to-reach spots need seeing to?"

He handed her the towel, which left him naked but for his grin. "I could name a couple."

Later, when all was quiet, there was a knock at the door. Sam dived below the bedcovers.

"Yeah?" Ramsay called out. "Who is it?"

"Anders," came Søndergaard's voice. "I'm looking for Sam, but she's not in her room and Zaina says she doesn't know where she is."

"So why do you think *I'd* know?"

"I've asked everyone else. Can I come in?"

"No. No! I'm – er – I'm busy. I mean, naked. Busy and naked. What do you want her for anyway?"

"I don't," said Søndergaard. "Mr Landesman does."

"OK. Well, if I see her I'll be sure to pass the message on."

"OK. And maybe you and me, we can shoot some pool later on down in the rec room, how about that? I know I've got to beat you sometime."

"Dream on, Danish pastry. I used to spend all my downtime on base hustling the COs for beers and dollars. You're going to need several years of practice before you even get close."

"The law of averages says I must win eventually."

"The law of averages doesn't take my killer topspin into account."

After Søndergaard was gone, Sam poked her head out from under the covers.

"Oh God," she groaned. "I feel about nineteen years old again. Hiding in some man's bed. Haven't done that since uni."

"Fun, ain't it?" said Ramsay.

"I suppose." She climbed out and started hunting around for her bra. "Wonder what Landesman wants."

"Wild guess? He's gonna bust your balls about the Minotaur."

"What? He was all for bringing it here."

"On-comms he was. But that was only 'cause he didn't want to lose face in front of everybody. Privately's going to be a different matter."

"You think?"

"I hope not."

But what Ramsay predicted was what happened, more or less. In his office, in a voice like the bubble of a boiling kettle, Landesman told Sam that he believed she was making a mistake. He'd been reluctant to say so at the time. Hadn't want to undermine her authority. But, in his opinion, the Minotaur was pure beast, nothing else. It couldn't be, in her phrase, "won over." It couldn't be rehabilitated like a secure-wing psychiatric patient and converted into some kind of ally. The whole notion was preposterous.

Sam related what she had seen up by the lake in Corsica, the Minotaur's behaviour, its reaction to its own reflection.

"A budgerigar will attack the mirror in its cage," Landesman said, "thinking it's seeing off a rival budgerigar. No, I don't buy your theory at all, Sam."

"You won't even give me the benefit of the doubt?"

"I've let you lock the monster up downstairs. I think you could call that the benefit of the doubt. You have a week. One week. That's all I'm allowing you. You want to make a project out of that creature, fine, but you need to get results within a week. Not a day longer. When time's up, and you're unable to show us any proof of progress, I'm sending Hyperion in there with his rocket launcher and he isn't coming out 'til the Minotaur's in pieces. Understood?"

Sam nodded. "I take it there won't be any ops for a week, then. That's good. Everyone could do with a break."

"Oh no, ops are going to continue. We've built up a good head of steam. It'd be a shame to lose it."

"I can't do both, deal with the Minotaur *and* lead an op." She saw the look in Landesman's eye, and everything became clear. "I'm being relieved of my command, aren't I?"

"You're being temporarily reassigned."

Same difference. "And Rick's going to be team leader in my absence. No? Then who?"

"You're looking at him."

"You, Mr Landesman?"

"Is there anyone else in the room?"

"But..."

"But what? I'm too old?" Landesman laughed. "*Au contraire.* I am, as I believe I may have mentioned at some point, in top physical condition for a man my age, and my mental faculties are, I'm sure you'll agree, unimpaired."

"But training..."

"I've trained long and hard in the TITAN suit. I was proficient in one long before you lot arrived."

"Cronus," Sam said, a lightbulb popping on in her head. "Of course. *You're* Cronus. That's why no one else has been found to wear that suit. You've been keeping it back for yourself."

"Spot-on. And now seems the opportune moment to make the move – to join the ranks. It always was my intention to. I've simply been waiting for the rest of you to gel as a unit, so that I could feel safe fitting in. And my presence on missions might have had an inhibiting effect before now. As things stand, I'm confident the Titans can accommodate me in their midst without it upsetting the balance of their functioning."

"Even though you've had no field experience?"

"I'll pick it up as I go. I'm a quick study."

"Will the Titans take orders from you, though?"

"They do already, to some extent. The only difference now will be I'll be right there beside them, not miles away. Sam, you can raise all the objections you like, but this isn't negotiable. This is just how it's going to be."

"And when I come back after a week, what then?"

"We shall figure out a way of meshing together seamlessly, you and I."

"I've been doing OK on my own so far."

"There's absolutely no slight intended here on your leadership qualities. Those have been all but impeccable. This is about taking the Titans to the next level. Our biggest battles lie ahead. I like to think that the addition of me to your number will strengthen your – our – effectiveness."

"Well," said Sam frostily, "you're the boss."

"Indeed I am."

"And Darren Pugh," she said. "Would I be wrong in thinking he was never going to be Cronus? It was never likely?"

"Ah, Pugh. Yes. He was more of a... Do you know the word libation?"

"Long word for a drink. Popular with pompous pub landlords and real-ale bores."

"Bit more than that. It's an offering. In classical times, before wine was served at a feast some of it would be poured out onto the ground, to appease the gods. The same at sacrifices, so that the gods would be propitiated and whatever the sacrifice was being made in aid of would be granted. Now I of course don't believe in any of that nonsense literally, but I thought it would be a nice idea – appropriate – if in this classically-based enterprise of mine I followed the precedent. Instead of a wine libation for good luck, a human libation. One of you. One I could afford to lose, even wanted to lose. I selected Pugh as the twelfth invitee secure in the knowledge, or let's at least say ninety-nine per cent certain, that he would back out before we'd even got going. He didn't have the incentive or the temperament to commit to the cause. And sure enough, he did exactly as anticipated. In addition, I'd been havering somewhat over whether I ought to enrol myself as a

Titan. I was treating Pugh as a kind of test of fate. If he baulked, that would confirm that I was meant to be Cronus. And so he did, and so I was."

"A rigged test. You chose him mainly because you knew he *wouldn't* sign up."

"A test weighted in my favour, perhaps. But then it never hurts to give fate a little helping hand every now and then. That's something I've learned in business over the years. Good fortune is a case of playing the odds, and only an idiot plays poor odds."

"And Pugh was also there to consolidate the rest of us," Sam said. "He helped us make up our minds, by being such a wanker. We thought, *Let's not be like him. Let's do the opposite of what he's done.*"

Landesman raised a sage eyebrow. "Such an accusation! Now would I do a thing like that? Deliberately expose you all to someone whose actions would, through contrasting example, lend impetus and validity to *your* actions?"

Sam stood. "All right, Mr Landesman. This is your show. You can run it however you like. I *will* prove you wrong about the Minotaur, though. And I'll do it within a week easily.

"And don't think I don't realise that taking away my prefect's badge is just another way of playing me. Now the pressure's on and I'll be twice as determined to get the Minotaur onside. You're an arch manipulator, and that's fine. I just want you to know I *know* I'm being manipulated, and I'm only going along with it because it serves my purpose."

Landesman acknowledged this. "For what it's worth," he said, "I'd never make anyone do anything they didn't already –"

He broke off. Sam was half out the door and, he could tell by the tension in her upper body, poised to bang it shut behind her as hard as she could.

"Please!" he cried. Then, more softly, and imploringly: "Please. Don't."

"Don't...?"

"Slam it. There's nothing I can't abide more than a door being slammed. Alexander, my son... Towards the end, that was all he ever seemed to do – slam doors on me. It was the soundtrack to the latter years of our relationship, like drumbeats getting faster and faster, until one day the front door slammed, loudest of all, and that was that. He left, never to return. So I... I have a thing about it. It's painful not only on the ears, and I'd appreciate it if you... well, didn't."

Sam was tempted.

But then she wasn't some stroppy, spoiled rich kid with parental-neglect issues, was she?

She departed quietly; closed the door gently.

From the other side came a "Thank you!" and there was something about it that made Sam pause. The tone was ever so slightly smug.

She couldn't help wondering: had she just been manipulated again?

37. UNARMED

Suited up, Sam prepared to enter the pen. In one hand she held an enamel pail full of pieces of raw chicken; in the other, one full of corncobs. Nobody had any idea what the Minotaur ate, so she was hedging her bets. The Minotaur might be a ruminant, in common with all bovines, but its aggressive nature suggested carnivorousness. One thing she was sure of: she wasn't going to offer it beefsteak, as Barrington had proposed. That would be too close to cannibalism for comfort.

Mahmoud, also battlesuited, stood by the wheel handle that operated the door.

"There was quite a bit of mooing and thumping around in there just before you turned up," she told Sam. "Things have quietened down, but still, you should be careful."

"I will be," Sam replied. "And so should you. Close

that door on me the second I'm in, and then get well clear. I may have to come back out in a hurry."

"Got you. Best of luck, duck."

McCann had fitted the door with a disabling system, to prevent it being opened by means of the matching wheel handle on the inside. Whether the Minotaur was intelligent and dextrous enough to work the handle was unclear, but no chances were being taken. Mahmoud hit the lever that re-engaged the lock mechanism, then grasped the wheel and began rotating. The door groaned open. Sam heard the Minotaur grunt and stir inside the pen.

She stepped through. The door whumped shut behind her.

Smells hit her: Minotaur musk, urine, dung.

The monster itself was crouched in a corner, surveying her intently. It rose to its feet. A full height, its horns scraped the ceiling. It lowed with unmistakable hostility. It knew this human. Remembered her.

"Food," Sam said in as soothing a voice as she could muster. "Here. I've brought you food."

The Minotaur eyed the pails as she set them down on the floor. She searched for a flash of recognition, comprehension, on its face. Saw none.

"Eat." She mimed lifting food to her mouth. "Mmmm. Tastes good." She smacked her lips. "Yummy."

Performing this babytalk act made her feel an idiot. The Minotaur's blank look made the feeling worse.

The monster shook its head, as though pestered by a gnat.

Then it lowered its horns.

Oh shit.

It came, at speed, across the floor.

Sam, at greater speed, feinted one way, then jinked the other.

The Minotaur collided full-tilt, head-first, with the wall where she had been standing a split second earlier. It reeled backwards, crashing over onto the pails and scattering chicken meat and corncobs.

While the monster lay stunned, Sam made her exit.

She gave the Minotaur an hour to calm down. Then she nerved herself to re-enter the pen. She would be presenting Landesman with a tame beast even if it killed her.

"Here we go again," said Mahmoud. "Don't forget your matador cape."

This time the Minotaur was lying in wait. It sprang as soon as Sam crossed the threshold, ramming her sidelong, sending her sprawling. She scrambled to her feet and met the monster with a reciprocal attack, thrusting it backward with her shoulder until it struck a wall. She left the Minotaur winded, heaving for breath, as she hurried out the door a second time.

"This is not working," she confessed to Mahmoud, peeling off a slab of chicken breast that had got stuck to her arm.

"You don't say."

"The Minotaur associates me with hurting it. I can't win its trust as long as it looks at me and thinks of pain."

"Why don't I try going in? It mightn't remember me."

"You sure? You'd be prepared to do that?"

Mahmoud went in. There was a scuffle. She came out again, Sam swinging the door shut just in time before the Minotaur could follow. The Minotaur hammered on the inside of the door, making it boom like a gong.

"OK, well, we're definitely not at home to Mr Happy this afternoon," Mahmoud said. "And, by the way, you didn't tell me that room's minging in there. Little warning please, next time I'm about to walk straight into a farmyard."

Sam gave the Minotaur another couple of hours to settle itself. Then she said to Mahmoud, "It's the suits."

"What about the suits?"

"The Minotaur sees them and knows we're the enemy."

"So?"

"So I have to go in without my suit on."

"D'you know, I knew you were going to say that, and then I thought, *No, she'd never. Nobody would be that daft.*"

"It's the only way. In my suit, I'm the bad guy."

"And without your suit, you're toast," Mahmoud said. "You're not doing this, Sam. I won't let you. Talk about suicidal!"

"If it sees me as a person, it might just hold off from attacking."

"Why? Persons are what it attacks. That's what it does."

"Not if I make it clear I don't pose a threat."

"Your mind's made up, isn't it? OK, what if I go in with you then, with the coilgun, just in case."

"A gun's as bad as a battlesuit," said Sam. "This needs to be me, alone, suitless, unarmed."

"Unarmed as in the Minotaur's going to rip your ruddy arms out of their sockets."

"I don't think so. I think I'll be all right."

"Weren't those Julius Caesar's famous last words as he set off for the Forum? 'I'll be all right'?"

"Can you trust me on this?"

"No. But yes. If you say I must."

"I do."

Sam felt naked, not simply suitless, as she approached the pen for the third time. She felt as terrified as – no, more than terrified than – she'd felt when setting out on her first op, against the Hydra. Ramsay would pitch a fit if he knew what she was up to. She had absolutely no protection here. The Minotaur could finish her off in a heartbeat. Standing before the door she experienced a moment of wooziness followed by a moment of sheer wanton panic. *What are you doing? What are you doing? What are you doing?* It was a supreme effort to turn to Mahmoud and give her the nod to open the door. It was an even greater effort to make her feet move one in front of the other and walk into the pen. And when the door closed behind her, her fear became a visceral thing, a cold relentless clenching of the gut.

The Minotaur fixed its crimson gaze on her, and Sam knew she was dead.

38. BULLS AND BULLIES

"I'M EMPTY-HANDED," SHE told the monster. Her voice seemed to come from a distance, from elsewhere, not her own mouth. "See? No battlesuit. No weaponry. Nothing. Just me. Because I know you don't want to hurt me. I know there's intelligence somewhere in there, there's a mind that knows that hurting and killing is not what you want to do."

She doubted the Minotaur understood a word, but what she was saying didn't matter so much as how it was said. She was adopting as soft and unthreatening a tone as possible, and her whole manner was designed to give the monster no sense of antagonism or loathing. She held her head down and her hands open, palms out. This was the way she'd been taught in the Met to deal with hostile behaviour. Meet it with reasonableness, and let just enough of your fear show through that the other person knew you were intimidated but not to the point of quivering-jelly terror. Bullies and lunatics thrived on other people's terror. It was their drug, and the trick was to give them a tincture of it, enough to keep them happy but nowhere near enough to ignite a narcotic frenzy.

She kept talking, even as the Minotaur began to stalk closer to her. She kept talking because there was nothing else she could do.

"Were you a man once? Before you became a man-bull? Did someone turn you into this? Did they take you and do something to you that made you a monster? Did they do it against your will? I think maybe they did. And then they trained you like a fighting dog. They used threats and brutality to make you violent. I think you used to be ordinary, a human being like me, and you can remember that. From time to time the memory of what you were floats to the surface, and you realise what you've become, and it causes you distress. I'm sorry about that. I'm sorry, too, that I hurt you back in Corsica. There's so much pain in your life, and I only added to it. I want to make up for that. I want to help."

The Minotaur continued to close in on her, but it was moving slowly. It appeared to be listening. And it hadn't attacked her yet, which was definitely something. Definitely progress.

"Look." She bent and picked up a corncob. "Food." She proffered it. "This is for you, if you want. You must be hungry. If it's not what you like, I can get something else. Water too. I bet you're thirsty. I could fetch a nice big bowl of water."

A flicker in those red eyes. A glimmer. A spark?

"I'm not your enemy. I could be your friend, if you'd like."

The Minotaur loomed over her. For several moments – very long moments – Sam could see some kind of struggle going on within it. A part was telling it to crush her like a bug. Another part was telling it not to.

Then, with a snort, the monster slapped her hand aside. The corncob went flying, and Sam bit back a yelp of shock and pain.

The Minotaur spun round and strode off to a far corner, where it hunkered down with its back to her.

Sam's hand throbbed.

But the Minotaur had held back, she knew. It could easily have shattered every bone in her hand and hadn't.

The monster had just given her a message.

Not corncobs. Something else.

39. NON-ACROBATIC

HER HAND WAS numb as she entered the pen yet again. Puffy, too, the back of it starting to swell up in a lovely sunset-coloured bruise.

She placed a plastic sink bucket brimming with water on the floor and a bale of hay beside it. The Minotaur studied both items from afar. Then up the monster got and over it came, shambling across the room. It bent to the bucket first and slurped up water sloppily. Then it turned to the hay bale. After a moment's contemplation, fleshy nostrils flaring, it kicked the bale aside, then urinated on it for good measure.

"OK, OK, I get it, I can take a hint," said Sam.

She returned with a selection of raw vegetables. These, to her relief, met with the Minotaur's approval. It fell on them greedily, munching down handful after handful.

Next she tried some fruit, and that, too, found favour.

"Well, we've established that it's a veggie," she said to Mahmoud at the end of the day, as they headed off to get some food for themselves. "Might make life easier. Veggies are peace-loving hippy types after all, aren't they?"

"Except for that Hitler bloke. I've heard he had a bit of a nasty streak."

"I think it was missing a testicle that made him that way."

"That certainly isn't the Minotaur's problem," Mahmoud said with a giggle. "I mean, ruddy 'eck! Have you seen the size of its you-know-whats?"

"Can't say I noticed," Sam said.

A sly look came over the other woman. "Probably just me then. Maybe if I'd been getting some action lately, I wouldn't have noticed either."

"What's that supposed to mean?"

"Oh come on, Sam. Don't play dumb."

Sam glance furtively ahead and behind. The corridor they were in was empty. She lowered her voice anyway. "How did you know?"

"I didn't," said Mahmoud, gloating. "'Til now. All I had was a hunch, which you've just gone and confirmed."

"You cow."

"And you did come to our room very late last night. Not that I blame you, mind. Rick's lush. Not my type, but still lush."

"You can't tell anyone."

"I won't. Scout's honour. So, when did it start? Corsica, I'm guessing. That's when the flirting stopped between you."

"Flirting? We were flirting?"

"You may not have realised it but you were. Even when you were in a grump with each other and not talking, that was a kind a flirting. And now you're both so formal around each other in public, there just has to be something else going on."

"Does anyone else suspect, do you know?"

"Not as far as I'm aware. What's the problem? There's nothing wrong with him and you hooking up. Why do you need to keep it a secret?"

"I don't know. I just do. I think it would look bad, the team leader sleeping with one of the team."

"Or maybe, if nobody else knows, you can pretend it's not happening."

"Why would I want to do that?" Sam asked stiffly.

"Because you had someone once," Mahmoud replied. "You've never talked about him but I know you did. He was The One, and you don't want to admit to yourself that anybody could ever replace him. So it's arm's length for poor old Rick, and probably for every other man you're with from now on."

There was flint in Sam's voice. "Bollocks. That's bollocks."

"Is it?"

"You know nothing, Zaina. Nothing."

Mahmoud understood she had overstepped the mark. There were some truths Sam wasn't prepared to hear.

"No, of course," she said, mollifying. "My mistake. So, er..." She changed the subject clumsily. "More Minotaur tomorrow, then?"

"Yes."

"Pretty soon you'll have that thing eating out of your hand."

Sam decided to take this literally, as an inspiration and a challenge. The next morning she brought in a single apple, which she held out to the monster. The Minotaur sniffed suspiciously, reached for the apple, then withdrew its hand. Sam offered the fruit again, telling the Minotaur there was nothing wrong with it, it was delicious. The Minotaur still wouldn't take it. Finally Sam took a bite out of the apple herself to prove it was safe. The Minotaur, letting out short, stertorous breaths, watched her chew. Then, abruptly, it snatched the bitten apple off her and retreated with it to its favourite corner of the pen.

A day later, Sam dared to squat down next to the monster as it ate. This was a bad move. The Minotaur reacted intemperately, believing Sam wanted to share its food and not liking that idea. It batted her aside with one sweep of its arm, then slapped her a few times as she tried to get up. Sam staggered out of the pen feeling pummelled and dazed.

That night, Ramsay noted that she was moving stiffly and wincing as she undressed. When the fresh contusions on her body were laid bare, he scowled.

"El Toro not treating you right?" he said.

"My fault."

"Spoken like a true battered housewife."

"I took a step too far too soon."

"Even so. The Minotaur keeps this up, I might have to go and have words with it."

"I'll sort things out."

"Playing *Born Free* with that monster is all very well, Sam, but one false move..."

"I'll sort things out," Sam insisted. She climbed into bed beside him. "God," she groaned. "I ache too much to be up for anything acrobatic tonight, Rick. Sorry."

"Never mind. Least we get to spend the whole night together, now that Zaina's in the loop. You just lie here, get all snug and cosy."

"I didn't say I wanted to just sleep. I said nothing acrobatic, that's all."

"Ha! Well, I've no problem with non-acrobatic."

"Really? Prove it."

"You lie still and I will. Now, nice and gentle. No moving around while I do... this."

"Ah."

"And this."

"Ohh."

"Uh-uh. Still no moving around. Now, how about...?"

And then Ramsay was not in a position to talk any further, and his silence, for Sam, was blissfully golden.

40. RUMBLINGS OF BELLIGERENCE

IN THE COMMAND centre, Landesman had an announcement to make.

"I am going to be Cronus," he told the Titans. The techs and Lillicrap were in attendance as well. "You know that already. Some of you may have suspected it for a while. I just want to say it's going to be a privilege working directly alongside you in the field. Over the past few weeks I've watched you cohere as a unit. I've watched you work wonders in all your various permutations. As a fighting force, you've impressed me no end. You've become better than I could ever have hoped. You've exceeded every aspiration I ever had for this project, and I intend to be every bit as good as you. I will not be the weak link in the chain. I will be an aid, an asset, an addition, an adornment, and doubtless lots of other words beginning with 'a.'"

"Arsehole?" offered Barrington.

"Thank you, Dez. I gave you that one for free."

"I know. My pleasure."

"I must also tell you," Landesman continued, "that it would appear that your efforts so far, not to mention the sacrifices of Soleil and Nigel, have cumulatively yielded victory. According to news reports this morning, the Olympians have recalled their monsters. Yes! All the ones that were still out there in the world, still at large, have been brought back to Olympus. Summoned back to the fold. Not that there were many of them left, admittedly, but it isn't the numbers that matter so much as the significance of the decision. It tells us something very important."

"Zeus has blinked," said Tsang.

"Precisely, Fred. Zeus has blinked. Our adversaries have conceded the round to us. They're taking their pawns off the board because they realise we've got the better of them. They know that if they carry on, they're only going to lose those few remaining monsters. What's more, there haven't been any further reprisals. Obviously that tactic didn't work last time, so they're not repeating it. In other words, ladies and gentlemen, phase one of the campaign is over and the clear winner is us. You may, if you like, give yourselves a hand. In fact I think you should."

They did, Titans and techs alike; Lillicrap too. The only exception was Sam, not fond of public displays of self-congratulation.

"Now," Landesman said, as the applause died down, "for my next point of order, you may be interested to learn that a spat has broken out between Prime Minister Bartlett and General Sir Neville Armstrong-Hall, who is, for those of you among us who don't know, the Chief of General Staff, i.e. Britain's highest-ranking military official. The argument is being conducted in the media – via TV interviews, newspaper columns and suchlike – and the wording is very coded and subtle. Neither man is saying exactly what he means but each knows the other will read him loud and clear.

"The ostensible bone of contention is Bartlett's newest round of defence budget cuts, with Armstrong-Hall complaining that these will expose his troops to unnecessary danger in case of conflict and Bartlett saying, basically, what conflict? Now, top military personnel don't, as a rule, speak out publicly and criticise the executive unless they have an ulterior motive, and in this instance, reading between the lines, it's not hard to infer what Armstrong-Hall's is. I've chatted to a few of my contacts within the MOD, reliable sources all, and they've confirmed it. Armstrong-Hall, it seems, is spoiling for a fight with the Pantheon. He thinks they're on the ropes right now, thanks to us. Hit 'em while they're reeling, is his view. Kick 'em while they're in disarray. The time is right."

"Like Bartlett's going to go for that," Mahmoud snorted.

"Of course he isn't. He'd rather circumcise himself with a pair of rusty nail scissors. But the fact that Armstrong-Hall is lobbying in this way, however covertly, is remarkable in and of itself. It speaks of a shift in mood among the military, a newfound eagerness for a scrap. Armstrong-Hall isn't alone, either. Generals in other countries are making similar noises, I'm told. I believe, if we continue as we have, we may find that these first rumblings of belligerence will grow into a groundswell."

"You mean we could start getting military backup?" said Søndergaard.

"It's too early to say, Anders. But you never know. At least our example is firing up others, not just the general population but people in high places as well. I can't say I was counting on this happening, but I was rather hoping. And on the subject of continuing with our campaign..."

Landesman's geniality faded. His tone turned grave.

"From now on we will be going after bigger and more dangerous game – the Olympians themselves. Next to them, the monsters are going to seem like the proverbial cakewalk."

"We know," said Ramsay.

"It needs saying nonetheless. To utilise the parlance of your countrymen, Rick, we're in the big leagues now."

"Just tell us," said Hamel. "Who's the first target? Which of the Pantheon do you have in your sights?"

"It has to be Hercules," said Landesman.

Barrington snapped to attention. "*Now* you're talking, Landy. That shit-stabbing drongo? Beauty!"

"Hercules is still in Manhattan, still partying and causing drunken havoc. So that's who's going to be our first proper Olympian takedown: Hercules in New York."

41. PUBLIC WORKS

HERCULES, AS IT turned out, was no longer partying, and was in fact intending to atone for the drunken havoc he had caused.

It was not in his nature to do something like this willingly, and he would still have been carrying on in the usual manner had Zeus not travelled to New York and taken the roistering demigod aside for a quiet word.

Quiet word? Actually it was more of a vicious row in the middle of Central Park, witnessed by countless Manhattanites and tourists, and it culminated in the senior Olympian calling down a thunderstorm on Hercules's head in the middle of Central Park, pelting him so hard with rain and hail that he could barely stand. Then he hauled the battered, bedraggled Hercules to his feet and urged him to do his bidding, on penalty of death. Hercules consented, not because he was scared by the threat, he said, but because he could now plainly see that what Zeus was suggesting was the right thing to do.

Zeus then, a day later, addressed a hastily arranged press conference in the shadow of the World Trade Center. Standing on the open-air plaza beside the large fountain with its granite base and bronze sphere sculpture, he informed the hacks of the world that Hercules would be performing a series of tasks in and around the city in order to make amends for his recent untoward behaviour. These would be practical, helpful, large-scale public works that would signally improve the lives of New Yorkers and their urban environment. The mayor had already given the scheme his blessing.

One bright young spark from *Vanity Fair* piped up: "Would I be right in thinking this is kind of a new Twelve Labours?"

Zeus nodded, smiling. It was often best not to spell things out for journalists. If a thing was obvious, let them spot it for themselves. That way they would feel clever.

"And Hercules," said the Olympian affairs correspondent for the *Financial Times*, "how do you feel about the idea? Looking forward to getting stuck in?"

"Delighted," said a grudging, truculent Hercules. "Couldn't be happier."

"Do you think this will help New York citizens forgive you for the damage you've done?" said a woman from the *Herald Tribune*. "And maybe the rest of America for your part in defacing Mount Rushmore?"

"Maybe."

"What about the two TV reporters you killed?" asked a stringer from the *Corriere Della Sera*, dressed with ostentatious nattiness as only an Italian could.

"What about them?"

"Is this how you are saying sorry to their families?"

Hercules grimaced. Zeus stepped in. "Hercules is not here to respond to questions about his past actions. He's interested only in discussing the near future and this generous gesture of reparation he's about to make. A dozen feats of prodigious strength will be accomplished during the next few days in this great city, and you, ladies and gentlemen of the Fourth Estate, not to mention the good folk of New York, will have a ringside seat."

Someone else in the throng of journalists raised a hand. "Zeus? Jennifer Konchalowsky from Fox News."

"Yes, Miss Konchalowsky?"

"O great Zeus the High-Thundering, the Aegis-Bearing, the Dispenser Of All Things To Men, God Of Gain, may I say what an honour it is to be speaking with you."

"We in the Pantheon always have time for the Fox network."

"And we at Fox always have airtime for you. First of all, can I ask, are you and Hercules intending on heading on over to the Capitol while you're here? I understand there's an open invitation to the White House. Also, President Stavropoulos has offered the Pantheon the freehold on Mount Olympus in Washington state as a gift, if you're interested in setting up a second base of operations Stateside. It's also a gesture to show there are no hard feelings about San Francisco and Mount Rushmore. Care to comment?"

"We have no social plans at present," said Zeus, "and picturesque though your Olympus is, ours is the original and best, in addition to being somewhat warmer and less snow-covered. Mike Stavropoulos, I must say, is a good and generous-hearted man, and next time we have a chance I'm sure we'll take advantage of his hospitality."

"And as a follow-up question, if I may," Konchalowsky continued, "what's with these guys who've been killing your monsters? The ones in the Agonides clip?"

"Agon-eye-dees, Miss Konchalowsky. Not Agon-ides."

"Oh. Sorry."

There were sniggers.

"And the point you're making is...?" Zeus said.

"Well, are you going to do anything about them? And if so, what?"

Zeus gave a tolerant sigh, although overhead, faintly, a crackle of thunder could be heard rippling above the summits of the Twin Towers. A Stars and Stripes, limp on its flagpole, swelled into life.

"We have," he said, "as a precaution – and I stress, only as a precaution – transferred Typhon and Scylla to Olympus for safekeeping. Cerberus, of course, is there already. We felt they would be exposed to undue risk if we left them where they were – we would be unable to guarantee their protection. It's a temporary state of affairs. This particular matter will, I promise you, be resolved shortly."

"But resolved how?" said Konchalowsky, who was one of those TV reporters whose glamorousness sheathed a steely tenacity. She looked all fluffy bunny but was all pushy vixen underneath. "This is a well organised outfit who've effectively taken thirteen of your monsters off the grid, at the last count, and forced you to mothball the rest."

"I wouldn't say we've mothballed –"

"So what's the plan? Bending the Eiffel Tower and smashing the Sydney Opera House didn't work. It didn't flush them out, didn't make them think twice. You must want these people bad. How are you going to get them?"

Thunder churned overhead again. Cloudless April skies were turning leaden grey.

"We will, Miss Konchalowsky, get them," said Zeus. "Let there be no doubt about that. The how and the when of it will be at our choosing. And I am not prepared to talk about this any further. Let's focus on Hercules and his New Labours, shall we?"

Konchalowsky would not be that easily dismissed. She persisted with her line of interrogation, even as her colleagues around her grew increasingly restless and resentful.

"Fox News is the Olympians' friend," she said, "you know that, Zeus. I'm not trying to be difficult here."

"So stop pestering him," someone nearby hissed, and someone else hissed, "Are you trying to piss him off?"

She ignored them. "I'd just like to know – I think everyone would like to know – that the monster killers are going to be dealt with before they cause even worse trouble. Some of us don't like it that there are people making the Olympians mad."

"Like you, you mean?" grumbled a man next to her.

"What do you say, Zeus?"

"What do I say?" Zeus barked. He had had enough. "What do I say? I'll tell you what I say, Miss Konchalowsky. They are flies! Gnats! That's all they are to us. A stinging, buzzing nuisance, and we shall swat them and squash them, but we shall do it in our own way and at our own convenience. We will not be goaded by these nobodies into acting before we are ready to act. Do I make myself clear?"

At that moment, before Jennifer Konchalowsky had a chance to reply, the heavens opened. The rain was like a billion buckets of water being tipped out at once, all of this downpour concentrated on the WTC plaza and a few hundred square metres around. Journalists scattered, making for cover. The thunder that accompanied the deluge was earth-shaking, the lightning blinding.

At Bleaney, watching a live broadcast of the press conference lapsing into rain-battered chaos, Landesman burst out laughing.

"Temper, temper," he told the sodden Zeus, who one camera showed retreating hurriedly indoors with the equally sodden Hercules. "Oh, you're well and truly rattled, aren't you? This whole Twelve Labours PR stunt – that's surely the mark of a desperate man. And," he added, "you've pushed Hercules out of the trenches into the firing line. Another egregious error. Our job has just been made ten times simpler."

Sam, beside him, couldn't help but sound a note of caution. "What if he did it on purpose?"

"The thunderstorm? No, Sam, that was pure lack of self-control."

"Hercules, I mean. These New Labours. What if it's... well, I hate to say, but a trap? What if Hercules is simply bait?"

"Dangerous bait, don't you think? Like putting dynamite on the hook instead of a juicy worm."

"Dynamite still brings home dead fish."

"Fair point. But no, I don't believe Zeus would be prepared to risk sacrificing one of his own, merely to get us."

"Why not? He's not that fond of Hercules. Hercules has always been a liability, a loose cannon. If there was one Olympian Zeus would consider expendable, one he wouldn't mind if he lost, Herc is it."

"Sam." Sternly.

"I'm just saying."

"I know. Don't you have a Minotaur to attend to?"

Sam stopped herself from going on. Obstinacy could be confounded by only one thing: greater obstinacy from someone else. Landesman was in charge. He had always been in charge. She was coming to understand that her leadership had been a token, his to grant, his to rescind at will. Landesman had used her to get the Titans to this point. She'd captained the ship out of harbour. She'd navigated through the early, relatively calm part of the voyage. But now, with rough seas ahead, he was very firmly taking the helm.

She went straight from his company to the Minotaur's, and of the two it was the latter she found more congenial. Five days into her allotted week, she was sure she had gained the monster's confidence. Its eyes, though still fearsome in their redness, looked at her now with something like trust. The monster almost seemed glad to see her whenever she entered the pen. At first she'd thought this was because she brought food – a straightforward stimulus response, animal conditioning. But then she'd tried going in empty-handed, and still the Minotaur seemed glad. It approached her expectantly, but wasn't angry or disappointed to discover she didn't come bearing sustenance.

That afternoon, after butting heads with Landesman, she plucked up the courage to touch the Minotaur. She placed a hand on its brow, taking time over the movement so as not to startle the beast. The Minotaur, to her surprise, didn't object, didn't toss her hand aside. Instead it crooned softly at the physical contact. Sam began to stroke and scratch the knotty tuft of hair between its horns. The Minotaur almost cooed with delight.

She knew then.

She had mastered the monster.

42. THE NEW LABOURS OF HERCULES

THE FIRST NEW Labour that Hercules performed was demolishing a condemned tenement building in Brooklyn's Bedford-Stuyvesant district. He collapsed the derelict three-storey brownstone with his bare fists, and took tangible delight in doing so. Then he cleared away the rubble, piling it by the armful into a fleet of municipal dumper trucks. The site was slated to be turned into a play park and sensory garden for kids in the neighbourhood.

The second New Labour involved a hunt for one of the urban-legendary giant alligators reputed to lurk in the New York sewer system. Much to everyone's surprise, Hercules returned from his jaunt into the underworld hauling the corpse of just such a beast, a caiman some 25 feet long from nose to tail which was taken to the American Museum of Natural History on Central Park West to be stuffed, mounted and put on display.

New Labour number three was a somewhat controversial one. Hephaestus had fashioned a statue of none other than Zeus himself, 112 feet tall, one foot taller than the Statue of Liberty, and similarly made of copper. Hercules helped hoist the Zeus statue into place on a plinth on Governors Island so that it gazed across the Upper Bay towards Manhattan and dominated the view southwest from Battery Park much as the Statue of Liberty did. Naturally, plenty of New Yorkers grumbled. They all knew what the Statue of Liberty symbolised. What did the statue of Zeus stand for? Some, however – people who were perhaps of a more sentimental outlook – felt that after all these years of solitary spinsterhood it was high time ol' Lady Liberty had a mate.

Hercules's fourth New Labour was unplanned and impromptu, and occurred just as he'd completed the third. One of the Staten Island Ferry boats got into difficulties coming in to dock at Manhattan. The captain would later profess himself mystified as to what happened. He'd made the back-and-forth trip countless times and thought he knew the tides and currents in the bay intimately. He could have berthed that boat blindfolded. But then a sudden, inexplicable and very powerful rip caught the ferry, twisted her round and began pushing her sideways towards the pier at great speed. Nothing the captain could do would impede her progress or correct the profound list to starboard she had developed. Two likely outcomes awaited: either the ferry would hit the pier broad abeam, crushing dockworkers and possibly holing herself and sinking, or she would roll over and capsize. Neither was, to say the least, desirable.

Then, salvation.

It came in the form of Hercules, who had just alighted from a coastguard motor launch and who now leapt into action, bracing himself between the ferry's hull and the pier. With his immense strength he halted the boat, staved off a collision, and averted disaster. A couple of hundred commuters cheered and the captain hooted his foghorn in appreciation. Hercules took a bow – hero of the hour.

That night, in a comedy club just off Times Square, a young rising star of the circuit made an observation that drew boos and jeers and caused a number of his audience to walk out in high dudgeon. What if, he mused, the ferry "accident" hadn't been accidental? What if Poseidon had been lurking somewhere on the sidelines and had created the freak current that imperilled the boat? What if, in other words, the whole event had been staged? A put-up job?

But you didn't say such a thing, not so soon after a near-calamity and not when your audience was made up of locals who were becoming increasingly enamoured of Hercules and were inclined to forgive him for his past misdemeanours. You might *think* it, but you certainly didn't say it. Or, if you were going to say it and you were in a comedy club, you should at least try to make a joke out of it.

New Labour number five seemed trivial by comparison with the previous one: laying the foundation stone for a new shopping mall in

Rockaway. A half-ton foundation stone, admittedly, the hefting and placing of which by one man, unaided by machinery, was no mean feat. But still, after he had saved all those lives, somewhat underwhelming.

The sixth New Labour was begun but never finished.

43. OSCILLO-KNIVES

THEY WERE DIGGING up the roads around Gramercy Park. They'd been digging them up for weeks. They dug them up day and night, night and day. Resurfacing was in progress. Soon there would be new silk-smooth asphalt. But in the meantime, as the stressed, bleary-eyed residents of the area knew all too well, there was digging-up. Jackhammers clank-clattering away well into the small hours, interspersed with truck-reversing warning klaxons and the sound of workmen hollering. Arc-lights that glared at the dark and made it go away. Continuous racket and hassle, meaning no sleep in the city that never sleeps.

Hercules came one evening to help speed things along. He stamped on the old asphalt, breaking it away in chunks from the layer of Portland cement concrete below, and then he tossed the chunks into skips to be carted off at a later date. Workmen leaned on their idle tools and were duly impressed, although their union representative did put in a call to his boss, the general president of the local Teamsters chapter, just to check whether Hercules's voluntary contribution to the project would affect his men's overtime bonuses. He was told that the mayor had promised it wouldn't.

The Titans sprang their ambush just as Hercules was prising up a particularly sizeable lump of asphalt. The Olympian's hands were full. He was preoccupied. A black-armoured figured zoomed in at blazing speed, a shadow in the arc-lights, and Hercules stumbled, dropping his burden. He cursed, and noticed that his arm hurt. He looked down and saw a gash in the bare skin of his right biceps, a wound that widened before his very eyes, exposing subcutaneous fat, then raw muscle, and then the shiny whiteness of bone.

Hercules roared, as much in indignation as pain. His biceps! His big, beautiful biceps! Ruined! He was proud of his physique. He knew how impressive his body looked. Many a young man had openly admired Hercules's naked self, gasped at those abs, run fascinated fingertips over those quads, and spent a long time in close-up, salivating appreciation of those fine dimpled glutes. But of his biceps muscles Hercules was particularly fond. They were superbly defined and, he thought, defined him superbly.

And now, somehow, one of them had been slashed through to the bone, all but cleaved in two.

Blood came, welling up like oil from the desert, filling the wound and brimming over.

"Hey big guy, you OK?" one of the workmen asked.

"I don't know," said Hercules. His brain was fuddled. He had no idea what was going on.

Then a shadow flitted towards him. A human figure. Something in its hand.

This time Hercules actually heard the wound being inflicted – heard the sound of his own skin being split, his own flesh being parted, a wet hiss, a slick unzipping of living tissue. It was presaged by a brief hum, which he had no way of identifying as the noise of an oscillo-knife, a Landesman-devised weapon whose razor-sharp 10-inch ceramic blade was given additional cutting power by means of 3,000-Hertz micro-pulses generated by a compact vibrational unit in the hilt. To this knife, any substance up to and including solid concrete was butter. Flesh, even the extraordinarily dense and durable bodily tissue of the godling, presented no obstacle.

The second wound was to Hercules's left flank, just below the ribs. A third caught him on the calf, narrowly missing severing his Achilles tendon. The shadow figures were coming in from all directions. They criss-crossed him like cars around a police officer directing traffic at an intersection. His back was raked. His left pectoral was sliced. Hercules turned this way and that, snarling spittle and spite.

"Slow down, you fuckers!" he railed. "Slow down so I can see you! Stop and fight like men!"

He got his wish.

One of the shadows decelerated to a halt in front of him, going from vague blur to solid three-dimensionality. Hercules saw a man sheathed in protective gear, helmed, visored, with a pump-action shotgun in his hands.

"Who," he growled, "the fuck are you?"

The armoured man pursed his lips as though in sympathy. "Bleeding pretty badly there, mate," he said in an Australian accent. "Of course, it's nothing Demeter couldn't fix. Only, your healer Sheila's not going to get here in time."

Hercules eyed the shotgun contemptuously. "You can't kill me with *that*."

"Reckon? Maybe, maybe not. But I bet this'll hurt heaps."

The shotgun belched. The skin was flayed from Hercules's right trapezius. The Olympian staggered but stayed upright. He was dimly aware of the workmen, who only moments earlier had been looking on with pleasure as he did their job for them, running away now as fast as they could, hightailing it out of there, ditching their hardhats and high-viz vests to lighten the load.

Another shotgun round shredded Hercules's other, treasured biceps.

"I'll kill you," he snarled at his assailant. "Fucking strangle you with my bare hands until your head pops off like a champagne cork."

"Vivid image," said the Australian. "Shame neither of your arms is working properly any more."

"Then I'll chew your head off with my teeth."

"Yeah, yeah. I had a brother, you know. Malcolm was his name. Malc."

"So?"

"Lived in Sydney. You killed him with a car. You don't even know you did, but you did."

"Do you think I care?"

"I think you do now."

Hercules's laugh was a caustic croak. "All you mortals are so feeble, so frail. You're like strands of spun sugar, and I am a hammer. I break you. It can't be helped. I brush past you and you crumble. I'm used to it. So should you be."

"'I break you'? This from the fella who's being cut to ribbons."

"Even like this," Hercules said, "I can pulverise you."

"Come on then, you big beardy shirt-lifter. Come and have a go."

The Olympian let out an enraged "Gnaaarrrhhh!" and lurched forwards as emphatically as his mutilated body would allow – which wasn't a lot. He was hit by yet another shotgun round, he had no clear sense where, he hurt all over so one further source of pain did not much make of a difference, it was one amongst a chorus of screaming voices – and then his target vanished from view.

After that, Hercules found himself on his knees in the broken roadway. He was howling in helpless fury, a baited bear hounded by dogs. The black-clad figures swooped in again, again, again, cutting, cutting. He was being made an example of. He was being made to suffer. Crucified. Tears sprang to his eyes. The injustice of it. His blood soaked the shattered asphalt around him. Genteel Gramercy Park had a new sound to keep it awake, the keening wail of a beleaguered, dying demigod.

And then one final, muffled shotgun blast brought hush.

44. AMBUSHING THE AMBUSHERS

Shortly before the op commenced, the latest mythoporn extravaganza showing on Blue Eros came to a climax. *Perve-seus And His Winged Stallion Poke-ass-horse* exhaustively documented the sexual permutations that could be achieved between man and equine, and in one scene extended the range by having the pair copulate while in flight, although cheaply rendered special effects and the patently fake pair of wings tacked onto the horse's back somewhat diminished the boundary-stretching majesty of the moment.

The movie was playing on one screen in mission control at Bleaney while the other screens were dedicated to the visor-cam feeds from the five Titans who were lying in wait in various places of concealment all round the site of the roadwork. Ramsay was trying to pay attention to the op-in-progress but kept finding himself drawn to the filmic bestiality, then repelled by it, then drawn, then repelled, over and over. His expression was at times so incredulous that his face looked as if it was melting and sliding downwards.

"Fuck," he breathed as the final credits rolled and, in yet another Pyrrhic victory for low-budget CGI, Perve-seus and mount soared off unconvincingly into the sunset. "I mean, Jesus. That was some sick, sick shit."

"I don't know, looked like true love to me," said Patanjali. "Of course, if you were that offended, Rick, you could always have asked me to change channels."

"I guess I thought I was broadening my horizons or some such, but now all I've got is a vision of a man drinking horse spunk stuck in my head."

"All right, quiet, people," said Sam. "It's started."

Much of the visor imagery was an unintelligible muddle, the Titans travelling too fast and their motion too shaky for the cameras to cope with. Time and again there were glimpses of Hercules flitting in and out of view at the corner of a screen as everybody took their turns with their oscillo-knives, Coeus then Phoebe then Rhea then Cronus, in a well-choreographed sequence. Iapetus had his moment of face-to-face confrontation, delivering shotgun rounds to Hercules's shoulder, arm and finally groin, and then the darting knife attacks resumed. The Titans were whittling the Olympian down. It was the only way to tackle an opponent so physically powerful – swift harrying strikes that gradually and increasingly disabled, like fighter planes strafing a dreadnought. Hercules tried to lash out at his assailants. On several occasions his blows nearly connected, but he was slowed down and made clumsy by the knife slashes, hamstrung, and he was flailing rather than fighting, and anyway at full speed the Titans were all but unhittable targets.

At last he was entirely helpless. On his knees, still somehow upright, but sagging. His lion-skin cloak tattered and dripping with blood. Unable to lift his limbs. Scarcely able to hold his head up. Once more he became a steady central object in Iapetus's visor-cam, as Barrington approached him, shotgun to the fore.

"Sorry now, you lousy mongrel?"

Hercules's brimming eyes suggested he was, if only for himself. The tears mingled with the blood spatters on his cheeks, turning from clear to pink as they trickled down.

"The other... Olympians," he gasped. "My family. They... will kill you. All... of you."

"Maybe," said Iapetus. "But you won't be around to see it."

He lodged the end of the shotgun barrel between Hercules's teeth.

"I'd ask if you have any last requests, Herc," he said, "but I can see you've got a gobful. Just the way you like it."

"Do it, Dez," Sam muttered, off-mic. "Enough tormenting. Get it over with."

"My brother was worth a hundred of you," Iapetus declared, and squeezed the trigger.

Hercules's cheeks were lit up from within like a jack-o'-lantern. Then his face seemed to collapse in on itself. His eyes bulged dumbly. His body slumped.

"There you go, Malc," Iapetus said softly. "She'll be right. Rest easy, mate."

The other four Titans joined him beside Hercules's lifeless body.

"Good work, one and all," said Cronus. "Iapetus, I trust you're pleased."

"Ripper, boss. Couldn't be happier."

"Then we should think about making tracks." Cronus's visor-cam viewpoint swept from one end of the street to the other. The roadway was deserted, as were the sidewalks, but faces were visible in almost every lit window overlooking the scene. "Before we attract any more attention."

"Fair go."

"We rendezvous at –"

"All Titans." This was Sam, into the mic. "Look north. I think I just saw…"

The visor-cam images all swung in the same direction.

All showed that something was coming.

A man.

Fast as a car.

Sam had spotted him appearing round the corner at the far end of the street, just as Cronus had been turning to look the other way. Cronus had missed him but she hadn't.

Loincloth. Winged sandals. Winged metal helmet. Staff with a pair of snakes wrapped around it.

Hermes, brandishing his caduceus.

None of the Titans had time to move, or even to cry out.

Then the visor-cam image from Coeus spun, showing brown night-time city sky, buildings, ground, sky, buildings, ground, until it finally settled on just sky, with blobs superimposed on it, splashes of something ink-dark and wet...

"*Scheisse*," Phoebe hissed. "*Sein Kopf. Sein verdammter Kopf!*"

"Go!" Sam yelled.

"His head..." said Iapetus, numb, aghast. "Clean off."

"Go!" Sam repeated. "He'll be coming back for another of you. It *is* a trap. Go! Split up! Run! As fast as you bloody can – run!"

45. RUN

THE FOUR TITANS scattered, Iapetus northward, Cronus, Phoebe and Rhea west. At the first intersection they came to, Cronus and Phoebe continued west while Rhea turned south. All four of them used road as well as sidewalk, slaloming between people and cars, going wherever a gap presented itself. Pedestrians yelled in protest as they were accidentally bumped into or barged aside. Drivers slammed on the brakes and honked their horns as black-clad figures shot by in front of them. Taillights flashed. Headlights flashed. Some very ripe language erupted in each Titan's wake, as if they were farmers sowing quick-sprouting seeds of profanity. For every person who was alarmed or startled to see an armoured, paramilitary-looking figure rushing past at astonishing speed, there were ten who were simply annoyed or indignant.

"Hey, asshole, go shoot your goddamn sci-fi movie somewhere else!" "Extreme sports is California, dude!" "Fuck you, buddy!"

New York.

"Where is he?" Cronus yelled. "Where's Hermes now?"

"No idea," Iapetus replied. "Bastard's got to be chasing one of us."

"Somebody look over their shoulder."

"Not me, mate. Too busy running. At this speed I've got to concentrate on where I'm going, or – shit! See? Nearly hit a mailbox just talking to you."

"Peripheral expansion mode," said Sam. "All of you."

"It's even harder to run in a straight line when that's on," said Rhea.

"Just do it. Keep looking forwards, blinker out the rest. I'll be the eyes in the back of your head."

One after another the visor-cam images jumped into warped widescreen. Buildings on either side ballooned from the vanishing point then tapered off again to the edges. Parked vehicles, railings, front doorsteps, shop windows, passers-by – everything swelled and shrank away as though viewed through a crystal ball travelling rapidly a few feet off the ground.

A quick scan of the screens told Sam all she needed to know.

On the far right-hand side of the feed from Cronus, and the far left-hand side of Phoebe's, there was a tiny, pale shape in motion. Sam could make out arms pumping, legs flickering, the gleam of streetlights reflecting off a shiny silvery helmet.

"Cronus, Phoebe, it's you. He's on your tail."

"Dammit!" Cronus spat. "Dammit all to hell!"

"Just keep going, both of you. You can outrun him."

"No, we can't," said Cronus. He was breathing heavily already, and Phoebe had begun panting hard, perhaps in panic. "Hermes has a top speed of well over fifty. We can barely manage forty."

"The suit goes faster the faster you go. Pour it on. Run flat out. *Sprint*."

Cronus and Phoebe accelerated. Their tachometer readings crept up above 40 mph. 45, 46, 47...

But Hermes was still gaining.

"Why doesn't he just teleport ahead?" Ramsay wondered.

"He can't do both at once," Patanjali replied. "It's not safe for him. He can only teleport from a standing start. Otherwise, when he reappears his stored momentum could carry him slap-bang into a brick wall or whatever and splatter him to pieces."

"And that would be a shame."

"Quite."

"Base, I'm going to double back." It was Iapetus. "I've got a lock on their whereabouts. Maybe I can intercept."

To Patanjali, Sam said, "Where's the GPS map? Why's it not up? Pull it up."

"No sooner said than done," the computer programmer said, and did.

A blue-on-black street map of Manhattan winked into life, with four moving red dots tracking the four Titans' positions.

"All right, Iapetus, try," Sam said into the mic. "Judging by your relative locations, I don't think they should count on you making it, though. Cronus, Phoebe," she continued. "I have you headed along West Eighteenth Street. You've just crossed Sixth Avenue. Now, if you continue on that course, you're going to run out of city and hit the Hudson River in a couple of minutes."

Cronus groaned.

"No, it's all right. Just listen. You can't attempt evasive manoeuvres yet. All the turns here are right-angles and you can't afford to slow down as much as you need to in order to take one without wiping out. Hermes will catch up for certain if you do. But once you hit the edge of the island there's an expressway, the, er, the West Side Highway it's called, also known as the Joe DiMaggio Highway. There's bound to be sliproads onto that, or some kind of broader junction to help you get on it without decelerating too much. It'll give you more room to run and a bit of breathing space. At some point, though, you're going to have to stop and turn and make a stand."

"Hermes is too fast a target for us to –"

"No, Cronus, *listen*. This is not negotiable. This is just how it's going to be. I know we weren't planning on dealing with Hermes today, which is why no one's packing the relevant armaments. Yes, he's fast, he can teleport... but his only tactical weapon is that caduceus of his, and it's only useful at close quarters. You two have guns – long-range capability. That's your edge, and it's going to make all the difference. It's going to save your necks. So keep moving, keep running. I don't care how tired you're feeling, how much your legs ache or your lungs hurt. You can do this. Phoebe? Do you read me?"

"I read you," Phoebe said, between gasps.

"I'm going to get you through this, both of you, I promise. Your side of the deal is simply to keep listening to me and do exactly as I say."

She covered the mic with her hand.

"Fuck. How *am* I going to get them through this?"

"You're doing great, Sam," Ramsay said. He was reaching out to touch her, but remembered himself in time. "Stay with it. Don't lose your nerve."

"But look at him." Hermes was less than 50 metres to Cronus's and Phoebe's rear, although distances were hard to judge in the fish-eye distortion of peripheral expansion. "And Kerstin's flagging. Her speed's dropping."

"Keep talking to them. That's what they need the most – your voice, telling them to be cool, everything's OK. If they lose it, they're gone."

"Base, Rhea. Anything I can do?"

"Hold on, Rhea, let me think. Yes. Sorry, but I want you to go back to Gramercy Park and retrieve Coeus's body. It's not the pleasantest task but it has to be done, and now, before someone else gets to it. I'd be surprised if Hermes is the only Olympian in New York at the moment."

"Roger, base. I'm on it."

"Base, we've just passed... Ninth Avenue, I think," said Cronus. "How much further to the... expressway?"

"Quarter of a mile. Less."

"I'm really... getting winded."

"You're fine. You and Phoebe, you're both staying ahead of him. Although, Phoebe, you might want to pick up the pace a fraction."

There was no reply from Phoebe beyond rasping ins and outs of breath, but her tachometer registered a slight uptick in speed. Other readouts indicated that her suit's battery life was down to 25% and the servos were hotting up, although their temperature remained within tolerable levels for now.

Her visor-cam showed Cronus in front of her, to her left, and Hermes now just a few paces behind her. Hermes ran with all the lean, sinewy grace of a top-flight athlete, the scissoring of his arms and legs sublimely co-ordinated, no part of him moving a millimetre further than it needed to. He seemed a thing designed to be at speed, furnished for it by nature, like a cheetah – biomechanical perfection. Every joint, every muscle, every tendon meshed precisely and for just one purpose: to propel him forwards, fast, without fail. It was something Sam couldn't help but admire even as she loathed the lethal intent behind it. The wild fixity in Hermes's eyes as he inexorably shaved the distance between him and his quarry, the bared, clenched teeth, the rhythmic flaring of his nostrils – these all spoke of a man who had never come second in a race and of a predator who was never unable to overtake his prey. Hermes the Luck-Bearer. Hermes the Ready Helper. Closing in.

Up ahead a four-lane road appeared, traversing 18th Street diagonally.

"That's it," Sam said. "The intersection. Take a right when you get there. It's a less sharp turn than left."

Traffic was flowing smoothly across from 18th Street. The lights were in the two Titans' favour. Everything was looking good, until they actually reached the intersection. At that moment green went to red, and WALK became DON'T WALK.

"Don't stop!"

Cronus burst onto the crosswalk just as vehicles on either side of him started to roll. He swung right in a wide arc which took him out past the median strip and head-on into the southbound traffic on the expressway. Luckily for him, it hadn't properly got going yet. He was able to insert himself between the two near-stationary queues and start to build up speed again.

Phoebe was not so fortunate. Coming to the intersection a couple of seconds later meant she wound up in the midst of traffic that was revving away from the lights in both directions, drivers impatient to make up for the half-minute delay that being stuck on red had just cost them. She dodged around a bus, then tried to skirt a UPS truck but clipped its rear bumper, lost her footing and went into a skid. From nowhere a yellow cab loomed.

The *karrrump!* of impact nearly blew the speakers at Bleaney. Phoebe was sent sliding sideways across the asphalt, making helpless gurgling and grunting sounds as she went. She came to rest some ten metres from the yellow cab. Her visor now had a crack across it but was still functioning, giving a view of the world canted at an acute angle.

The traffic halted. Sam watched the cabbie, a turbaned Sikh, get out. Looking infuriated, he went to inspect the front of his car. The radiator grille was stove in, the bumper deeply dented, the bonnet crumpled like a piece of half-finished origami. He cursed, then straightened up and started rubbing the back of his neck. Either he'd suffered whiplash or he'd been in the taxi trade long enough to know that, in the event of an accident, it was vital to feign the injury for the benefit of witnesses, so that any later claim for compensation or sick leave would look authentic. Only then, after he had taken care of these important formalities, did he think to check up on the person he had just run into with his cab.

"Phoebe," Sam said as the cabbie strode over to her, still busy with his neck rubbing. "Phoebe, you have to get up. You have to move. Phoebe! Do you read me? Over."

Phoebe gave a groan. "*Ich bin...* I'm OK."

"Good. Now on your feet. I don't know where Hermes is, but –"

She saw the cabbie falter in mid-stride, then start backing away. Hermes stepped into view at one corner of the screen. The peripheral expansion distended him, making him seem a giant – huge legs, narrowing torso, pin-sized head.

"Oh God, he's behind you, Phoebe, he's right behind you, right there..."

Shakily, Phoebe tried to rise. Hermes, with an almost solicitous air, extended one hand and helped her up, turning her around as he did so.

"He's touching her so he can teleport with her," Patanjali said. "Shit, he'll take her somewhere, anywhere. Olympus. They'll make her talk. She'll tell them everything."

"Phoebe, you can't let yourself be taken captive," Sam said. "You've got to get away."

The visor-cam image shuddered. Phoebe was reaching for a weapon. She pulled the pistol attached to her hip but Hermes swatted it from her grasp with his caduceus.

"Not quick enough on the draw," he told her, smirking. "And you never will be. To me, everybody moves in slow motion, and so clumsily, like an arthritic tortoise. So, out with it. Who are you, you people with your weapons and your fancy armour? What's your game here?"

"Our game is killing you, *Schwanzlutscher*," Phoebe replied.

"Ha!" exclaimed Hermes. He might not have known the German for *cocksucker* but, given how she'd spoken the word, no translation was necessary. Then, suddenly, Phoebe's head jolted from side to side, the visor image flipping crazily. Hermes was hitting her in the face with the flat of his caduceus, the blows coming as fast as a string of firecrackers popping.

"Cronus," Sam said. "Phoebe is in serious trouble. Turn back and help her."

No reply. Cronus kept on running north along the West Side Highway.

"I'm nearly there," said Iapetus, but his transponder told a different story. He was somewhere up past Madison Square Garden and still had a mile to go. It would take him at best a minute and a half to get to Phoebe. Far too long.

"Well, my little German hellion," Hermes was saying to Phoebe, "we'll find out all about you soon enough. Let's go on a trip to meet my kin, shall we? My great-aunt Aphrodite will get to work on you, and when she's done with you and you've spilled every secret you have she'll hand you over to my cousin Ares – a little gift to her lover. Likes a mortal woman now and then, does Ares, though I should warn you, he can get rather rough. Doesn't always know his own strength, if you know what I mean."

"Cronus!" Sam tried again, urgency fraying her voice.

"Maybe he can't hear," Ramsay said. "I hope to God that's it."

"Few mortals get the privilege of travelling with me, *fräulein*," Hermes said. "One moment we're here, the next – blink! – somewhere else. I understand it can be unpleasant if you're not used to it and not an Olympian. You'll probably feel rather sick afterwards. But a small price to pay for the once-in-a-lifetime experience. Ready?"

He closed his eyes, summoning his concentration.

And that was when Phoebe struck.

She headbutted him, ramming the brow of her helmet onto the bridge of her nose. Hermes shrieked, and blood spurted from his nostrils. He didn't let go, however. He blinked, and then in retaliation he started to hammer at Phoebe's helmet with his caduceus again.

The blows coming rattlingly fast, like hail on a roof. Phoebe, it seemed, was helpless, with no choice but to endure the attack. But then Sam heard, distinctly even though it was a tiny sound amid all the commotion, the metallic *tink* of the pin being pulled from a grenade.

"Kerstin..." she sighed. Resigned. Knowing there was nothing she could do, and nothing else Phoebe could do.

Hermes ceased battering her. His nose had begun to swell, and a slick of blood coated his mouth and jaw.

"That really hurt, and it's going to cost you, bitch. One teleport? How about twenty? You'll be puking yourself inside out by the time we're done."

There was a blizzard of onscreen static, and then Olympian and Titan were on a high hilltop somewhere, perhaps New Zealand. Lush grassland below. Pasture, with maggot-sized sheep.

Another blizzard of static.

They were in a desert. Copper-coloured sand dunes. Magnesium-flare sun.

More static.

An icy waste. A howling wind. Endless whiteness. Bleached blue sky.

And all Sam could think was, *The grenade. He doesn't know.*

Static.

Some city. Not New York. The other side of the world. Broad daylight. A dusty marketplace. Vendors yelling. Flies swarming over foodstuffs. India?

Static.

A rainforest. Liquid jungle sounds.

And then a burst of sharp light.

And then just static. Constant sizzling static, filling the screen from edge to edge.

46. THE MYRMIDON PROTOCOL

"BASE, IAPETUS. Is Phoebe...?"

"Just get to the rendezvous point, Iapetus," Sam said, voice sick and weary. "There's nothing you can do now."

"Shit."

"Base, Rhea. What happened?"

"Phoebe's gone. But I think she might have taken Hermes with her."

"For sure?"

"Don't know. Looks that way."

"Coeus *and* her. My God."

"I know."

"Then I don't suppose more bad news is going to make any difference." Rhea was speaking in hushed tones. "I'm back at Gramercy Park. Can you see what I'm seeing?"

Sam could. Coeus's decapitated body lay where it had fallen, the head nearby still staring skyward, not far from Hercules's remains – and standing over the Titan's corpse, with their backs to Rhea, were three Olympians. Rhea was some way off from them, lurking in the shadow of an awning of the kind the smarter New York apartment blocks often had outside their front entrances. Nevertheless, even at a distance, Sam had no trouble identifying Zeus, Poseidon and high-helmed Athena.

"Please don't tell me you want me to engage, base."

"Of course not. Get out of there, and try not to be seen."

"Roger that."

As Rhea loped away from the scene, sirens could be heard honking and caterwauling in the background. Blue and red light splashed off building façades to the rear of her.

"Cronus, base. Come in, Cronus," Sam said.

"Cronus here."

"Phoebe is down. Do you copy?"

His pace was slowing. He knew already. "I gathered."

"Were you aware that I asked you to go and help?"

"I... I must have missed that. I was running so hard – I assumed she was still with me."

Sam hesitated. No, this was not a conversation they should have on air. Later. In person. Alone. It would wait.

"Understood, Cronus. Make rendezvous as soon as you can."

"We got two of them, base," Cronus said. "That's not bad going for a day's work."

"Only one of the kills is confirmed," Sam replied. "And they've got Coeus's body."

"Yes, about that. Here's what you'll need to do. Implement the Myrmidon Protocol."

"The what?"

"One of you there knows what I'm referring to."

Baffled looks from Sam and Ramsay were met with a not so baffled look from Patanjali.

The IT wizard shifted uncomfortably in his seat. "Before I say anything else, it wasn't my idea. It's nothing to do with me. I didn't come up with it, I just made it possible."

"What is the Myrmidon Protocol, Rajesh?" Sam demanded.

"It's, er... It's preset remote reprogramming of the battlesuit nanotech. We send a command signal to the bots that reassigns their function from defence and camouflage to, um, to a process of intromittent erasure."

"In English," said Ramsay.

"Basically? We turn them into eating machines. They consume their way through everything they come into contact with for a period of exactly five minutes, self-replicating as they go, making new bots that are also eating machines. 'Everything' means battlesuit structure, weapons and, um, other stuff. Then, when time's up, they deactivate and go inert. They turn into a big heap of grey goop."

"It's a self-destruct mechanism," Sam said.

"In layman's terms, yes."

"In anyone's terms."

"And the body," said Ramsay. "Anders's body. That gets eaten too."

"Superficially," said Patanjali. "Enough to make identification difficult, if not impossible. It's pretty brilliant, really. Don't you agree?" Their faces told him they didn't. "In a cold-hearted way. I mean, obviously, from a certain viewpoint it could seem kind of callous. But to repurpose the nanobots like that – inspired. They become like ants, submicroscopic ants, munching their way through their environment. Myrmidons were a band of mythical Greek soldiers, led by Achilles. It's in the *Iliad*. Their armour made them look like ants. Myrmex – that's Ancient Greek for ant. Hence the..."

He trailed off.

"This is a problem for you, isn't it?"

"Damn straight it's a problem," said Ramsay. "You haven't been wearing those battlesuits. We have. And all along there's been a self-destruct mechanism in there no one told us about?"

"You weren't told about it," said Cronus, "because it's intended to be used only under these precise circumstances, when a Titan dies and his or her suit is about to fall into enemy hands. And the protocol needs to be implemented right now, for Coeus. That is an order."

"Just hold on a moment here..." Ramsay began.

"*Now*, base," Cronus snapped. "We can discuss the ethics of all this another time, if we must, but the protocol has to be put into effect while Coeus's suit remains more or less intact. Should the Olympians start dismantling it, the command signal could fail. You know what to do."

This was directed at Patanjali, who immediately opened an onscreen window, tapped in a password, and waited for a prompt to appear.

Myrmidon Protocol – Callsign: Coeus
Execute?
Yes   Cancel

The "Yes" was highlighted. Patanjali hit Enter, and up popped the inevitable precautionary message:

Are you sure?
Yes   Cancel

Again, the "Yes" was highlighted. Patanjali's finger hovered over Enter. He looked at Sam. With her lips pressed together so hard that they whitened, she nodded. Patanjali hit the key, and a timer appeared, counting down from 5:00, while a message came up saying "Myrmidon Protocol sequence active" and a hollow percentile bar gradually filled up from left to right with a strip of black. Rhea was no longer on-site to transmit a visual, so there was no way of seeing the reactions of the three Olympians as Coeus's battlesuit and its wearer began to disintegrate before their very eyes. Via the feed from Coeus's helmet, however, Sam heard Athena gasp softly in sudden amazement and say, "What's that? It's starting to... dissolve?" Then one of the two male Olympians, almost certainly

Zeus, advised stepping back from the body just in case. Moments later the audio stuttered and hissed, then went silent. The visual – still that view of nocturnal New York sky, which Anders Søndergaard's own eyes were past taking in – persisted a little while longer, becoming overlaid with tiny white scratch-marks, as though filaments of spider silk were falling across it.

"The bots," said Patanjali. "Eating into the visor."

Soon the scratch-marks were so numerous and so densely packed together that the image was almost wholly opaque. And then the nanobots must have chewed through a connection, as Coeus's screen abruptly went static-filled, like Phoebe's.

The timer ticked down to 0:00, the percentile bar was black from end to end, and a message announced "Myrmidon Protocol sequence complete."

It was midnight, GMT.

Not much later, the first live news broadcasts started coming in.

NYC's Night Of Chaos.

Manhattan Under Siege.

Gramercy Park Horror.

Hercules Dead, Hermes Missing.

Olympians In The Firing Line.

For Sam, the one abiding image out of the multiplicity of on-the-spot reports was not, as it was for many, footage of a forensics unit from the FBI examining the mutilated carcass of Hercules. Nor was it Athena pontificating to a reporter, with great gravitas, on the nature of the people who had the sheer gall to murder an Olympian in full public view in one of the busiest cities in the world – an Olympian, moreover, who was engaged in helping the inhabitants of that selfsame city.

No, what struck home for Sam was a brief, long-lens shot of two piles of grey dust in the road, one roughly the size and shape of a headless body, the other of a head. As a breeze caught the dust, some of it blew away, exposing blood-smeared bone beneath – a part of Søndergaard that the nanobots hadn't had time to consume.

When, shortly before dawn, she crawled into bed with Ramsay, she asked him to hold her. That was all. Just hold her.

She felt cold, cold to the marrow, and thought she might never feel warm again.

47. MEDIA PASTE

THE WORLD'S MEDIA gorged on the events in New York for days afterward, chewing over each and every morsel then regurgitating and chewing it over again, until what was left was a paste of facts, opinions and suppositions so thin and watery as to be almost devoid of nutritional content. There remained, however, a few gristly segments which no amount of intellectual mastication could break down to a palatable consistency. How, first and foremost, had the slayers of Hercules been able to kill him? How had they come by weapons capable of harming a demigod? And how could they move at such speed? Then there was the matter of Hermes. Where was he? Was he alive or dead? And, although he had come to Hercules's rescue, could he not have arrived sooner? For that matter, how was it that Zeus, Poseidon and Athena had turned up in Gramercy Park shortly after Hercules was killed? Their presence in New York that night seemed to imply they'd suspected an attempt was going to be made on his life. If so, couldn't they have taken steps to prevent it?

The awkward questions would not go away, and so Zeus agreed to guest on America's top-rated daytime chatshow, with Hera, to set the record straight.

The show's hostess, Paulita Dominguez, started out deferential, as you did with the Olympians, liberally deploying their godly epithets – Zeus the Sign-Giving, Hera the White-Armed, Zeus the Far-Seeing, Hera the Purple-Belted, and so forth. The longer the interview went on, though, the bolder and more pugnacious she became. Neither Zeus nor Hera, side by side on a tasteful beige leather sofa on a set decked out to look like someone's living room, seemed to be giving her acceptable answers. Zeus spoke of unfortunate timing. He said he had had an inkling that Hercules might be a target for these people – these "scuttling cockroaches," as he called them – but had had no idea they would be quite so audacious as to attack him out in the open, with eyewitnesses on hand. No sooner had it become apparent that Hercules was in difficulties then Hermes had raced to the scene, but, fast though he was, he had arrived too late to do anything except punish the perpetrators.

"He could have teleported," Paulita suggested.

"Yes, a good point," Zeus replied, "but you see, he wasn't sure where Hercules was. That is to say, he thought he was somewhere but in fact he was... well, not there, but somewhere else."

He appeared to be floundering. Hera leapt in. "What my husband is trying to say, Miss Dominguez, is that there were too many variables. Hermes didn't believe he could teleport in safely. He thought it better to come in running, so that he could assess the situation as he approached."

In general, Zeus's performance on *Paulita* was uncharacteristically listless and unconfident. Hera did most of the talking, and kept trying to divert the hostess from confrontational lines of questioning towards a more personal, domestic agenda.

"I'm sure the audience here and your viewers at home want to hear how we're dealing with our shock and grief back on Olympus," she said at one point, and at another said, "I'd prefer to be discussing Hercules's legacy, not his death but his life. Hercules was my stepson but like a son to me. A wayward one, but lively and loveable in spite of it." And on the subject of Hermes: "We hold out hope that he will find his way home safe and sound. My heart aches to think about a stepson – another stepson of mine – lying somewhere, in a remote corner of the earth, injured, perhaps in great pain. Argus is searching high and low for signs of him, and we pray for his return."

"Pray?" said Paulita, intrigued. "Who exactly does an Olympian pray to?"

"Figure of speech," said Hera.

"Are you scared?" This was Paulita's closing question. The floor manager was making winding-up motions, while in the production gallery they were telling her over her earpiece to reel the interview in. There was a sense of disappointment in the air. This edition of the show hadn't turned out to be as riveting as everyone had hoped. Paulita had one last chance to dredge up some TV gold.

"Scared?" said Hera as though unfamiliar with the word, let alone the concept.

"Of these people, these paramilitaries, these terrorists, whatever you care to call them. They've killed most of your monsters. They've killed at least one of you, maybe even two. All I'm saying is, if I were you, I'd be at least a little nervous about stepping foot outside Mount Olympus now."

This roused Zeus from his torpor. "But you are *not* us, woman," he thundered. "You are mortal, prone to insecurity. You know fear all the time, whether it's fear of your ratings slipping or of people thinking you're fat, or most of all the deep-down fear that you're hideously overpaid for doing a job that a trained monkey could do, and better, what's more. You are a seething mass of anxieties and inadequacies, and I am not. I am king of the Pantheon and I fear nothing and no one!"

Then, having insulted his hostess, although Paulita's desperate grin tried to convey that her skin was thick enough to take it, Zeus found a camera, gazed deep into the lens, and said, "Above all, not *you*. I am not scared of *you*. I know who you are now, and I will tell you this. '*Mai phunai ton hapanta nika logon.*'"

On the next news bulletin on the same channel, an Associate Professor of Classics and Ancient Mediterranean Studies at Harvard was consulted. He claimed he could identify the quotation. It was

Sophocles, *Oedipus At Colonus*, a line from the antistrophe to one of the later Chorus interludes, and it translated as "Not to be born is, past all prizing, best" – although, the distinguished academic added somewhat archly, Zeus's pronunciation of Ancient Greek left something to be desired.

The significance of the quotation was much debated in newspaper columns and on TV and radio discussion programmes. It was generally agreed that Zeus had simply been threatening his opponents. *When I'm finished with you*, he'd been implying, *you'll wish you'd never been born*. No deeper interpretation of it was needed than that, or could be divined.

Meanwhile, the great vox pop that was the internet spoke. From habit, it spoke guardedly. Argus was the ever-present ear at the door, the ever-present eye at the keyhole, and a careless comment, a blog entry or chatroom post that was overtly anti-Pantheonic, might lead to unwelcome consequences. Argus could smash a website to pieces, reducing it to a shambles of corrupted code with one of his unstoppable, sledgehammer viruses. He could crash servers and wipe hard drives. And a persistent offender could expect something much worse – a knock at the front door, a personal visit from an Olympian for a terrifying "polite word."

Still, there were ways to state your true feelings that didn't automatically alert the Hundred-Eyed One, or at the worst would result in the relatively mild rebuke of him blocking out the offending comment with his icon – a peacock in full tailfeather display – accompanied by a pro forma warning: *I am watching*. For instance, a set of nicknames had been devised for the Olympians that were so banal as to be unobtrusive. Zeus was "Jerry," Hera was "Jane," Ares "Joe," Apollo "Jack," Artemis "Jill," and so on, meaning that those in the know could write about them in a derogatory or defamatory fashion without fear of censure. Argus had not cottoned on to that particular ruse, the J-Series Cipher.

Nor did he seem to be in on any of the Olympian-uncomplimentary acronyms that were doing the rounds, such as WADWAH (Weak As Dionysus With A Hangover, usually used in reference to a bad joke or a movie that failed to meet up to expectations), MHB (My Hercules's Bitch, a favourite among online gamers, as in "I'm going to beat you at this level and make you MHB"), and LLH (Lame Like Hephaestus, something shoddy or inadequate being compared to that Olympian's physical disability).

Other acronyms were less humorous, less widespread, and more specific in their aim. They were the online equivalent of a Freemasons' handshake, a method of sounding out whether an e-correspondent was a fellow traveller on the path of anti-Pantheonism. These included DODO (Dump Olympians, Destroy Olympus) and GMA! (Gods My Ass/Arse!). Slip one of them into the "conversation" and pretty soon you would know whether you were in sympathetic company or not. The Agonides resorted to them frequently, and Argus remained ignorant of their meaning.

On the internet a broad consensus was developing. The Olympians were, for the first time ever, looking vulnerable. Their iron grip was loosening. The perch they sat on, which for so many years had seem so lofty as to be unassailable, now seemed as though it might be within reach, since someone had managed to knock a couple of them off it.

The doubters had, for once, real fuel for their scepticism. The pessimists were converting to the church of optimism. The cynics were laughing. The scoffers were turning serious. Could this be it? The beginning of the end? Was the closing chapter in the saga of Pantheonic rule being written?

"Jerry was LLH on *Paulita*," ran a typical post. "The J's don't know what's hit them," ran another. "Whoever the guys in the super-suits are, they're MHB-ing the Pantheon," was a common refrain.

More and more, the New Labours of Hercules were coming to be regarded as a cheap ploy by Zeus, a bid for public kudos, an attempt to save some face by winning hearts and minds. It was almost taken as read, now, that Poseidon must have been behind the Staten Island Ferry near-disaster, and some were speculating whether the 25-foot alligator in the New York sewers hadn't just been planted there for Hercules to find. That 'gator was a kind of monster, after all, and the Olympians knew a thing or two about monsters, did they not? It stood to reason.

As for Hercules himself, a certain grudging pity was in evidence. "Jessie," as he was dubbed in J-Series Cipher, was judged to have been a patsy in the whole affair. Zeus had dangled him out there in front of the noses of the monster killers, setting him up as their first Olympian target. They'd taken the bait, and all along Hercules had been oblivious, innocently obeying Zeus's orders, until out of the blue the attack had come. "Jim," a.k.a. Hermes, was never meant to have arrived in time to save him. Zeus had, in other words, sacrificed Hercules in the hope of killing or capturing one or more of the enemy in exchange. Herc the Jerk was a perennial embarrassment for the Olympians. His death was no real loss to "Jerry." Get rid of him, get rid of some of the opposition at the same time – two birds with one stone, win-win, all that. Only, the scheme had backfired, and "Jim" was now MIA. One of the Pantheon's major assets, gone. Little wonder "Jerry" had been in such a grump on the chatshow. He'd made a bold play, and the other team had spanked him.

So ran the sentiment within humankind's electronic collective consciousness, and whether the internet shaped or only reflected the mood out there in the real world, its users were certainly becoming more strident in their views, more daring, more willing to stick their necks out and say what they thought. There was a fever building. The Titans, though no one apart from them knew yet that that was their name, had started the infection, and now it was incubating nicely, replicating, spreading. At last it seemed possible that Pantheonic rule was finite. The future wasn't going to be just year after year of the same old arrogant tyranny, the same old squirming submission.

A tantalising prospect. No more Olympians. If everyone could just get together, following the example of those unknown champions in their strange high-tech armour. If ordinary people would just rise up. If national armies would just unite and march on Olympus. If, if, if...

And as the fever grew, the temperature online rising and the internet buzzing and thrumming with a febrile radical zeal, hardly anyone noticed a brief, anonymous email that was lodged in the Comments and Suggestions section of the British government's official website. Hardly anyone noticed because such emails were routinely discounted and discarded. The UK's leadership had little interest in learning what the common man had to say about the way it ran the country, and even less interest in putting any of the common man's ideas or proposals into practice. The civil servant whose daily chore it was to delete each of these missives didn't even glance twice at this particular one, despite it having as its subject heading the words "I KNOW WHERE OLIMPAN KILLERS R HIDING." All sorts of crazy people wrote in to parliament, and emailers were often the worst. They were the new green-ink brigade. "Disgusted" of wherever-it-was had access to a computer now and no qualms about bombarding those in power with whatever nonsense happened to percolate up in his or her pea-sized brain that day. The poor grammar, the capitals, the misspelling of Olympian, and the textspeak "R" all confirmed that this particular email was the work of yet another uneducated, semiliterate nutcase. The civil servant opened it, ignored the content, pressed Reply, pasted in the stock answer template – "The Prime Minister thanks you for your concern and will address the valid issue you raise as soon as time permits" – then Send, Delete, done. Next!

Someone did sit up and pay attention, however.

Argus.

The email snagged at the fringes of his awareness. His enormous, globe-spanning ether-self felt a tweak, a faint, distant niggling as some lexical filter or other that he had set up years ago probed the content of the communiqué and was made curious. With intangible tentacles the software plucked the email from oblivion, much like a librarian retrieving a tome from the basement or a truffle pig snuffling out a fungal delicacy in the depths of the forest, and brought it winging to the forefront of Argus's mind, for his closer attention. Thousands of operations like this occurred every hour of every day. Argus's life was a perpetual assessment of data, an unending sorting of the relevant from the irrelevant, the pertinent from the impertinent, the tolerable from the intolerable. He would sift everything down further and further until only the finest-graded stuff remained – the credible threats to Pantheonic control, the most insulting or seditious opinions given voice to, the matters that demanded immediate action. He would then inform Zeus, leaving it to the king of the Olympians to determine the appropriate response.

The email in question read:

DEAR MR CATSBEY BARTLET

 I CAN TELL U XACTLY WERE THESE PEOPLE R HANGING OUT IT WILL COST THOUGH, IM TALKING MABE A MILLION

"NUMBER 12"

It was the tone of it more than anything that temporarily arrested the billion-baud flow of Argus's thoughts – the certainty, the crude confidence, the cool sincerity. The sender of the email was either a fraudster with nerves of steel or someone with genuine insider intel.

Argus elected to take matters into his own hands, to a degree. Zeus was absent from Olympus at present. A face-to-face consultation would not be possible until his return, and the email merited, Argus felt, face-to-face. In the interim, he had authorisation to let the sender know that the Olympians themselves were taking an interest. It was standard procedure with potential informants. He despatched a peacock icon back along the filepath of the email. It pinged up in the sender's inbox.

Sitting at a terminal in an internet café in south-east London, Darren Pugh at first frowned. Then, as the full implications of the peacock icon dawned on him, his face broke into a broad, feral grin.

48. DETECTIVE WORK

AT ANOTHER TERMINAL, underground on Bleaney, Sam sat. Mahmoud sat beside her.

"You're sure about this?" Mahmoud said.

"I'm not sure about anything, Zaina," Sam replied. "All I know is, there's something Landesman's not been telling us. It's been nagging at me for a while. Little things here and there. Like when I was talking to Lillicrap and he used the word 'vendetta.' He tried to make out it was a slip of the tongue, but I don't think it was. And Landesman's behaviour on the whole. I don't buy the whole 'billionaire on a mission to save the world' bit, not any more."

"And this isn't just because you're pissed off with him, after New York?"

"Not just because of that, although I swear to God he knew Kerstin was in trouble and he didn't even think about turning back to go and help her. I'm also pissed off with him because he's been busy avoiding me ever since."

"Due to 'work commitments'?"

"What bloody work commitments? Being a Titan is his job now. What else does he have to do?"

"He still has a business to run. Daedalus Industries is still a going concern."

"Nothing he can't delegate," Sam said. "It's been three days. He's hiding from me. He knows it. I know it. And he knows I know."

"Maybe he's embarrassed. His first op as leader wasn't exactly a roaring success."

"Whatever. The point is, I'm convinced he's been holding out on us. It was watching Zeus on that programme with the chubby woman that clinched it for me."

"Paulita, chubby?"

"Don't you think so?"

"I'd describe her as healthy-looking. Latinas are always quite rounded anyway. Bit like Arab-ethnic women."

"You've got a great figure, Zaina. I'd kill to have boobs like yours."

"Bless you, duck."

"But, if I can get back to my argument..."

"Of course."

"I've lost my thread, actually."

"Zeus on *Paulita*."

"Oh yeah. You see, it set my cop instinct tingling."

"Cop instinct? Is that like Spider-Man's spider sense?"

"Almost identical."

"I'm not certain I ever had one. Don't you have to get bitten by a radioactive policeman?"

"Are you going to let me explain?"

"Sorry. This is making me nervous, and I gabble when I'm nervous." Mahmoud mimed buttoning her lip.

"Now, is that door locked?" They were in one of the facility's R and D labs, surrounded by electronics equipment, tools, components, and steel-frame shelves bearing mounds of microchips and snaky nests of fibre optic cable.

"No one's unlocked it since you asked me the same thing five minutes ago," Mahmoud said. "But I still don't see why all the secrecy. And why do you need *me* here?"

"For a second opinion. To confirm my hunch or else tell me I'm being a paranoid loon. And as for the secrecy, if I'm wrong then I'm wrong, and no harm done. But if I'm right, I don't want anyone else knowing yet. Not 'til I've decided what to do with the information. The *Paulita* clip, that'll be on YouTube, right?"

"I should imagine so."

Sam tapped keys. Broadband access was fast on Bleaney, for all the island's isolation. Patanjali had devised dozens of methods for boosting bandwidth and download speeds, such as installing powerful swap memory caches and ultrafast glass-based photonic circuits in most of the bunker's computers. Within seconds Sam was rerunning the moment at the end of the chatshow when Zeus had looked into the camera and rumbled his threat in Ancient Greek.

She played that segment of the clip a couple more times, studying it hard.

Then she said, "How old do you reckon Zeus is?"

"Some would say ancient. Thousands of years old."

Patiently: "How old would you say that man there on the screen is? How old does he look?"

"I don't know. Forties? Fifties?"

"It's the hair. It ages him. Silver hair like that – it can add at least a decade. A bushy white beard too. Look at his face. Look at it closely. His skin. No way is that the skin of a middle-aged man. That's the skin of someone in his thirties, I'd say."

"Maybe he has a good grooming regime. Moisturiser and that. Some men do, you know."

"Or maybe being an Olympian, having all that power, somehow keeps you looking young," said Sam. "But let's assume it doesn't. Let's assume Zeus isn't some perpetually ageless immortal. He's a bloke in his thirties whose style makes him look much older and who also acts like a much older person."

"So? Where are you going with this?"

"I'm going where my suspicions are dragging me. Now, next question. Does he remind you of anyone?"

"Who, Zeus?"

"Yes. Keep an open mind. Look at him talking there. His features. The way he holds himself. His mannerisms. Anyone at all?"

Mahmoud was nonplussed. "Er, no one as such. Who's that American actor, the one who always plays cowboys and bar owners and the like? Never without a cheroot. Name's on the tip of my tongue."

"I know the one you mean."

"Younger version of him. But it could be the hair again. They both have the same hair."

"Try to ignore the hair." Sam paused the clip. "There. That's a good shot. You really can't see it?"

Mahmoud placed her hands on the screen, cupping out Zeus's snowy-white locks. She squinted. "Nope, not ringing any bells."

"OK, let's try another tack." Sam opened up a new tab and input a name into Google Images.

"Who's he?" Mahmoud asked. "That surname. Is he anything to do with...?"

"You'll see. Or rather..." The search, somewhat to Sam's surprise, returned no worthwhile hits. "You won't. Damn. He must be out there. He can't have absolutely no internet presence. That would be..." She thought about it. "Well, it wouldn't be inconceivable, I suppose. Not if you happen to know someone who could eradicate every trace of you online if you wanted it."

"You're being very enigmatic here, duck. Or is it me? Am I being slow? Is there something glaringly obvious I'm missing?"

"If there is, it's something we've *all* been missing. Right, how about this?" Sam inputted another similar name, and this rustled up dozens of valid results. She selected one. "That's a good shot of him. Now, compare that face to this one." She clicked between tabs: first Zeus, still paused on the YouTube clip, then the image she had just Googled. Back and forth. Click, click. "See it?"

"Am I looking for a resemblance?"

"You are."

"I really don't –" Mahmoud stopped herself. Her mouth formed itself into a perfect O. "Or perhaps I do," she said slowly. "The noses. The noses are almost identical. The shape of the eyebrows too. They're like those French accents, whatchemacalls, circumflexes."

"Something about the jawlines as well."

"Yes. Sort of."

"And then there's the body language," Sam said. "My DI always used to tell me to watch out for that. Study faces, he said, but study posture and gesture as well. People give away so much about themselves unconsciously, and I'm still in the habit of noticing those little tics and giveaway cues." She un-paused the clip. "Zeus has this sturdy self-assurance about him."

"As well he might."

"As well he might. But it's so like someone else we know, isn't it? Also, he holds himself very erect. See? Even when sitting. He's not quite as tall as he'd like to be, but he keeps his back straight. Tall people have a tendency to stoop. Small people are the opposite. They have a tendency to keep their backs straight in order to try and make themselves look taller."

"And *he's* not tall," Mahmoud said, referring to the other man.

"Correct. What does it for me most, though, is Zeus's eyes. You may not have, but I've seen a photo of someone with big dark eyes like that. Two people, in fact."

Mahmoud sat back in her chair. "So let me get this straight. You're saying they're related? Him and him?"

"I'm saying I think there's a strong likelihood of that being the case."

"Ruddy Nora. It can't be – can it?"

"In context, it makes sense. I know for a fact that they have history. There's no love lost between them."

"But to take it this far...?"

"No one can hate quite like family can hate."

"But..." Mahmoud could think of a whole host of further objections, and wished that any of them was strong enough to withstand the weight of Sam's evidence. If what her friend and colleague was saying was true, then the Titans had been very much misled.

"I am," said Sam, "so much less quick on the uptake than I should be. This has been staring me in the face for weeks."

She gestured at Zeus onscreen.

"Staring me in *his* face."

49. MINOTAUR ON THE LOOSE

"MR LANDESMAN! MR Landesman!" Lillicrap hammered on the door, sounding frantic. "It's broken free. It's smashing up the refectory."

"It? What it?"

"The Minotaur, sir."

Landesman came out of his office. "Well, where the bloody hell's Sam? It's her pet. She should be dealing with this."

"I've no idea where she is. I've no idea where any of the Titans are. The techs are running around like headless chickens. So's the chef. Nobody knows how the Minotaur escaped, but it's complete chaos downstairs. Panic stations."

"The other Titans – they're *all* missing?"

Lillicrap shrugged so hard his shoulders touched his earlobes. "I've looked all over. I thought if they could suit up, they could contain the monster, maybe kill it. But they're nowhere to be found. That's why I came to you."

"Right. Then I should go down and get my Cronus gear on, shouldn't I? Or..." Landesman paused, pondering.

Lillicrap said, "Don't you think it would be better to abandon the bunker, get to the surface, call Captain Fuller to come and fetch us?" It was clear he favoured this alternative. His beloved boss's personal safety, and his own, were priority one for Jolyon Lillicrap.

"No," said Landesman, with a calm, slow-spreading smile.

"No?"

"Clever girl, Sam." Gritted-teeth admiration. "Very well, let's get this over with."

"Sir?"

Landesman strode off down the corridor. "Follow me, Jolyon."

"Where to?"

"The refectory."

"Sir! The Minotaur –"

"– is no danger to us."

"With all due respect, sir, I beg to differ."

"This is Sam's doing. She let it out. She controls it. She wants a confrontation with me, and this is her rather dramatic way of engineering one."

"Are you positive about that?"

"It's what I would do, were I in her position and had I the tools at my disposal that she has." Landesman sighed elaborately. "Serves me right for hiring smart people, Jolyon."

Lillicrap chose to interpret that as a compliment. "Er, quite, Mr Landesman."

The crashing of crockery resounded along the corridor that led to the refectory. Landesman couldn't suppress another smile as he neared the source of the ruckus, with Lillicrap tagging along reluctantly behind. If the Minotaur laying waste to the flatware was Sam's idea of a joke, it wasn't a bad one. Bull in a china shop.

"All right!" he called out. "All right, I'm coming in. Don't let that thing attack me. I come in peace."

As he entered the refectory he felt a twinge of misgiving. What if he was wrong? What if he'd entirely misread the situation and the Minotaur *was* on the loose, unrestrained by its mistress?

Debris lay everywhere. Tables had been overturned. Chairs were scattered about, lying on their backs with their legs in the air like dead animals. Shards of glass and crockery littered the floor, forming a crazy mosaic along with pieces of cutlery and condiment containers. And in the thick of it all the Minotaur was stomping to and fro, snorting furiously as it crushed fragments to smaller fragments underfoot.

Landesman couldn't see Sam anywhere, and then the Minotaur rounded on him, fixing him with its crimson gaze, and all at once his misgiving sharpened into dread. What had he done? He'd just blundered straight into danger. The monster started to move towards him, and Landesman did a smart about-turn and made for the exit.

Then a voice came from a corner of the room.

"No. Stop."

Landesman heard the Minotaur halt in its tracks. He turned again, to see Sam emerge from behind a shelving unit, one of the few items of furniture in the room still standing upright. She crossed over to the monster, which preened at her approach, offering her its head much as a cat might do when greeting its owner.

"That's enough," Sam said, scratching the Minotaur between the horns. "We have Mr Landesman's attention now."

Landesman recovered his composure, some of it. "Really, I should deduct this from your wage packet," he said, waving at the mess. "It's what any other employer would do. Luckily for you, I'm not that petty. Now, you're quite certain you have that beast fully under your command? It's not going to take against me all of a sudden and charge?"

"That depends. If you're uncooperative, the Minotaur might sense it and not be happy. Then there's no telling what it'll do."

"I don't believe that," Landesman replied. "You're many things, Sam Akehurst, but reckless isn't one of them. Especially when it comes to the welfare of others."

"I don't know. Perhaps you should try me and see."

Landesman eyed the Minotaur, then her. "No," he said firmly. "I'm perfectly safe." He picked up a chair, righted it, dusted off the seat, and sat with his arms folded and ankle on knee. "So. What shall we talk about? What is it you want? This is about New York, I'm assuming. You're of the opinion that I handled the op poorly. I waltzed us straight into a trap. You even warned me beforehand that you thought Zeus might be setting us up, and I pooh-poohed the notion, and look where it got us. It was a miscalculation on my part. I could have managed things better. There, I've admitted it. Is that good enough for you? I messed up. I shan't again, though. Once bitten, and so on. Happy?"

"No." Sam took the Minotaur by the arm and steered it to the far end of the room, near the hatch through which meals were served. The massive, hulking creature let itself be led, docile as a donkey. She fetched a dish of fruit and vegetables for it, and the monster got to work noisily and indiscriminately, stuffing apples and broccoli florets into its mouth, green beans and whole tangerines with the skins still on, raw potatoes and handfuls of red grapes. Then she returned to face Landesman, who understood that she had just holstered her gun but could still draw it any time and use it on him. Not that she would. It wasn't in her nature – was it?

"Then what are you after?" he said. "Need I remind you that New York, although it cost us two of our own, also cost the Olympians dearly. And, furthermore, it appears to have garnered us considerable public support and acclaim. It's even fired up some politicians. Only this morning the new prime minister of Japan announced he's sending a fleet of warships on exercises in the Mediterranean. I say fleet. They're only got about five in total left. But the Mediterranean! A place of about as much strategic important to Japan as the moon. What possible motive can Mr Akiyama have for sending ships there other than to rattle a sabre at the Pantheon? You mark my words, those warships will sail into the Aegean and as far up the north-east coastline of Greece as they can, 'til they're within shelling distance of Mount Olympus – and then Poseidon will sink them. But still. The world will see. The message will have been sent, loud and clear. Japan isn't afraid. Japan is prepared to forfeit its last few naval vessels to show the Olympians how unafraid it is. And where one nation leads, others will surely follow. The New York op has effected a sea change, Sam, a seismic shift in the global mood. Yes, we had to lose Anders and Kerstin in order for that to happen, and it's something I deeply and sincerely regret, but for God's sake, just look at the benefits!"

Sam said nothing.

"I see. Not New York," said Landesman. "The Myrmidon Protocol. Is that what's got you so hot under the collar? OK, perhaps I should have come clean. Perhaps I should have shared that little nugget of information with you right from the start. But honestly, would it have helped? You might have refused point-blank to put the battlesuits on, knowing what the nanotech could do, knowing that it wasn't solely there for your protection. I made a judgement call, and on balance I think I got it right. After all, it was possible that the protocol would never have had to be implemented, and then you'd have been none the wiser."

"Ignorance is bliss, eh?"

"It's not always such a bad principle. Doesn't it tell you something, though, that *I* am quite happy to put a TITAN suit on, Myrmidon notwithstanding? If I'm not bothered by it, then neither should any of you be. It's only ever to be used in a worst-case scenario, when the suit wearer is long past caring, and there's a failsafe in place to stop it going off accidentally. The suits have built-in cardiac monitors. Myrmidon will not work if the CPU is measuring heart rate activity in the wearer."

"You know, maybe it says something about me, about how I've changed since becoming a Titan, but I don't actually find the Myrmidon thing that difficult to come to terms with," Sam said. "A few months ago I'd have been disgusted. Now, I'm able to see the need, even if the whole idea of it doesn't exactly give me a warm, fuzzy feeling inside."

"You're a more pragmatic person than you used to be."

"In some respects, yes. I'm more able to see that means are justified by ends. Scruples have to be discarded in order to get the results you crave. You, I imagine, were born knowing that, but it's something I've had to learn."

"You think all I am is a businessman without scruples? How shallow of you, Sam. If that's really the case, why the Titan project? Why am I here haemorrhaging money over this thing, and now putting my life on the line as well, if I am, as you seem to be implying, an ethics-free zone? What is this campaign I've embarked on if not a selfless, public-spirited act, intended not for my own good but for everyone's?"

"Well, there you have it, Mr Landesman. There we get to the nub of it."

"I remain in the dark. What has been my sin, Sam? I'm as committed to the cause as you are, isn't that obvious? *More* committed, I'd say."

"Some might debate that," Sam said. "Some might say that if you were truly committed, you'd have gone to Kerstin's aid in New York instead of just carrying on running up the West Side Highway."

"I told you at the time," said Landesman, face reddening, "I didn't know Hermes had got her."

"And I told you he had."

"And I didn't hear!" he barked.

The Minotaur looked up from its meal and grunted a query at Sam. She patted the air, telling it everything was all right.

"It's protective of you," Landesman murmured. "Amazing. You have that creature wrapped around your finger."

"I said I could tame it, and I did," Sam replied.

"And I never truly doubted you. But as for Kerstin – I swear, if I'd realised, I'd have done something. It's an oversight that will haunt me to my grave. Although, one could argue, could one not, that a leader is entitled to focus on his own safety, to the exclusion of all else, in order to be able to continue to lead."

"No. One could not argue that. That's not leadership as I understand it."

"Well, anyway," Landesman said, "if my shortcomings in the field are evidence that I'm not worthy of being a Titan, I'd humbly submit that you are in error, and I shall prove it on our next op. So, are we done now?" He made to stand up. "Only, I have plenty of other matters to attend to."

"Nearly done." Sam motioned Landesman to retake his seat, which, somewhat to his own surprise, he did. "We just have one last thing to discuss, and it's what I brought you down here for."

"Fair enough. Out with it then."

"Selfless, you said a moment ago. Public-spirited. For everyone's good."

"I did say that."

"Well, forgive me, Mr Landesman," Sam said, "but I've never heard such a crock of shit."

Landesman's circumflex eyebrows shot up. "I beg your pardon?"

"The truth is, you've lied to us. You've been lying from the start. We're not fighting the Pantheon for some high-minded notion of freeing the world from the yoke of oppression."

"No," Landesman said, nodding, "not solely. Revenge is a factor as well. We all know that. It's why I chose you. You have a personal stake in seeing the Olympians brought down. All of you do. So what?"

"What you haven't told us is that you have a personal stake too."

"I do?"

He almost – almost – managed to get the words out smoothly, deadpan, with nothing other than a mildly startled note in them. Almost. But a split second of hesitation betrayed him. Sam caught it, and the look in her eyes told Landesman his bluff had been seen through and could not sensibly be sustained.

He heaved a great sigh, slumping a little in his chair.

"Somehow," he said, eventually, "I knew it would be you, Sam. You'd be the one to figure it out, if any of you were going to. In hindsight, perhaps I revealed too much. Gave away too many clues. But that's not to denigrate your achievement. Detective Sergeant Akehurst strikes again."

"Zeus is your son, isn't he, Mr Landesman?" Sam said. "He's Xander. The son who walked out on you. The son you haven't spoken to in years. All this, the Titan project, Titanomachy II, everything – all it really is is a spat between an estranged father and child. Am I right?"

"I can see how you might draw that conclusion," Landesman said. "However, you couldn't be more wrong."

"Then what is the truth, Mr Landesman? Why don't you explain it to me so I can understand?"

"Very well. As you insist. I shall."

50. XANDER

"WHERE TO START? I loved that boy. He was so beautiful as a baby, quite the most exquisite thing I'd ever laid eyes on. Sometimes, when he was asleep, I'd sneak into his nursery and just gaze at him lying there in his crib. Hardly moving, hardly even breathing, it seemed. So relaxed, so deep in the arms of Morpheus that he could almost have been dead. Alexander, my son. I'd never thought of myself as father material, but the moment he arrived I vowed I would look after him to the very best of my abilities, make sure he had the very best life imaginable, and every night when I looked in on him sleeping I'd renew that vow. You don't have children, Sam."

"So?"

"It wasn't an accusation. I know you don't. I know everything about you. You were pregnant once, and you lost the baby, and for that you have my sincerest condolences."

"Kind of you. Go on."

"I think you will make an excellent mother, and I think one day, *deo volente*, you will *be* one. Let me tell you, the sense of duty that parenthood brings, it's indescribable. The burden of care which it places on you and which you willingly shoulder – you're quite transformed by it. It makes you try to become the kind of person you never thought you could be."

"Yeah, yeah. Having kids is wonderful, life-changing, et cetera. Everyone knows that."

"Let's not be snippy."

"I just don't see the relevance of any of this."

"I'm trying to show you that I am not a heartless and cruel man, although later on you may get the impression that I am. Please be assured that I never ever intended for Xander to despise me or for me to despise him in return. Of course I didn't. I gave that boy everything I could. Not just in material terms, though he lacked for nothing in that respect. I gave him as much of myself as I could, as much time and attention as I could spare.

"But it was hard, especially after Arianna died. With his mother gone, a crucial plank of stability was wrenched away from him, and instead of giving him the extra support he could have done with, I threw myself into my work in order to cope with my own loss, or run away from it. Work became my consolation and my displacement activity. I spent less and less time with Xander when I should have been spending more and more. I wasn't consciously neglecting him, I just found that I had to retreat into doing what I knew best, running Daedalus Industries, to save my own sanity.

"It didn't help that we were winning some huge contracts at the time, churning out mind-bogglingly vast amounts of product. Jolyon will bear me out on this. The company had gone into overdrive, and I couldn't simply leave underlings to deal with it all. That's never been my way. I'm a hands-on kind of employer, as you are well aware by now. I like to roll up my sleeves and get stuck in."

"It took you a while, though, here. To step up and become Cronus, I mean."

"I waited, in order to be sure. I had no desire to rush into anything."

"You wanted us to lay the groundwork first. To field-test the suits and iron out any kinks."

"Which you did, incomparably well. Shall I get back to my narrative?"

"Be my guest."

"Thank you so much. Now, I'm not making excuses for myself. I'm simply relating what happened. I never ignored Xander. I never shut him out. Every minute of free time I had, I devoted to him. But there wasn't a lot of it to devote. When you have manufacturing plants on three continents, a workforce of several thousand depending on you, innumerable suppliers to court and clients to schmooze, it consumes you. It leaves you with very little else.

"Xander never lacked for company as he was growing up. Our huge house was never empty. An army of staff, mostly female, tended to him day and night. His every minute, when he wasn't at school, was occupied with play, sports coaching, swimming, horse riding, music lessons, extra tuition. You name the extracurricular activity, Xander did it. But he was lucky if he saw me, his dad, for more than a few hours a week. I tried my utmost to be there for bedtime, to read him the stories I loved and I thought he loved, the classical tales of gods, heroes and monsters.

"But I only made it perhaps every other evening, if that. Visiting politicians from abroad do so like to be taken out to dinner, you know, and it's only polite to make videoconference calls with subcontractors in Asia when it's their daytime and our night. Xander was never alone. Perhaps it would be more accurate to say that he was never *left* alone. The one person he really needed to be with, however, was hardly ever around."

"I feel sorry for him."

"You should. I do. Poor lad. My God, I loathed my own parents sometimes. Uptight, restrictive pair of cretins, they were. But I'd still rather have had them there than not. So many times I wished them dead, but equally I knew I would have been devastated to lose them. My mother smothered me, my father was a passive-aggressive bully. And then there was our rabbi, who seemed to be constantly around at our house, like a third parent. A pox on them all, but I wouldn't have done without them, even without Rabbi Rabinowitz, a kindly man in person but wrapped up in his Torah.

"And Xander had no one like that. No one he could rely on to the point where he was heartily sick of them. He had just me, absentee dad, whose chequebook was always open even if his appointments diary was not. And still he forgave me. Still he loved me. Small children do that. They have that capacity. They will love you boundlessly, unconditionally, whatever your faults and your shortcomings. And if you are good and attentive and you nurture their love, it will last. But if you aren't and you don't... don't..."

"Take your time."

"Thank you. This is pure self-pity. That's the only emotion that can still choke me up. I can go on now. Awkward moment over. Is this like one of your criminal interrogations, Sam? Am I like a suspect you need to crack?"

"I already cracked you, Mr Landesman. This, now, is just paperwork. Tying up the loose ends."

"Maybe I should ask for my lawyer."

"Only the guilty ask for their lawyers."

"Then I should definitely ask for my lawyer! Especially with 'bad cop' over there glowering at me. I hope we're not in for some of that police brutality one hears so much about."

"Just keep going, Mr Landesman."

"So, Xander continued to be my number one fan until he was about eight or nine, even if often he was adoring me down the phone or during a scant hour or two of together time that I could snatch on a Sunday afternoon."

"You'd even work on Sunday?"

"I was a driven man, Sam. Beyond workaholic. My job was me. I was my job. *Forbes* profiled me once. 'Captain Industrious' they called me in the headline, 'the hands-down most dedicated employer in the business world,' next to a ten-year-old publicity still that was the most up-to-date picture of me they could find. They weren't actually terribly flattering in the article itself, but that was mostly resentment because I kept refusing them an exclusive interview. I hate all that stuff, as you know. Always have, always will.

"But back to Xander. Our problems began – or rather, I began to be aware there were problems – when I started getting calls from his prep school headmaster. Xander was in trouble. Fighting other boys. Being disruptive in class. Stealing. He'd take money from the bursar's office. Break in, raid the petty cash tin, then trot off to the local village shop and splurge on sweets. I thought, 'Oh, this is harmless enough, it's a phase, it'll pass,' though I had a few stern talking-to's with him and pointed out to him that if he needed money as he had to do was ask. The Bank of Dad was never shut. Which, of course, was completely missing the point. Xander wasn't stealing because he needed money. He was stealing because he needed attention. My attention. It was the classic cry for help, and I in my stupidity and blinkeredness was completely blithe to it.

"Then he went to public school, and things just got worse. I sent him to Eton, naturally. What else do you do when you're filthy rich? The most expensive school in the land, where a year's fees set me back, oh, half a day's income, if that. Xander lasted four terms – 'halves,' I should say – before he was, ahem, invited to leave. After that it was a succession of schools – Harrow, Bedales, Charterhouse – working down the list until we were in the second division, and it was a miracle if Xander saw out a full term in any of them.

"And then even the second-division ones started refusing to take him, which is remarkable in that within the independent system there are usually no conditions of entry other than making sure the parental cheque doesn't bounce! But headmasters were talking to headmasters, and frankly Xander was getting such a bad reputation that nobody wanted him as a pupil. If it wasn't smoking, it was drinking, and if it wasn't drinking it was thieving, and if it wasn't thieving it was disruptive behaviour.

"One time, he stole a teacher's moped and rode it through the dining hall during lunch. Another time, he set fire to his desk in a history lesson – poured lighter fuel over it, struck a match, and chucked textbooks onto the flames to stoke them. He punched a French teacher who awarded him an F for a dictation – gave the man a lovely *oeil au beurre noir* – and nearly gassed an entire chemistry class by emptying a vat of sulphuric acid on the floor. Naturally I was able to soothe furrowed brows by offering handsome donations. I daresay there are several new science blocks and music faculties up and down the land that ought to have plaques on them bearing my name. And all the time, I was trying desperately to convince myself that Xander would grow out of it, that he was not a bad boy, beneath it all he was just hurt and misunderstood, he would come good eventually."

"And we all know how that turned out."

"Until you have children yourself, Sam, be slow to judge the parenting abilities of others. Xander ended up at an international academy in Geneva. His notoriety, thank heaven, hadn't extended beyond British shores. They took him in, and I braced myself for the inevitable explosion – and it never came. Something about the school, the environment, the Swiss climate, the polyglot peer group, I don't know what, seemed to have a calming influence on him. Maybe it was just being in a different country, putting some distance between him and all he was used to. It gave him perspective. That was what I thought, anyway.

"Xander knuckled down to his studies. He proved to have a great aptitude for the sciences, and in particular biology. He passed his International Baccalaureate in that subject with flying colours. I allowed myself a sigh of relief, letting out a long-held breath. The worst was over. We had weathered the storm. A place at Oxford beckoned for Xander. His future looked bright, and mine looked, well, certainly a little less vexing. I'd been right, I felt, to give him time, to let him work things out in his own way. My wait-and-see approach had paid off. This, as you might gather, was me justifying my own inaction to myself. I believed Xander cured of what was plaguing him..."

"Whereas in fact the problem had just gone deeper inside."

"Exactly! He'd figured out that acting up wasn't going to get him what he craved."

"Your full attention."

"Which equated to my love. He wanted me to show him I loved him, and to show it in ways that didn't involve shovelling cash at him, and he'd come to see that misbehaving only got him more of the latter and none of the former, so he adopted a different tactic. He decided to challenge me. I deduced this after the fact. If he couldn't get love from me to fill the void in his life, how about respect instead? He would make himself formidable, my rival, perhaps my better. He would become someone I couldn't fob off with money, someone I simply couldn't ignore. He resolved to excel in a single discipline and use it to compete with me and win. We had argued about many things, Xander and I."

"All those slamming doors."

"Yes. At first, as an adolescent, he would mouth off at me and I would scold him and we would row about that and also about how much or how little freedom he had, how I was trying to restrict him, how much he hated the schools I kept sending him to. Typical teenager stuff, really. All parents go through it. It's expected, *de rigueur* at a certain age. Adolescents stretch their wings, and their parents teach them the limitations of flight. But once all that was over the arguments turned ideological. Xander found that he didn't like what I did for a living. He thought it morally indefensible. Any number of times, I rehearsed the reasons why I have no problem with the arms trade – dirty job but someone's got to do it, and so forth. I also pointed out that my making weapons put food on our table and clothes on our backs. Would he rather we starve and go naked?

"But he wasn't having any of that. His riposte was that I was a clever man, I could have made my fortune in any of dozens of industries that didn't lead directly to murder, mayhem and maiming. Why arms? Why did death and devastation have to be my trade? And I would say to him that I personally did not pull the trigger or press the launch button, that was other people's doing. All I did was provide them with the means. It was their choice whether to use it or not."

"I bet that convinced him."

"You're right. It didn't. Not one jot. But I doubt any case I'd made would have. Xander had determined that I was in the wrong and that my career, my entire existence, was predicated on death. Worse, that I somehow relished death. That I was pleased to create the things that destroyed. He'd satisfied himself that the matter was that cut and dried, and nothing I said was going to shift him from this entrenched viewpoint. He simply dug himself more deeply into it as time went by.

"He was doing extraordinarily well at Oxford, flourishing there. His tutors, whom I made a point of being in personal contact with, reported astonishing progress. It seemed to them they had a budding genius on their hands, one of the biology greats, possibly a future Nobel winner. His discipline was terrific. He was attentive in his tutorials, thorough in his practical work, a regular habitué of the lab. In fact their only concern about him was that he seemed a little too devoted to his researches and experimentation, a little too fixated on work. They were worried that he lacked a social life. He was never at the pub or the JCR, he never attended 'ents' events at his college, he didn't do sports, he was the undergraduate least likely to be found parading around with a traffic cone on his head or dressing up in women's clothing as part of some rag week stunt or generally doing any of the oafish student things that so endear 'gown' to 'town.' He focused on work, nothing else. It was as if he had something to prove."

"And he did. To you."

"Indeed. By his final year at Oxford, Xander was specialising in pure genetics. That was his core interest. His obsession, one might say. He was using the facilities at the biology faculty to pursue various theoretical avenues that he kept his administrators mostly in the dark about. He'd tell them just enough to pique their interest and assuage their curiosity, the things they needed to hear in order to convince them to let him get on with it unmolested and unsupervised. He handled them cunningly. The budding genius got all the solo lab time he wanted and all the supplies and material he required, and not too many questions were asked.

"Which is why a senior professor had a hell of a shock one night when he walked in on Xander and found him in the process of trying to euthanase a lab rat. Not such a strange occurrence, you might think, only Xander wasn't attempting to put the creature down humanely by gassing it in a carbon dioxide chamber or injecting it with an overdose of barbiturates. He was chasing the thing round the room with a fire extinguisher, doing his best to club it to death with the base of the cylinder, and looking somewhat frantic about this too.

"Because the rat would not die. The rat took the fiercest blows he would deliver with that fire extinguisher and came up smiling. He was bashing it hard enough to crush every bone in its body, and all he got in return was an indignant squeak and a baring of fangs and a rodent that scurried away ever keener to escape the lab and its would-be executioner.

"Finally, still unaware of his professor staring incredulously from the doorway, Xander managed to imprison the rat under an upturned plastic sink bowl, which he then had to stand on to keep it in place while the captive rat hurled itself at the bowl's sides, desperately trying to break free. And almost succeeding. It had prodigious strength. It was able to shove the bowl along the floor even with Xander's full weight bearing down on top of it, nearly knocking him off-balance. The sides of the bowl were starting to bulge outwards, such was the force with which the rat rammed against them. It was only a matter of time before it burst through. This was not, the professor correctly intuited, any ordinary laboratory creature."

"Xander had done something to the rat."

"Very much so. The professor later confided to me that the animal's strength and resilience had been amplified tenfold, perhaps twentyfold. Xander had boosted its toughness at a cellular level, through manipulation of its DNA."

"Super Rat."

"Ha! Yes. Now, I'm a technology man myself. Engineering, physics, things that can be built from scratch out of manmade materials, things that are solid and fixable and that have predictable effects – these I understand. These are my métier. The organic world, nature, flora, fauna – simply not my sphere. Xander applied himself to biology precisely because of that, I'm sure. Because it was the antithesis of his father's forte.

"And so I can't give you chapter and verse on what Xander actually did to the rat. His professor barely could either, and he was supposedly one of the leading experts in that field of knowledge. Isolation of genes of interest, molecular cloning, transgenesis between unrelated species, prokaryotic vectors to aid transformation of the target organism, and a whole lot of other terminology was wheeled out by him to explain to me what Xander had achieved, or at any rate what the professor thought Xander must have achieved. He theorised that Xander had inserted genetic material from some other creature famed for its durability – he suggested a cockroach or an ocean-bed tubeworm – into the rat, in viral carrier form, and had used advanced restriction enzymes to facilitate the spread of the new genetic material through the rat's body. He'd managed to overcome one of the main obstacles to genetic transformation, rejection by the immune system.

"Though not completely. Not yet. All at once, the professor told me, the rat desisted in its efforts to batter through the sink bowl, let out a spine-tingling squeal of pain, and then went quiet. Moments later, blood came oozing out from beneath the bowl's rim. Xander tentatively stepped off, lifted the bowl, and peeked in. The rat was lying on its side, stone dead. The blood was gushing out from all its orifices. It was only then that Xander realised his professor was standing nearby and had borne witness to the whole escapade. A week later, Xander was sent down. The gates of the university were closed behind him. He was out on his ear."

"But that wasn't the end of it."

"Sam, it was barely even the beginning. Xander wasn't about to let a small thing like being turfed out of one of the most prestigious higher-education establishments in the world stand in his way. Not now that he had a goal in life: besting his old man.

"For several months he moped around the house, not doing much, brooding. I kept encouraging him to go out, have some fun, be with friends. What I failed to appreciate was that Xander had no friends. With all his shenanigans, moving from school to school, and then his intensive work habits at university, he'd not got round to making any. Least of all did he have a girlfriend, despite there not being any shortage of potential candidates. He was a handsome lad, and wealthy. Young ladies would throw themselves at him – and then bounce off, rebuffed by his indifference. His hair had started silvering prematurely, as mine did, but that didn't make him any less attractive. It lent him a distinguished, wiser-than-his-years air. But he did not capitalise on his many personal assets. He did not, as they say these days, 'get a life.' He refused to. He just stayed at home, and he was this awkward presence on the property, like a human thundercloud constantly hanging overhead and darkening the atmosphere.

"And still we would clash, he and I. A lot of the time we were civil to each other and you could almost have mistaken us for close acquaintances. Not friends, and definitely not father and son, but two people who shared a grudging mutual liking. Largely, though, we were at war. That ideological stuff again. Not simply about my line of work any more. Broader-ranging subjects. Politics. Religion. The state of the world. The ultimate fate of humankind. The big questions. Whatever stance I took on a topic, Xander would automatically take the opposite stance, regardless of whether he believed in it or not. After a while it didn't seem to matter to him if he was spouting nonsense, so long as the nonsense ran contrary to my opinion. The practice of opposing me became so ingrained, it turned into his reality, and he could no longer tell the difference between what he was pretending to think just to be antagonistic and what he genuinely thought.

"If, therefore, I said I thought the human race would survive, because our ingenuity and knowhow would enable to us to meet all the challenges thrown up by overpopulation, environmental degradation and the rest, Xander would flatly disagree, saying we were doomed. If I said, being something of an optimist, that I could foresee a time when liberal democracy would be universal, there would be a supreme governing world body and war would become a thing of the past, Xander would insist that history would continue on in its current, shambolic, violent way until eventually we wiped ourselves out. Almost in the same breath, however, he might add that some form of pan-national rule could be humankind's salvation. If someone powerful enough was in charge, if some strict global authority took control, then order could be maintained, problems curbed, and the future ensured."

"He wasn't above contradicting himself."

"Nor above espousing an orthodoxy that ought to have been abhorrent to someone with his heritage. My parents were refugees, you know. They quit Austria just before the *Anschluss*, in the nick of time. I reminded Xander of that fact often – how his grandparents had had to leave behind everything they knew, home, possessions, and quite a few of their loved ones, and seek sanctuary in this country, and then had had to watch helplessly as friends and relatives were rounded up and taken away by the Nazis, never to be heard from again. A powerful leadership of the kind he was advocating, running the world by force, was not simply morally repugnant, it was an insult to his own ancestry. His notion of saving the world by enslaving it was the one thing he said that truly irked me, the one thing guaranteed to make me lose my temper with him, and so it goes without saying that it was the viewpoint he voiced the most often and the most vehemently. He'd found a chink in my armour and kept stabbing his sword there."

"Was that what you had your final argument about? The one that led to Xander storming out and never coming back?"

"That? No. That was about money, of all things. Xander turned twenty-one, and at that point came in line to inherit a substantial trust fund which I had been building up for him. I, however, was not convinced he should have it, so I set about amending the terms of the trust so that it would remain under my custodianship for a further four years. By that time, I reckoned, Xander would have conquered his inner demons and be mature and responsible enough to handle being quite so rich.

"When he got wind of what I was trying to do, he went berserk. He threatened to sue me. He engaged the services of a firm of vicious Inner Temple Rottweilers and warned me that if I didn't let him have the money he would drag me through the High Court and make sure that the case was highly publicised, that every reader of every newspaper and lifestyle magazine in the land knew what a rotten father I was and how miserable I had made his life, how callously plied my evil trade and how I laughed at the suffering my weapons brought to the world. This was no mere bluster, either, I had no doubt on that score. Xander would do it. He'd do it all, and worse. He'd expose me to the full glare of public scrutiny, and the consequences would be grim, both for me personally and for Daedalus.

"So I had no choice. No choice at all but to be blackmailed by my own son into handing over a small fortune in gilts, blue-chip stock and property."

"How much in total?"

"People are so fascinated with figures, aren't they?"

"Only the large ones."

"I'd estimate the fund was worth something in the region of one hundred million sterling."

"Phew."

"Enough, more than enough, to leave Xander in a very comfortable position for the remainder of his life. So what did he do with it? He only went and cashed in the lot, incurring, I might add, a hideous amount of capital gains tax along the way. And then, bank account groaning with readies, he disappeared. Just disappeared. For five years there was neither sight nor sound of him. I put out feelers, asked people who might know where he was if they'd seen him, even hired a private investigator for a while.

"But Xander was gone. He had vanished utterly. That much money can buy you a great deal of privacy and anonymity if you use it right. It can also buy you the time and the wherewithal to carry out further scientific research and to perfect certain methods you have already established."

"He was carrying on with his genetic manipulation experiments?"

"Clearly he was. At some undisclosed location – I suspect in South America, where laws are generally lax and lawmakers bribable, but possibly China – Xander got very busy. And made great strides. And the results are now in evidence for all to see."

"The Olympians."

"The Olympians. I imagine the non-human monsters were Xander's earliest successes, his prototypes and his first concrete results – splicing various different animal species together or super-enhancing existing ones. Once he'd made them work, and they didn't die as that rat had, similar hybridisation techniques with human subjects would be the next step."

"For example, the Minotaur."

"That malodorous beast over there, yes. It would have been a man once, as your instinct told you, Sam, until Xander got his hands on him. Who? Who was the person that now resides within that bull-like form? I've no idea. The same with all the other humanoid monsters, and with the Olympians themselves. Who used they to be, before? I do not know. Volunteers, one must assume, if not all then at least some of them. You'd have to ask Xander himself for the full answer.

"All I know is, at the Olympians' very first public appearance, when they gatecrashed that General Assembly session of the United Nations, I recognised Zeus and fathomed immediately what my son had been up to during those five wilderness years. It was obvious to me, too, what he intended to do thereafter, and sure enough the world was soon under the jackboot of the kind of powerful, authoritarian leadership he'd spoken of so often and with such relish.

"What's more, what was worse as far as I was concerned, was that Xander had dressed himself and his cronies in the guise of the Greek pantheon, from the weaponry right down to the ringleted hair and the peplos gowns. It was a personal insult, a direct slap in the face to me. 'Here,' he was telling me, 'these are the myths you love, Dad. Look what I've done with them. See how I've perverted them. See what I've turned them into.'

"I'm not ashamed to admit that it was when this sank in – the way my son was making a mockery of something dear to me – that I felt for the first time true loathing for him. That is not a thing a parent will do lightly, hate their own offspring. You can resent your kids, be exasperated by them, wish they were less spiteful, be driven to distraction by them, but beneath it all you keep on loving them. But not me, not any more.

"Now I hated Xander. I hated him beyond all compare. Beyond all enduring. It was agony to me that I hated him so much. It made me physically unwell. But there was nothing I could do about it. I couldn't help myself. I wanted to wring the vile, contemptuous, ungrateful little wretch's neck. And that feeling only got worse as the Olympians began rampaging all over the earth, behaving far more intemperately and irresponsibly than their mythical exemplars ever did. Gods unfettered. Deities who treated humans with no more care or respect than we do ants. The Obliteration... I watched the reports of that with sickness in my heart, more so than anyone else, I'm sure. Not only was it unspeakably appalling, but to some extent I was to blame. I was to blame for that and for all of the Olympians' acts of bloodshed. Because the Olympians' ringleader, their progenitor, was my son. My own flesh and blood, who had spurned me, who had used money I'd given him to finance this grandiose exercise in super-powered fascism, and who was, as a happy by-product of his mission to 'save' the planet, rendering my business empire increasingly invalid and driving it almost to the brink of bankruptcy."

"So you decided to fight back."

"Absolutely I did."

"You couldn't just have tried to unmask him publicly instead? Gone on telly and told everyone the truth about the Olympians?"

"Would anyone have believed me? And might Xander simply not have had me silenced if I had? Besides, that was not my way. I knew what I must do. Where Xander had used biotechnology, I would use plain old technology. Where he had turned people into living weapons, I would give people weapons. Where he had enhanced them from the inside out, I would do it from the outside in. Whatever he had achieved, I would achieve too, in inverted form. I would take him on at his own game and I would win!"

"Which brings us to where we are now."

"In the throes of Titanomachy II. And not doing too badly so far, either. Tell me, Sam, what was it that made you finally twig? About Xander, I mean. Was it something I said? What about the mural? Did that have anything to do with it?"

"There is a whole fathers-and-son theme in evidence here, Mr Landesman. You and Xander, the mural – it's all there. But what actually made something click in my brain was Zeus quoting Sophocles on TV."

"Ah, Xander's classical education showing through. He did pay attention in some of his lessons other than biology."

"Not only was it a line about wishing not to be have been born –"

"A sly dig."

"– but it was from a play about Oedipus."

"A tragedy centring on a son who, among other things, murders his father."

"A veiled threat from Xander to his own father."

"Not so veiled, if you're the person being threatened and the threat is couched specifically for you alone to understand."

"Dez also noticed that you and Zeus talk alike."

"The apple doesn't fall far from the tree, much though the tree might wish it otherwise."

"And the two of you are physically similar. The resemblance is there if you look for it. So it was a combination of all those things, but the Sophocles line was the key, the rope that lassoed them all together."

"Well, now that everything is out in the open and we've cleared the air, Sam, what next? What do you propose to do?"

51. WELL AND TRULY SNOOKERED

IT WAS A question Sam had done some considerable soul-searching over.

"I know what I personally am going to do," she told Landesman. "But I think that needn't concern you so much as the rest of the Titans and what *they're* going to do."

"I was rather hoping they might not have to find out about any of this," Landesman said. "I was counting on you agreeing to be discreet."

"Discreet? You mean keep the others in the dark. Lie to them."

"If that's how you want to put it. It could be a secret between the two of us."

"The three of us."

"The Minotaur?" said Landesman, eyeing the monster sceptically. "I don't believe *it* can –"

"Not the Minotaur. Jolyon out there in the

corridor. Who's been listening in all this time."

"And who knows the truth anyway."

"Of course he does. He accidentally let slip that he does, too, not so long ago. But," Sam went on, "I really can't let it stay our secret. Couldn't even if I wanted to."

"I'll up your pay."

"It's always about money with you, Mr Landesman! Not everyone can be bought."

"They can't?"

"No, and what I'm trying to tell you is that the other Titans already know by now."

"Oh really?"

"Look over there. On that shelf. Among the stacked dishes. Do you see?"

Landesman squinted, frowned uncomprehendingly, then did see.

A battlesuit helmet lay half-hidden among the crockery, visor facing out.

"That helmet," Sam said, "has been transmitting a feed back to the command centre, and that feed is being relayed to a laptop which the others are gathered around watching somewhere up on the surface. You've had an audience, Mr Landesman. I don't think you're completely in shot, but even if they can't see you they've been able to hear every word you've said. Why not lean forward and give them all a wave!"

Landesman smiled serenely but deep down – Sam could tell because she knew him well enough by now – the man was fuming. He did as bidden, offering the visor-cam a sardonic, somewhat chagrined salute.

"I've been well and truly snookered, haven't I?" he said.

"Perhaps if you'd been honest with us from the start, all of this malarkey wouldn't have been necessary."

"Honesty would not have been effective. The truth would not have endeared you to me."

"Oh, but catching you out in a lie has?"

"I never lied, Sam! All I did was keep one or two salient facts from you."

"Which is lying."

"If you insist. Fine, I am a liar. But does it really change anything? The cause is still there. Our goal is a common one, even if our motives for achieving it differ."

"It doesn't bother you that killing the entire Pantheon will mean killing your own son?"

"If that's what it takes to liberate humankind. Anyway, I've long since ceased to regard Xander as a son."

"He's just the enemy now. The man who metaphorically castrated you, like Cronus castrating Uranus."

"Why can't you see that we can still be allies, in spite of all this?"

"Why can't you see that we can't?" said Sam. "It's simple, Mr Landesman. I can't work with you any longer. I can't go on with this."

His face fell. "You're serious?"

"As cancer. I'm quitting. Count me out."

"Now, come along. We can discuss this, surely."

"Over cognac and cigars, like you did with Nigel? No thanks. Not the gentlemen's club type."

"Then perhaps if I could raise the subject of money again without you leaping down my throat..."

"Money doesn't matter to me!" Sam exclaimed hotly. "How can I get that through your head? Not everyone in the world has a price. I know. Astonishing. But it's true. You could offer me my own weight in gold, but I'm not staying."

"I believe you're already getting paid a lot more than that. How heavy are you? Gold's at around a thousand dollars per troy ounce, so if we multiply that by –"

"Funny," Sam cut in. "My point is, I can't be a part of this, now that I know what 'this' really is. Up 'til now I was glad to be a Titan because I felt we were better than the Olympians. We were everything they weren't – united, noble, morally superior. Turns out that we're not, though. Turns out our boss is as venal and corrupt as any of them."

"Harsh."

"A user. An exploiter. Self-interested. Prepared to say anything to get his way. Stop me when the description doesn't fit."

"Self-interested? And there's no self-interest for *you* in being a Titan, Sam? Not even punishing the Olympians for the death of your beloved Adrian?"

A low blow, mentioning Ade, as Landesman well knew. Sam was incensed enough, however, not to feel it strike home. She had a battlesuit of emotion on.

"Maybe revenge isn't a worthwhile reason after all," she said. "For doing anything. I could lose more chasing after it than I could ever hope to gain. I already feel I'm missing a lot of what used to make me me. I'd like to leave before I completely lose sight of who I am."

"But who were you, Sam, before? Be honest. Until you came here, you were nobody. Nothing. You were adrift, an empty lifeboat. Being Tethys has given you strength and purpose like you've not known in a long time, and perhaps like you've never known. I've seen that. I look at how you are, and I think back to the woman who came to this island at the beginning of this year, and there's no comparison. It's a tiger next to a cat, a shark next to a minnow. You have become... *incredible*. No other word for it. And now you just want to pack it all in? Now, when we – when you – have come so far?"

Oh, it was silver-tongued stuff, but she was not going to be swayed. She was immune to smarm. Impervious to charm.

"My mind's made up," she said.

"What about the others?"

"They're grown-ups. They can make their own decisions. Stay, leave – whatever they choose is up to them and fine by me."

"But surely they won't want you to go."

"They can manage without. It's not like I'm team leader now or anything. Cronus runs the ops." She nearly added, "Runs *from* the ops," but unlike Landesman she wasn't going to stoop to taking cheap shots.

"Everything may fall apart without you," Landesman pleaded.

"If it does, it does. Not my responsibility. I'm done."

She headed for the door.

"Sam!"

The Minotaur lowed, echoing the tone of Landesman's cry.

Outside the refectory she shoulder-butted past Lillicrap and kept on walking.

PART 2

ONE MONTH LATER

52. COLD TURKEY IN KENSAL RISE

IT SEEMED THAT she had had a family for a while, briefly. A man who'd shared her bed, a childlike thing that had been dependent on her, partners who'd been like brothers and sisters, even a father figure, self-serving and untrustworthy though he'd turned out to be. It seemed that she had been happy in her life with these quasi-kin, although some of them had died and that had brought a measure of sadness.

Their home had been an underground warren, the polar opposite of the Olympians' mountaintop eyrie. From the darkness they had emerged to scrap with that other ersatz family and had shown them they were not the apex predators they thought they were. Those weeks of that existence, it had been a grand time. Often terrifying, just as often exhilarating. There had been laughter and despair.

It had been like living.

But now it was all over.

It was definitely all over.

Kensal Rise was grey and stagnant. Summer kept not quite coming to London. Every day began with a warm morning which never managed to catch alight and blaze. Noon clouds would gather, the sunshine would fade, the air would cool. The Met Office put on a brave face, cheerily promising better weather ahead, but it didn't come and behind the forecasters' grins there was desperation and disappointment. They took it personally. They wished they could do better. Like the national cricket team, currently getting trounced in the Ashes. Like Catesby Bartlett's government, already starting to renege on last year's election promises. Letting the country down.

As if any of these things were surprises.

Sam, in a desultory fashion, busied herself. The house, neglected and unoccupied since January, needed spring cleaning and sprucing up. The neighbours hadn't kept an eye on the back garden as they'd agreed to, so it was now a mass of weeds and parched unwatered plants and the shaggy lawn was dotted with half a ton, give or take, of fox excrement. She was out there every morning with hoe and rake and rubber gloves, restoring life and order and hygiene. She read books. She watched too much daytime TV, "too much" meaning "any." She trudged along to the shops on Chamberlayne Road and trudged back again with just enough groceries for today and tomorrow. On several occasions she picked up her mobile and speed-dialled DI Prothero's private line, only to stop before the number reached its last digit. Once, she got as far as listening to the dial tone trill twice, before hitting Disconnect. She wouldn't have minded hearing his voice, even if it had only been his voicemail message. Those roundly singsong Swansea syllables that conveyed a lilt of warmth, however chilly the message of the words they comprised. She missed it. Missed him. Prothero, however, she was sure, had moved on. She doubted he ever even thought about his one-time protégée now. He had a new DS, someone else to chide and coax and mould. She was on her own. As she had been before. As, perhaps, she had always been.

She watched the news. Of course she did. Assiduously, religiously. BBC Breakfast, the ITN lunchtime bulletin, Channel 4 News in the evening. Like a monk observing matins, sext and vespers.

Nothing.

Nothing about the Titans.

The Olympians were keeping quiet too. There would the odd sighting of one of them every now and then. Hephaestus, say, visiting an Athens scrapheap to gather car parts and other metal detritus, for reasons he wouldn't divulge; Artemis fulfilling a longstanding commitment to attend the ceremony announcing the winner of the bid to hold the next Olympic Games (this time round, as it happened, the lucky bidder was the New Democratic People's Republic of North Korea). Other than that, they maintained a low profile, and some observers commented and other commentators observed that with Hermes still missing in action the Olympians were getting out and about much less. Not for them any more the luxury of instantaneous teleportational travel to any point on the globe. Instead, the slight indignity of flights on private chartered aircraft, although at least they were always waved straight through at customs and never asked to present passports or visas. They were Olympians. Who was going to query *their* travel credentials?

The Japanese navy, such as it was, completed its exercises in the Med. As Landesman had predicted, all five ships travelled far up into the Aegean to the Thermaikos Gulf, bringing them within spitting distance of Olympus. A well-aimed missile from the *Takanami*-class destroyer the JDS *Inazuma Maru* could have reached the Pantheonic stronghold some 20-odd kilometres inland, not that the weapon would have been permitted to complete its journey had it been fired. After sailing in circles for several days without getting sunk, the fleet turned for home with everyone on board, from admiral to lowliest rating, astonished and delighted to still be alive. The Greek navy – one frigate, the HS *Plataia* – played escort down through the Cyclades, politely but pointedly showing the Japanese the way out.

At the newsagent's on the corner, Sam's eye was caught by a headline one morning. It was on the front cover of the *Daily Mail*, a paper that liked to take an occasional libertarian poke at the Pantheon when it was feeling brave.

CHASTENED?

the headline ran, in 40-point capitals, above a library photo of Zeus looking curmudgeonly and disgruntled. Against all her better judgement Sam bought a copy, but the article turned out to be nothing more than a few paragraphs insinuating that the Olympians might be a little cheesed off about losing their monsters, Hercules, and Hermes. All of it was furtively and carefully worded so that there was no reasonable way anybody could take offence. The copy got no further from the newsagent's than the litter bin on the pavement outside.

She was bored, she had to admit it. Day merged into day and nothing much changed. As her time as a Titan receded further into memory, she found it harder and harder to believe that she had wielded guns, punched through walls, run at extraordinary speeds, and stood face-to-fang with nightmarish creatures and expunged them from the world. But if that all seemed so dreamlike and unreal now, how come ordinary life wasn't acceptable? Why was everything drab and pointless here in Kensal Rise? Why, having been Tethys, was it so difficult to go back to being just plain Sam?

A phrase came to mind: *cold turkey*.

She'd been on a wild, dizzying trip. She'd come back down to earth with a bump.

It had been her choice to end it, though. She had to keep remembering that. No one had forced her out. She'd taken that step entirely on her own and, indeed, against everyone else's wishes.

And so, like a habit-kicking junkie, a reformed alcoholic, she was having to learn not to look too far ahead or expect too much, to take each day as it came.

Until the day *they* came.

Ramsay and Mahmoud.

53. DRIFTING SHIPS

SHE WAS MAKING lunch – chicken salad – when they appeared on her doorstep.

"Dead posh round here, isn't it?" was the first thing Mahmoud said when Sam opened the door.

Sam immediately went on the defensive. "Didn't use to be. Past ten years, we've been getting the overspill from Notting Hill and Ladbroke Grove. People priced out of the market there but still wanting to be close to all the trendiness. All the bloody celebs as well. When I was young, Kensal Rise was famous for was murders and Irish navvies. Now it's all gastropubs and organic greengrocers. I keep meaning to sell up and move." She avoided meeting Ramsay's gaze. "So, to what do I owe the pleasure?"

"Oh come on," said Mahmoud. "Isn't it nice to see us? It's nice to see you."

"Did Landesman send you?"

Ramsay snorted. "Nope."

Sam relented, a little. "Then it is nice to see you. Come on in."

She made lunch for them too. Mahmoud explained that they had come entirely off their own bat. Landesman didn't even know they were here. In fact, not having Sam's address, and not wanting to ask Landesman or Lillicrap for it, Mahmoud had had to ring an old friend on the force and ask him to look it up for her on the internal police database.

"Mr Landesman thinks I'm just taking Rick sightseeing for a couple of days."

"Shucks, I just lurve your quaint li'l ole country, ma'am," said Ramsay.

"He must suspect something, though," Sam said.

"Well, if he does, so?" said Mahmoud. "Sam, I won't beat around the bush. We want you back. Please. It's not been going all that brilliantly without you, duck. Not to put any pressure on you or anything, but... No, I will put pressure on you. Frankly, it's been crap at Bleaney lately."

"What's happened? What have you been up to, mission-wise?"

"Zip," said Ramsay. "And that's just the problem. We've been sitting spinning our wheels. Getting on one another's nerves, and worse. Kayla and Thérèse – Christ, we've had to separate those two a coupla times. Going at it like cat and dog. Once they nearly came to blows, and believe me, angry like they were, I did not much want to have to step between them and break it up."

"Kayla's been starting it," said Mahmoud.

"Yeah, but Thérèse ain't exactly been turning the other cheek. The least thing can set them off. And then there's Dez."

"Dez has been..." Mahmoud mimed tipping a bottle to her lips. "A lot. Upset about Anders, but also just bored. We've been hiding the booze, and confiscating his own stash of it when he's not looking, but he always seems to be able to get his paws on more. Cadges off the techs, we think, or maybe bribes Captain Fuller to bring him some over from the mainland. Every night he's sloshed, every morning he's in agony from a hangover. Neither's pretty."

"Why no ops?" Sam asked.

"Landesman," said Ramsay. "Says leave it be for now."

"But he was all about keeping the momentum going."

"Was. Now? My guess is he's lost his nerve. New York, then you, and all that stuff about his son. Not that he shows it, but he's rattled as all hell."

"And the Minotaur? Is it OK?"

"Pining," said Mahmoud. "Sits in his pen, eats just enough to keep going, but he looks so sad all the time. Bereft. He tolerates me feeding him, but he'd rather it was you."

"It's a he now?"

"I'm kind of fond of him. And with privates like those – I mean, how can he *not* be a he?"

"Ah, they're not so impressive," Ramsay quipped. "I've seen bigger. In the shower this morning, as a matter of fact."

"Oh?" said Sam. "So who were you sharing the shower cubicle with?"

"Oof! The Akehurst slam dunks another one!"

Sam did not smile. "Nobody else quit? It was just me?"

"You upset about that?"

"No. I just thought, once you all knew who Zeus really is and why Landesman wants to topple the Olympians so badly…"

"…we'd turn our noses up and walk away?" said Mahmoud. "I can't say the idea never crossed my mind. But having sat and thought about it, I decided Landesman's motives aren't so different from my own. It'd be hypocritical for me to pull out just because he turns out to have a personal involvement in the campaign too."

"Also, he upped our pay," Ramsay said, "and I'm sorry but I don't have your high standards when it comes to money, Sam." His quick glance round her modest but well-fitted kitchen was a kind of footnote: *We don't all have terraced houses in central London with no mortgage.*

"Fred did almost bail," Mahmoud added. "He was in two minds for a while, but then he said something like, 'Leaving won't change anything. Staying, I can still do some good.' I think, like the rest of us, he hasn't got a lot to go back to. Bleaney's as much home to him as anywhere."

"Landesman hired himself a bunch of drifting ships," said Ramsay, "and gave us fuel for our tanks. Whatever his flaws, whatever kind of a man he really is, we owe him for that. Myself, I still want to see this thing through to the end. I couldn't stand to leave the job half finished. That'd be harder for me than pulling out. I respect what you did, Sam, and I know you did it 'cause you felt you had to. But I'm here – we're both here – to ask you to reconsider. As a friend," he said, "and I think we are friends if nothing else, I'm asking you to get back with us and give Titanomachy II a kick-start to get it going again."

"You seriously think Landesman will have me back?" Sam said. "After the way I dealt with him?"

"I seriously think he doesn't have a choice. He's waiting for you. That's why nothing's happening. He knows the Titans aren't half as good without you. We could try but it wouldn't be the same, and it'd probably only lead to another New York. He'll swallow his pride if you come back, I know he will. He's a pragmatic man. One eye on the bigger picture and all that."

"What if I can't swallow *my* pride?"

"You don't have to. Just come waltzing in to base, swagger around a bit, make as if you own the place – you'll get a hero's welcome, and no one'll even mention about you being gone, they'll just be so damn glad to have you there again and to have things return to normal."

"No."

"That's it? Your final answer?"

"You wouldn't like to phone a friend?" said Mahmoud. "Ask the audience?"

"Zaina, I can't carry on working for a man without conscience or scruples – a man who's planning on killing his own son, for God's sake!"

Ramsay had had enough. "This is not the time to come over all pious!" he snapped. "We Titans are the best – the only – chance mankind has got against the Olympians. And thanks to you, we're about to blow that chance for good."

Mahmoud shot him a look. "What Rick is trying to say is we appear to have them on the back foot still. Plus, we've got global goodwill behind us. Everyone wants us to win, and we can, the eight of us, still. Especially with Hermes out of the running, no pun intended. The eight of us, including you. It's still not too late."

Sam knew what lay behind Ramsay's outburst. He was hurt by how easily she'd been able to leave Bleaney, how casually she'd been able to turn her back on them, the two of them, as an item. It was clear he hadn't managed to compartmentalise the way she had. She felt sorry. Guilty, too, which suggested that her own compartmentalisation hadn't been entirely successful.

"Look," she said, "I've no wish to fall out over this. I just don't believe in Titanomachy II any more. I don't believe in what we were doing, because we were doing it for all the wrong reasons. We were misled from the start. We were even misled into thinking that revenge would make us feel better. Does it? Has it, Rick? Now that the Lamia is dead, is your life complete? Are you calm at heart? Has your pain over Ethan gone?"

"It ain't any worse," he mumbled.

"If we've managed to give the Olympians a bloody nose," Sam went on, "and if, as a result, they're going to behave more leniently, as they seem to be doing right now, then maybe we've done all we can and all we needed to. We've restrained them. Under the circumstances, I'd call that a win."

"I can't believe you're saying that. You're no better than your prime minister."

"There's no call for insults. I'm only making the point, Rick, that killing all the Olympians, even if we could, isn't going to help us and might not help anyone else either."

"All right then," said Mahmoud, nodding. "We go to Plan B."

"And what's Plan B? Clonk me on the head and drag me back to Bleaney kicking and screaming?"

"Nope," said Ramsay. "From what you've just been saying, I reckon Plan B might be right up your alley."

54. THE LOTUS EATERS

THE BLACK CAB dropped them off in the southern part of Mayfair, between Piccadilly and Pall Mall, outside a Georgian building with a discreet brass plaque that read The Hellenium – Members Only. A white-gloved doorman greeted them with a tip of his top hat, polite because they looked the part. Ramsay wore a Savile Row suit and hand-stitched shoes. Sam and Mahmoud were in Donna Karan evening gowns cut in the fashionable Doric *chiton* style and accessorised with Louboutin ribbon sandals and Givenchy clutch bags. To the casual passer-by they certainly were dressed like people who would belong to a club like the Hellenium, or at any rate be friends with someone who did.

"We're guests of Mr D and Miss A," Ramsay said.

The doorman's expression altered a fraction, just perceptibly hardening. "Welcome," he said, part opening the door for them, but not all the way.

A clerk at a desk in the foyer likewise stiffened as Ramsay repeated the code phrase. "This way," the clerk said, leading them a private lift which he summoned by turning a key chained to his belt. "The basement."

Creaking downwards in the elderly lift, the three Titans exchanged apprehensive glances.

"Into the lion's den," said Sam. "They could kill us at any moment."

"I don't think so," Ramsay replied. "My gut says they're on the level. The offer's genuine."

"In any case, we're carrying protection," Mahmoud said, tapping her clutch bag. "We just have to be quick enough with it. By the way, Sam, *rocking* that dress."

"True that," said Ramsay appreciatively.

A bell dinged. The lift halted. The cage-like metal doors concertinaed open.

Another doorman waited to check them over. This wasn't a courteous old retainer like the one upstairs. This was a thick-necked bouncer type, ex-military to judge by his razor-edged crew cut, who made little effort to hide the shoulder holster he wore beneath his jacket. He frisked them from top to toe and rummaged through the women's bags. Both bags contained, among other requisites, plastic tampon holders. Sam and Mahmoud exchanged a quick glance of concern, but the man could barely bring himself to touch the tampon holders, let alone open them to check inside.

"Right," he said, jerking a thumb. "I don't recognise you, so that means you must be them. The special visitors. Go on in."

Above street level the Hellenium was an entirely respectable establishment. Judges, civil servants, politicians, captains of industry, bankers, and others of the British upper crust drank in its bars, dined in its restaurant, and dozed in its wingback armchairs before blazing fireplaces with glasses of port wilting in their hands. The Hellenium had its own club tie, an exorbitant membership fee, and a ten-year waiting list. To join, you had to be recommended by no fewer than seven current members, and a single word of dissent from any other member would instantly and indelibly scupper your chances. Only the most stainless and well connected could get in.

Downstairs, however, was another story. For nigh on a decade the Hellenium's basement had played host to an event whose existence was a secret even to many of the club regulars. Down there, perhaps once every four months, perhaps less frequently than that, the Lotus Eaters congregated.

They didn't necessarily have to be members of the Hellenium. They didn't necessarily have to be British or even European. The criteria for being a Lotus Eater were simple. You must be powerful, not just influential, not just some elected official, truly powerful, which in almost every instance equated to being rich. And not just the ordinary kind of rich – fabulously, insanely rich. The kind of rich that rich people dreamed of being. Rich enough to have the ear of statesmen, the attention of generals, the adoration of supermodels, and the fawning respect of luxury yacht salesmen and high-end real estate brokers everywhere. You also had to have no shame.

Shame was a commodity that ill befit a Lotus Eater. Shame, if you carried any about your person, had to be left at the entrance with the thick-necked doorman, along with firearms, knives, any other weapons, sharp implements, and narcotic substances.

Beyond the entrance, in the basement's many chambers and partitioned-off subchambers, you became someone else. You shrugged off care and inhibition. You slipped out of the skin of your life and surrendered yourself to euphoria and carnal indulgence the likes of which could be found nowhere else on the planet.

As Sam, Ramsay and Mahmoud moved through the basement they saw, through open doorways, sights that would have had the editors of downmarket tabloids wetting themselves with glee. Here was the most successful director in Hollywood history lolling languidly on a divan with his flies open, fondling his tumescent (if still rather unimpressive) cock while a pair of prostitutes cavorted in front of him, pouring honey over each other's immaculately depilated bodies. Here was a billionaire Russian oligarch letting himself be rigorously penetrated with a gold-plated dildo strapped to a gimp-masked dominatrix. Here was the lead singer of the top-selling rock act of all time happily fellating a man who closely resembled, but surely could not be, the present incumbent of the Throne of St Peter. Here was a diva-esque fashion house owner who, having just had three young men ejaculate on her suspiciously smooth face, was now inviting them to rinse their semen off with their urine.

It was a jaw-dropping parade of famous and notorious personalities engaged in acts of depravity and self-pollution, all with smiles of pure bliss irradiating their faces, all with dreamy, delirious looks in their eyes, as if never before had they scaled such peaks of ecstasy and never before been so totally not at home to themselves. Their actions were slow, almost robotic, reminiscent of animatronic mannequins at a theme park ride. Time had wound down in the Hellenium's basement, the world's elite operating at a mere fraction of their usual meteoric pace of life, squeezing a minute's worth of joy from every second, relishing the prolonged savour of normally fleeting pleasures.

Incense covered up the smell of the emissions and effluvia that spurted all around – or almost did. But the miasma of rank sourness was pervasive, and choking, and somehow, in its way, more offensive than the deeds that gave rise to it. Sam struggled not to gag. And she thought the stench of the Hydra had been bad...

All the corridors in the basement branched off a central hub, and in this central hub was the source of the glazed looks and the heightened orgiastic sensitivity.

Dionysus and Aphrodite were perched on two thrones, side by side. A mismatched pair if ever there was one: plump, jocose Dionysus, slender, exquisite Aphrodite. Before them stretched a line of the ultra-wealthy, all queuing up to make their obeisance and receive the boon of the Olympians' powers. As the three Titans arrived, a bearded British entrepreneur who'd made his millions franchising a single brand name was on his knees before the god and goddess, promising to honour and serve the Pantheon with all the assets at his disposal. Dionysus beamed twinklingly down at him, Aphrodite nodded graciously, and then both of them closed their eyes and the bearded entrepreneur shuddered as their combined benison flooded into him. When it was over he tottered upright and left the room like a sleepwalker, already loosening his shirt buttons as he headed off towards whatever sexual scenario he had scheduled for himself tonight.

Next in line was the heiress to a prestigious hotel chain, but before she had a chance to prostrate herself, pet Chihuahua and all, Dionysus raised a hand.

"So sorry," he said to the young woman. "It will have to wait. I see we have newcomers, and if I'm not mistaken they're here in answer to a certain invitation that Aphrodite and I extended."

He was looking at Sam, Ramsay and Mahmoud.

"*Am* I mistaken?"

"You aren't," said Ramsay.

"Then come," said Dionysus. "Let us repair to a private room."

He and Aphrodite stood, to a collective groan of disappointment. The hotel heiress huffed and pouted and stamped her foot, but was ignored.

"Follow us," Aphrodite told the three Titans. "This is a highly significant moment, and one, I believe, that may resolve a great many things."

55. CONGRESS

"Wine?" said Dionysus. He proffered a carafe of red.

"Thanks," said Ramsay, "but no."

"Mind if I help myself?"

"You go right ahead."

The two Olympians were one side of a small table, the three Titans the other. The room had been set aside specially for this congress. Congress of a different kind could be heard going on all around, muffled grunts and groans and gasps echoing through the walls.

Sam still couldn't get her head round the notion that she was sitting less than a couple of metres away from two of the enemy. She found herself longing for her battlesuit, for the invulnerability that came with being Tethys. Longing for a weapon, too. Just in case.

"Wine clouds most men's judgement," said Dionysus, quaffing liberally, "but mine it clarifies.

Claret, especially, clarifies." He tittered at his little
bon mot, and quaffed some more.

"So," said Aphrodite. "Three of our foes. Hmm."
She appraised. Sam appraised back. Aphrodite really
was one of the most beautiful women she had ever seen.
Even close up, there were no flaws. Pristine skin, clear
eyes, full lips, a toned but still curvaceous body. She tried
to hate her but could only envy. She wondered what
this ravishing creature made of the comparatively plain
Sam Akehurst. To someone as perfect as Aphrodite, did
everyone else look disfigured, malformed?

"I'm more impressed than I thought I was going to
be," Aphrodite said at last. "Three ordinary people
– I mean no disrespect by that – ordinary, seemingly
unremarkable, and yet you have caused us no end of
trouble. Brave, too. To come here tonight, unarmed.
What makes you think this isn't a trap?"

"What makes you think we don't think it is and
we're not prepared?" Sam replied.

"Ah, the spokesperson. The other two defer to
you, I can see that. I like a woman who takes charge.
I like your hair, too. Such a striking shade of red."

"Thank you," Sam said, then rued it. She wasn't
here to accept compliments about her looks.

"Natural as well," Aphrodite went on. "You don't
get coppery highlights like that out of a bottle."

"Listen," Sam said. "I'm well aware what you're
capable of, Aphrodite, and if I detect the slightest hint
of funny business, if I even suspect that you're trying to
snake-charm me and my colleagues, I have this." She
produced a rape alarm from her bag. "Hundred and

fifty decibel siren. It'll drown you out and give us plenty of time to make an exit. Same goes for you, Dionysus. Any of us starts to feel the least bit merry or light-headed, then these come into play." She uncapped a tampon holder and tipped out a couple of small, single-use hypodermics with a clear liquid inside. They were part of the Titans' array of countermeasures, a specific defence against Dionysus, and Ramsay had pocketed a few of them before leaving Bleaney. "Solute epinephrine, with added cortisol to speed up the absorption rate. Enough of a dose to negate the effect of your intoxication power, at least until we can get out of range. So, if you want to discuss the possibility of a truce, fine, let's discuss it. The first whiff of treachery, and this is over."

Dionysus and Aphrodite glanced at one another.

"Well-prepared," she said.

"And so businesslike," he said, somewhat reproachfully.

"Not everyone has your laidback attitude, Dionysus." Aphrodite turned to Sam. "My admiration for you increases. May we know your names? What should we call you?"

"Tethys," Sam said. "And he's Hyperion, she's Mnemosyne."

"Titans," Aphrodite said, quick as a flash. "Of course. The ancient enemy. Obvious. Apt. But how about some real names?"

"You give us yours, we'll give you ours."

"You know ours. Dionysus, Aphrodite."

"No, that's who you want everyone to think you are. You were born human. You know that."

"I was born from the sea," Aphrodite said. "When Cronus cast Uranus's severed genitals into the ocean, the waves swirled and foamed around them, and I emerged fully-formed from that foam."

"Whereas I was born not once but three times," said Dionysus. "First, to my mother Semele, a princess of Thebes, whom Zeus impregnated. She died while I was still in the womb so Zeus removed me from her body and sewed me up inside his thigh, a second womb where I grew to term. Then as a child I was killed, at the behest of jealous Hera, by none other than the Titans, the real ones. They rent me limb from limb, roasted me and ate me, but Athena and Zeus buried my heart and my other remains and Rhea re-combined the parts and brought me back to life, my third birth. Thus, like the grapevine dying each winter and flourishing again each spring, I can be seen to embody the cycle of death and resurrect–"

"Yeah, yeah," said Ramsay. "This isn't you talking. This is stuff outta some Greek myth textbook."

"I assure you – Hyperion, is it? – I assure you, Hyperion, I speak nothing but fact."

"And Athena sprang from Zeus's brow," said Sam, "and Hera gave birth to Hephaestus through parthenogenesis, in retaliation for Zeus not conceiving Athena with her, and so on and so on. All these old stories, they're not true, and they're not how you Olympians really came to be."

"Oh?" said Aphrodite, narrowing her starry-lashed eyes. "And how did we come to be, if not in those ways which the poets and bards have long enshrined in song?"

Sam studied the two of them. She was usually pretty good at spotting liars, and neither was giving any of the telltale signs. Yet they were no more genuinely Dionysus and Aphrodite than Xander Landesman was genuinely Zeus. Did they not understand that they were impostors? And if not, how not?

Not germane to the matter at hand, said the voice of DI Prothero in the back of her mind.

"It doesn't matter," she said, "and anyway it's off-topic. You two put out word that you wanted a friendly meeting with us."

"Yes," said Dionysus. "How did you get to hear? Was it directly from one of the Lotus Eaters? No point cultivating an association with these people if we can't put them to work for us every once in a while."

"I'd rather not say." In the event, the message had come via a roundabout route, from a Lotus Eater who was an acquaintance of Landesman's. According to Ramsay, the Lotus Eater had mentioned it in passing during a phone conversation – an invitation from Dionysus and Aphrodite to their anonymous opponents to come for a parley – and Landesman had in turn mentioned it to Lillicrap, who'd just happened to let it slip to a tech within earshot of Ramsay. Ramsay had no idea whether the last had been a setup deliberately contrived by Landesman or just mere happenstance. Either way, he'd decided that here was an opportunity too good to pass up.

"We get to scope out two of the opposition at first hand," he'd told Sam, "and if it turns out the Olympians really are desperate for peace, then we'll know for sure that we've got 'em scared." A tap of his forehead. "The mental edge."

For her part, Sam had begun to wonder whether a truce might not be the best solution available. A compromise, yes, but better than the alternative, which was a war of attrition she didn't believe the Titans could win.

"Would I be right in thinking," she continued, "that you're doing this without Zeus's permission?"

"Without even his knowledge," said Dionysus, rubbing his head in such a way that he accidentally nudged his wreath of entwined vine stems. For the rest of the meeting it sat cocked at an angle, no longer the dignified symbol of dominion. "This is purely our own initiative, mine and Beautiful-Buttocked Aphrodite's. You don't mind me using that particular epithet, do you, Aphrodite?"

"There are worse."

"Mighty Zeus would strike us down with a thunderbolt if he got wind of what we're up to," Dionysus went on. "He is consumed utterly with hatred of you people. He shan't be content until you're all dead. You should hear him ranting on about you. Your hubris! Your impiety! Ares and Athena are absolutely on his side, as is Hera, of course, and the Twins. Hades too. Even Aphrodite's husband Hephaestus spits tacks whenever the subject of you comes up on Olympus, as you can imagine happens quite often."

"We two," said Aphrodite, "like to think we're more reasonable than the rest of the Pantheon. More kindly disposed toward mortals, as well. We're actually rather fond of you lot, on the whole."

"Both of us like a bit of fun," said Dionysus, "and don't you mortals too? After all, without intoxicants and fornication, how dull would life be? Our Lotus Eaters understand that. One needs to let go from time to time, go wild, take leave of one's senses, otherwise existence is an airless tomb that slowly suffocates."

"Dionysus the Blossoming and I believe," said Aphrodite, "that you – you Titans, as we now know to call you – and we Olympians could keep going at one another hammer and tongs, and all that will result will be just more unpleasantness, more bloodshed, more deaths. There is another way. There must be. Hopefully, you and we can establish some common ground here this evening. We can lay the foundation for further talks in which we can work out a way for Olympians and Titans to coexist. What, for example, is your ultimate goal? Tell us. Perhaps it's something that can be achieved through negotiation rather than conflict."

"Killing all of you is our ultimate goal," Ramsay said.

Aphrodite's lip curled delicately at his bluntness. "But say you accomplish that, Hyperion. Unlikely, but say you do. Then?"

"Then, speaking for myself, I retire to the West Indies and spend the rest of my days deep-sea fishing, drinking piña coladas out of coconut shells and reggae dancing with girls with big round behinds."

"And you, Mnemosyne?"

"Get on with my life again. Maybe run a delicatessen. That was my dream as a little girl."

"What about you, Tethys?"

"I don't have a plan as such," said Sam. "Haven't thought that far ahead."

"Some might call that a lack of foresight. Others, a lack of confidence."

"I'd call it being pragmatic."

"And as a group do you Titans have a strategy for what happens if you do destroy us? Can you imagine how a post-Pantheonic world would operate?"

"Can you?"

"I don't have to. There will be no such thing. We're immortal. We will rule for ever."

"Immortal, yet you can be killed."

"Hercules was only a demigod."

"And Hermes?"

"He hasn't been confirmed dead."

"But you fear death. You don't like it when people come gunning for you. You retaliate hard."

"A natural reaction. Nobody, not even a god, wishes to be hurt or harmed."

"I have already died once," Dionysus said, "as I explained just now. I have no great desire to repeat the experience."

"You believe all of this stuff, don't you?" Sam said. "You're thoroughly convinced you're divine beings."

"Belief implies the absence of fact," Aphrodite replied. "I don't need to be convinced of anything about myself. One look in the mirror is all it takes. I am Aphrodite, Laughing Aphrodite, Aphrodite the Dark-Eyed, the Silver-Footed and, yes, the Beautiful-Buttocked. I have always been, will always be. I fear, however, that this digression isn't getting us anywhere. Calling my and Dionysus's godhood into question may be childishly satisfying for you but it's hardly diplomacy, and that, after all, is what we're here for, isn't it? Diplomacy? Otherwise I might act undiplomatically myself and point out that there's a certain irony in someone who calls herself Tethys but knows she really isn't accusing someone of not being Aphrodite who knows she really is."

"I'm glad to hear you wouldn't do that."

"Love is forgiveness," said Aphrodite, with magnanimous grace, "and I am the goddess of love."

"So," said Dionysus, "is there any way we can persuade you that not trying to kill us might be a good idea?" The wine was starting to take effect. His speech had begun to slur: *sho, pershuade, ush*. "Can we tempt you with something? Is it money you want? Land? A kingdom to rule over yourselves? I'm sure it could be arranged. Perhaps you'd like Britain. We could afford to let you have it, I'm sure. Nice enough place, bit too damp for my liking and no viniculture to speak of, but architecturally impressive and the British, as a race, have a scrappy tenacity that one can admire if not necessarily warm to. All we'd have to do is ask Bartlett to step down and have you installed in his place. Not difficult. Would that suit?"

"Throw in Outer Mongolia and you've got yourself a deal," said Ramsay.

"Really? Oh. No. I see. Flippancy."

"I was going for sarcasm but, hey, flippancy'll do."

"We're not in this for material gain, Dionysus," said Sam. "If you want to offer us something, how about unconditional surrender?"

Dionysus almost popped with laughter. "What, we shuffle off to Olympus and stay there for ever and never bother anyone again?" he said, refilling his glass for the third time.

"Pretty much."

"And who would keep an eye on things? Who would suppress the oppressors and tame the tyrants and generally keep humankind on the straight and narrow? Because, let me tell you, if it weren't for us this world would be in a very sorry state indeed. You surely couldn't expect us to sit on our hands and do nothing while injustice and inequality and greed and environmental despoliation all rear their ugly heads again. With our powers? Our strength? What is the *point* of us if not to save you from your own worst impulses?"

"The point of gods, surely, is not to punish people for doing wrong but encourage people to do right by setting an example," Sam said. "Gods should be an inspiration, something to aspire to, not a bunch of bullies throwing their weight around."

"Jesus Christ and that Mohammed fellow certainly claimed as much," Dionysus said, "but then they were men mediating on behalf of a supreme being, trying to reconcile his will with human hopes, and when you get down to it that monotheistic deity of theirs was hardly a poster boy for virtue and tolerance, now was he? Floods. Plagues. Ferocious edicts against homosexuals and women. Ring any bells?"

"But you could be different. You could be the first gods truly deserving of worship. Instead of just slaughtering anyone who disagrees with you or opposes you, you could show compassion and forb– forb– What's the damn word?"

"Forbearance?"

"That's the one." Sam paused to check on herself. Was Dionysus bringing his power to bear on her, fuddling her wits, or had she merely misplaced a word she was looking for, as you did from time to time? She felt OK, she thought. Heart rate a little elevated, which was only to be expected, but otherwise normal. The hypos were within easy reach. Proceed, then, with caution. "Forbearance. You could take a constructive rather than destructive approach. Help out. Be kind." She looked significantly at Aphrodite. "Show love."

"Love must sometimes be stern," Aphrodite said. "A mother must chide and scold, no matter how profoundly she adores her children – *because* she adores them and wants them to learn rules and manners and do themselves no harm."

"What was the Obliteration, then?" said Ramsay. "Hell of a chiding, if you ask me, and it wasn't even like Hong Kong had done anything to offend you."

"An example had to be set. A city was chosen, one that had prestige and status and seemed to embody everything that mortals hold dear: wealth, ambition, success, acquisitiveness. We had to demonstrate exactly what we were capable of and how far we'd be prepared to go to subdue resistance and bring peace."

"At a cost of seven million lives?" said Sam.

"Any fewer and you might not have sat up and taken notice. And they had to be civilians, because up until then the Pantheon had caused tens of thousands of military casualties and nobody seemed any too bothered by that. The Obliteration was expedience, on a necessarily grand scale."

"And you wonder why we hate you," Mahmoud seethed, "why we want to depose you. To talk so coolly about a massacre, a holocaust..."

Aphrodite aimed a placid look at her. "Have you ever owned a pet?"

"No. Why?"

"If you'd owned a pet, you'd know that if it becomes terminally ill, the kindest thing you can do is have it put down. It grieves you but it must be done. That is how we felt about the Obliteration – tragic but unavoidable, an act of love that would appear, on the surface at least, cruel, but was well intentioned. We love you mortals. Truly, we do. We want only what's best for you."

"And *you* determine what's best," said Sam.

"Someone has to. You seem so incapable of doing it yourselves."

Sam rose.

"Oh," said Dionysus, wine glass halfway to lips. "Are we done? So soon? I thought we all seemed to be getting along."

"I've given you our terms," Sam said. "You Olympians stand down. You no longer interfere. In return, we leave you be."

"You drive a hard bargain," said Aphrodite. "No concessions? No room for manoeuvre? We can't make a counteroffer? It's that or nothing?"

"Believe me, this is me being generous. Go and tell Zeus what's on the table."

"He won't like it," said Dionysus.

"Use your influence on him, both of you."

"We wouldn't dare to."

"Then try appealing to his good nature, if he has one. It's for your own good, yours and the whole Pantheon's."

"We will at least consider it," said Aphrodite. "I promise we will give it great thought. Won't we, Dionysus? We will also sound out the Cloud-Gatherer, circumspectly, to see if there's any likelihood at all of him budging in his viewpoint. If I know my nephew, there won't be, but we can always hope. And maybe, in a day or so, we can meet up again?"

"Maybe."

"How should we get in touch with you? Passing messages via the Lotus Eaters isn't the most reliable method of communication. If you were to let us have a phone number...?"

Sam deliberated. "I don't know."

"We won't try and trace it, if that's what you're worried about. I swear."

Finally she relented. She scribbled her mobile number down on a scrap of paper. A mobile was less easily traced than a landline, and as long as she kept the conversation brief she doubted Argus would have time to pinpoint her whereabouts.

Before handing the scrap of paper to Aphrodite she said, "The Olympians keep the world honest through fear. Perhaps the Titans can keep the Olympians honest the same way. Perhaps that's the best we can hope for, détente, a balance of power, a kind of new Cold War."

Aphrodite, in answer, flashed a white and dazzling smile.

Even her teeth were perfect. The bitch.

56. THE CALL

"You were bluffing," Ramsay said in the taxi back to Sam's house. "All that stuff about a Cold War, a balance of power – psyching them out, yeah?"

"Well, to work, any good bluff has to have an element of sincerity."

"But détente – doesn't that mean they have to believe we're a force equal to them?"

"As long as they believe it, then it makes no difference whether we are or aren't."

He whistled through his teeth. "You are some piece of work, woman. You've got even me thinking there could be a nonviolent solution to all this, and I'm a 'shoot first, don't bother asking any questions' type of guy. This comes off, and a certain former billionaire we all know is going to be mighty pissed."

"And I care what he thinks because...?"

Ramsay downpipe-gurgled, and Sam realised

she'd missed that wonderful ugly sound.

"Can we trust those two back there, though?" asked Mahmoud. No one was mentioning any names. The partition between the taxi driver and his passengers was shut, but it was as well to be discreet.

"I trust their sense of self-interest," Sam said. "And I think, by their own standards, they're trying to do what's best for all concerned."

"So now we wait for them to call."

"We do. It all depends how far they get with their leader. I'm not holding out much hope, but you never know."

"A part of me doesn't like the idea," Mahmoud said, "them not being brought to book for what they've done."

"Your brothers?"

"And all the rest of it. But another part of me thinks your proposal could actually be the right thing under the circumstances. It shows that we're better than them. We're not descending to their level. As a cop I was never in favour of the death penalty, even for the worst kind of murderers. Bang them up for life, yes, but don't kill them. The law shouldn't stoop to the level of the lawbreakers, it should rise above. I felt differently after what happened to my brothers and what that did to my dad and mum, but now, if there really is an alternative available, I think I could live with it."

Back at Kensal Rise, Sam put her mobile on charge and left it switched on, and a day passed and the only call she got was from her phone service provider enquiring whether she would like to upgrade to a pricier and staggeringly more complicated tariff. Another day passed, and still no word from Dionysus and Aphrodite. Her initiative appeared to have failed. She was disappointed but, if she was honest with herself, not that surprised. It was doubtful that Zeus could be persuaded to surrender his authority, his position, all he had gained, just like that, whatever the perceived threat to him and his cronies. Xander Landesman had dedicated five years of his life to plotting revenge against his father and a further decade to seeing it through and consolidating his grip over the world. Such a fire of spite and pride burned inside him that nothing short of death, it seemed, could extinguish it. And what he decided, all the other Olympians, beholden to him for the gift of their extraordinary powers, would loyally go along with.

"At least you tried," Ramsay said to Sam on the evening of the second day, over beers in the back garden. It was actually warm out, something of a miracle. The first proper good weather of the year, and they'd celebrated it with a barbecue on the patio and two six-packs of Samuel Adams which Ramsay had found at a local, specialist off-licence and pounced on like a man lost in the desert finding water. Now, on deckchairs, beneath a purple sky streaked with flamingo-pink contrails, slightly drunk on the beer, he and Sam were consoling themselves. Mahmoud was indoors, catching up on *Corrie*.

"Shot for the moon and missed," Sam said.

"More like Pluto than the moon. But still worth trying."

"I take it you mean the planet, not the cartoon dog."

"There's a planet called Pluto?"

"Don't think so any longer, actually. Hasn't it been downgraded to a dwarf planet or some such?"

"Oh, so now it's Dopey, not Pluto."

Sam laughed. "By the way, did you hear about those astronomers who want to rename the planets? It was on the news just the other day. They want to switch them from their Roman-god names to their Greek-god equivalents. Neptune to become Poseidon, Jupiter Zeus, Mars Ares, et cetera. Can't believe it. It's not enough that the Olympians have the earth, they have to have the solar system as well?"

"Ah, it's just whackjob scientists trying to be controversial, get noticed, maybe hoover up some extra funding," said Ramsay. "It'll never gain any traction."

"But why, even still, are there people who want to suck up to the Olympians? We were changing things, weren't we? Turning everyone against them, even the waverers. What happened?"

"We stopped. The campaign went into hiatus. That's what happened. Halfway through the game us guys suddenly walked off the field, and now folks in the bleachers are all confused. Who do they support? They thought the underdogs were going to bring the league champions down. The Olympians were the team they hated to love and they were just beginning to love to hate them, and think it was safe to, and then..." He flapped his lips, making a noise like a deflating balloon.

"All over, so maybe they should start to hate to love them again." A shrug. "Crowd psychology's not one of my strong suits, but that would be my guess. We've let them down when we least needed to. I'm sure we can pick up from where we left off, though."

"Is this you trying to re-recruit me?"

He held out a fresh bottle of Samuel Adams. "Right now I'd settle for us, you and me, getting back to where we were not so long ago. The rest I can take or leave."

"I'll consider it," she said, twisting off the cap. Beer foamed, and for no good reason she thought of Aphrodite and her mythical birth in a turbulent froth of divine semen and sea water.

"Thank you for that," Ramsay said. "Not least 'cause sleeping on that couch of yours is giving me a hell of a crick in the neck."

"So all you're after is somewhere comfy for the night. How romantic."

"I thought romance didn't enter into this."

"You have me there," Sam admitted.

Indoors, her mobile rang.

She and Ramsay exchanged glances.

"Probably just another sales call," she said, starting to get up.

"I'll go!" Mahmoud shouted from the house.

"Would you mind?" Sam shouted back. The deckchair was proving tricky to extricate herself from. She was perhaps a little tipsier than she thought.

The twiddly melody of her ringtone halted and she heard Mahmoud say, "Yes?"

Then there was silence.

A long silence.

That got longer still.

Sam and Ramsay exchanged glances again.

"Zaina?" Sam called out. "Did you pick that up? Did they ring off? Who was it?"

No reply.

A chilly breeze prickled the back of Sam's neck.

Except that there *was* no breeze.

She and Ramsay levered themselves out of the deckchairs and crossed the lawn. Ramsay looked as apprehensive as Sam felt, and as puzzled about it too, for there was no cause for apprehension, was there?

The back door led through a utility room extension into the kitchen, where Sam's mobile lay on the countertop, still hooked up to the mains. Of Mahmoud there was no sign. Sam grabbed the phone and checked the memory. Whoever had rung a couple of minutes ago had withheld their number.

"Zaina?"

A creak of a floorboard, overhead.

Ramsay pointed in that direction, then aimed two fingers at his eyes for *look*, followed by a pumping of the fist to indicate *move out*.

Sam would have laughed at him, but somehow, as things stood, the use of military patrol hand signals didn't seem so absurd. Not least because at that moment she noticed something. A knife was absent from the knife block next to the toaster. The slot where one of the large carvers was normally sheathed gaped empty.

She drew Ramsay's attention to this.

He looked a question at her: *you're sure?*

"Don't think we used it tonight," she whispered. "It should be there."

"But not for definite?" he whispered back.

"If it's not there, I don't know where else it would be."

"Shit." He rolled his eyes. "OK, there could be a perfectly innocent explanation for all this. That was a wrong number and Zaina's gone up to her room to get a book or something and the knife's been mislaid and you and I are making a big deal outta nothing."

The fearful note in his voice undermined everything he said.

"Why hasn't she answered me then?" Sam said.

"I'm trying not to think about that. Come on."

They headed up the stairs single file, stealthy. The guest room, which Mahmoud was using, lay directly above the kitchen. It used to be Sam's bedroom when she was a girl, and still visible on the door were the shapes of eight wooden letters that had spelled out her name, bright white against the surrounding age-yellowed paintwork. She kept meaning to sand the door down and repaint it, get rid of the ghost name. She had repapered the walls of the guest room itself to cover up the greasy Blu-Tack residue which marked where posters of Take That and the Spice Girls – and, later, Jarvis Cocker and Blur – used to hang. The door had been next on her to-do list, but somehow she couldn't bring herself to erase every last trace of her childhood from the house.

Now the door stood slightly ajar and the white letter silhouettes seemed to be calling to her, beckoning her in. The light inside the guest room was not on. Yet she knew Mahmoud was there. She could sense her, a waiting presence in the dark.

Ramsay rapped carefully with one knuckle, just above the second A of SAMANTHA.

"Zaina? You OK? Sam and I were wondering if there's a problem of some kind. Who was that on the phone? Was it, maybe, Aphrodite?"

Please not, Sam said to herself, but she had been thinking exactly the same thing. Aphrodite had called and had spoken to Mahmoud in her special way, her influential way, and had ordered her to do something – something that involved a carving knife.

"Zaina, we're going to come in," said Ramsay. "Nice and gentle. This is me and Sam. Your friends."

"Titans," came Mahmoud's voice from the dark. The word rose and fell, eerily neutral, neither quite interrogative nor statement.

"Yeah, Titans. Like you. So is it OK? Us coming in?"

No answer.

Ramsay eased the door inwards, a hinge squeaking softly. He and Sam peered into the darkness, trying to make out as much detail as they could by the twilight glow coming in through the uncurtained window. Bed, wardrobe, dresser, chair, fireplace, radiator – but nothing of Mahmoud.

"Zaina, if Aphrodite's been speaking with you, whatever she's said to you I want you to ignore. It's lies, all of it. You have to remember, Sam and me, we're the good guys, and so are you. We're on the same side. We –"

Sam glimpsed the glint of the blade an instant before it came jabbing through the gap between the door's hinges. She yelled out a warning, but not in time. The knife slashed down Ramsay's arm, raking it from shoulder to elbow. Ramsay recoiled with a shout, colliding with Sam and sending them both asprawl on the landing carpet. He rolled off her, clutching his arm in pain. Sam leapt to her feet.

Mahmoud came out from behind the door and stood framed in the doorway, bloodied carver in her hand. Her eyes were unnaturally wide and staring. Her smile was likewise unnaturally broad. She looked lost and dazed and at the same time serenely happy.

"Oh Sam," she said, shaking her head slowly from side to side. "I cut your man. I penetrated him. Just like he penetrates you, when you let him. Doesn't like it, though, does he? Being penetrated. Look at him."

Ramsay was struggling to get up but he was in shock, grey-faced, gasping. Blood gushed from a deep, foot-long wound in his arm, soaking the carpet.

"Zaina, put the knife down," Sam said. "It's not you doing this, it's Aphrodite. You have to fight it. She's told you to attack us, kill us, but you know you don't really want to. Deep in your heart you know."

"My heart?" echoed Mahmoud. "Yes, Aphrodite is in my heart. She loves me, I love her, and I'd do anything for her. You don't know much about love, do you, Sam? You've got a man to fuck, and that's great. Everybody needs a good fucking. Me especially. I haven't had a good fucking in ages, and to be honest I'm jealous of you, you with your big stud there. Wish I'd been able to get him to fuck me. But love? You don't do love, do you, duck? It's not in your vocabulary any more. You've forgotten what it means. You've shut yourself off from it, ever since you lost that other fella of yours, that Ade. Let me open you up to love again, Sam." She reaffirmed her grip on the knife handle. "Let me open up your heart."

She ran at Sam with the carver held out at chest height. Sam stepped smartly to one side, as she'd been taught in her training at Hendon. Avoiding the impetus of the blow, she parried at the same time, shoving Mahmoud's arm aside. Mahmoud's momentum carried her forward, but she quickly wheeled and came back. Sam knew she ought to use one of the more vicious control techniques she knew to bring Mahmoud down, but couldn't bring herself to. This was her friend. In the event, all she could do was catch Mahmoud's wrist double-handed, just preventing the knife from plunging into her. The two of them slammed against the landing's wooden balustrade. Mahmoud bore down hard on Sam, forcing her to bend backwards, away from the knifepoint, which quivered over her sternum.

The balustrade was old, an original feature of the house from the late Victorian era. Sam's parents used to caution her often about putting too much weight on it, in case it broke.

Now, with too much weight being put on the balustrade, her parents' prediction came true. Several of the spindles snapped free from their sockets, the handrail cracked in two and gave way, and Sam and Mahmoud plummeted through onto the stairs. Sam took the brunt of the impact with her shoulders, then together she and Mahmoud, with the carver still between them, slither-rolled down to the foot of the flight. Mahmoud tumbled free at the bottom, spreadeagled across the parquet floor. The knife remained in her clutches.

Sam lay upended, stunned, her neck and shoulders in spasm, and though she kept telling herself to get up, get going, because the danger was far from over, her body felt numb and unresponsive and stubbornly refused to move. She looked up, and there was Ramsay peering out over the lip of the landing through the broken balustrade, face tight and pain-wracked.

"Sam..." he groaned. Then, with sudden, bug-eyed urgency: "Sam!"

Mahmoud appeared, looming over her, the knife poised above her throat.

Sam had no idea how she managed it, but somehow, through some panicked miracle, she found herself scrabbling up the stairs feet first, on all fours, on her back, faster than she would have ever thought possible, like some sort of human crab. Mahmoud came charging up after her, but Ramsay intercepted, reaching out from the landing and seizing her knife hand with his one good arm. She twisted out of his grasp easily, but the delay gave Sam just enough time to reach the top of the flight and right herself and turn.

Mahmoud aimed a couple of ferocious stabs at Ramsay's face, which he barely succeeded in evading. Next moment, Sam hurled herself down the stairs in a headlong lunge, slamming into Mahmoud. The two women staggered all the way to the bottom and crashed together onto the hall floor. This time it was Mahmoud who, being underneath Sam, got the worst of it. The impact jarred the knife from her hand and sent it skidding under the small round table near the front door on which Sam left her house keys and her unopened post.

Sam straddled Mahmoud, pinning her wrists to the parquet.

"Zaina! Listen to me! Snap out of it!"

"This is kinky, isn't it?" Mahmoud's wheedling tone was accompanied by a leery grin. "I always suspected you'd be an on-top kind of woman. But girl on girl? Isn't that more Thérèse's thing?"

"Shut up. This isn't you. This isn't the Zaina Mahmoud I know. Aphrodite's turned you into a... a *thing*. A perverted thing. You have to remember who you are."

"Such a beautiful voice, the goddess has," Mahmoud crooned. "When you hear it – hear it properly – you can't help but listen. It's still in my head, and my heart. She loves us, us Titans. Loves us so much. But we can't carry on. We can't carry on hurting the Olympians. She can't let us. Zeus doesn't want it, and she is his aunt after all. His doting aunt. She wants me to kill as many Titans as I can, then myself. And she's right to want that. It's the best way, the kindest way. Like putting down a pet, remember? Euthanasia."

"Zain–"

But with a sudden, startling burst of strength Mahmoud lunged upwards, shoving Sam off. She scrambled on her hands and knees to get to the knife. Sam sprang after her, but Mahmoud was faster, nearer, and snatched up the carver from under the table and began twisting round to meet her opponent. Sam dived on her back, driving her onto the floor. She'd hoped to lodge the knife securely beneath Mahmoud's body, flat, out of harm's way. That had been the plan. Put the weapon beyond immediate use, then hold Mahmoud down, applying minimum restraint techniques – armlock, wrist flexed round, one knee on her back. Continue trying to talk her round from Aphrodite's bewitchment. Failing that, keep her secured in place until the spell wore off. As a rule, Aphrodite's commands had a life of half an hour or so, after which their influence rapidly waned. Sam was willing to hold Mahmoud down for that long, longer if she had to. With Ramsay's help, perhaps she could truss her up with bedsheets or something until her mind was fully clear again.

But Mahmoud had stopped moving, had gone entirely limp, and even as Sam bore down on her with her full bodyweight she knew the truth. The truth had been in the angle of the carver's blade as she had landed on Mahmoud. The truth was in the soft rattling croak that now escaped Mahmoud's throat, followed by utter silence. The truth began leaking out on either side of Mahmoud's torso, a seeping dark flood that submerged the parquet tiles, erasing their unevenness with its thick, oily smoothness. The awful crimson truth.

Sam clambered off her friend and crawled to the edge of the hallway, clear of the spreading blood and the motionless body. Knees to chest, knuckles to mouth, she began to choke. Then she began to sob. For the first time in a long while tears came to her eyes, burning as they brimmed and spilled. Soon she was howling, and shaking uncontrollably, and it felt terrible but it felt good as well, for as much as she was filled with grief, she was filled with hatred too. The old familiar hatred but a new strain of it – stronger, hotter, purer. A hatred so intense that, like some all-dissolving acid, it seemed nothing could ever contain it.

That was how Ramsay found her as he came limping down the stairs, his belt lashed around his bicep as a makeshift tourniquet. Sam was hunched up, in torment, and hating as she had never hated before.

57. DI PROTHERO

HE CAME AS soon as she rang. Off-duty, enjoying a quiet night in with a DVD of all-time great Welsh rugby victories and a bottle of single malt, but he came straight over without hesitation or qualm.

"Akehurst, Akehurst, Akehurst," he said, sadly, sternly. "What the hell kind of a mess have you got yourself into here?"

He didn't appear to have aged much in the three years since she'd last seen him. A few more speckles of grey in his hair perhaps, and he seemed shorter than she remembered, but essentially no change. If the sight of a body lying in a pool of blood in her hallway shocked him, he didn't let on, and that was no change either. It took a lot to perturb DI Dai Prothero.

"So who is she? Intruder? Stalker? Neighbour complaining about your raucous sex parties? What?"

"She is – was – a friend," Sam said.

"If this is how you treat your friends, Akehurst, maybe I should leave."

You couldn't be a cop and not develop a gallows humour.

She took him into the living room, out of sight of Mahmoud's corpse. She sat him down and offered him a drink, which he declined, saying he'd had a couple of snifters already and he had a feeling he was going to need a clear head from this point on.

"Come on, then," he said. "I'm bracing myself. Out with it. What have you done?"

What had she done? She told him everything. If she couldn't confide in this man, who could she confide in? Everything. The cryptic invitation, Bleaney, Landesman, Titanomachy II, the monsters, Hercules, Hermes, Xander Landesman, Dionysus and Aphrodite, Mahmoud. She unburdened herself of it all to the one person she had faith in to keep his cool and not disbelieve her. For a time, as he sat there listening, it was like it used to be, the old days, the two of them together, master and pupil, her trust in him implicit, his unflappable calm her lodestone, her magnetic north.

She'd loved Prothero like a second father, and known that he loved her back in his own way, and now that love was still strung tightrope-like between them, perhaps a little less taut than it once was, and dusty from disuse, but still there. His presence here confirmed it, as did the fact that he didn't butt in once during Sam's narrative, even though the temptation must have been immense. He didn't query anything she said or mutter a phatic "Yes?" or "Really?" to prove he was paying attention. He simply paid her the respect of letting her talk, uninterrupted.

When she finished, he was quiet for a few seconds, then said, "This American bloke, Rick Ramsay – sounds like a hardboiled private eye in a movie, name like that – where's he now?"

"I packed him off in a cab to St Mary's Paddington. Hopefully they're stitching him up there even as we speak."

"Poor fellow. Submitting himself to the tender mercies of the NHS."

"He can take it. He was a soldier."

"Even so. Some British hospitals are worse than war zones. What's he telling them about how he got injured?"

"Accident with a lawnmower. He was fixing the blade back on, slipped, fell against it, cut himself. He's going to play the dumb Yank. He can do that quite well."

"Can't they all."

"We reckon a busy, overstretched A and E doctor isn't going to enquire too deeply. The wound does look like a knife wound but the lawnmower story's just about swallowable, especially since Rick's had a beer or two and they'll smell the alcohol on his breath. Drunk and American..."

"Chances are they won't report it as suspicious."

"Chances are."

"We-e-ell now..." Prothero took a deep breath. "First things first. I think I will have that drink after all. Whisky if you've got it. Doesn't do to mix. Second of all, I'll tell you this. No word of a lie, it did occur to me that you were caught up in what's been going on lately, the monster killings, the attacks on the Olympians, all that. Don't ask me how, but a couple of times it definitely flitted through my mind, like. 'That could be Akehurst,' I said to myself, 'out there giving the Pantheon a bloody nose. That'd be just the sort of thing she might do.'"

"Really?"

"Really. Which is partly why none of what you've been telling me comes as a total surprise. The Agonides clip had something to do with it too. I watched that, and blow me if one of the armoured figures in it didn't move just like you do. You know me, how I am about posture and bearing and all that. *That could easily be Akehurst, look you*, I thought, because we Welsh even think in stereotype phrases like 'look you.' *Sounds like her as well*, I thought, though the dialogue was pretty hard to pick up on. And you've phoned me a couple of times lately, according to my caller ID. I didn't call back because I felt you'd leave a message if you wanted to chat – when you were ready to chat. But to phone me at all, out of the blue like that, after such a long silence..."

He sipped the whisky she had just brought him.

"So all in all," he continued, smacking his lips, "the evidence has been pointing pretty firmly in a certain direction, though not so firmly that I've been able to go 'eureka!' – 'til now. You should have come to me earlier, *bach*. You should have known you could share all this with me and I wouldn't breathe a word of it to anyone else."

"I've come to you now."

"Now that you need my help."

"Sorry."

"No, it's fine. Nice to be needed by someone. Especially by the best DS I ever had. You should see this new chap they've got me working with. Barely looks old enough to shave, and if the good Lord gave him any brains at all it was only as a token effort, just so's he'd have something to put in his skull. His reports are atrocious! University degree, and he can't even spell 'forensic.' Puts a 'k' at the end, which, I grant you, has a certain ironic aptness but is hardly a ringing endorsement of the quality of modern higher education. Doesn't even bother him that the spellchecker underlines it. I'd have you back in the job like a shot, Akehurst, if that was a possibility." His expression clouded. "Only it isn't a possibility, is it? Not now. Not from the way you've been speaking. You're set on rejoining the Titans, is that right?"

"I am."

"And kicking yet more Olympian arse."

"Yes."

"And what you want from me is to make this" – he gestured towards the hallway – "go away. Is that it? Remove the body. Baffle any investigation. Keep your record clean so that you can carry on with your mission, which you now feel more fervently about than ever."

"No. I mean, yes about the mission. You're dead-on there. I'm going to get the Olympians back not only for Ade but for Zaina. They turned a friend against me. They made me kill her. And, worse, if I'd been the one who'd picked up the phone..." The sentence trailed off into a shudder.

"It was an accident, the way you described it. Self-defence. Your friend was not in her right mind, and she fell on the knife while you were trying to restrain her."

"Still, I was the one who pushed her onto it. I as good as stuck it into her."

"The Aphrodite defence has been used successfully in courts of law. The mob that killed that would-be assassin in Corsica, for instance. They were held to be not responsible for their actions, not of sound mind, because of Aphrodite, and it applies here too, the other way round."

"I don't care. I'm not trying to wriggle out of this, sir."

"I'm not 'sir.' I'm not your boss any more."

"Nor," Sam went on, "am I hoping you'll help me cover this up, sir. I wouldn't dare ask something like that from you. Wouldn't dream of it."

"That is, I must admit, a relief," said Prothero. "Call me old-fashioned, but I have this thing about being police and not perverting the course of justice."

"I'd be ashamed if the thought even crossed my mind. All I want is for you to know that I did not commit murder here. When the body is eventually found, when it comes out that the police are searching for former detective sergeant Sam Akehurst in connection with a suspected homicide, when the story hits the headlines and the shit hits the fan, I just want it known by you that I'm innocent. I don't care what anyone else thinks, so long as one person, you, is in possession of the full facts."

"Akehurst... Sam... I'm truly not liking the way this sounds."

"How does it sound?"

"Permanent," said Prothero. "Irreversible. Like you're heading down some path you don't think you're coming back from."

"Well good, that's how it's supposed to sound. What happens to me isn't important any longer. It's what happens to *them* that counts."

He surveyed her over the rim of his tumbler. She could see thoughts churning behind those bright, penetrating blue eyes of his, affection wrestling with duty, past vying with present.

Finally he said, "I'd be a fool to try and talk you out of this. I'd be wasting my breath. Your heart's set, and frankly I pity those poor Olympians. They've mucked with the wrong lass, and they don't know what's coming. You can't expect me not to call in the discovery of a dead body, though."

"No, of course not."

"So here's what I'm going to do. I'm going to give you ten minutes. You phoned. You sounded peculiar on the line, a bit 'off.' I came round to see you. You let me in. Then, while I was standing in the hall goggling at the corpse, you ran. Gave me the slip, scarpered out the garden way, over the fence and along the alley at the back. Wheezy, paunchy, middle-aged Prothero gave chase but there was little hope of him catching young, slim, nimble you. OK so far?"

"And why did I phone you?"

"To get me over here, to... confess to your old guv'nor, I suppose. Only, you must have had a last-minute change of heart. Took one look at me. Panicked. Fled."

"Who is the woman in the hallway?"

"A friend who you had a falling-out with, will be my assumption. Over a man. Yes?"

"Sexist but acceptable."

"You'd rather it was over a knitting pattern?"

"A man gives me reasonable motive. There'll be no clear evidential history between me and Zaina Mahmoud, though."

"You said she was a cop. Maybe that's how you two knew each other. Met and bonded at some training seminar a while back, then ended up dating the same fellow. Another cop perhaps, or a mutual friend, someone who commutes between London and – where did you say she was from? Manchester. The thing is, the why of it won't be anywhere near as significant as the fact that her body is lying in your house with your knife in her and your fingerprints all over her. *That's* the picture everyone'll see, that's what'll stick in people's minds, and by comparison the background details will hardly matter. Besides, crimes of passion so often are random-seeming. There's not always a direct, unambiguous trail linking one person to another. You know this."

"I do."

"So now I'm sitting here, having helped myself to a glass of your whisky, and I'm getting my breath back and also reeling because I'm stunned – stunned – by what my erstwhile protégée has done. And in ten minutes' time I'm going to finally muster up the mental wherewithal to phone Despatch and get them to send Scene of Crime over and the rest. You have ten minutes to clear the area and get on your way to wherever you're going, Sam. I'm sorry it can't be longer, but we have to make this as realistic a timeframe as we can, don't we?"

"I'm just glad you didn't ask me to punch you, so that you can say we had a scuffle and that's how I got away."

"Come now," said Prothero with a wry half-smile. "I have my manly reputation to consider. Stopped by a punch from a woman? The boyos back at the station would be ribbing me mercilessly about it for months. Mind, the way I'm feeling right now, getting hit's probably what I need to bring me to my senses."

"How about a hug instead? Would that be all right?"

They had never hugged before. He took her in his arms, tightly, and she buried her face in his jacket collar, which smelled of dry cleaning fluid and him.

"Thank you," she whispered. "For everything."

"Ah now, let's not have any of that."

"You didn't have to agree to do any of this for me. Lie for me."

"No, and I'd much rather be telling everyone the truth, because that exonerates you. But then everyone would start wondering why the Olympians targeted you and your friend, and that'd lead to some unwelcome complications. Your face is going to be on TV soon, there's nothing I can do to prevent that, and Dionysus and Aphrodite will recognise you, and if you stayed here to face the music and clear your name the Olympians would know where you were and come after you in force. So you have to go on the run. It's the only way you'll be free to fight your war. And that's what matters to you, so it matters to me too."

He eased her away from him, holding her at arm's length, clasping her shoulders.

"Go get the buggers, Akehurst," he said. "Hurt them. Make them pay."

She hadn't been seeking Prothero's blessing, and didn't need it, but Christ she was pleased to have it.

58. PRODIGAL DAUGHTER

SAM AND RAMSAY aboard Captain Fuller's fishing smack, again, but now beneath a gleaming blue early-summer sky, and the swell in the strait gentle and sparkling. A pod of porpoises accompanied them for part of the journey, sporting in the boat's bow wave, and the harbour town they left behind was getting into the swing of the tourist season – freshly painted shopfronts, bunting laced across the streets, the amusement arcades whizzing and popping, fish and chips on every corner, ice cream for sale.

Signs of brightness and hope everywhere, but not on Sam's drawn, brooding face, nor on Ramsay's, who winced every time the smack bucked and jarred his bandaged arm.

Black-and-green Bleaney loomed out of the sea, solemn, shining. Nobody was on the jetty to greet them. Captain Fuller began unloading boxes of supplies and humping them up to the bunker entrance on a porter's trolley. His two passengers went ahead and disappeared underground.

McCann was the first person they came across, and his unconfined joy at seeing Sam again almost managed to raise a smile from her.

"The boss told us you were coming back," he gushed, "but I said I wouldn't believe it 'til I saw you with my own eyes." His grin faded. "I heard about what happened with Zaina. Horrible. That Aphrodite bitch. And your face has been on the news, did you know that? Wanted woman, you are. Fugitive from justice. Police keen for you to help them with their enquiries. That's got to feel weird, jumping the fence like that, hasn't it?"

"As usual, Jamie, you never quite know when to stop talking."

"No, I don't, I know. I'm sorry."

"Don't be. We wouldn't have you any other way. Where is Landesman?"

McCann shrugged. "You could try his office."

En route there, they bumped into Patanjali, who offered a courteous nod, and Hamel, who enfolded Sam in a fierce embrace then, without a word, carried on her way.

Landesman was at his desk. He rose.

"Sam... I don't know what to say."

"As long as you don't gloat, you can say anything you like."

"Why would I gloat? This is a moment for celebration, not recrimination. I'm delighted to have you back. The prodigal daughter returns. Finally we can get things rolling again."

"Before we do, I have two conditions."

"Name them. Anything."

"One: Aphrodite is mine. No ifs, ands or buts. I want Apollo and Artemis as well, but Aphrodite is top of the list."

"Done."

"Two: as before, no ops without me."

"Also done."

"That means you take orders from me. Tethys outranks Cronus at all times and in all places."

"I don't foresee having a problem with that," said Landesman.

"One more thing I need to clear up. You meant for me to go to the Hellenium and parley, didn't you? It was no accident Rick overhearing Lillicrap mentioning Dionysus and Aphrodite's invitation."

"In a spirit of full candour," said Landesman, "yes, I did hope that Rick would pass on word to you about the parley offer, and I did anticipate that you would go."

"Why?"

"So you would see that nothing would come of it, that talking peace with the Olympians is futile. Please believe me, though, when I tell you that I had no idea the outcome would be as it was. I know how close you and Zaina had become, and what Aphrodite did is unforgivable. It was never my intention that a Titan would suffer as a result of you meeting with her and Dionysus. I simply wished to make a point."

"You made it well. Better than you could ever have imagined."

"I won't deny that I'm glad this has brought you back into the fold," said Landesman, "and left you more resolute than ever. Sometimes the darkest clouds have the most brightly silver linings."

Sam glanced at the desk. The photo of Xander Landesman and his mother had been removed.

"Yes," said Landesman, following her gaze. "And with it goes any last vestige of sentimentality I may have had towards the boy. At the back of my mind there's always been the hope that, in spite of everything, Xander and I could have some sort of rapprochement. Enough of me remembers the joy he used to give me, the happiness I found in him when he was small, that I still harboured notions of bringing our dispute to an amicable conclusion. Or certainly, that's how I used to feel. I was clinging to the idea that, at the last, we would find some way of settling our differences that didn't entail the death of one or other of us. But" – a profound, heartfelt sigh – "it's not to be. Not now.

"Zeus gave Aphrodite the order to brainwash one of you over the phone, I'm sure of it. She wouldn't have done it except on his say-so. And to me that is the final straw. A truly unacceptable, insidious act. The mark of a coward and a rat. When he was a boy, I adored Xander. Now he's an adult, and has turned out the way he has, I believe more than ever that the only responsible course of action is to wipe him off the face of the planet."

If he was trying to elicit agreement or sympathy from either Sam or Ramsay, he got none. "I'm going to check on the Minotaur," Sam said.

The monster, languishing in his foetid pen, leapt to his feet and capered with glee the moment he laid eyes on Sam. His – yes, his – excited lowing sounded like peals of laughter, deafening in the confined space. He had lost weight, a lot of it, and sores had broken out on his muzzle and chest. Sam spent several minutes scratching the top of his head; he wouldn't let her stop. And it was only after being petted for some considerable time that he thought to eat the food she had brought.

Sam noted the heaps of untouched, rotting vegetable matter that littered the floor of the pen. "Hunger strike, eh?" she said. "You poor thing. I don't blame you. But I'm back now, and I'm not abandoning you again. I'm staying 'til this is all over."

The Minotaur snorted approvingly, as if he understood, and resumed munching a head of cabbage.

Then, mid-mouthful, he stopped.

He looked up. Cocked his head.

His red eyes were wide and wary.

"What is it? What's up?"

Stupid to ask questions of a speechless and uncomprehending beast, but Sam did it anyway. She was unnerved. The Minotaur had become agitated, as if he sensed something, detected something she could not. Something wrong.

Then he let out a deep, growling low. The ridge of coarse hair leading down from his scalp to between his shoulderblades bristled.

Danger.

Sam was on her feet in an instant, making for the command centre. The Minotaur lumbered after her.

And at that point, all through the bunker, alarms started to sound.

59. RAID ON BLEANEY

THIS WAS NOT a drill.

The Titans had rehearsed what to do in the almost inconceivably unlikely event of the Olympians launching an attack on Bleaney. Make for the command centre, suit up as fast as possible, go out to repel invaders.

All seven of them converged now in that large chamber, along with the techs and the Minotaur. There were moments of clamour and chaos as Patanjali and others checked the island's perimeter cameras to establish who and where the threat was, while the Titans scrambled into their battle garb. They had their armouring technique down to a fine art now, but still none of them could achieve full combat readiness in under ten minutes.

"South promontory secure," Patanjali announced. "Nothing there. Looking at the eastern shoreline now. Nothing on any of those cameras either.

Come on, come on, show yourselves. It's got to be Olympians. With our facial recognition software, this can't be a bunch of boat trippers landing for a picnic. The emergency alarms wouldn't've triggered. Scanning along the western shoreline now... oh shit."

"Which of them?" Landesman barked, strapping on his chestplate.

"Uh..."

"Come on, out with it. How many?"

Patanjali had paled. "A lot, sir. Too many."

On the large screens, they were coming up one of the mainland-side beaches, striding purposefully across the shingles. Sam counted six in total. Not the full Pantheonic complement by any means, but enough. Enough. Ares, Apollo, Artemis, Hades and Zeus. Naturally Zeus. All the big guns, the heavy hitters. And sauntering behind them, was that... could it be...?

Hermes?

Hermes. It *was* him. Caduceus, winged helmet and sandals – all present and correct. Alive after all. Looking unharmed, intact, as if he'd been nowhere near Harryhausen's grenade when it went off. He had Demeter to thank for that, no doubt.

And yet, Sam thought, it wasn't Hermes. Not quite. There was something about him, something different but at the same time naggingly familiar...

No time to worry about that. She slapped her helmet on and triggered the visor display. The suit ran its preliminary diagnostic, and she felt the servos humming around her, and she was armoured again, and Tethys, and powerful, and it was good.

Not just good.

Fantastic.

"This is it," she heard Sparks murmuring beside her. The other woman was fumbling with her own helmet, hands trembling. "This is really it. O Jesus, Lord, saviour of my soul, I ask you this morning to protect me and keep me and let me defeat these heathens who profane the word 'god.' I pray for your guidance and blessing in this, our hour of tribulation."

Sam helped her fit the helmet on. "Just do what you can, Kayla – Theia. Take the fight to the Olympians. Give them no quarter. If this is to be our final clash with them, let's make it a battle to remember."

"How the hell did they find us, that's what I want to know," said Ramsay, now Hyperion. "Somebody sell us out?"

A terrible thought came to Sam. Prothero? Could it have been? She had told him everything about the Titans, after all.

But Dai Prothero would never betray her. Never. She dismissed the possibility outright, although the fact that the idea had even occurred to her left a bitter mental aftertaste.

"Ah, who cares?" said Barrington, Iapetus, slotting shells into his pump-action shotgun. "We're taking the bastards on, face to face, man to man. It's what we wanted, isn't it? Up to now all we've been doing is skirmishing. About time we had a proper ding-dong go."

"I couldn't agree more," said Tsang, Crius. "They've come here in numbers. That'll just make it easier to obliterate them."

"Jamie!" Cronus called out.

McCann came bounding over. "Sir!"

"Whatever happens out there, I want you to commence evac procedures."

McCann blinked. "Sir?"

"We can't guarantee the integrity of the bunker, especially with Hermes back in action, and our location has been compromised anyway. You know what to do. All noncombatant personnel up top, along with the bare essential support equipment. We're in luck – Captain Fuller's still moored at the jetty. Get everything and everyone on board the boat and set sail. We'll keep the fighting as far from you as we can. Come on, hop to it. Time's wasting."

McCann whirled and started doling out orders to the techs: dismantle this, unplug that. All at once he no longer seemed boyish.

Sam approached the Minotaur, who was bewildered by all the noise and confusion and the scent of dread in the air. He shrank from her in her battlesuit.

"It's me," she said soothingly. "You know my voice. Me."

The monster relaxed a little.

"I need you to stay put. For your own good. You can't come with me. Stay down here where you'll be safe."

But the Minotaur tagged along after her as she headed for the exit with the other Titans.

"No," she insisted, thinking this was like something out of a Lassie movie, "you can't come. It's too dangerous."

"Dangerous?" said Hyperion. "For a four-hundred-pound beast?"

"Or for us," Sam told him. "Who knows whose side he'll be on? Once he sees who's up there..."

"He'll be on our side," Hyperion stated firmly. "He'll be on whatever side *you* are on."

"You think?"

He nodded. "And we could surely do with the extra muscle."

Sam turned back to the Minotaur, who was showing absolutely no intention of doing anything but go with her.

"Fine," she said, and on she and her fellow Titans went, the Minotaur too, up to the entrance, where the Titans mustered in a line as the main door rolled apart in front of them.

"Comms on," Sam said. "Titans, sound off. Tethys."

"Cronus."

"Hyperion."

"Rhea."

"Crius."

"Theia."

"Iape-bloody-tus."

The Minotaur grunted.

"Out we go, then," Sam said. No big speech. No pre-battle rallying address. Nobody needed reminding how grave the situation was. All knew.

Six Olympians were marching northward up the island.

Seven Titans, and a monster, strode south to engage.

60. SCREAMERS AND RUMBLERS

A SHALLOW VALLEY, a long spoon-scoop in the island's surface, became the battlefield. At the northern end of it there was the broken black ruin of a croft, where the Titans embedded themselves, hunkering among the jagged runs of wall and tuning their suits' camouflage to appropriately dark hues. The Olympians approached from the other end, striding in a confident phalanx. Artemis with her silver spear shouldered, her twin brother Apollo with an arrow nocked, their half-brother Ares swinging his battleaxe – these three formed the front rank. Zeus came next. Hermes and Hades hung back, the rearguard. Clouds were darkening the firmament. Drumbeats of thunder sounded.

Sam was sure of only one thing: she might be about to die but she would not sell her life cheaply. Oddly, hearteningly, the fear was not as great as she'd thought it would be. What she felt was relief more than anything. This looked like being the final showdown, the culmination of all the guerrilla attacks, the climax of the war's gradual escalation. In a way it seemed the most honest method of settling the thing. Titan versus Olympian, out in the open, in broad daylight. No more skulking around, no more hit-and-run sneakiness. Today Titanomachy II would be resolved one way or the other. In terms of raw power the Titans were outmatched, there was no question about that, but then again, so far the battlesuits hadn't been pushed to their absolute limits, nor had every weapon at the Titans' disposal been used in the field yet.

"We see you!" Ares boomed across the length of the valley. "Lurking there. Come on out. Show yourselves like proper warriors. I ache for combat. I yearn to bathe in the blood of my enemies."

"And I yearn to stick this shotgun up your arse," Iapetus muttered.

Ares beat a fist against his breastplate, making the copper ring like a gong. "How impatiently have I awaited this moment," he went on. "Since first you began your challenge to our supremacy, I have wished for nothing else. Come out and face me, you snivelling weaklings, and learn what war really means."

"Titans," said Sam. "Shock and disorientation to start with. We go out and hit them hard, screamers and rumblers on. Theia, Hyperion, Rhea, you're with me. The rest of you stay down, cover us at the flanks. Enfilading fire to keep the Olympians hemmed in. Got that? Good. On my mark. Three, two, one... *Now!*"

The four Titans sprang from hiding, simultaneously tapping their wristpads to activate inbuilt sonic assault arrays. High-frequency squeals shrilled like invisible drills from shoulder-mounted directional speakers, while deep bursts of infrasound pulsed outward, reverberating below the threshold of audibility, felt rather than heard, like an earthquake in the bones. The battlesuits afforded some insulation against the effects of this aural battery, but still it was like being at the heart of a squall, the world shrieking and thrumming and unsteady. Sam plunged across the grass towards the Olympians feeling as though she might stumble at any step. It didn't help that there were tussocks and rabbit holes everywhere, threatening to trip her. She forged on, and she could hear someone howling like a banshee, as loud as if not louder than her suit's screamer, and she thought it might be her.

The Olympians staggered and reeled. Apollo kept trying to loose off an arrow but his golden bow shook in his hands and he was unable to draw the string. Artemis had her hands clamped over her ears, as did Ares, while Zeus attempted to summon lightning but could not marshal his thoughts to do so, and Hades was on his knees, retching. Then bullets began to rake the hillsides to the left and right, and the Olympians instinctively closed together, a sense of survival penetrating the pain and nausea brought on by the decibel hell the Titans had unleashed.

Screamers and rumblers, however, could not be deployed for long. The infrasound bursts, in particular, were indiscriminate, affecting the suit wearers more slowly but just as surely as they did the suit wearers' opponents. The moment Sam felt her stomach start to churn, she knew it was time to shut the noise down. At least she and the other three were now within decent range of the Olympians. She went down on one knee, bringing up her recoilless submachine gun.

Plenty of targets to choose from, but with barely a second thought she singled out the twins, Apollo and Artemis, and then narrowed it down to Artemis.

The hunting goddess, or genetically-enhanced simulacrum thereof, was recovering her wits, raising her spear, getting ready to strike. A stutter of rounds from Sam came stitching across the grass towards her. Quick as anything, like some jungle-wary predator, Artemis vaulted aside, launching her spear at the same time. The throw, for all that it was made while taking evasive action, was astonishingly accurate. Sam just managed to hurl herself flat as the spear hissed over her and impaled itself into the ground directly behind.

Then Artemis was sprinting towards her, covering the distance in a few lithe, pantherish leaps. So fast. Too fast. She snatched up the spear and brandished it above her head. Her eyes flared, her teeth flashed, the sinews in her arm flexed, and Sam rolled over, hoping to get onto her back in time to fire but knowing, even as she did so, that she wasn't fast enough.

The spear came down, aimed at her waist, in between sections of the suit. Sam felt a sudden terrible pressure in her stomach, a discomfort that expanded all at once into sharp, rooting agony. Her trigger finger spasmed, but the shots sprayed wild. Artemis grinned fiercely and, left hand joining right on the spear, brought all her weight and might to bear. Sam heard a low, helpless moan coming out of her throat, and she could feel – *feel* – the spearpoint skewering through her abdominal tissue, worming down towards her innards, splitting, bursting things as it went. Her hand involuntarily slackened, the gun slipping from her grasp.

"There, that should hold you," Artemis said. "Now where's – ?"

Then thudding footfalls, a roar, and a huge black blur came barrelling into Artemis. Sam wailed as the spear was wrenched sideways out of her flesh. She saw, blurred as though through a veil, two figures moving close by, grappling, locked in combat. One was Artemis, the other she identified as the Minotaur, who had come to her rescue. She heard his grunts and snorts as he beleaguered Artemis with blows. Artemis, in return, kicked and wrestled with the monster, her face a leer of disgust. Her spear was still in her hand, its tip dripping with Sam's blood, but the Minotaur was pressing in hard, keeping the Olympian at too close a range for the weapon to be useable.

Elsewhere on the battlefield Sam could see Rhea dodging to and fro at full TITAN suit speed while Zeus strafed her with lightning bolts, missing but keeping her off-balance and preventing her from getting near enough to hit him with her flamethrower. Hyperion and Thea, meanwhile, were trying to pin down Apollo, who answered their gunfire with a volley of arrows, which he plucked from his quiver one after another and sent on their way with inhuman swiftness and precision. As Sam watched, an arrow struck Theia in the elbow, piercing the vulnerable, unshielded join between upper arm and forearm. It went clean through, fully half of its shaft emerging from the other side. Theia groaned, staggered, but then, all credit to her, kept up the assault on Apollo, firing her coilgun one-handed while her arrow-transfixed arm hung useless at her side.

Dreamily, bobbing on waves of pain, Sam swivelled her head and looked towards the croft, where Ares was now taking the fight to the three Titans emplaced there. His battleaxe rose and fell, rose and fell, gouging chunks out of the tumbledown walls as he rousted Cronus, Iapetus and Crius from hiding. Sam could not help but marvel at the Olympian's relentlessness and tenacity. His copper armour bore the marks of shotgun rounds, he was bleeding in several places, yet none of it seemed to bother him or hinder him. Like some living siege engine he hammered away at the Titans' meagre, makeshift fortification, driving them out into the open by whittling it to pieces.

And waiting for the three Titans as they retreated was Hades and Hermes, who had teleported into position on the other side of the croft, upslope. Cronus, Iapetus and Crius backpedalled blindly towards where the two Olympians stood. They were firing at Ares as they went, concentrating solely on him, so that they didn't perceive the danger from another quarter until they were almost on top of it. Sam tried to warn them over the comms, but could manage only a whispery, unintelligible croak.

Hades flourished his bare hands out of the sleeves of his cloak as the three Titans blundered within reach. Hermes darted behind the nearest of the three, Crius, and tore off the Titan's helmet. Then Hades leaned in and – casually, almost – brushed fingertips over Cruis's face. Hermes returned to Hades's side before Crius had even started sagging to the ground. Then in an eyeblink, with a kind of spiral twisting of the air, both Olympians were gone. Cronus and Iapetus scarcely had time to register what had happened. They watched their comrade keel over face first onto the grass, and over the comms Sam heard Iapetus curse: "Fuck no. No. Fred. The poor bastard."

Then another twisting of the air, as though space itself were being unwound, and there stood Hermes and Hades again, back for more.

This time, however, Iapetus was too quick off the mark. As Hermes reached for his helmet, the Titan squirmed sideways. Then, with a gloating "Hah!," Iapetus squeezed off a shot at the other Olympian. The round hit Hades in the gut and sent him flying backwards. In the time it took Iapetus to pump and reload, however, Hades vanished. Hermes grabbed him and teleported out of there, and Iapetus blasted nothing but the innocent soil of Bleaney.

Sam returned her attention to the nearest conflict, the struggle between Artemis and the Minotaur. Artemis was a hellion, clawing and spitting like a cornered cat as she fought. The Minotaur's superior strength and brute force counted for nothing against the naked ferocity of the Olympian – not least when a well-aimed knee jab from Artemis caught him square between the legs. The Minotaur let out a moan that would have cracked iron and staggered away from Artemis, clutching his large, prominent and all too unprotectable genitals. He doubled over, almost weeping, and Sam could tell what was coming next and knew she must somehow prevent it. Only she would be able to. Her submachine gun lay on the grass just inches away, and all she had to do was turn over onto her side, but she couldn't turn over onto her side, she just couldn't, this simplest of manoeuvres was beyond her, physically impossible, but she *had* to, because Artemis was lofting her spear, set to run the Minotaur through with it, and the monster was still helpless with pain, no idea what was about to happen, past realising, and Sam had just a split second in which to act, and so she turned over, even though it felt like muscles were tearing and her stomach was splitting open, she turned over, and her fumbling hand found the gun, but then she seemed to have nothing useful inside her gauntlet, nothing that could bend or grab, a bunch of bananas in place of fingers, so that her hand flopped onto the gun but couldn't pick it up, and Artemis levelled her spear and with cool, cruel deftness lanced it into the monster.

Such was her strength that it went in through his chest and out through his back as easily as if she had been piercing putty. The Minotaur cried out, loud, then louder still as Artemis yanked the spear out and smartly rammed it home again. This time she got him in the midsection, and as the spear was withdrawn it tugged out a blue-grey tangle of intestines with it. Then the Olympian plunged the sleek silver weapon into the Minotaur's chest once more, hard enough that ribs could be heard splintering.

"How they turned you against us, beast, I don't know," she said. "But all living creatures are fair game to Artemis the Untamed. Man, animal, or both, you're mine to hunt and kill."

The Minotaur met her look of haughty triumph with a contemptuous crimson stare. Blood and drool bubbled around his lips. Then, lowering his horns and planting both feet firmly, he thrust himself toward her. The haft of the spear sank further into him, while the point protruded further out behind. Artemis was too startled to let go of the weapon. She'd thought the Minotaur done for, finished, still standing only because her spear was holding him up. Too late did she understand that the monster, though fatally wounded, had resolved not to die alone or unavenged. Now, pushing himself along the spear, he got to within arm's length of her. His massive black hands seized her by the head, took a firm grip, and clenched. Artemis's scream was high-pitched and unearthly, like steam whistling from a kettle, but, ghastly as this was, it wasn't nearly as ghastly as the sound of her skull being crushed – a ripple of firecracker pops that ended in an abrupt, eruptive *squish*. Wet pink spongy stuff spewed out over the Minotaur's fingers. Artemis's body twitched, then went limp. The Minotaur dropped her and a moment later himself fell, toppling forwards onto her supine form. Briefly he shuddered, then lay still, with the spear poking up vertically from his back like some hideous, gore-soaked flagpole.

Elsewhere, lightning continued to flicker and explode. Gunfire ripped through the air. There was the heavy *kerrump* of a grenade going off, followed by the patter of clods of earth raining down. Just by her ear, and yet as though from miles away, Sam heard Hyperion calling anxiously for her, for Tethys. In the midst of all the mêlée he couldn't see that she was lying not so far off from him, beside the fallen Minotaur and the remains of Artemis, whose head was like a trodden-on pumpkin. She wanted to speak up, tell Hyperion where she was, but a strange and wonderful numbness had set in. Icy fire burned in her belly, licking along her veins, suffusing her with soothing coldness, and with every heartbeat she seemed to grow calmer, more detached, remoter from herself. The ground was like water, something you could float on, and nothing mattered. Life, she saw, was such a small thing. All its strains and efforts were immaterial. It felt good to be able to rest at last. Perhaps that was all she had ever needed, just some rest. A good, long sleep.

Her eyes were on the point of closing when a face hove into view above her, peering down.

Hermes, with his shiny winged helmet, like a cross between a dove and a hubcap.

Sam smiled, then frowned.

Why did Hermes have someone else's features?

Why did he look a lot like – no, exactly like – that twelfth Titan candidate, what was his name, the one who dropped out right at the start? Darren Pugh, that was it. Why was Hermes a dead ringer for him?

She couldn't work it out.

Then Hermes reached down with one arm, and said, in Darren Pugh's voice, "Time to go," and clasped her wrist, and next thing Sam knew she was being turned inside out, flipped like a pillowcase, then flipped again, and/

/not Bleaney/

/enclosed, quiet/

/ceiling, not sky/

/where?/

Here?

Her?

Er...

61. A VIEW
FROM ON HIGH

THEY REMOVED HER TITAN suit at some point.
Shortly before that, or maybe it was after, someone
placed hands on Sam, touching her stomach where
Artemis's spear had gone in. This hurt abysmally.
The pressure of the hands was almost unendurable.
Then something warm and sparkling seemed to flow
into her, like liquid summer-night stars, and the
pain went away and was replaced by a deep-seated
sensation somewhat like a tickle and somewhat like
an itch but neither, and better, and worse. Sam prised
open her eyelids just enough to catch a glimpse of a
woman she had never met but recognised all the same
– a woman with unruly hair and plain, outdoorsy
looks, her complexion coarse and plum-coloured,
her cheeks jowling over her jawline. Demeter.

The Olympian stood up after her ministering
was done, and swayed for a moment, as though

suddenly emptied of all energy, then tottered out of sight, and Sam tried to track her as she moved away but darkness closed in and she plunged back into unconsciousness, although not before hearing Demeter murmur to someone, curtly, "She'll live."

Later, there was food being spooned between her lips. She took it in – some kind of soup – in grateful slurps. Who was feeding her? Was that Zeus himself?

Later still, voices in the room. Hushed. Heated. Arguing over her. About her. Why keep her captive? Why heal her? Why let her live? Why not simply kill her?

"Because it is my will," was the final, definitive answer to all these questions, and it came from – him again – Zeus.

And then, just like that, Sam found herself fully awake, and alone, and feeling better than she had in ages, refreshed as if after the sleep of a lifetime. She was stretched out on a couch in a bedchamber furnished in the ancient Hellenic style. Drapes billowed. There were urns and amphorae everywhere, patterned in orange and black, some with figures painted on them – warriors, huntsmen, poets with lyres. Repeating zigzag and spiral motifs ran along the top of the walls, and a mosaic by the door depicted... she wasn't sure what, until she inspected it close up and worked out that what she was looking at were scenes from Tartarus, a panorama of the torments of the damned.

Here was Sisyphus, eternally and unsuccessfully pushing that boulder up that hill. Here, Tantalus, unable to slake his thirst from the pool he stood in or eat the grapes that dangled just out of reach overhead. And here, Ixion, strapped to his ever-revolving fiery wheel.

Turning away from this rather charmless piece of décor, Sam went to the window, which was small and unglassed, the source of the thin, cold draught that nudged the drapes. She looked out, already knowing what she would see, just needing it confirmed.

A view from on high.

From a mountaintop, across folds of pine-forested crag and foothill to a far-off, urbanised plain and beyond, in haze, a coastline, the sea.

The view, she knew, from Mount Olympus.

She tortoised her head out of the window. Below her lay a long, straight drop into a deep cleft, whose far side was capped with battlements. Both faces of the cleft were smooth and precipitous. Sam peered hard, but potential handholds and footholds were few and far between. Climbing out of here was simply not an option.

"There is no exit that way," a voice behind her confirmed.

Sam whirled. Zeus had entered, accompanied by Ares.

"At least," he added, "not unless you consider falling to your death an exit. Which you might, but it would be a pity and a waste. How are you, Tethys? Well, I trust?"

"All right."

"You'll have noticed that your wound, which was a fatal one, is troubling you no more. Gone as if it never was, I think you'll find."

Sam's hand went to her stomach, reflexively, and stroked it through the cotton of the *peplos* someone had dressed her in. The skin was perfectly smooth. There was no trace of injury, not even any scar tissue. Nor did she feel any residual internal ache. Nothing.

"Demeter," said Zeus, "has never seen fit to use her powers on a mortal before. You should feel honoured."

"Remind me to thank her," Sam said, "when I next see her and I'm kicking her teeth in."

"Oh, Tethys, Tethys. Or would you prefer I call you Samantha Akehurst?"

"Sam, if you must."

"Your aggression does you credit, Sam. It's made you a remarkable foe. But surely you can see that the time for such petulant posturing is over. Besides, you don't have your fancy suit of armour. You pose no threat to me, or to anyone here."

"Oh yeah? Then why have you come along with Tall, Dumb And Clueless there? If you're not afraid of me, send the big hairy goon out of the room and we'll chat alone."

Ares scowled, unfolding his arms menacingly.

"No, no," Zeus said, staying him with a hand. "Sam shouldn't be punished for speaking her mind. She has a point. Am I afraid of you, Sam? No I am not. Of course not. But were I to have come in here by myself, and you were to attack me in some kind of maenad frenzy, it would be inconvenient and undesirable to have to deal with."

"And lightning bolts don't work so well indoors," Sam said.

"There is that," Zeus conceded. "Hence an escort, as a precaution. One that, I am sure, will not be necessary. Eh?"

She shrugged. "So why am I a prisoner? And what happened back at Bleaney after Hermes kidnapped me? Where are the other Titans? Are they here too? Oh yes, and why does Hermes not look like Hermes used to?"

"So many questions. Perhaps you'd like to shove me into an interview room and shine a lamp in my face while you're about it."

"Watched many TV cop shows lately?"

"Let me take your first enquiry first. You're here as our guest" – he laid emphasis on the word – "because I'm hoping to persuade you how reckless and misguided your war against us has been. As for the results of our little island fracas, I can show you shortly. And on the subject of Hermes – well, frankly I'm not sure what you're getting at. Hermes is still Hermes. His helmet, his sandals, his caduceus, his speed, his ability to teleport, all the things that make him the Divine Messenger, the Luck Bringer, the Conveyor Of Souls, are there."

"All the things," said Sam, "except *him*. *He's* changed. Face, body, voice – they all belong to someone I met once a while back."

"I really don't know what you mean."

"In the same way that your face and all the rest of it belong to a man called Xander Landesman."

"Never heard of him." Zeus was beaming benignly, as one might when conversing with a person whose sanity one was beginning to doubt. "Xander... who?"

"Landesman. Don't act like you don't know what I'm talking about."

"No acting here. I honestly don't."

"You are Alexander Landesman," she said, spelling it out, "son of Regis and Arianna Landesman, and you're probably something of a genius because you invented a way of genetically –"

Zeus, still beaming, overrode her. "Do *you* have any idea what she's on about?" he asked Ares.

Ares twitched his massive shoulders. "Search me, O Cloud-Gatherer. Mortals. They do get some strange notions in their heads sometimes."

"Right, I see," Sam said. "That's how we're going to play it, are we? You *are* gods. The original Dodekatheon, newly emerged in the twenty-first century. Not a bunch of biotechnologically souped-up human beings, but the genuine article."

"That is so," said Zeus.

"OK. Then the obvious thing to do, as I have this opportunity, is ask where you've been for the past couple of thousand years. Why's it only recently that you decided to come out into the open?"

"We," said Zeus, "were biding our time. Before the arrival of what is known as the Common Era, belief in us was waning – had, indeed, dwindled almost to nothing. Other faiths, other creeds, had sprung up to take the place of us, and so rather than linger on, superfluous, like party guests who have outstayed their welcome, we went into recess. We withdrew from the world, ceased to have any truck with mortals, left you to go on your way with your Yahweh and your Allah and your Krishna and your Buddha and their ilk. It was a period of what one might call, I suppose, divine hibernation. Did you not hear my speech to the United Nations all those years back, when we returned? I explained all this then."

"Obviously I wasn't paying close enough attention. Maybe I was too busy marvelling at Ares's great godly forearms. Or buffing my nails, I can't remember which."

"The woman cannot keep a civil tongue," Ares growled. "Let me at her, O Father Of Gods And Men. I'll teach her how to show respect."

"No, restrain yourself, Ares the Slaughter-Stained," Zeus said. "She is trying to provoke us. Let's not give her the satisfaction of rising to the bait. We are her superiors, after all. Her elders and betters. Sam, our worshippers began looking elsewhere for their divine guidance and we simply didn't feel we were needed any more, so we left this earthly plane, although we continued to keep an eye on things here from afar, because we were, and remain, rather attached to you mortals. A millennium passed, then another, and we perceived what a mess you were making of things. Your religions seemed to be leading you down all sorts of terrible paths, to inquisitions, to pogroms, to endless internecine wars. At their best they were being used as methods of mind control, enslaving the masses with the promise of a reward in the life hereafter, and even where they were rejected there was still wholesale torture and slaughter. The atrocities of Communism, for example, were inflicted in the name of a political system predicated in no small part on atheism.

"In the end, we could no longer stand idly by. Enough was enough. Somebody had to take the world by the scruff of the neck and set it straight again. Somebody had to drag you people out of the mire into which you had got yourselves and down into which you were remorselessly sinking further and further every day. At my instigation, we Olympians manifested in the mortal realm once more, taking fleshly form as we so often did of old. Our role this time was to be proactive and change things for the better. This, I would submit, we have achieved. Not without cost, but is there not some wise contemporary adage about omelettes and eggs?"

"Yes, Xander, there is."

"I told you, I know of no person by the name of Xander... Landman, was it? Please stop trying to insinuate that I am something less than I am. You're taking some poor innocent's name in vain. Perhaps, because you yourself have pretended to Titanhood, you feel I pretend to godhood. In fact, now I recall Aphrodite telling me how you levelled a similar accusation against her and Dionysus. You are, in this regard, quite clearly delusional."

Sam almost laughed. "*I'm* delusional? All right, let's say for argument's sake I am. I still don't see why, if everything you're claiming is true, you didn't step in sooner. I mean, what about the Second World

War? Where were you when Hitler was rounding up and gassing the Jews? That, surely, was the time to get involved. You didn't have to leave it another sixty years."

The reference to the Holocaust didn't appear to faze the man who was Xander Landesman, grandson of Austrian Jewish refugees. He simply said, "And what about the hundreds of other occasions we could have stepped in? What about all the other despots and fanatics throughout history? Should we have returned from limbo to smite Attila the Hun, Genghis Khan, Torquemada, Stalin, Pol Pot? No. We considered it but held off. On balance, in spite of these tragedies and injustices, humankind still seemed to be thriving, progressing. It was only at the turn of this century that it became apparent that this was no longer the case. That was when we realised that mortals were, indisputably, on course to their own doom, spiralling downward into the abyss with no hope of salvation or rescue – apart from us. And so we came. At the eleventh hour, perhaps, but better late than never. And now, Sam, speaking of late, evening is fast falling and I would dearly love to take you on a tour before the sun is gone."

"A tour?"

"As I said, I have things to show you, and things to persuade you of. Come with us and see what very few other mortals have been privileged to see. Come and see Olympus!"

62. OLYMPUS

SAM WAS HARDLY in a position to say no, and anyway it would have been foolish not to say yes. A tour was a chance to spy out potential escape routes, and there was, too, a part of her that was curious to take a look round the place. Who wouldn't be curious? *Olympus*, for heaven's sake.

Zeus was eager to impart the statistics and data as he and Ares showed her around. The Pantheonic stronghold had been modelled on the Acropolis, with added ramparts and stockades. It occupied 3.5 square kilometres of mountainside, on a tilted plateau between the ridge of sharp peaks that constituted Olympus's summit and the secondary peak known as Ilias, at an altitude of some 2,500 metres above sea level. It was built, just like its exemplar, of Athenian limestone and marble from the Penteli region, and comprised several clusters of private quarters, a temple dedicated to each member of the Pantheon and one dedicated to them all, a central *agora* or meeting place, and countless courtyards, colonnades and cloisters. There was a sunken amphitheatre where the more martially-minded Olympians practised their weaponcraft, a menagerie for the monsters, and a pool for communal bathing. Water was provided by snowmelt, while food was helicoptered in from the nearby city of Katerini, courtesy of the Greek government, which had also provided, likewise for free, the materials and manpower for the stronghold's construction.

"Ordinary food?" said Sam. "I thought you lot only ate ambrosia and nectar."

"If the locals wish to pay tribute in this way," Zeus replied blithely, "who are we to turn down their largesse? Not that the gifts the Greeks come bearing are given entirely selflessly. We have brought renewed prestige to their country. Our presence has put what had become a minor, some might say inconsequential, European power firmly back on the map. It's a more than fair exchange, in my opinion."

"The Greek government may think that. The people aren't so sure. They don't like their taxes being spent on you."

"The building work was costly, I grant you, but nonetheless a small fraction of the national GDP. And the food is a very modest outlay indeed."

"Even so, other nations are forever grumbling about how Greece mollycoddles you."

"Mollycoddles?" Zeus looked amused. "Pure jealousy. The whingeing of the wishful. Besides, correct me if I'm wrong, but I've not heard anything to that effect from your own Mr Bartlett."

"I said nations, not leaders."

"Are leaders not the mouthpieces for nations?"

"Not always," Sam said. "And only a totalitarian dictator would make that assumption."

"Sticks and stones may break my bones, Sam..." said Zeus.

"Not mine they don't," Ares averred.

The tour continued, and as they walked Sam kept casting surreptitious sidelong glances at Zeus. He was unmistakably his father's son. Close up, in the flesh, the resemblance was marked. Cut the hair, trim the beard to a goatee, and you'd have a younger Regis Landesman, only with Arianna Landesman's dark eyes. The body language was a match as well.

What was this absurd pose, then, that he wasn't Xander? A bluff? An attempt to deny any connection with his past, sever himself entirely from his despised father? Or was there a deeper, stranger explanation? Had he somehow made himself forget who he'd been, and done the same to his fellow Olympians? If so, how?

Above and beyond these puzzles, though, what perplexed Sam most of all was why Zeus was being so polite and hospitable. Dionysus had told her that Zeus was consumed utterly with hatred of the Titans and wouldn't rest until they were dead, or words to that effect. Yet here she was, a Titan, alive, having been brought back from the brink by Demeter at Zeus's request, and he was treating her with a courtesy that bordered on deferential. What was going on? What was his gameplan here? She couldn't fathom it.

A sweeping flight of stone steps took them down to the stronghold's main gate, which was immense, several trees' worth of wood planed and planked and dovetailed together. The gate's rear, reflecting pictures Sam had seen of its front, was embossed with bronze plaques. Each plaque carried the emblem of an Olympian – a thundercloud for Zeus, an owl for Athena, an anvil for Hephaestus, a bunch of grapes for Dionysus, and so on.

The towering gateposts on either side were topped with platforms, and here Harpies perched. One of the monsters took flight as the three neared. It soared on batlike wings into the dusk-purpled sky and circled a few times, letting out shrill cries that resounded out across the sheer slopes below and down into the valleys. When it returned to its roost on the vacant gatepost it found another Harpy had moved in to take its place, and a vicious altercation broke out, the two bird-woman creatures going at each other with beak and talon until finally the interloper, with a flustered squawk, beat a retreat and flew to a platform further along the battlements. There, in a true demonstration of the meaning of "pecking order," it turfed off the Harpy already sitting there and settled down in its stead.

"Should you be contemplating some kind of breakout," Zeus informed Sam, "I wouldn't advise it. Our Harpies are incredibly vigilant. When I say they sleep with one eye open, I mean it. They do. And such eyes, too. Sharp as a hawk's, with night vision to rival an owl's. So even supposing you were able to open the gate, Sam, which I very much doubt, you would not get far on the other side. A dozen Harpies would be on you in a trice."

"They have, after all, been exceptionally well trained," said a female voice.

It was Hera, who sidled up to join them, accompanied by a three-headed dog on a triple leash – Cerberus.

"No one," she said, "comes within a mile of here on foot. From bitter experience people have learned better than to do that. Death by Harpy is neither quick nor painless."

"My dear," said Zeus, "may I introduce Sam Akehurst."

"I'm well aware who she is," Hera replied, giving Sam a disdainful once-over. "One of the monster killers."

Cerberus gave a threefold growl and strained on its leashes towards Sam. A trio of large, near-spherical heads came within inches of her, so close that the slobber from the knifelike fangs flecked her dress. Sam couldn't help but shy away, much to Ares's amusement.

"Scared of a stupid mutt?" he scoffed. He patted one of Cerberus's heads, which suddenly rounded on him and bit his hand while the other two heads kept their attention fixed on Sam. "Ach! You fucker," Ares hissed, shaking the hand in the air.

"Your own fault, Ares," said Hera. "You startled him. He doesn't like people coming at him from the side."

"Yes, well," Ares said, sucking his hand, "let that be a lesson to you, Sam. That dog's got a hell of a nip on him. Didn't even break my skin, mind, but if it'd been you, you'd be looking at the bleeding stump of your wrist."

"So I was sensible to be scared of him then?" Sam said tartly.

"Hmph," was Ares's reply.

"If I had my way, Miss Akehurst," said Hera, with a doughty swell of her chest, "Cerberus would right this very moment be feasting on your vitals. The way you Titans massacred my menagerie was unforgivable. Quite, quite unforgivable. However..." A glance at Zeus. "My husband is adamant that you are not to be harmed, and what the Aegis-Bearing decrees, all must obey."

"Spoken like a good little wifey," Sam murmured.

Hera flashed a glare at her. "You would do well to mind your manners, mortal. Zeus is prone to whims and fancies, like any male, but that which he gives he can also take away. Without his protection, trust me, you would not last long here."

She stalked off, dragging the thrice-whining Cerberus with her.

Zeus chuckled indulgently. "Hera the Ox-Eyed does not like it if even I so much as look at another woman. I have a history of dalliances, of course, I won't deny it. But what she ought to know by now is that I always come back to her in the end. All said and done, she is the only one for me."

Sam was aghast. "Oh my God, is *that* what this is? You've taken a shine to me? I'm just another of your 'dalliances'?"

"Certainly not."

"That's repulsive. It's never going to happen, you hear me? One hundred per cent never."

"Hera spoke out of turn," Zeus said, spinning on his heel. "Now come. There's still more to see."

Sam turned incredulously to Ares. "Please tell me I'm not a dalliance."

"Zeus has always had a taste for nubile mortal females," said Ares, "and ever since he saw your picture on television he's been going on about capturing Titans if possible, rather than killing them. Although," he added, "that could just be coincidence. The main thing as far as you're concerned is that, while you don't annoy him, you get to live. So, if you want my advice, try not to annoy him."

"OK," said Sam. "But no way am I sleeping with him, ever, and if that means I'll be signing my own death warrant, fine."

Ares nodded, perhaps with a touch of admiration. "Nobly put. When the time comes, should the Fates decide that I am to be your executioner, I promise I shall do you the honour of making it swift and clean."

"Thanks for that, much appreciated," said Sam, and she set off to catch up with Zeus.

63. ARGUS

THE FINAL STOP on the Olympus tour was a chamber hewn deep in the rock of the mountainside and reminiscent in many ways of the command centre at Bleaney. Here, as there, could be found a plethora of screens and cables. The former provided the only illumination in the room, a wavering bluish glow, while the latter fed, presumably, to the meter-diameter parabolic antenna dish which Sam had spotted outside, nestled between two buildings, an incongruous sliver of modernity amid all the Classicism.

A smell reached Sam's nose as she followed Zeus and Ares into the chamber, a drab, musty odour that put her in mind of a teenage boy's bedroom. It was worse inside the chamber itself, stronger and more noxious. It spoke of unwashed flesh and fungal growth.

The source was – could only be – the corpulent figure who reclined in the centre of the room on a mound of silk cushions. He was near naked, his modesty preserved by a cloth draped across his groin, and his pallid, vein-marbled skin looked like it hadn't seen the sun in ages. It also looked like it hadn't seen soap and water in ages. There were blotches all over it that could have been food stains, encrustations that could have been rashes, a whole host of scummy dried-on marks of indeterminate origin. The covers of the cushions the figure half sat, half lay on were similarly bespattered and besmirched.

What was even more repellent about this bloated monstrosity, though, were the wires protruding from his head. A score of them were plugged into his hairless scalp, sticking out at all angles like rubber-insulated dreadlocks, and around the point at which each wire pierced the skin there was inflammation and scabbing. It reminded Sam of something from an anti-vivisection poster, a laboratory monkey with electrodes implanted in its brain.

He was slumped there with his eyes closed, as though blissfully asleep. However, as Sam drew (reluctantly) closer, she saw that his eyelids were puckered at the join, like pursed lips, and concave, sunken. There were no eyeballs beneath them.

"Argus?" said Zeus softly. "O Hundred-Eyed One? Can you hear me? Are you with us?"

Argus did not stir, but all round the chamber the screens flickered and changed. They had been displaying websites, live news broadcasts, CCTV footage, webcam images, a range of data input streaming in from across the globe, but now all at once each showed the same thing: a computer-generated peacock, its tailfeathers fanned, and the eye markings on the fan actual human-style eyes, different-coloured, intermittently blinking.

"Greetings to you, O mighty Zeus," said a warm, mellow voice that came from several directions simultaneously. The words echoed, cascaded, overlapped. "And to you, Ares. And to you too, Samantha Akehurst, former detective sergeant, resident of Kensal Rise, London." The voice proceeded to list Sam's driving licence and National Health numbers, gave the name of the high street bank she banked with, and threw in her credit rating for good measure. "Currently wanted by the London Metropolitan Police for questioning," it added.

"And my dress size?" Sam asked, trying not to sound unnerved.

A pause. Then: "You look like an eight to me."

"Actually I'm a ten."

"It's always wise to underestimate."

As the voice said this the man on the cushions, eerily, smiled.

"Argus," said Zeus, "Sam is, as you know, a member of the resistance group who were until not so long ago our mortal enemies – in more senses than one."

"Ah, yes, the Titans," said Argus. Several of the screens shifted from the peacock image to display stills from the Agonides clip, a blurry security-camera shot of a Titan haring through Manhattan, several newspaper pictures of dead and decaying Olympian monsters, a forensics photo of Søndergaard's skeleton half-buried in the dust of his battlesuit, and Titan-related soundbites from the press conference Zeus and Hercules gave in the shadow of the World Trade Centre and from Zeus and Hera's appearance on *Paulita*.

"There's more," he said, and a number of websites popped up on other screens, all of them festooned liberally with his peacock censorship-icon. "Titan-advocating sites and blogs and homepages. These are the ones I've allowed to continue to exist, the ones where the approval expressed is only moderate. The more ardent ones I have, of course, wrecked beyond repair."

"Still there are people rooting for you," said Zeus to Sam, "in spite of everything."

The words sent a small chill through her. "What do you mean, in spite of everything?"

"I mean, with no justification there are some poor misguided souls who still feel that the Titans are going to oust the Pantheon."

"Aren't we?" said Sam. "Just because you've taken one of us captive... Ohhh." Light dawned. Hope fluttered. "That's it, isn't it? I'm a hostage. You think the Titans won't dare attack again, as long as you're keeping me here. Well, newsflash, Zeus. It won't deter them. They know I'd rather die than have them abandon the mission. Do what you like to me, but the war will go on."

"You're misreading the situation completely, Sam," said Zeus. "You're not a hostage. To hold someone hostage implies that there are those for whom that person's continued survival matters."

"Which in this instance there are."

"She just isn't getting it, is she, Zeus?" said Ares, snickering. "I think you're going to have to give it to her in words of one syllable."

"Better yet, in pictures. Argus?"

"Yes, Zeus?"

"Bleaney Island, please. Everything you've gathered over the last three days."

"Your wish is my command."

The screens stuttered, altered, refreshed. Now there were shots taken from various news helicopters, showing Bleaney from several different angles. Some focused on an expanse of charred, blackened, churned-up ground which Sam was just able to identify as the site of the battle with the Olympians. Others were more distant views of the island, all of them featuring a vast column of smoke that was roiling up from, if Sam's guess was correct, the entrance to the bunker.

Argus turned up the volume on one screen where a microphone-toting reporter from CNN was doing a piece to camera on the landing jetty.

"...and as you can see behind me," the reporter was saying, "there's still a huge amount of smoke coming from below ground, and we can only imagine the kind of inferno that's raging down there. This is the closest we're allowed to get to the subterranean complex, a former Second World War listening post which, reports suggest, the Titans were using as their base of operations. It hasn't been confirmed how the Olympians uncovered this fact, but what we do know is that yesterday they came here in force to put paid to the Titan insurgency once and for all. And it would appear, certainly on the available evidence, that they have succeeded…"

Argus cross-faded to footage of another reporter, from the BBC this time, conducting street interviews with residents of the harbour town across the strait from Bleaney.

"…dreadful noise it were," said an old lady. "Bangs, crashes, explosions. You could hear it across the water, clear as day. I said to my husband, 'That's on Bleaney,' I said, 'and I bet it's them Olympians. *Something's* going on there,' I said. You could see this big black stormcloud hanging over the place, and the lightning was coming down like you wouldn't believe, flash, flash, flash, like that, that quick. Never seen the like!"

Cut to a bespectacled middle-class dad wrangling a restless toddler: "Yes, we've always been a bit suspicious about the goings-on over there. 'Research into cold fusion' we were told – keep still, Harry – but everyone was convinced there was more to it than that. For months people kept saying they'd heard, well, muffled gunfire, and no one believed them, but clearly they were right. Who knew? It's amazing what can go on right beneath your nose. Harry! No ice cream now. Later."

Cut to a couple of acne-speckled youths in sportswear, hair gelled to a slick gloss. One did the talking while the other sipped from a can of the energy drink Ichor and grunted agreement every now and then: "Yeah, right, it's crazy, innit, like these people was right on our doorstep – so to speak – and nobody knew nuffink, kinda makes you proud, like they was goin' out all over the world and smackin' them Olympian w[*bleep*]ers up and comin' back to Bleaney of all places, like that lump of rock out there in the sea where there's nuffink but rabbits, but it's pretty cool to think they was right here 'cause nuffink happens round here, knowahmean?"

Cut back to the BBC reporter herself. "So there you have it," she said, "a flavour of the local opinion about the astonishing events of the past twenty-four hours. To recap, the Olympians have attacked the island the Titans were calling home, just off the coast here, and from what we've seen and from what coastguard and police are saying, there are no survivors. No bodies have been found, but no Titans have been spotted alive either. We don't know where they are, where they've gone to, assuming any of them are left, but the likelihood is, given how thorough the Olympians are known to be, that the Titans are simply no more."

And now another reporter, from ITN: "...must presume that the Titans' bold, perhaps foolhardy stance against the Olympians has come to its inevitably bitter end..."

And now none other than Jennifer Konchalowsky from Fox News, flown over to England specifically to cover the breaking story: "...this is what you get for sowing whirlwinds. The Titans have reaped themselves a deadly harvest of Olympian wrath. They poked the hornets' nest, and boy have they got stung."

And Prime Minister Bartlett, in Downing Street: "I'm sure I'm not alone in hoping that once and for all a line has been drawn under this scandalous and sordid chapter in modern history and that we can look forward to a future of continued *entente cordiale* with our friends in the Pantheon. The Titans may have been based in Britain but I can't emphasise enough that their antics were in no way representative of British policy and our Great British values..."

And President Stavropoulos: "A buncha Limeys. Who woulda guessed?"

And finally, Jennifer Konchalowsky again: "It's over. *Finito.* The Olympians have flushed the rats out of their hidey-hole and exterminated them. We can go back to living our lives again as normal. Time's up, Titans. You had your shot and you blew it. Goodnight."

Argus faded the volume down to zero, and the chamber was filled with nothing but the hum and whine of the screens. Zeus and Ares stared expectantly at Sam. She kept her face rigid, her expression inscrutable. Inside, though, she was crumbling.

"No bodies," she said finally. "No bodies equals no proof. They could still be alive. Did you actually kill them? Did you actually, personally see them all die? Well? Did you?"

Ares looked at Zeus, Zeus at Ares.

"We can account for one death for certain," Zeus said. "Hades used his death touch on one of you, and the man fell."

"I saw that. I also saw Hades get shot."

"He's better now. As for the other Titans, after Hermes whisked you from the battlefield I unleashed the full might of the lightning."

"Scorched earth policy," said Ares.

"I blasted every inch of ground. It was spectacular, if I say so myself. I can't remember when I last let rip like that. Not since Sjælland, that's for sure."

"My ears are still ringing," said Ares.

"Naturally, your teammates were routed. They panicked. Started lobbing smoke bombs."

"White phosphorus grenades."

"I kept up with the lightning strikes. It was pandemonium for a while."

"Chaos!"

"But at last it was done, and the smoke thinned, the air cleared, and there was nothing left of our enemies, not even smithereens. We searched all over the island, just to be sure. As the reporter said, we're nothing if not thorough. Then we entered that bunker of yours."

"And had some fun," said Ares. "Nothing beats a bit of rampant post-victory vandalism."

"All your equipment, your belongings."

"Bashed. Smashed. Trashed."

"A rather grand-looking office, ruined."

"Your mission control, all that technology, shattered beyond recognition."

"And afterwards we set a fire. A fire that burned through the whole place, reducing it to cinders, turning your dream to ashes, and then we informed the media of what we had done, and you've just watched the fallout." Zeus studied Sam. "Do you get it now? That Konchalowsky woman, empty-headed language mangler that she is, summed it up pretty well. It's over. *Finito*. Goodnight, Titans. You're the last one left, Sam, the only survivor. We've won."

Sam did all she could to keep her emotions in check, but the very effort of doing so set her body trembling.

"She's sad," said Argus's everywhere-at-once voice.

"Don't be sad," said Ares. "You were valiant to the end, all of you, despite the fact that there was never any doubt that you were going to lose. It was a glorious defeat. Courage like that should be celebrated."

Sam continued to say nothing. All she could think was: *no bodies equals no proof.* That was the one last flimsy scrap of hope she had to hold on to. Ramsay, Barrington, Hamel, Sparks, all dead. Landesman too. But *no bodies equals no proof.* Captain Fuller's boat – it was just conceivable that the Titans had got to the jetty and joined Lillicrap and the techs aboard and got away. She had to believe that.

No bodies equals no proof.

She repeated it in her head like a mantra.

No bodies equals no proof.

Because otherwise, what else was there for her? What else was left?

64. THE MUNDANE LIVES OF GODS

DAYS CAME AND went on that chilly mountain peak, and Sam drifted along, numb, observing the mundane lives of gods.

The Olympians endured her presence among them with varying degrees of acceptance. Zeus was by far the friendliest, Hera by far the least friendly, and the others ranged along a scale between these two extremes but tending more towards the Hera end. Aphrodite and Dionysus did a marvellous job of pretending they were delighted to have Sam there but she could almost hear their smiles vanish the moment they turned their backs on her, and her own loathing of Aphrodite made smiling back out of the question. Hephaestus, meanwhile, seemed to grumble about almost everything, so it was hardly out of character that he grumbled about her ("Mortals have their place, and this isn't it."). He mostly kept to himself in his own temple, however, from where could be heard, now and then, the clank and groan of metal being worked.

With Apollo Sam had very little interaction, and that was probably just as well, since the sight of him, proximity to him, made her feel physically unwell. He spent all his day honing his warrior skills at the amphitheatre, or else exercising, pumping weights, running, swimming, often in the company of Ares. He paid Sam no heed – she was beneath his dignity. If he considered her in some way responsible for the death of his twin sister, there was no sign of it, although she couldn't help noticing that, a few days after she arrived on Olympus, one of the mannequins he used for archery practice had received a splash of orange paint on its head, a crude approximation of auburn hair. Whenever she passed, this mannequin was always pin-cushioned with arrows.

Poseidon was an infrequent visitor to Olympus. He regarded himself as an outsider, the one hard done by, the perpetual black sheep, although when he came he expected to be welcomed with open arms and made a fuss of. Otherwise, he got huffy and muttered about lack of kinship and respect. He didn't have much to say to or do with Sam.

Would that Hades had been the same. He liked to hang around her and engage in conversation about the most trivial, inane things, all the while eyeing her up and licking his dry lips. With his cadaverous looks and those black leather gloves he reminded Sam of the kind of man who loitered outside school gates or got caught with unforgivable jpegs on his home computer hard drive, and she made every effort to avoid him if she could, but it wasn't easy. Wherever she went around the stronghold, Hades would sooner or later appear, smiling his far too toothsome smile. "Why, hello, Miss Akehurst. Fancy bumping into you." Or: "So we meet again. People will talk." It was hard to tell what he wanted from her, beyond a few minutes of stilted chitchat, but Sam couldn't escape the impression that he was sizing her up for something. What, she dreaded to think and wasn't keen to find out.

Ares she quite liked – didn't despise so wholeheartedly, at any rate – and he in turn adopted a sort of prison officer attitude towards her. Formal, not at all kindly, but you knew where you stood with him. As long as you didn't give him any nonsense, he wouldn't give you any grief.

Athena was an altogether different matter. The least well-known of the Olympians, the one who shunned the limelight as a rule, she was stern and no-nonsense and quite frank in her resentment of Sam. Just as Sam could seldom steer clear of Hades when she was out and about, she couldn't evade the contempt-filled looks that Athena sent her way, most often during meals, which were taken in the *naos* – the main central courtyard – of the communal Pantheonic temple. Every time Sam so much as glanced her way across the table, there was Athena, high-browed and haughty, glaring. Usually Athena would then lean over to Hera and whisper something, still with her eyes on Sam, and Hera would nod grimly. As Sam understood it, these two Olympians were not supposed to like one another. In the myths, being the offspring of Zeus and his first wife Metis had earned Athena the undying enmity of her stepmother. But, assuming the myths had any relevance here, the two of them looked to have overcome their differences. Possibly their shared dislike of Sam was helping bring them closer together.

Demeter was also in the staunchly anti-Sam camp. So was Hermes, which didn't bother Sam in the least, since she was staunchly anti-Hermes. He was Darren Pugh, after all. Looked the same. Spoke the same. Walked the same. He might be dressed up as Hermes, and possess the requisite powers, but there wasn't a shred of doubt in her mind that this was the ex-con who had threatened her back on that first day at Bleaney and had then taken Landesman's cheque, agreeing to go away and not tell a soul about the invitation or the island.

Only, he hadn't stuck to his promise, had he? It didn't take a genius to work out how things had gone. Maybe the money had run out, trickling through Pugh's slippery fingers faster than he could hold on to it, or maybe not but he had nonetheless spotted an opportunity to make some more, or just gain himself a leg-up in the world.

She confronted him about it one afternoon, when she was heavily premenstrual and in a combative mood. Hermes was alone on the steps of his temple, burnishing his helmet with a cloth. Sam strode up and said, "Do you really not remember me?"

Hermes looked blank. "Until I hauled you off that island, I'd never seen you before in my life."

"January. In the bunker. I pegged you as a jailbird from the off. You got shirty and called me 'ginger tits,' then went off in a strop with a lot of Regis Landesman's money. Which you then, I bet, pissed away on booze, women and horses, am I right?"

The blank look remained, although the phrase "ginger tits" seemed to spark something, albeit momentarily. In his eyes had there been just that tiniest flash of recollection?

"Woman, I am Hermes the Thrice-Great, He Who Presides Over Contests," he said. "That's who I am and who I have always been."

"And after the money was gone," Sara continued, "what? You saw something about the Titans on the telly and your cunning little mind put two and two together. You remembered the bunker, you remembered what Landesman was promising us, and next thing you're in touch with the Olympians, saying you know where we can be found. But you wanted something in return for that information. You probably asked for money but they made you a better offer. Power. They needed a new Hermes, so they offered you the job. That's what happened, isn't it?"

"I've heard that you're not quite right in the head..."

"That's what happened," Sam insisted. "You traded our whereabouts for speed, teleportation and that tin helmet there. You sold us out."

Hermes smiled and shrugged. "Zeus has said you're not to be harmed, but I'm sorely tempted to take you up to a very high crag and –"

"Have they done this before?" Sam cut in, musing aloud. "Replaced an Olympian who's died with a substitute? It's conceivable. Maybe one of you was killed in action but the death was covered up and along comes a new face shortly afterwards, same outfit, same powers, but no one's looked further than that and spotted that it's an impostor. The brand continues, original packaging, new content. That really would make each of you immortal, after a fashion."

"I'm going to go now," said Hermes.

"And your memories get wiped, too. How does Zeus do that? I'm assuming it's Zeus behind all this. He gives the powers, takes away your past, somehow makes you convinced you're genuinely a Greek god..."

"Really am going."

"...and you're left none the wiser. Can it be done? More to the point, where is it done?"

"Goodbye."

Hermes vanished.

"Yes, off you go," Sam said to the empty space where he had just been sitting. "Run off and polish your helmet somewhere else. I know who you are and what you did, Pugh. You're on my shit list too, you know."

Empty as this threat was, she felt better for saying it.

Later, Zeus drew her aside for a quiet word. "Hermes tells me you were haranguing him today with this – I can only call it conspiracy nonsense. That's him in addition to me, Ares, Aphrodite,

Dionysus... Anyone else? Just please desist, Sam. None of us is interested. Your convictions aren't convincing. We don't believe your disbelief. It's irksome and tiresome, and frankly your position here is tenuous as it is without you imperilling it further. Try and fit in and behave. That's all I ask."

"My position?" Sam retorted. "And just what position is that, Zeus? Because, me, I have no idea. Why am I even on Olympus? I hate it here. Everyone hates *me*. Why are you keeping me around? Am I a pet? Spoils of war? What? *What the fuck do you want from me?*"

Zeus took a step back, eyeing her with a lofty, paternalistic gaze. Behind it, though, she thought he looked hurt.

"I want nothing from you," he said, "that isn't given voluntarily."

"And that's supposed to mean...?"

He didn't elaborate.

"Zeus, either kill me or set me free. Those are the only two things I'm after. One or the other, you choose. I don't much mind which it is. Anything rather than stay on here with this dysfunctional so-called family of yours, half of who hate my guts and the rest of who either don't even notice me or else keep sniffing around me like a dog on heat."

"Who keeps 'sniffing around' you?"

"No one."

"Hades? It is, isn't it? Is he bothering you? I've seen him and you together a lot. I'll have words. You won't have to worry about him any more."

And from that moment on, she didn't. Hades kept his distance, although she often felt the weight of his stare on her, sulky now, baleful, offended. She noticed, too, that he had started making a point of removing his gloves in her presence and articulating his fingers, like a pianist warming up, practising invisible arpeggios in the air. It was a show for her benefit, and she resolved to be more careful around him from now on. A single touch of those skeletal fingers and she'd be dead in a flash, as had happened to Fred Tsang, as had happened to countless others. It didn't even have to be deliberate. A chance collision, an accidental misstep that brought her skin into contact with one of those hands, and it would all be over.

That she was anxious about Hades's hands told her a truth about herself.

She wasn't willing to die, for all that she had claimed she was.

She wanted to live.

And that meant escaping.

65. CRATES

BUT STILL SHE couldn't see *how* to actually escape. There was no way in or out of the stronghold except via the gate, which lacked an operating mechanism and indeed seemed designed to be openable only by hand. And the hand that opened it would have to be an Olympian's. So huge a portal would yield to the strength of an Ares, say, or a Hercules. Not, though, to the comparatively feeble strength of a Sam Akehurst.

Then, of course, there were the Harpies to take into account.

Gate apart, the one other route out of the stronghold worth consideration was the freight helicopter which came once a week, on Sundays, bearing a crate full of supplies. The crate, an eight-foot plywood cube with Greek script and right-way-up arrows stencilled on it, was winched down into the *agora*, then an Olympian, normally Hermes, would detach the cable and hook it to the previous week's now-empty crate for the hovering chopper to take away. If, Sam thought, she could somehow get herself into that empty crate without being seen, she could be flown to Katerini and safety.

It was a very big if, though. Each empty crate was sealed up in readiness the day before pick-up, usually sometime in the morning but never later than the evening. Assuming she managed to clamber inside and not be discovered during the sealing-up process, there was still the problem of her absence being noted over the course of the Saturday night – and it would be, by Zeus if nobody else, and he would raise the alarm, and then perhaps Hera would set Cerberus on her trail, all three of its noses sniffing out her place of concealment...

No, she had to accept that that particular crate plan was a non-starter.

Then how about leaping onto the empty crate and clinging on as it was being hoisted away?

This had potential. Except, the Sunday helicopter drops were a source of great excitement to the Olympians. Almost the entire Pantheon would turn out to watch the chopper fly in and out, and then be on hand for the opening of the new crate, the unveiling of all the essentials and luxuries inside. Sam would never make it onto the departing crate without one of them seeing, and Hermes would have her back down off it and onto the ground in no time.

Each time the helicopter arrived Sam steeled herself to put this plan into action. Each time, the sheer unfeasibility of a success overwhelmed her and left her paralysed.

Then all she could do was watch, crestfallen, disappointed in herself, as the Olympians clustered around the new crate and pried it open. There would be delight at some fresh seasonal delicacy the Greek government had decided to treat them to, disgust over some unfavoured foodstuff, affront that a particular item had not been included even though it had been on the request form which Argus had emailed to Athens the previous Monday. Then there was the division of the crate's non-edible contents, which really showed the Pantheonic hierarchy in operation. Hera had first pick and snapped up the best of the boudoir products for herself – this fragrance, that lip balm, those bath salts – before any of the other female Olympians got a look-in. Zeus likewise had first pick of the male-orientated toiletries. Then it was Athena's turn, then Poseidon's if he was there, then Ares's, then Demeter's, and so on all the way down to Dionysus and Hephaestus. Fortunately Dionysus was interested only in wine, which none of the others had quite such a penchant for, so he was quite happy to get dibs on the Beaujolais Nouveau or the retsina and forgo all else. Lame old Hephaestus, however, was invariably left with little, the dregs of the crate, and just as invariably he would fume and grouse about this to anyone who would listen, which was no one, until his wife Aphrodite told him to be quiet.

The weekly airdrop was a highlight of the Olympians' week, and it became clear to Sam, as her stay on the mountaintop wore on, that if there was one thing that characterised the general mood of the Pantheon, it was boredom. They had set the world to rights and now, interruptions like the Titans aside, there wasn't much to do except monitor the global situation and make sure the lid stayed tightly pressed down.

That, then, would be why they loved to argue amongst themselves so much – it helped pass the time. Bickering at table was commonplace. In fact, it seemed almost compulsory. Hardly a meal went by without someone dragging out some long-held grudge for an airing, and more often than not Zeus was the one who instigated these spats.

"Ares, remind me again," he said one lunchtime, seemingly *à propos* of nothing. "Your little fling with Aphrodite, how did that end?"

"It ended," declared Hephaestus before Ares could reply, "because I ended it! Caught them out, didn't I? Ares seduced her, soiled her, my own wife, with his grubby, hairy paws, but I –"

"Seduced her?" Ares said, a scornful bark. "Oh, believe me, He Who Dwells In Etna, nobody seduces Aphrodite. She was willing, let me tell you. More than willing, downright eager. Couldn't keep her hands off me. Could you, O Beautiful-Buttocked? She craved the touch of a real man, a man with vigour and stamina, having had to suffer the attentions of a stunted, crippled blacksmith for so long. Tell me, Hephaestus, does 'limp' apply to everything about you or just the way you walk?"

"Oh, how funny," Hephaestus said. "Haven't heard that one in a long time. But I got you back. Got you back good and proper. With my bronze net I trapped the pair of you in bed together, and then the rest of us gathered round and how we laughed." He roared with laughter, to illustrate.

Aphrodite, throughout, kept her head down and her gaze fixed firmly on her plate.

On another occasion, again after a spot of none-too-subtle nudging from Zeus, Demeter started having a go at Hades for his having abducted her daughter and dragged her down into the underworld to be his queen.

"My poor dear Persephone," she said, "forced to be a consort in such a gloomy, sunless place when she was born a creature of the daylight, the breezes, the sky."

"She gets all that in spring, summer and autumn," Hades said. "She spends only the three winter months with me. That was our deal, after she ate three of the twelve seeds in that pomegranate, and it seems a more than reasonable one. If there's anyone you should feel sorry for it's me, deprived of the comforts of a wife for three quarters of the year. Besides, the kingdom of the dead isn't so bad, once you get used to it."

Sam was tempted to ask where this Persephone was right now? Did she even exist? And what about the underworld? As far as she could tell, Hades spent all his time on Olympus. If he was the ruler of some other realm, he was very much an absentee monarch.

But a look from Zeus forestalled her before she could pipe up. He sensed exactly what was going through her mind, and a subtle sideways flick of his head indicated that it should remain there, if she knew what was good for her.

One suppertime, over a roast suckling pig cooked to perfection by Demeter, Hera turned the tables and embarked on a sustained critique of Zeus and his many infidelities. It seemed light-hearted at first, a piece of teasing, wife trying to embarrass husband even though knowing that he felt no shame. She couldn't, however, keep a trickle of venom from entering her voice.

"Antiope, the river god's daughter," she said. "What form did you take in order to attract her, Zeus? I can't remember, was it a satyr by any chance? How charming. A short, hirsute man with stubby little goat legs – I can't think of anything more alluring. And Europa. A white bull, wasn't it? Innocent little virgin, she wasn't to know any better. I wonder, did you woo her or *moo* her?"

Athena and Demeter both chortled archly at the witticism.

"And then there was that silly thing Leda," Hera went on, "who fell for you while you were playing at being a swan. Swans can break a man's arm with their wing, but all you managed to do was break her heart. And after she went to the trouble of laying a couple of eggs for you! And what about Callisto? At least you came to her in the shape of a man, without bothering with all that animal disguise nonsense.

Although, hmmm, didn't you turn *her* into a bear after you'd had your wicked way with her, so as to hide her from me? And then Artemis hunted her down and killed her."

"Artemis," said Apollo. "Ha! That was just like her. Couldn't see a bear without wanting to chase after it." He tore some pork off the bone with his teeth, eyeing Sam all the while. "I miss her," he added, chewing morosely.

"Then there's Semele, Danaë, Leto, Alcmene, Io..." Hera checked off the names on her fingers. "The list is endless. You should count yourself lucky, Zeus, that you have a wife who's prepared to put up with your philandering."

"Dearest Hera," said Zeus, "'put up with' is hardly how I would describe your behaviour towards some of my conquests and their offspring. Take Io. I transformed her into a cow so that she would escape your notice and your ire..."

"A cow. So gallant of you."

"...and what did you do? Turned yourself into a gadfly and so tormented her with your stinging that she galloped halfway round the world in a maddened frenzy. If that's 'putting up with,' I'd hate to see what you're like when you truly take against someone."

"Speaking as Semele's son," said Dionysus, very drunk as was customary by this point in the evening, "I admit that my stepmother and I have had our misunderstandings, but we have managed to overcome them. Yes, she arranged for me to be torn limb from limb, and yes, she wasn't best pleased when I was presented to her dressed as a girl in the hope that she wouldn't recognise me and realise I had survived her murder plot. Weren't fooled for a moment, though, were you, O Hera the Fulfiller? But then I'd never make for a very convincing female, not with this beard."

"Maybe with those fat man-breasts of yours you would," said Ares.

"Thank you and fuck you," said Dionysus. "All I'm saying is, Hera can be forgiving, in the end. The fact that I am here, in the bosom of the family, regarded as close kin, proves it. Same goes for the twins. For Demeter too. There aren't many wives who'd happily sup at the same table as one of her husband's ex-lovers, let alone become good friends with her."

"I can be forgiving," Hera agreed. "But forgiveness is never boundless, Zeus. You'd do well to bear that in mind. There comes a point when enough is enough. An extramural indiscretion is one thing, but to flaunt it, to rub our noses in it, is quite another."

She didn't look at Sam when she said this, but then she didn't need to. Everyone present was aware who was the true focus of these remarks.

"There are acts no wife should be expected to support or tolerate," she added, laying down her napkin and pushing back her chair. "Decide sooner rather than later what it is you want to do, my husband, or the decision will be made for you, forcibly, permanently, and in a manner that will cause considerable distress to one of the parties concerned. Do I make myself clear?"

So saying, she left the dining hall, and Athena and Demeter followed her out in a show of solidarity.

Zeus broke the ensuing awkward silence. "Well. I, for one, have no idea what all that was about? Does anyone else?"

The joke fell flat. Only Dionysus found it funny, but then he was so deep in his cups that anything and everything seemed funny to him.

Hades, however, seemed very pleased by the turn of events, as though Hera's threat to Sam promised some kind of windfall for him.

66. MARTYRS

SAM STAYED IN her room for the next couple of days with a feigned illness, lying low, venturing out only to grab leftover food from Demeter's kitchen and scurry back to eat it alone. She had no desire to mingle with the Olympians, not now that Hera had so openly declared her hostility. Anyone could see that Zeus had been set an ultimatum. Whatever his intentions towards Sam were, he had better act on them, otherwise his wife would step in and cut through this particular Gordian Knot herself.

The impulse to escape, and the impossibility of it, warred within Sam, the one hemmed in tormentingly by the other.

On the morning of the third day, beginning to get stir crazy, she headed out into the frigid dawn air. No one else was around other than the ever-present, ever-vigilant Harpies, cawing and cackling on their roosts.

She roamed, enjoying the semblance of freedom that being on her own gave her. Her wanderings took her eventually to a corner of the stronghold she hadn't explored before. Here she came across a low-built edifice, like a large mausoleum, sandwiched between a tall rock outcrop and the inner flank of the stockade. This had not been on the itinerary of the tour Zeus had given. Curiosity piqued, she tried to door, tugging on its large round brass handle. The door, banded with iron, did not budge. There was no evidence of a lock but something, certainly, was holding it fast. She circuited the building but found no other entry point, not even a window. Returning to the front, she searched for some outward sign of the structure's purpose but found none. It had one unusual feature, a copper lightning rod attached to the vertex of the roof, two metres long and greened with oxidation. Other than that the place was plain and nondescript, almost ostentatiously so, given the general grandeur and ornateness that could be found everywhere else in the stronghold.

Perhaps it was some kind of storage unit.

Or perhaps this is where they're keeping my TITAN suit.

The thought galvanised Sam. She'd given up her battlesuit for lost, assuming Zeus would have destroyed it by now, but if by chance it was here, if she could be reunited with it, then a bid for freedom stood a substantially improved likelihood of success.

She resolved to come back after nightfall armed with something she could use as a crowbar to pry the door open.

Moving on, she shortly found herself passing the entrance to Argus's lair: a gap in a rockface surrounded by a carved-out portico, with giant bas-relief peacocks standing sentinel on either side. She had no intention of going in. Even the thought of Argus – that blubbery malodorous body, that wire-sprouting head – gave her the willies. But then a low, rippling voice called out from within: "Who's there? Someone's there. I'm picking up the sound of footsteps. I'm glad you've come. I need to talk to someone."

Sam started tiptoeing away, but Argus became plaintive and insistent. "Please. You must listen to me, whoever you are. It's urgent. Something important is happening. The mortals are up to something."

That was too intriguing to ignore. Turning, and bracing herself for the smell, Sam entered the chamber.

"Oh," said Argus. "It's only you, Samantha Akehurst."

"Only me."

"I need Zeus. Would you fetch him? I have intelligence I need to share."

"What's it about? I could pass on a message."

Sam glanced around as she said this, and noticed that several of the screens were tuned to surveillance satellite images – orbital views of Greece and the Mediterranean – while on others there were news broadcasts showing smartly dressed people, quite possibly diplomats, stepping out of limousines and walking quickly into imposing buildings. One screen featured warships at sea, another a series of military transport aircraft taking off. This was as much as she could take in before, with an "ah-ah-ah!," Argus swapped all these feeds for his peacock insignia. Hundreds of feather-mounted eyes glared reprovingly at Sam.

"Zeus," Argus said. "Not you. Kindly go and get him."

She came back shortly with a yawning Zeus. He didn't tell her to wait outside, so she went in with him.

"A bit early for our morning update, isn't it?" Zeus said to Argus.

"I regret getting you out of bed, but it just couldn't wait. Although," Argus added, "perhaps this should be for your ears only."

With a look at Sam, Zeus said, "Perhaps I should be the judge of that."

"But she's a mortal."

"So she is. But presumably what you have to tell me is news from the mortal world, meaning other mortals will know about it already, so why not her too? Besides, Sam is one of us for the time being, whether she likes it or not. Your tact is commendable, Argus, but unnecessary."

"As you wish, Cloud-Gatherer." The screens reverted from the peacock to the disparate images they'd been showing before. "This began late yesterday evening. I've been monitoring developments overnight."

"What am I looking at?"

"We have what amounts to a military coup taking place in the United Kingdom."

"What!?" Zeus exclaimed.

"General Sir Neville Armstrong-Hall is the instigator," said Argus. "Although he's calling himself Field Marshal now, because he believes Britain is on a war footing. He's invoked a law drawn up during the Cold War that's become redundant but hasn't been removed from the statute books. It was drafted to allow the mobilisation of British armed forces without parliamentary authority in the event of a Soviet nuclear strike."

"Mobilise them to do what?"

"Anything they like, more or less. In this instance, move on Olympus."

Sam saw Zeus's mouth drop open. "Preposterous! They can't. Why would they do that?"

By way of answer, Argus pulled up footage of a trim, grey-haired old soldier holding an impromptu press conference at an airbase, surrounded by a jostling mob of reporters all yelling, "Sir Neville! Sir Neville!"

"It's a nettle that needs to be grasped," Field Marshal Armstrong-Hall said, "and now seems to be the time to grasp it. People at home should rest assured that this is not, I repeat not, a declaration of martial law. Parliament is only being pre-empted, not supplanted. This is military action against an outside power, in retaliation for an attack that took place on British soil a few weeks ago – an attack that was, in my view, no less disruptive and impactful than a nuclear warhead would have been. I am simply doing now what the vast majority of the British public wish to be done and what our elected representatives, shirking their democratic mandate, have stubbornly refused to do. I regret that it's come to this. Since Bleaney Island I have been holding frequent behind-the-scenes meetings with Mr Bartlett, urging him to harden his stance towards the Olympians, but frankly I've been wasting my breath. Now, at a time when the Olympians have been proved to be vulnerable, and after an example has been so bravely and tragically set to us by these Titans, *now* is the moment to be decisive and take action of the kind that, God willing, has a decent prospect of success."

"There's more," Argus said. "The Americans are offering logistical support. The US Joint Chiefs of Staff have issued a statement in the past hour backing Armstrong-Hall."

At the Pentagon, a much-medalled general at a podium was addressing a rowdy press pack. It was 11pm Eastern Standard Time.

"We're pledging the Brits all of our Chinooks," the general drawled in iron-edged Texas tones, "plus ordnance, body armour, because we know how underequipped those fellas can be in that department, and last but not least the use of our one remaining aircraft carrier – the *Nimitz*-class USS *Prometheus*, which happens to be in the eastern Atlantic even as we speak, just off the Straits of Gibraltar – as a floating command post and field hospital."

"General! General! General!" the reporters cried.

"That's as much matériel as we can spare for now," he continued, "but we'll be keeping a weather eye on things, and should the situation alter radically we'll be prepared to maybe escalate our involvement further."

"What about the President?" somebody shouted.

The general's gimlet eyes glinted. "What about him?" he said, dismissively, and quit the podium amid a blitzkrieg of camera flashes.

"The Japanese navy is sailing back this way," Argus said, "and there've been reports of other nations putting their armed forces on a state of high alert."

"How could this all have sprung up so suddenly?" said Zeus.

"The pressure has been building for some while. If the internet is anything to go by, the global consensus has steadily been turning against us."

"Yes, I was aware of that, but I assumed that would die down eventually. It normally does."

"But it seems to have come to a head instead," said Argus. "And if you think you're having trouble believing what Armstrong-Hall has done, take a look at Mr Bartlett."

A late-night emergency session at the Commons. A harassed Bartlett was standing at the despatch box, trying to make himself heard above a House packed with restive, baying MPs.

"Mr Speaker, I would ask Sir Neville, beg him, to reconsider. He – he is knowingly endangering – *knowingly endangering* the Great British public. If he persists in these actions, it will place this country in the firing line. He cannot go down to Greece. He cannot position troops on the territory of – on the territory of another sovereign nation without their consent. That is a violation of international law. More than that, it's sheer folly, and I will not stand for it!"

The cry, Sam thought, *of an impotent man*. Bartlett knew there was nothing he could do but bluster and remonstrate. He'd been undermined by events. The ground beneath his feet was crumbling. He had become a victim of his own lily-liveredness.

"Can we all not just –" Bartlett went on, but the rest of what he had to say was drowned by massed bleating from the ranks of the Honourable Opposition, Shadow Cabinet and backbenchers alike.

"Baa!" they all went, "Baa! Baa!," taunting him like playground bullies, until the Prime Minister had no choice but to drop back into the seat behind him and sit there with his arms crossed, red-cheeked and fuming.

Argus said, "Other communications chatter I've been intercepting suggests that paramilitary organisations are throwing their hats in the ring as well. The Resistenza Contru-Diu Corsu, to name but one."

Galetti! He'd told Sam the RCDC owed the Titans a debt of gratitude. Now, if a little late to be of direct benefit to them, it seemed he was going to pay it.

"And the Agonides are podcasting about sourcing themselves weapons and volunteering."

Zeus rubbed his brow hard. Outside, distantly, thunder growled.

"Here," he said. "They're coming *here*."

"RAF planes have already touched down at Larisa and Tanagra airbases. The Greek government hasn't granted them permission, but the Hellenic Air Force hasn't lifted a finger to turn them away."

"Fellow travellers. They're in on it too."

"Not against it, certainly."

"Don't these people understand?" The thunder crackled louder, sharper, clearer. "They'll never win. They cannot."

"It's your own fault," said Sam.

Zeus swivelled round. "Excuse me? Who asked your opinion?"

"Nobody, but I'm going to give it to you anyway. You Olympians have brought this on yourselves, by killing the Titans. You made martyrs of them, and if there's one thing people love, it's a martyr."

"But we've killed countless others over the years. What makes the Titans so different? Why were they – you – special?"

"Because we hurt you," Sam said. "We did what no one else had done and showed there were chinks in the Olympian armour. That raised us in people's estimation. We gave the world what nobody else had been able to before – hope. You stamped down on us and crushed us out of existence, but it was too late. Hope's a pesky thing. You only have to think of Pandora. Hope won't stay in the box. Once it's out, it's out, and nothing you can do will put it back in or stop it spreading." She was mangling the myth somewhat but Zeus didn't seem to notice.

"But what good is this hope, if all it's going to do is create thousands more martyrs?"

"That's not the point, is it? People have been inspired to rise up against you again, *en masse*. And if they die, that's likely to inspire still others. Hope's like that."

"I do not accept this!" Zeus shouted, and a thunderclap detonated right overhead, making the chamber shake. Zigzags of static fizzed across all of Argus's screens, and the images on some rolled upwards, vertical hold lost.

"O God Of Gain, if you wouldn't mind," said Argus, sounding pained. "You're interfering with my signals..."

Zeus's eyes blazed. Sam wondered if she hadn't pushed him too far.

Then, slowly, he calmed. His jaw unclenched. The storm abated.

"Lay siege to Olympus then, would they?" he said. "Well, let them. Let them come. Let them try. All they'll find here is nemesis, divine retribution. Argus, keep abreast of events, figure out how long we've got until the first troops reach our doorstep. I'm going to call together the Pantheon. We need to discuss strategy. But before that – Sam." He grabbed her roughly by the arm. "You are coming with me."

67. THE SHRINE OF APOTHEOSIS

THIS IS IT, Sam thought as Zeus frogmarched her out of Argus's lair. *It's over. I'm done.*

A formal execution? Perhaps. Ares with his axe. A beheading. Or maybe Zeus would opt for something slower and more gruesome. Evict her from the stronghold and let the Harpies have their way with her. Or else he'd just fry her himself with a lightning bolt. She only had herself to blame. She had provoked him. She had spoken out of turn. Her own big mouth had got her into this. It was either that or Zeus simply didn't want her around any longer, now troops were on their way to mount an attack on Olympus. He didn't want someone in his camp who'd be sympathetic to the enemy's aims, a potential Fifth Columnist. Whatever the reason, Hera was about to get her wish. Her husband's latest dalliance, such as it was, was at an end.

As in the run-up to the battle at Bleaney, Sam felt calm, fatalistic, resigned. She didn't want to die but you had to accept that which you could not change. Death had hovered over her life since her late teens, when her parents were taken from her. Death had been omnipresent during her police career, when scarcely a month went by without her being confronted by some corpse or other – a murder victim, an accidental drowning, an overdose, a suicide. Then there was Ade's death, and her own subsequent flirtations with ending it all, and following that the progressive, one-by-one deaths of the Titans, climaxing with the Pantheon's mass destruction of those of them that death had so far spared, all save her (except: *no bodies equals no proof*). Death had been stalking Sam over the years, at times breathing down her neck, at other times standing off at a distance but still at the periphery of her consciousness. Now, having flagged her up for special attention, it was zeroing in, coming to claim her once and for all.

Zeus dragged her back along the route she herself had not so long ago taken, to the low windowless building she had stumbled upon earlier, the storage unit or unmarked temple or whatever it was. They halted outside the door, and Sam understood that this structure must in fact be what it most resembled, a mausoleum, a place of death and entombment. Handy for Zeus to have had it included in the plans for the stronghold. This would be where he disposed of his ex-lovers and other nuisances. Hence the lightning rod. She envisaged an electric chair inside, wired up so that Zeus could provide the juice for it himself with his divine powers, delivering a personal send-off to his strapped-in victims. It would have been absurd if it hadn't been so grimly plausible.

"This, Sam," said Zeus, "in case you're wondering, is the Shrine of Apotheosis. It is for my own private use. None of the other Olympians can readily gain access to it, not that they would dare even try. They know and fear my wrath."

Yeah, yeah, thought Sam. *Let's just get this over with, shall we?*

"The door is secured with a magnetic clamp lock, which responds only to a single charge of some hundred million volts. The size of current that the average lightning bolt provides."

With that, he conjured a small cloud out of nowhere in the clear alpine sky, and an instant later there was a flash, a static crackle, and Sam felt all her hair stand on end. A blue glow wreathed the lightning rod briefly, and from the door there came a loud, resounding *clank*. Zeus dispersed the cloud, then reached for the brass ring handle.

As the door opened, lights flickered on inside. Zeus thrust Sam in ahead of him, and slammed the door shut behind them.

This wasn't a place of execution, that much Sam gathered straight away. There *was* a kind of chair, however.

The room filled the entire volume of the Shrine and was of similar dimensions to the interior of a trailer park home. In the very middle stood a padded leather chair with a tubular steel frame and a curved headrest. It looked not unlike something you'd find in a dental surgery. Sam could see that it articulated in at least two places and was controlled by two pedals attached to its pedestal base.

Around the edges of the room there were medical refrigeration cabinets with glass doors, through which were visible shelves laden with test tubes, flasks and phials. All these were stoppered, labelled, and filled with various different-coloured opaque serums. Other furnishings included a metal desk with a laptop on it, a washstand, an alcohol gel dispenser for hand disinfection, several wheeled tray-stacks full of stainless steel surgical implements, and, the truly sinister touch, a set of restraints hanging on the wall – wrist and ankle cuffs made of leather, with perforated straps and buckles.

"Sex dungeon," Sam said. "Zeus, I'd never have pegged you for the S and M type. Hercules definitely, but not you."

She was able to quip, but only because her inner ice had melted, thawed by a sudden, unexpected flare-up of hot terror, which she needed to control. Death was one thing, but she sensed she had just been ushered into a torture chamber. That the room reeked of antiseptic only added to this impression. Things had had to be swabbed up in here, bodily fluids and the like. The walls were thick – solid stone. The Shrine of Apotheosis was set well apart from the main section of the stronghold. Screams that emanated from this building would be heard by no one.

Not that she was going to be screaming. No way was Zeus fastening her to that chair. Never in a million years. She would kill herself first. Beat her own brains out against the floor if need be.

"Sam," said Zeus, "first of all, whatever you're imagining this room is, one thing it is not is a place of cruelty. Please trust me on that. Suffering has occurred in that chair, yes, but suffering in a good cause, endured in the name of self-enhancement and the fulfilment of greatness. Do you know what apotheosis means?"

Sam fumbled for an answer. "Isn't it the epitome of something? A perfect specimen?"

"It can be used in that auxiliary sense, but its original, principal definition is deification. The attainment of divinity. From the Greek *apo*, a prepositional prefix meaning 'towards,' and *theosis*, 'godhood.'"

Sam said, "Zeus has left the building. I'm talking to Xander Landesman now, aren't I?"

Without missing a beat, Zeus said, "Of course."

"And I always have been."

Again: "Of course."

"And this is where it happens. This is where you do it. Where you make Olympians."

For a third time, veneered with a smile: "Of course."

"Fuck," she breathed. "Fuck me, I knew it. I knew you lot were faking. I knew it!"

"Oh, I know you did," Zeus said. "You've been telling us that constantly. Trouble is, no one has been listening. You're like Cassandra, blessed with the gift of accurate prophecy, cursed with the inability to convince others that what you're saying it true. It's been amusing, and heartbreaking, watching you try and trip us up, make us admit we're not gods. Thwarted every time. Coming up against a wall of incomprehension again and again."

"They have no idea, do they?" Sam said. "The rest of them."

"Not a clue. Only one person in the whole wide world knows the truth about the Olympians. Me. Make that two people now. Although, the knowledge won't remain yours for long."

"Ah. You are going to kill me after all."

Zeus shook his head wonderingly, bemused. "Don't you see, Sam? Don't you get it? I have no wish to kill you. Not any more."

"You don't?"

"Nor harm you in any way. Right now, all I want to do is make myself understood to you. Will you hear me out?"

"Do I have an alternative?"

"Not as such."

"Then go ahead, talk."

68. AN AUDACIOUS LIE

"MY FATHER MUST have told you all about me," said Zeus. "How else could you have known that someone called Xander Landesman ever existed? Not that he does any longer. I had Argus wipe every trace he could find of that person from the public record. There may be scraps of paper here or there in some national archive confirming that a Xander Landesman once walked the earth, but nothing easily located. From the databases that people habitually consult, he is gone. That was necessary to do before the Olympians went public, partly so that my wretched father couldn't stand up and say, 'Wait. That's not Zeus. That's my son.'"

"He still could have," said Sam. "Why not? Even if you'd left nothing to prove Xander was alive, plenty of people would surely remember him – schoolmates, teachers, staff at your father's house. Your dad could've found someone to back him up."

"I'd disappeared for five years, and come back looking nothing like I used to. My hair was long and had gone completely silver. I'd grown a beard. And memories are short. I'd passed through various educational establishments like a poltergeist, causing plenty of havoc but never staying long enough to leave a lasting impression. Also, the turnover of staff *chez* Landesman was quite rapid. I was counting on all that preventing people from recognising me, and I calculated that my father would realise he'd have difficulty backing up his claims about Zeus's true identity and so would refrain from making them."

"Maybe he'd be too embarrassed to, as well, after you Olympians started throwing your weight about."

"That would be for him to say. As for other people, past acquaintances – well, after five years, if it ever occurred to anyone to wonder what became of Xander Landesman, they'd no doubt assume from the absence of evidence that he was dead. Another poor little rich boy gone off the rails, lost to some addiction or other. Another privileged life flushed down the gold-plated toilet. More to the point, who'd care who Zeus really was, who'd even think to ask, when Zeus was so self-evidently *the* Zeus? With those powers, who else could he be?"

"OK," said Sam. "I'll buy that, just about. You gambled that nobody would connect Xander and Zeus, or be able to, and it paid off."

"It did, and that was crucial to the success of the whole enterprise. The same applied with the rest of the Pantheon. As long as they looked and acted like the gods of Greek myth, as long as they could do what those gods used to, few would think to look past that and probe deeper. Fewer still would consider that these gods might formerly have been ordinary people. And anyway, as with me, Argus had purged the relevant records, leaving the electronic slate wiped clean. It was an audacious lie, presenting ourselves to the world as deities, but if told convincingly and with impressive feats to back it up, it was a lie that could easily be swallowed."

"Especially if only one person involved knew it was a lie."

"And I've maintained the deception assiduously," Zeus said. "None of the other Olympians even suspects that I am anything other than king of the Pantheon, the Cloud-Gatherer, God Of Gain, and all the rest. I've made sure of that."

"How? With all those arguments over the dinner table, rehashing stories from the myths?"

"That helps reinforce the indoctrination."

"Indoctrination? You've brainwashed them?"

Zeus rolled his eyes. "That makes it sound like something from an old spy movie. With psychedelic lights and whirly music and a sinister reverbed voice repeating statements over and over – is that how you think it was done? Much subtler than that, Sam. And more sophisticated."

"Some kind of hypnotic suggestion, though."

"Implantation of concepts at a somatic level, yes, while the subject is in a state of deep relaxation. The ideas take root and propagate in the unconscious, growing until they overtake the conscious mind and turn subjective reality into objective. Bolstered by neurolinguistic programming techniques, it's surprisingly effective. Here, listen to this."

He went over and switched the laptop on. While the machine booted up, Sam's gaze strayed towards the door. She could make a run for it, but where would she go? The stronghold itself remained a prison. Part of her, besides, itched to know the full story behind the Olympians. She might as well stay put until Zeus had revealed all.

With a few keystrokes Zeus triggered a playback of an audio recording. It was his own voice, reciting part of a myth.

"...Actaeon made the grave error of approaching the lake where you were bathing and spying on you from a thicket. Can you see the lake? The thicket? Your keen instincts alerted you to his presence, however – a tiny snap of a twig underfoot – and in outrage you changed the mortal voyeur into a stag. He's changing now. Now he is a stag. Can you picture his antlers? Actaeon's own hunting hounds then set on him and gave chase, and soon caught up with their transformed master and tore him to pieces. You can hear the dogs' savage snarls, the sound of his flesh ripping, hear his screams..."

Zeus hit Stop. "I have over a hundred hours' worth of material stored here," he said, "culled from the major literary sources, each section filed according to which member of the Pantheon it pertains to. Those questions and observational remarks that break up the narrative? That's NLP. It forces the subject to visualise events in the story, making them more immediate and anchoring memory recall to these specific verbal stimuli. But beyond simply having the Olympians listen to stories about themselves while in a trance state, I availed myself of gene number VMAT2, popularly known as the 'god gene.' It's a gene encoded with an integral membrane protein that carries neurotransmitters around the immune system. Tests have shown that it's also responsible for rendering humans susceptible to belief in mystic forces and a higher power. Manipulation of VMAT2, a sneaky bit of reassignment, made my Olympians compliant, more liable to believe in *themselves* as gods. It gave them a sense of their own transcendence. Because, of course, genetic engineering is what this is really all about."

"So your dad said," said Sam. "He told me about your rat."

Zeus chuckled, recollecting. "Ah yes, the rat. It was quite a thing. Scared the life out of me at the time, but with hindsight it was my eureka moment. That was when I understood that I could actually make this whole thing work, that the theoretical was practicable. Most of my five wilderness years was spent advancing and perfecting the processes which had led to the creation of that freakishly strong rat. I isolated and cross-spliced and developed and tested and tested and tested once again until anything was within my reach, anything at all. I became a choreographer of the genome. More artist than scientist, I could make those chromosomes and nucleotides dance and prance and cavort. I could enhance and improve any living thing.

A housecat with the speed of a cheetah? No problem. A chimpanzee with the strength of a silverback gorilla? Easy. A brown trout with the aggression and killer instinct of a great white shark? A breeze."

"A trout that thinks it's Jaws?"

"You should have seen it, Sam. It attacked anything in its tank that moved. It had no idea it wasn't a fearsome pelagic predator. Its self-delusion was entire. A river fish that was utterly convinced it was some kind of piscine god."

"But isn't it a bit of a leap from tinkering around with animals to giving human beings super powers?"

"Not really," said Zeus. "If I can augment animals, why not humans too? It has long been my belief that we all of us possess untold, hidden abilities. Embedded somewhere in us, latent, right down at the most primal level, are extraordinary faculties. In the past some people have been able to tap them, and then perform what have generally been regarded as miracles, astonishing feats of strength, telekinetic manipulation, healing, endurance, bilocation, pyrokinesis, and more. Some have been hanged for doing so, or drowned on ducking stools, or of course crucified. Others have been hailed as divine and worshipped. Finding and identifying the genes that generate these paranormal abilities was the task that preoccupied me over the five years. The result was... well, I've no need to tell you what the result was. You know full well."

"Where were you at the time you were doing all this?" Sam asked. "Your father thought South America."

"And how right the old man was. South America is the ideal continent for those who wish to go about their business unmolested by the law and unhampered by rules, ethics bodies, oversight committees and the like. You can buy anything, south of Mexico. Stump up enough money and whatever you need, whatever you desire, it's yours. A fully equipped lab. Animal test subjects. Even..."

"Even...? You were about to say human test subjects, weren't you?"

Zeus smiled. Bared his teeth, at any rate. "Prostitutes and feral gang kids from the *favelas* – who was going to miss them? Certainly not the local law enforcement, who shoot them as a matter of course and are only too happy to save bullets and supplement their income by abducting them to order instead."

Sam's stomach turned. "Are you sure you weren't adopted and your real father was a Nazi vivisectionist?"

"Playing the Jewish card again, Sam? Didn't work last time, won't now. Just because my father was of the Tribe, doesn't mean I am. Judaism is matrilinear, and Mum was Greek. Greek Orthodox, for what it's worth. Although for my dad it was enough that she was Greek, him with his passion for all things Hellenic."

"A passion his son seems to have inherited."

"No," Zeus corrected her, "he shoved all that stuff down my throat. I couldn't give a damn about Greek myths."

"Except where it suits your purpose."

"Well, yes."

"Your father was well aware that you chose the Greek pantheon, out of all the other pantheons, deliberately. To piss him off."

"He'd have been stupid not to realise that."

"And, by the way, one of the Titans you killed on Bleaney" – *remember, no bodies equals no proof* – "was him. Your own father."

Not even a flicker in Zeus's expression. "You say that like it's a bad thing."

"Patricide usually is."

"Usually. Now, shall I continue, or are you going to keep on sidetracking me?"

"I'm not sure I want to hear any more, now that I know where the human portions of your monsters came from."

"Squeamish?" said Zeus. "Squeamishness is a luxury no true pioneer can afford. Suffice it to say that I gave those whores and street kids the kind of power and invincibility they'd hitherto thought they could get only through a needle or a firearm. They were my foundation stones. On them and on countless dumb animals I built the edifice of a grand dream. A dream of saving humankind from itself. *This* dream."

"And getting one up on your father at the same time."

"A fortunate corollary."

"As well as gaining absolute authority for yourself. Misunderstood misfit Xander Landesman, appointing himself supreme leader of the world. Revenge of the dropout."

"Your obstreperousness is one of the things I like most about you, Sam. It's quite endearing. Exasperating, but endearing."

"Maybe we should just cut this short," Sam said. "If the only reason you've brought me here is to brag on about how clever and ruthless you've been, with your dancing DNA and your Greek myth storytime audiobook, then maybe –"

"Sam!" Zeus burst out. "Heavens, woman, just stop and think for a second. You're not here so that I can crow about my achievements."

"And not here to be killed either. So, what, then?"

"Could I make it any more obvious? Why not ask yourself why I had Hermes pluck you from the battlefield. It was because I had a feeling about you, Sam, based on what Dionysus and Aphrodite told me about you and my own subsequent researches, after your identity became apparent. And my hunch has been confirmed over the past few weeks. You're stubborn and obstinate and awkward in every way, not to mention resourceful and smart. That makes for a worthy foe. It also makes for a worthy ally."

"Ally?"

Then she saw it, and everything in her seemed to sink. Not just her heart, her whole self, as though her soul was draining out of her, seeping onto the floor.

"Godhood, Sam," said Zeus. "I'm offering you your very own apotheosis. Transformation from mortal to divine. Exaltation. I'm asking you to join us and become an Olympian."

69. COUNCIL OF WAR

ARGUS PINPOINTED POSEIDON'S whereabouts. Hermes fetched him. The twelve Olympians sat in session in the *naos* of the main temple. Zeus presided. Sam looked on from the sidelines.

A council of war.

"We go nuclear," said Athena. "Argus has control over the world's atomic arsenals. It's high time we took advantage of that. We bomb London. That'll halt this thing in its tracks. You know this, O Zeus."

"I can't countenance it, O Athena the Owl-Eyed," said Zeus.

"Why not? I'm the one you consult when it comes to tactics. Have I not advised you well in the past? Have I not helped steer you successfully around countless potential pitfalls? So this is what I am recommending now. Wipe out London with one of

Britain's own ICBMs, and this new insurgency we're seeing will melt away – gone in a flash."

She hadn't always been Athena. Once, she had been a brilliant business strategist, a consultant whom corporations hired at staggering expense to tell them how to get one over on the competition and expand their own interests. Then she tried to play off two rival pharmaceutical giants against each other, for the sheer pleasure of manipulating them both, and got caught at it.

"I agree with my stepsister," said Dionysus. "Why must we exert ourselves over and over again quashing these uprisings when there's a far less effortful option open to us? All Argus need do is think it, and the deed is done."

Dionysus had been a vintner and *bon viveur* who hosted lavish, booze-sodden parties that could last for days. The good times ended for him after one of his guests killed another with a broken bottle in a drunken brawl.

"Typical!" barked Ares. "You're soft in every way, Dionysus. Soft and lazy. I, myself, will gladly take on these mortals hand to hand on the slopes of fair, snow-capped Olympus. The clash and clangour of combat is my music. Bloodshed and screams are my meat and drink."

Before he was enlisted into the Pantheon, Ares had been a soldier, a good one, born for discipline and killing, if a little too apt to sacrifice the former in the name of the latter. His involvement in a massacre of civilians in some west African hellhole town prompted a dishonourable discharge and a descent into alcoholism. There were frequent arrests for affray, until Xander Landesman came along.

"And I will fight alongside my stepbrother," Apollo declared. "My arrows stand ready to pierce a thousand mortal breasts." He and Ares clasped fists, a sinewy display of shared philosophy.

Apollo used to be an Olympic-class archer, a toxophilite of the first rank, until he took a bribe from a betting syndicate and blew a contest he should have won easily. The scandal was hushed up but his career never hit the bullseye again.

"I'm minded to side with Athena and Dionysus on this one," said Hades. "In the thick of combat isn't a place I'm too comfortable being, and there's something rather elegantly fitting about using one of the mortals' own weapons of mass destruction against them. So much death in the space of a handful of seconds – I find the idea positively thrilling."

An embalmer by trade, Hades had been noted among his peers in the field of mortuary science for the skill and care he took over his work. With cosmetics brush and restorative wax he could render even the most unsightly corpse viewable. He prided himself on having saved many a family the distress of a closed-casket funeral. Unfortunately, it emerged that his affinity with dead bodies didn't end with smartening them up and making them look lifelike. A colleague caught him in the morgue one night, lavishing the wrong kind of attention on a recently deceased lingerie model on the slab. Vocational oblivion beckoned, but so did Xander Landesman.

"Perhaps," argued Aphrodite, "we should offer them one last chance. Set a deadline. Give them until, say, next Monday to reconsider and pull back, then if they don't comply, attack. Isn't it better to show forbearance and allow their better natures a chance to shine through?"

Aphrodite had previously been a madam running one of the most exclusive bordellos on the planet, a harem-like haven for playboys, plutocrats and princelings. Her abiding philosophy was that the relationship between prostitute and client was a sacred one, akin to true love, and in support of that, money was never mentioned on her premises. Credit cards were silently swiped and exorbitantly debited, and from there on in it was *l'amour* all the way. This didn't save her, though, when the inevitable police raid and prosecution for brothel keeping came. Her clients, showing anything but love, turned on her in order to protect themselves, and she had been facing a lengthy stint behind bars, until a certain arms dealer's son approached her with a tempting proposition.

"Hardly," sniffed Poseidon. "They don't *have* better natures, O Protectress of Births. Haven't you realised that yet? Give even an inch of ground and they'll think you're weak. Gods cannot be seen to be weak. Say the word, Zeus, and I'll capsize every warship out there."

So said a man who'd been a keen amateur yachtsman and also a shipping magnate who routinely overloaded his cargo vessels in order to maximise profits. Dozens of crewmen were lost at sea as his freighters foundered in rough weather, shipped water and sank. Eventually his avarice left him with nothing, no fleet of any kind except his own private 30-foot schooner, and when that was repossessed in order to help offset his legal defence team's costs, he knew he was going under. Xander Landesman threw him a lifeline.

"I wouldn't dismiss my wife's proposal so quickly," said Hephaestus. "Aphrodite is sensitive to what goes on in the hearts of men –"

"The hearts and the loins," Ares interjected.

"– and," Hephaestus went on, ignoring him, "she is right to hope that maybe, in this case, people will come to their senses before it is too late. However," he added, "should that not happen, I have something up my sleeve that will assist us in the conflict. Athena suggested I build this particular item, and I think, once you see it in action, you'll be impressed, both by her foresight and my dexterity."

He'd been a sculptor, an expert in metalcraft, praised for the way he could replicate the texture and flow of organic objects with inorganic materials. But as with many an artist, he was flawed, temperamental, prone to bouts of rage and depression. Like the stuff he worked with, he was either cold and inflexible or incandescently hot and dangerous. He lost friends, fell from grace, his creative fire sputtered out – and then, at the hands of the man who would be Zeus, he was forged anew in the crucible of science.

"In my view," said Demeter, "in this summer heat, we must reap when the harvest is ripe."

"And that means...?" said Apollo.

"Mortals are corn. You be the scythe."

"That's what I thought it meant."

Demeter was an ex-doctor, a member of the caring profession who grew complacent and stopped caring. Stopped caring to the extent that she neglected the patients whose health she was responsible for, especially the elderly ones. Many of them were left permanently damaged, and some even died, as a consequence of treatable conditions she'd failed to diagnose. She was struck off the medical register. Then came a chance to redeem herself.

"Demeter and I," said Hera, "see eye to eye on this, as on so many matters. Cerberus will enter the fray at my command, as will Typhon, Scylla and, it goes without saying, the Harpies. You must make the decision, my husband, but I'm sure you will make the correct one."

Hera had been a veterinarian, good with animals, but that wasn't Xander's only criterion for choosing her. She'd been married no less than four times by the age of thirty-five, always to unfaithful men, and he'd wanted someone who was familiar with the burden of the wronged wife – who even took a perverse pleasure from it.

"I am He Who Presides Over Contests," said Hermes. "If it is your will, Zeus, I shall preside over this one too, this clash between us and the mortals. Wherever you ask me to be, there shall I go."

Hermes had been Darren Pugh. His predecessor had been a getaway driver, of all things, a criminal who'd turned informant and had to go into witness protection. But Hermes the second, the replacement, was the erstwhile Darren Pugh. The elusive, slippery traitor.

Sam watched them as they debated, and superimposed over all of them was her knowledge of the people they had been, the lives they had led before Xander Landesman approached them with the tantalising prospect of godlike powers. What a sorry bunch. Losers, perverts, cheats, crooks, the lowest of the low, and Xander had taken them and elevated them to the highest of the high.

And now he was offering her the same opportunity.

"What do you say, Sam?" he had asked her in the Temple of Apotheosis, a few hours earlier.

Her immediate reply had been, "You've just described to me a dozen or so utter scumbags, and you're asking if I'd like to join them?"

"'Scumbags' they may have been, but they were also uniquely suited to the roles I'd planned for them to play. Each had the requisite characteristics, a background in tune with the abilities I intended to give him or her. Each, too, was in dire straits, at low ebb, with very limited future prospects."

"You made them an offer they couldn't refuse."

"*Wouldn't* refuse. It had to be consensual. Otherwise the indoctrination wouldn't take. No form of hypnosis can make a subject do something he or she wouldn't do naturally. That's another movie canard, the idea of the mesmerised victim becoming an assassin or whatever. My Olympians couldn't behave as they do if it wasn't already inherent in their psychologies. Athena's ruthless streak is that of the boardroom schemer she used to be. Ares's warrior aggression has been there since his soldiering days."

"Did they know, going in, that they would be losing all memory of their old selves?"

"It was made crystal clear to them that I would be rewriting their conscious minds, erasing their pasts so that they would know nothing about themselves other than that they were gods. All of them were happy with that. It was, I feel, one of the great attractions of the procedure for them. They'd all done things they weren't at ease with, things that had earned them opprobrium and shame. I was giving them the opportunity to start again, afresh, all sins forgotten, like a religious rebirth. That and supranormal powers – an irresistible combination."

"Not to me," Sam said. "I've no interest in forgetting who I am."

"Really, Sam? Strikes me there's a lot of past baggage you'd gladly let go of if you could. Your parents' deaths. You boyfriend's death. Your miscarriage. Your stalled police career. Perhaps also the Titans' abject failure in realising their objective. All that, I could whisk away from you, as though you were a soul in the afterlife drinking from the river Lethe, whose waters remove all remembrance of a person's time on earth. I could rid you of the pain you carry around inside you, the deep-seated traumas that have left you as you are – reserved, aloof, untrusting, cynical."

"I am none of those things!"

"You may not think so, but you do not see yourself as others see you. Have you ever loved anyone? Truly?"

"Not that it's any of your business, but yes."

"Adrian Walters?"

"Ade."

"One man. And before him? After?"

She nearly said Ramsay's name, but didn't.

"And *was* it love?" Zeus said. "Or more of a convenient arrangement? Ade was in the same line of work as you, therefore comfortably within the parameters of what you knew and understood. He was also inferior to you in professional terms, so not likely to threaten your self-image in that respect."

"You can't know any of that."

"I've done my homework, with Argus's assistance. I can read you, Sam, same as I read all of the candidates I chose for apotheosis. I can see into you. It's a gift I have. You're a smart but inhibited woman, with so much anger inside you, a well of frustration and aggrievedness. And I can save you from that. I can tap that well, relieve the pressure. I can unshackle you from your self-made chains, open you up to who you truly are and what you'd truly like to be. Come on, admit it, isn't that just the least bit tempting? The possibility of absolute freedom, absolute selfhood, a life lived without constraint or regret?"

Not tempting, no. Not at all.

Well, perhaps slightly.

"It does hurt," Zeus said. "It takes several days, it involves courses of injections and infusions, and the physiological alterations these cause are unpleasant while they are happening. But does the athlete not endure great hardship as he trains to become the best in his field? Does the ballerina not go through agonies as she distorts her feet and builds up calluses? If we are to become sublime, do we not have to pay first in sacrifice and suffering? You will sit in that chair and experience a sometimes unbearable level of discomfort and distress. The restraints may be necessary from time to time, if only to stop you harming yourself or me in the throes of change. And you will listen to the myths constantly while the procedure is in progress, until the transformation is complete and you are no longer Sam Akehurst but someone else, a greater being, superior in every way."

"Who?" said Sam. "Who would I become?"

"You are interested, aren't you?"

"No. Hypothetical question. Which goddess do you think I'm most like?"

"Well, it's a matter of serendipity more than anything. We have a vacancy. It just so happens that you'd be ideal to fill it."

"Artemis." She knew it. She'd known it all along, somehow.

"Artemis," Zeus confirmed. "The cool, calculating, vicious huntress. Lethal in a fight, and not one who likes to be slighted or wronged. That was a portion of her file I played to you just now. Artemis's revenge on Actaeon, who had the temerity to spy on her and saw her in her nakedness. Artemis was a virgin – inapplicable in your case, obviously, but for the ancient Greeks that was how they conceptualised her subsidiary function as divine patron of chastity and virtue. She was their idealised notion of feminine justice, untouched, untouchable, to be admired from afar but not to be roused to fury."

"The previous Artemis had dark hair."

"I believe there's such a thing as hair dye."

"She was a good three inches taller than me."

"Once you have her spear in your hands, no one will notice the height difference."

"I can't even use a spear."

"Apollo will teach you, and I will see to it that you have an aptitude for the weapon."

"And I'm no killer."

"Oh, and what were you doing in that suit my father designed if it wasn't killing? Did you not hunt down our monsters? Kill them?"

"And 'feminine justice'?"

Zeus widened his eyes. "To someone who was once a female detective sergeant, do I have to make the parallel any plainer? Sam, you *are* Artemis. Nobody could be the new Goddess of the Hunt better than you. You were made for it."

"Except..."

"Yes?"

"It seems like some kind of sick joke," Sam said. "I loathe Artemis. I've loathed her for so long. Since Hyde Park."

"Where this Ade of yours died."

"She killed him. Her and Apollo."

"From the accounts I've read, *she* didn't kill him. Neither did Apollo. He drowned. He died in the Serpentine, in a stampede, saving a girl's life."

"A stampede Artemis and Apollo caused. If it wasn't for them, he'd never even have been there."

"But did Artemis's spear go through him? Did one of Apollo's arrows? No. If anything killed him, it was his own bravery."

"But I hate her. I hate you all."

"And isn't it time to give that up?" Zeus said gently. "Where has it got you? Nowhere. Imagine if you were one of us instead. Helping shape the world. Making the future brighter, safer, better. Hating no one except those who would oppose you. Being part of the greatest force for good humankind has ever known."

A last counterargument, all Sam could muster at that moment amid the turmoil she was feeling: "Why didn't you use all *this* as a force for good?" She meant the chair, the serums in their phials. "Your advances in genetic engineering. Didn't it ever occur to you that, rather than make a handful of people gods, you could make everyone gods? Demeter can heal. Damn it, with a thousand like her, a few hundred even, you could set up hospitals all over the planet and cure every known disease. And think, if everyone could teleport like Hermes, there'd be no need for mechanical transport any more. No buses, no cars, no trains – no pollution. Poseidon – an army of Poseidons could irrigate deserts, make it so that crops can grow anywhere, help end famine and drought. You yourself – couldn't a host of people harnessing lightning solve the world's energy problems somehow?"

"Sam, ideas like those did flit through my mind briefly, once, before I dismissed them as the pure naivety they are. Could I have turned everyone on earth into a god? Should I? Well, apart from the impracticality and inordinate expense of attempting to do that, what do you think the result would be? Chaos. Utter chaos. People teleporting willy-nilly everywhere? What would happen to privacy, crime levels, the principles of territory and international borders? Hordes of Demeters curing all ills? So what about the population explosion that would ensue? Where would we find room for those billions of people who don't die when they're meant to?

"Say we decide to dole out the strength of a Hercules. Who to? A select few? Who'd choose that select few? So let's be democratic and give it to everyone. But if everyone is as strong as Hercules, what's the point? All it'll lead to is an exponential rise in property damage and personal injury, people literally not realising their own strength, breaking things and each other. Over and above all that, who would control this world of gods? How would it be policed? Someone even more powerful would be needed to oversee it, gods' gods. Which gets us back to where we are now."

He gesticulated with both hands, clutching empty air.

"It just doesn't work, Sam. It's not feasible. I recognised that from the start. What I could do to people needed to be done with precision and great forethought. It couldn't be universal, it had to be specific, targeted, a laser not a blunderbuss. Don't change everyone. Change a few who can change things for everyone else."

Sam could see the logic in this. It was inhuman logic, but logic nonetheless.

"So," Zeus said. "What's it to be? What's the answer? Yes or no?"

Another Landesman presenting her with another life-defining decision.

"I need time," Sam said. "Time to think."

Zeus leaned back. Sighed. "I feared you might say that."

"Just a few days."

"Sounds like a no to me."

"No, it's not definitely a no," Sam said, and was surprised to find that this was the truth. It was 99% a no, but somewhere in her that 1% of yes was whispering softly, wheedling, saying, *Why not? Why not?*

At last Zeus had relented. A few days. No, pin it down. She had to decide by this coming Saturday.

Sunday, Sam had said. Three whole days from now.

Sunday, Zeus had agreed. He couldn't spare her any longer than that. He needed his Artemis, especially with the mortals making their move on Olympus. This lot could be fought off, but if Sam was right and more followed in their wake, then he wanted the full Dodekatheonic complement of Olympians available.

Now, at the council of war, having heard out his fellow Olympians, Zeus delivered his verdict.

"I am of the view," he said, "that any attack on Olympus must be met with immediate and devastating counterforce. Let us wait, though, until whoever is coming has got here. Let us let the mortals assemble outside, and let us let them make the opening gambit. That will save us the trouble of going to seek them out and also make us look like the aggrieved party, the provoked rather than the provokers. Surely you can all see the beneficial aspects of that. Athena, a nuclear strike is simply not on. If we need to level a city – well, we've shown we can do that ourselves, haven't we, without recourse to manmade technological armaments. Having Argus assume control of the nuclear arsenals was to prevent their use, not commandeer them for our own purposes. It ill befits us as gods to drop bombs. What mortals can do, we cannot, and vice versa. That," he said, addressing all of them once more, "is my thinking on this. Let none demur."

None did. Athena looked disgruntled but resigned. The Cloud-Gatherer had spoken. His word was diktat.

"My daughter," he said, taking her under his arm as the meeting broke up, "don't be downcast. Your great mind will be vital in the coming days, apportioning our resources across the field of battle, deploying your family against the foe. Surely you relish such a challenge."

A smile played about Athena's serious lips. It seemed she did relish it, as a matter of fact.

Then Zeus came over to Sam.

"Three days," he murmured, too low for anyone else to hear. "I shall be patiently waiting."

"And if the answer isn't the one you want? Isn't this whole thing supposed to be voluntary?"

"You won't disappoint me," Zeus told her, genially but with the force of conviction. "I know you won't."

70. THREE DAYS

Friday.

British troops, nearly a thousand of them in all, were massing to the south-west and east of Olympus. Satellite imagery showed them bivouacked on the plains north of Larisa and along the coast in the mountain's shadow. American supplies were being airlifted in and distributed. Japanese ships, meanwhile, were cruising through the Straits of Gibraltar, bound once more for the Thermaikos Gulf.

Internationally, diplomatic efforts were under way to defuse the situation. Plenty of people weren't comfortable with the idea of armies taking action independently of their governments, but the unease was felt most keenly at executive level. Catesby Bartlett flew to New York to try to obtain a UN Security Council resolution forbidding Field Marshal Armstrong-Hall from going through with a siege of the Olympians' stronghold. The Prime Minister's hope was that fear of contravening the will of the UN, and of being branded a war criminal as a result, would deter Sir Neville. However, both America and Russia vetoed the proposal, China abstained from voting, and Bartlett's transatlantic trip was all for naught.

University students across the globe abandoned their lectures and libraries for a day in order to take part in protest rallies, but with one or two exceptions these took the form of pro- rather than anti-military demonstrations. The vast majority of the world's undergraduates were supportive of the stance taken by Britain's armed forces, which led to the unusual sight of youths carrying placards with crossed-out peace symbols on them and drawings of doves surrounded by a red circle with a diagonal red line through the middle, brandishing these as they chanted slogans such as "Hell yes – make a mess" and "All we are saying is don't give them a chance." On the more liberal campuses, such as Berkeley and Paris, scuffles broke out between the protestors and their professors, who were of the old school and angered that the ideals they themselves had once marched for, back in the day, were being so roundly spurned by the post-Olympian generation. As was often the case with academics, they'd failed to grasp that society around them had changed and they had not changed with it. The times were topsy-turvy now. The enemy was not the Man any more, it was the God.

Saturday.

The British troops' numbers were bolstered by the arrival of contingents from France, Australia, Spain,

Italy and Russia, along with handfuls of soldiers from Israel and several north African nations, all of whom had come of their own accord, without the express consent (but probably with the tacit approval) of their superiors. Freelancers, among them a couple of dozen RCDC members, swelled the ranks. All at once the landscape around Larisa was smattered with impromptu camps, rows of tents in oblongs like patches of corduroy on a jacket.

On that afternoon the Harpies spotted British scouts who had crept to within binocular distance of the stronghold in order to reconnoitre. The bird-women swooped, and the scouts were plucked from the ground and carried screaming into the sky, where the Harpies proceeded to tear them apart in a leisurely, almost playful fashion. Limbs were tossed from taloned foot to taloned foot, a gruesome game of catch. Entrails were flung high, snapped up as they fell, gobbled on the wing. The Olympians looked on from the battlements with some satisfaction, not least Hera. Sam, on the other hand, went to her room and stayed there until the whole ghastly spectacle was over.

Zeus came to her afterwards, to find out if she was any closer to a decision.

"Not yet."

"I have no wish to put any pressure on you," he said. "I just want to be sure that you're not prevaricating in the hope that some sort of salvation is going to arrive. Remember Penelope."

"Penelope?"

"Odysseus's wife. While her husband was off on his wanderings and widely believed to be dead, she was beset by suitors, so she told them she wouldn't consider marrying any of them until she had finished weaving a shroud for her husband's late father Laertes. Every day she wove a little more of the shroud. Every night she unpicked the work she had done during the day. It was in vain. She was found out eventually. And if this is all some ruse of yours, a way to buy time for yourself, rest assured that it, too, is in vain. Those troops gathering around us will not get within a hundred yards of this stronghold, let alone set foot inside. If what the Harpies have just done hasn't driven home that fact, it ought to have."

"I still have one more day."

"Tomorrow, then. If your answer's yes – and I believe it will be – you won't regret it, Sam."

"And if it's no?"

"Then regret will be the least of your concerns."

It was a long night. And bitterly cold. It never got truly warm up on Olympus, which didn't seem to bother any of the Pantheon but certainly didn't agree with Sam, especially when she couldn't sleep. She piled blankets on herself until there was such a weight of them she could hardly breathe, but still the chill seeped through. There was a chill inside her too, to match. An icy dread.

How much did she want to live?

That was what it boiled down to. The alternatives were: agree to become Artemis, or die.

Being Artemis would mean survival but it would be a kind of half-life at best. Zeus had promised an existence untrammelled by doubt or scruple, absolute godlike freedom. The price, though, would be the loss of everything that she had been up to that point, all her memories, her essential Sam-ness. Wasn't that, in itself, tantamount to death? The other Olympians had embraced the opportunity of oblivion, the chance to forget all their inadequacies and misdeeds, and she could see the allure of that. Her own life hadn't exactly been an unblemished catalogue of triumphs. But had it been so bad that she'd be prepared simply to dump it all and start again as someone else? Wasn't that just a little too easy?

Then again, wasn't taking the other option, death, also just a little too easy? If nothing else, as Artemis she would have influence. Not to mention power. The same kind of power she had enjoyed while clad in her TITAN suit, had luxuriated in, been exhilarated by. And it would not be just while she had the suit on but all the time. All the time. Power in perpetuity. To be able to spring and strike as she'd seen Artemis do, to wield that spear like a darting needle, to be preternaturally strong, indefatigable, a creature of enhanced senses and reflexes – that would be something, wouldn't it?

There was a third way, though. Tomorrow was crate delivery day. That was why she'd haggled with Zeus for an extra day in which to make up her mind. Assuming that the helicopter was still coming in as scheduled despite the rapidly changing circumstances on the ground, Sam could always make that desperate leap onto the departing crate and hope to be choppered clear of the stronghold.

Which would be the equivalent of giving Zeus a big no and would almost certainly lead to her death. But at least it wouldn't be a cheap death – an easy death – and that would count for something.

Tomorrow.

Sunday.

Sunday came, and with the dawn there arose one of those mists that often plagued Olympus, a dense white shroud that was turbulent and wind-tormented but also, conversely, brought a stillness and hush to the mountaintop, muffling the stronghold, cutting it off from the rest of the world. The moment Sam stepped outdoors into the damp milkiness of the mist, she felt a crushing sense of despair. The helicopter would not be coming. Not in these conditions, surely.

She wandered, disconsolate, hearing the cries of the Harpies as they called to one another through the mist, a sound that was deadened and distant and strangely forlorn. She noticed that the bird-women seemed agitated this morning, chittering querulously rather than screeching as normal. Perhaps it was the mist. Their primary sense of perception, their eyesight, was useless, and this unnerved them.

Ares was up early too. She came across him in the amphitheatre. He was clad in his full copper armour, swinging his battle axe, lunging at invisible foes, his feet kicking up plumes of the sand that covered the arena floor. He looked avid, aroused, like a young man on a first date.

"Athena says an attack is likely today," he told Sam, "and I believe her. I can smell it on the wind, can't you? The scent of impending conflict. Iron and blood. My axe will be dripping wet by evening's end."

She moved on, leaving him to his limbering up. Her footsteps took her eventually to the *agora*, where she sat and waited, even though it was pointless because there would be no helicopter. She sat and waited because there was nothing else to do. Time was up. Zeus needed to know if she was to be his new Artemis or not. She still wasn't sure, which suggested she was coming round to the idea. That was the thing about her and dying, Sam had discovered. Unless she had no choice in the matter, she invariably preferred living. As a certain sage individual, Dai Prothero no less, once put it: "There's only one place where death is worth more than life, Akehurst, and that's on the Scrabble board."

Shortly before nine, when the helicopter was due, the Olympians began arriving at the *agora* in ones and twos. Soon they had all assembled, and when Sam expressed surprise, Zeus said, "The delivery always comes, whatever the weather. The helicopter's a Super Puma, equipped with the full array of navigation sensors and synthetic radar imaging. A good pilot can fly by instruments alone, thanks to that. Takes a steady nerve, I understand, but these are brave men – and the Greeks wouldn't want to disappoint us, would they?"

In a lower voice, and with an expectant twitch of those circumflex eyebrows of his, he added, "So? Sunday is here. Are we near an answer?"

"Almost," said Sam, and Zeus seemed satisfied with this and turned away, and so did she. Suddenly all a-tingle, she focused her attention on last week's crate, which was sitting near the centre of the *agora*, ready for pick-up. It was sheathed in a cargo net whose corners were gathered together and attached to a figure-of-eight loop at the top. The cargo net's matrix of ropes would make it easy to scramble up the side and would provide something to cling on to as the crate was being flown away. If the pilot climbed quickly, Sam might just manage to disappear into the mist before the Olympians could react. Zeus wouldn't be able to zap the helicopter with lightning if he couldn't see it, and likewise Apollo, who was toting bow and quiver this morning, couldn't hit her with an arrow if his target was not clearly visible. As for Hermes, he might be able to teleport onto the crate but as long as she didn't let him grab her he couldn't teleport off again with her. He might, besides, think twice about landing on a moving object, especially if he was jumping blind and if the moving object was swaying around none too far from a set of whirring rotor blades. A slight miscalculation, and Hermes the Luck-Bringer would be Hermes the Headless.

The mist, then, far from being a catastrophe, might just be the best thing to have happened to Sam in ages.

All she had to go was get the timing right. Usually the Olympians were so eager to crack open the new crate that they didn't pay much heed to the old one as it was being hoisted away. She'd have to dash for it at the very instant it lifted off from the *agora*, though, and she'd have to keep an eye out, also, for Hephaestus. He alone never got particularly excited about the divulging of the new crate's contents, so his attention would not be fully on it. He, of all of them, might catch her in the act and raise the alarm. If she made sure to sneak round so that she was out of his line of sight... yes, then this could work. Sam could hardly believe it. Finally, *finally*, a chance of getting out of the stronghold. A slim chance, to be sure, the thinnest of slivers, but that was better than before, when there had been none whatsoever.

And now the beating of rotor blades could be heard, ever so faint but distinct nonetheless, like the purr of some gigantic cat, and the most wonderful sound in all the world as far as Sam was concerned. The sound of hope.

She sidled over to the perimeter of the *agora*, away from the Olympians, who were clustered together peering skyward, and then she diverted towards the empty crate, getting as close as she dared without it looking suspicious. The helicopter noise grew louder, becoming a pulsating roar, and then there it was, a dark shape looming overhead in the mist, a giant grey tadpole, and its downwash tore the vaporous air into sharp, spiralling vortices, and at last the Super Puma came clearly into view, searchlight ablaze, with the crate swinging below in its cargo-net papoose. The Olympians' robes whipped around them as the chopper descended, their hair thrashed in all directions, and then the crate touched down and Hermes darted on top of it and detached it from the winch hook. The cargo net slid away like a negligee, puddling around the crate's base. Hermes vanished and reappeared on the other crate, lifting up the figure-of-eight loop and beckoning to the pilot to come over. Ares, meanwhile, slotted the blade of his axe into the edge where two sides of the new crate met and started to jemmy them apart. The screech of nails being wrenched out of wood was audible even above the cacophony of the helicopter's vanes and turbines.

Sam braced herself. Thirty yards or so to the empty crate. How many seconds to sprint that far? Four? Five? She could do this. She just needed to choose the exact right moment to start her run. Wait for it. Wait for it.

The pilot seemed to be taking an abnormally long time manoeuvring over to the empty crate, or perhaps that was just how Sam perceived it with her adrenaline flowing and her heart rate speeding up with anticipation. The hook glided towards Hermes slowly, so slowly she began to think it was never going to get there.

In the meantime, Ares had set down his axe and was levering the side off the crate with his bare hands, and now it came free, and he stepped back to let it fall, and it did, an eight-foot-square slab of plywood boards swung outwards with a weird kind of grace, slumping flat onto the flagstones, and the Olympians craned their necks to look inside, and Athena was at the front, and Sam heard the gunshot, a loud and extraordinarily familiar percussive *snap*, and Athena's proud, large, magnificent forehead disintegrated, her helmet flew backwards as though yanked off by an invisible wire, and she reeled away from the crate with a shattered cavity where the front of her skull had been, and her eyes rolled white, and brains spilled like pink blancmange from a broken bowl, and she collapsed into Zeus's arms and he caught her, held her, and his expression was incomprehension, bafflement, as were all the Olympians' expressions, but not Sam's.

She understood.

Even before five TITAN-suited figures burst forth from the crate, she understood.

No bodies equals no proof.

Hyperion led the way, and he was yelling, "Trojan horse! Trojan goddamn horse! We're in! We did it! Now let's plug as many of these motherfuckers as we can before they figure out we're not the weekly drop-off from the Athens Stop And Shop."

71. RETURN OF THE TITANS

IT WAS THE enormity of it, the effrontery of it, that took the Olympians aback so. More than the fact that there were still Titans alive and they were pouring out of the crate with guns blazing: the sheer gall of these mortals, to hijack the Greek government's act of weekly tribute and use it as a method of gaining ingress into the stronghold.

The shock took several seconds to process, and during those seconds two of the Pantheon perished. Athena first, then Hades. As bullets began whipping towards the Olympians, the Lord of the Underworld raised his gloved hands defensively, as though somehow his death touch might ward off the hailstorm of ammunition and preserve him from harm. The bullets, however, raked through his hands, shattering them to pieces and also shattering the face behind them. His sallow, skeletal features disappeared as if flayed. He went down with nothing but a bloody mess between jaw and brow, jigsaw pieces of skull falling away, one eye socket a ragged hole, his other eye staring bleakly out through all the gore with a look that seemed to say, *This can't be happening. I give, not receive. This can't be happening to me!*

The less combat-orientated Olympians scattered to the edges of the *agora*, taking refuge among the colonnades of the buildings adjacent. The others – principally Ares, Apollo, Zeus and Poseidon – recovered their wits and marshalled themselves to retaliate. The five Titans, meanwhile, fanned out across the *agora*, still firing for all they were worth. Sam watched them with a dizzying mixture of gratitude and joy. They'd survived Bleaney. Not just Hyperion but Rhea, Iapetus, Theia and Cronus. All of them. They'd got away, and now they were here, heading up the international assault on Olympus.

And they'd infiltrated the stronghold in a time-honoured fashion, what's more. Xander Landesman, under any other circumstances, would surely have appreciated the irony.

Apollo nocked and loosed arrows, while Ares went on the offensive in his own way, charging at the Titans with axe aloft and letting out a battlecry as he went, a wordless ululation that was intended to intimidate but also to express a kind of ecstasy. He picked Iapetus as his target, but the Titan accelerated, side-stepping at speed as the axe came down. Blade sparked on flagstone, chips of limestone flew, and then Iapetus's shotgun shouted. The blast caught Ares between greave and thigh-plate, disintegrating much of the Olympian's kneecap. Ares roared and swung his axe sidelong. The blow was swift, and the shotgun was sliced in two near the top of its stock. Iapetus was lucky not to lose a hand. He backed off, fast, and Ares lurched after him, limping but not hobbled – too lost in bloodlust to be hindered by a small thing like a ruined knee.

The helicopter had risen swiftly once the crate deception was laid bare. The pilot wanted to get out of the vicinity as fast as possible, for fear of becoming embroiled in events below. Tragically for him, he failed. Hephaestus reached out with his mind and took hold of the Super Puma. First he stalled its engine, freezing the working parts. Then, with a furious scowl of concentration, he assumed full command of the great five-ton mass of metal, bringing it straight back down into the *agora*. The pilot struggled with collective and cyclic, stamped his anti-torque pedals, but nothing was working. He was in a dead weight of aircraft, plummeting through the mist. Rotors groaned, windscreens shattered, he was bucked about helplessly in his seat, and still he fought to maintain control and keep the helicopter aloft, a true professional to the end.

Cronus happened to glance up just in time and yell a warning. The Titans scattered as the Super Puma came hurtling down. It missed them all, bellying onto the flagstones with an immense, ground-shaking *crunch*. Parts shot everywhere like shrapnel.

Sam ducked for cover behind the empty crate as the tail rotor came cartwheeling past her. Several more fragments of chopper slammed into the crate itself, shunting it against her hard enough to send her sprawling onto the ground.

A brief lull, and then the gunfire resumed, and above it could be detected another sound, the trundle of massing stormclouds. The atmosphere became charged with static. Sam knew she had to get to her feet and move. Once Zeus started tossing lightning bolts around, anyone could be hit.

As she rose, a Titan appeared in front of her.

Hyperion.

Mostly she saw just his grin through his visor, but that was enough. More than enough.

"Sam," he said, reaching out to her, "you have no idea how good it is to see you again. And you have no idea how long I've waited for a chance to say these words. Come with me if you want to live."

72. FANTASIA OF GHOULISHNESS

SHE TOOK HYPERION's gauntleted hand, and together they ran, out of the *agora*, away from the oncoming electrical blitz. Behind them flashes lit up the air, turning the mist brightly pearlescent, and then came a tremendous crackle and clatter as the lightning struck, and the grinding of flagstones behind torn up, and beneath their feet the booming groan of the mountainside as it cavilled at the harsh treatment being meted out on it.

"Where are we going?" Sam yelled.

"Anywhere but there," Hyperion yelled back.

"And the others?"

"They've got their orders. There's a plan, believe it or not, and part of it is you and I need to get somewhere sheltered and safe. See this thing on my back? Santa's sack. I have a present for you."

She hadn't noticed in all the mêlée, but Hyperion had a large container strapped to his shoulders, somewhat like a hiker's backpack but made of solid plastic. It looked big enough to contain...

"My suit!" Sam gasped.

"Not quite, but good as. Now shut up and run."

She shut up and they ran, hand in hand, while the lightning apocalypse raged on in the *agora*. Hyperion appeared to be making a beeline for the amphitheatre but Sam had a better idea. With a tug she diverted him toward the nearest temple, which happened to be Hades's. They darted through the entrance, passing along a shadowy passageway and emerging into the *naos*.

Sam hadn't ventured in here before – had had no desire to – but she was not surprised to find the courtyard decked out with all manner of death-related paraphernalia. There were coffins, crematorium urns, headstones, skulls, wax death masks, embalmed foetuses in jars of formaldehyde, and even a lifesize mock-up, like a museum diorama, showing Charon the underworld ferryman punting his skiff across the Styx, the river represented by a sheet of rippled glass.

"Jesus," muttered Hyperion, "who did the interior design here – Tim Burton?"

The centrepiece of this fantasia of ghoulishness was a stone bier on which lay a naked woman, clad in diaphanous nightwear, garlanded with silk flowers and surrounded by candles. Hyperion approached the bier for closer inspection, assuming the woman was another model like Charon. Sam grabbed him by the arm.

"I wouldn't."

"It's just a waxwork."

"I don't think so."

Hyperion looked again, and his lip curled in revulsion. "You have got to be shitting me."

Not an effigy. A cadaver. The skin puffy in places, grey-tinged, not shinily smooth like the Charon replica's. The undersides of the arms and legs empurpled with livor mortis. The make-up overdone to compensate for pallor. The hair matt and listless but too thick and wavy to be anything but the hair of a once-living person.

Sam would have bet anything that Hades called this embalmed corpse Persephone, and what he got up to with it in the privacy of his temple didn't bear thinking about, although the half-used tube of lubricating jelly that lay at the foot of the bier was something of a clue.

She would have bet anything, too, that Hades had been considering her, Sam, as a substitute Persephone for when he got bored of this one here or the relevant parts of the corpse wore out their welcome. Hence his constant speculative interest in her. He'd been sizing her up as the next candidate for the role of necrophiliac fuck-dummy.

"Let's just do this quickly and get out of here," she said to Hyperion, suppressing a shudder.

Nodding agreement, Hyperion unshouldered the container and began fishing segments of TITAN suit out of it. Sam, with her back firmly turned on Persephone, shrugged out of her clothes and set to work armouring herself.

"It's Fred's, not yours," Hyperion said, "but he wasn't big. You guys were pretty much the same height and weight, so with a bit of adjustment it should be an OK fit."

"I don't mind," Sam said, tugging on the one-piece undergarment. "How did you know, though? That I was here? How did you know I was even still alive?"

"We didn't. We believed. We hoped. I hoped most of all. And believed most of all. The way Hermes took you, it looked like a planned kidnapping. We figured maybe Zeus wanted you for some reason, like as a bargaining chip or something."

"Worse than that."

"What?"

"I'll tell you some other time," said Sam. "It's been a long wait, Rick, but I never gave up on you lot. I never despaired." Although it had been close.

"Hey, you want to talk about long waits? Try spending two and a half hours in a sealed crate with Dez Barrington." Hyperion downpipe-gurgled.

The lightning bolts were still streaking down onto the *agora*, but now a deeper, louder sound resounded across the stronghold. It came from the direction of the gate, and resembled nothing on earth so much as the splintering *creak* then *crash* of some immense tree being felled.

"What the hell was – ?"

"That," Hyperion said, "is Rhea taking out the gate with a frostique charge. Least, it should be if we're still on-plan. Did you see her scooting off just before the helicopter fell?"

"No. Too busy getting out of the way."

"Hermes went after her, but she dropped countermeasures."

"Caltrops?"

"It was glorious. She plunked them down behind her like a handful of jacks. Asshole couldn't stop himself, trod straight on them. Spikes stuck right through his feet and he went over like a bowling pin."

"Wish I had seen it," Sam said, strapping the breastplate on. "Darren ruddy Pugh."

"Huh? What about him?"

"Again, I'll tell you some other time. So if the gate's breached..."

"...there's about fifteen hundred armed troops waiting out there in the mist to come in."

And as if to illustrate, a faint, far-off cry started up, a throaty bellow from hundreds of voices, a massed rallying call. Counterpointing it were shrill, indignant shrieks from the Harpies and a few sharp *cracks* of gunfire.

"God, this is really it, isn't it? This is the day the Olympians finally get what's coming to them."

"Don't jump the gun, Sam." Hyperion handed her a helmet. "It's looking good but it's far from decided. The Olympians are tough sons of bitches and shouldn't be underestimated."

"But three of them have been taken out already."

"*Two* of them. Two of the weakest. Hermes isn't out of action. He can still teleport, and if Demeter gets to him he'll be up and running again in no time."

"We need to take out Demeter. She's their most valuable asset, in a way."

"Hey, fearless leader, let's get you back in the game first before you start handing out orders again. How's the suit feel?"

"Odd." But right. Oh so right. She snugged the helmet on.

"Patanjali's reprogrammed the voice recognition to respond to your speech patterns rather than Fred's. Try it."

"Options menu up," Sam said, and the visor HUD sprang to life. Again, oh so right. The beautiful familiarity of those glowing symbols and characters.

She looked down at herself. The breastplate still carried the black-bordered "HK" that Fred had had put there, emblem of the Obliteration. A dead man's suit, but that didn't bother her. It was hers now, and she was Tethys once more.

As if to confirm it, she heard a familiar voice in her ear.

"That sounded like... Tethys? Is that really you?"

"It is, Jamie. How's tricks?"

"Not so bad. We're cooped up in some bloody wee Portakabin in the back garden of the boss's pad in London, me, Rajesh and a couple of the other guys. This is base now, and it's no Bleaney but it'll have to do. I'll be here if you need me."

"Gotcha."

She looked round at Hyperion and found him holding out a recoilless submachine gun to her.

She took it.

"Rick..."

"Hyperion."

"No. Rick. When this is over –"

"When this is over, Sam, and assuming we make it, we're going to get roaring shitfaced drunk and have a damn good time. Right now –"

"No."

She flipped her visor up, leaned forward, flipped his up too, and kissed him. It was awkward, a case of angling her head over to the side as far as it would go and extruding her lips as far as they would go. It was also fleeting, because the position was impossible to maintain for long. But it was tender, and soft, and meaningful, and she relished it right down to the scrape of his day-old stubble against the tip of her nose.

"And now," Sam said, flipping her visor back down and ratcheting her gun's cocking lever, "let's get out there and finish this."

"That's what I want to hear," said Hyperion, and he and Sam hustled out of the temple – Hades's little haven of morbidity, his celebration of all things deathly, complete with corpse bride – and into the mist-draped tumult of battle.

73. CERBERUS AND TYPHON

ONE AND A half thousand troops converged on the wrecked gate, with Field Marshal Armstrong-Hall leading from the front, putting both his life on the line and his money where his mouth was.

They were a makeshift army, so it wasn't pretty, no breathtakingly well-drilled unit here advancing in formation, more like a rabble of men and women, most in uniform, some not, slogging upslope through the mist, sinking ankle-deep in scree, crunching through patches of thin-crust leftover snow, tripping, stumbling, colliding, and now and then, alas, accidentally discharging their weapons and winging a comrade. But still, up they went, on they came, feeding out of the treeline and streaming toward and into the stronghold.

The Harpies descended as eagles on a flock of sheep, feet first, talons flared. Here, and here, and now here, somebody was hauled aloft, dangling from claws that hooked under the ribcage or clavicle or through the meat of the shoulder. Savage beaks went for throats or bellies, digging, rending, wrenching. A few of the bird-women's doomed victims, however, retained the presence of mind to use their guns even as their bodies were being lifted up and opened up. One Harpy spiralled to earth with a wing blown clean off, its slayer death-gripped in its talons. Another, dropping its burden, fell with the most of its head missing.

This made their "sisters" more cautious but didn't discourage them from further attacks. Now they swooped on the soldiers in pairs and, once airborne again, played wishbone with their prey.

But the Harpies totalled less than twenty, and the invading troops had numbers on their side. They could bear the losses the Harpies inflicted. They surged on, pouring in through the gate. Dozens of them entered the stronghold at other points, using ropes and grappling hooks to scale the walls. With the Harpies otherwise occupied, this was now a viable method of access.

Within the stronghold, the ragtag army met with the Olympians' next layer of defence.

In earlier days, before the Titans, Hera would have been able to assemble a daunting array of monsters from her menagerie. She would have gathered them all in beforehand from their various locations around the world and would now be countering the influx of mortals by unleashing a horde of nightmares – the Cyclops with its blunt strength, the Gorgons with their shrivelling stares, the Griffin with its naked viciousness, the Minotaur with its formidable rage, to name a few.

As it was, all she had left were Cerberus and Typhon. Not that Cerberus and Typhon were anything to sneeze at.

The three-headed dog, large as a wolfhound, stocky as a Rottweiler, cut a swathe through the invaders. It thought nothing of chomping on three of them at once, sinking teeth simultaneously into one man's arm, someone else's leg and a third person's privates. It accounted for nearly thirty fatal dismemberments before, at last, a British SAS lieutenant-colonel with a Minimi light machine gun was able to put the canine down.

Typhon was an even more perturbing proposition. Half man, half serpent, it slithered sinuously among the enemy ranks, spewing out a hideously corrosive acidic secretion. Xander Landesman had tried his level best to engineer a beast that could shoot flames from its eyes as the Typhon of myth had done, but this had proved to be beyond even his considerable prowess, a fantasy attribute too far. He'd settled for the ability to eject organic acid, by means of a delivery system derived from the venom-squirting glands of the spitting cobra. The acid, aerosolised by a gust of breath, burned flesh on contact and could eat through clothing in a matter of seconds. Typhon, moreover, habitually aimed for the eyes, and a great many of the attacking army succumbed to the monster in just that fashion, blinded, their eyeballs turning opaque and bursting, aqueous humour dribbling down their blistered cheeks.

Field Marshal Armstrong-Hall came within a hair's breadth of becoming one of Typhon's victims, but was saved by Rhea. The Titan threw herself between Sir Neville and the monster, taking the splash of acid on the back of her battlesuit. The nanobots raced to neutralise the acid's effects and managed to prevent it from doing any more than scarring the surface of her armour. Millions of them were sacrificed in this effort, however, and Rhea's visor display informed her that the suit's integrity had been compromised and its bulletproofing capacity reduced to 60%. Which wasn't so bad, in her estimation. She could live with 60%.

Side by side with Sir Neville she blasted away at Typhon. He had his army-issue SA80 assault rifle, she her Landesman-issue flamethrower. Between them, at a safe remove, they were able to pin the monster down. It spattered acid in all directions, snake body lashing to and fro like an unsecured high-pressure fire hose. Soon, though, it was bullet-holed and ablaze, and not long after that it was a long, thick coil of charred meat, twitching and rolling as it burned.

Sir Neville looked at Rhea. "You know," he said, "when your man Landesman got in touch, I had my doubts. I didn't think there'd be much to be gained by joining forces with a bunch of glorified amateurs."

"I hope you've changed your mind," Rhea replied.

"Too bloody right I have," Sir Neville said, and then the grizzled old veteran (DSO, DSC, MC, KCB, Gulf Medal) turned and waved his troops onward. "Come on! Fan out. Don't bunch up. Occupy any high ground you can find, and if you see an Olympian, do not hesitate, shoot to kill."

The orders were relayed, translated into other languages where necessary, disseminated by walkie-talkie, and for the most part obeyed. Sir Neville knew he was in charge of too many people, and a great proportion of them weren't strictly speaking subject to him in any way. Discipline was at a premium and frankly, though he hardly dared admit it to himself, it was a miracle he'd managed to get all fifteen hundred of them up onto Olympus during the night, let alone been able to get them to follow him *en masse* into the stronghold.

Working in his favour was the fact that he had become the figurehead for this latest and hopefully last act of anti-Olympian insurgency. Every single man and woman present here today knew who he was and had come largely because of him. That helped. They were willing to be commanded by him because he, in a single person, represented what they all stood for. Nevertheless it had been a hell of an administrative and logistical struggle. Sir Neville had hardly had a wink of sleep in seventy-two hours and was running on adrenaline and glucose-enriched power bars only. If he didn't have to fight, he was pretty sure he would collapse any moment through sheer exhaustion.

On he trudged, though, with Rhea alongside him, and several hundred serving soldiers, further into the stronghold, wondering what the Olympians had in store for them next.

74. TALOS

THE OLYMPIANS' NEXT line of defence came courtesy of Hephaestus. He called it Talos, and this was only a slight misnomer. In the myths Talos, the giant guardian of Crete, had been made entirely of bronze, whereas Hephaestus's version was constructed from much less noble matter – car parts, old refrigerators and tumble dryers, lengths of discarded pipe and ductwork, sink drainers, industrial offcuts, countless bits and pieces of metal scavenged from the scrapheaps and junkyards of Athens and brought back to Olympus to be merged and plaited and moulded together inside his temple, all in anticipation of an incursion like this.

Sam and Hyperion were among the very first to see Talos as it arose from within the temple. First they heard a series of stupendous creaks and groans, the sound of joints grinding as they moved. Next, they saw a colossal figure stand stiffly upright, rising above the temple rooftop. At full height it was close on 40 feet tall, and it was blockily humanoid, like some sort of cubist piece of monumental statuary. Patchwork too, its various different-coloured components thrown together with no overall aesthetic design, just fitting wherever they would go. A few freezers lashed together with cables served for one upper arm. The fenders and radiator grilles from several makes of car became a glittering chrome neck. Scaffolding poles and filing cabinets meshed to form the bulk of its chest.

It had no face, which made it look even more imposing and sinister. Its entire head was just a bumpy mass of hubcaps, office chairs, hood ornaments, shopping trolleys, hi-fi equipment and anglepoise lamps shaped into a rough oblate sphere, multifaceted and featureless. Eyes, nose and mouth would have given it character, might even have softened its appearance somehow. This towering metal *thing*, however, was utterly inhuman.

Now it clambered out over the entrance end of the temple, clumsy, crunching the roof underfoot and smashing tiles with its hands, which were the claw-tipped buckets from two Caterpillar excavators, and Sam and Hyperion looked on with equal parts disbelief and horror.

Hyperion summed it up when he said, "That is one seriously fucked-up Transformer robot."

No sooner had it set foot outside the temple than Talos began laying into the troops that were swarming around its legs. Bullets flew at it and pinged ineffectually away, the ricochets causing death and injury among the shooters. Even a rocket-propelled grenade did nothing much except put a dent in Talos's torso, and the damage repaired itself instantly, metal bending and buckling outward to fill in the smoking hole. The metal giant, barely impeded, swung its excavator-bucket hands left and right, scooping up soldiers and flinging them aside. Bodies fell screaming, limbs shattered and rubbery. Often Talos's sweeping hands severed its victims' legs at the shin, leaving booted feet standing on the ground while their owners flailed through the air gouting jets of arterial blood from stumps.

Talos lumbered on, with soldiers now scattering in all directions to get out of its path. Wherever they took refuge, though, the metal giant could still get to them. A group of men, cowering beneath the portico of Artemis's temple, died as Talos pounded the support columns and brought part of the edifice crashing down on their heads.

"We have to stop that thing," Sam said.

"Of course we do," Hyperion agreed. "Only one small problem. Fucking *how*?"

"Hephaestus is controlling it. Find Hephaestus, kill him, you kill it."

"I don't see him."

"He's got to be somewhere close. As I understand it, he has to be able to see something to manipulate it. He needs line of sight. His temple's as good a place as any to start looking. That's where the robot-whatever came from."

Exchanging a grim nod, the two Titans accelerated toward the temple, making sure to steer well clear of

Talos's thumping feet. Each of these was the shell of a Volkswagen Beetle densely packed with gym weights for solidity and stability, and was not something you would wish to be caught beneath, as more than a few of the invading troops had found to their great cost.

Hyperion spotted Hephaestus first. The Olympian was lurking in the shadows of the temple entrance, hunched over, his whole body trembling with the strain of controlling his creation. Sam was reminded of an orchestra conductor swept up in the throes of a particularly dramatic section of a symphony. Occasionally Hephaestus even mimed Talos's actions. He jerked an arm to the side; Talos's arm ploughed through yet more soldiers.

Hunkering down with Sam behind a pile of rubble from Artemis's temple, Hyperion lined up a shot with the coilgun. The range was less than 50 metres. He couldn't miss.

"Come on, do it," Sam urged, as Talos crushed a fleeing soldier with the flat of one hand. The man was cut in two like a pinched ant. Both halves of his body squirmed for a few moments before settling into stillness.

"Yeah, yeah, I'm going to," said Hyperion. "Only... Hephaestus is a person, you know. We should respect that."

"What?"

Hyperion's voice had thickened, becoming oddly husky. He swivelled his head from the gunsight to look at Sam. "Everyone deserves the right to live, don't they? We shouldn't be killing anybody. All life is beautiful."

"Have you gone stark staring mad? What the hell's got into you?"

"*You're* beautiful, Sam."

"Really, this isn't the time. Go ahead and..." Sam stopped and thought about it. Yes, she *was* beautiful, wasn't she? And how nice of him to say so. "Actually, you're pretty damn good-looking yourself," she told Hyperion. "And I love your laugh. It drives me crazy but I love it."

She had no idea why she was saying such things in the thick of battle. The setting could not have been more inappropriate. Yet they needed to be said. So many things needed to be said but never were. People, she realised, wasted their lives keeping in all the expressions of kindness and desire that they should be sharing out. They caged their feelings up when they ought to be giving them free rein. The world would be a far better place without all these inhibitions holding everyone back. If you loved someone, or even just appreciated them, why not simply admit it? What was there to be gained by being all cool and remote and sardonic?

"Rick," she breathed, "this is crazy but... I want to kiss you again."

"Yeah?"

"And not just kiss you. It's been a while. Maybe we can find somewhere private and quiet, away from all this, and..."

"Sounds good to me."

In her mind, as if from some fathomless inner canyon, a tiny voice was shouting *What is this? What in hell's name are you doing?* It was, in fact, Jamie McCann's voice, but she didn't recognise it as such, and it was easily ignored. Her stomach was doing flipflops at the thought of getting naked with Ramsay again. Her craving for him was a low-down ache, a heat-filled tide. She was wet, goddammit, wet *down there*, and she wanted to rip the TITAN suit off Ramsay's body and leap on him, *engulf* him, on this very spot. More than that, she wanted to burrow into him, unwrap him like a birthday parcel, shred him to bits in a frantic paroxysm of lust. She imagined her fingernails scoring tracks down his back, her fists grabbing handfuls of his flesh and tearing them away in bloody chunks, her teeth biting into his succulence and devouring every hot inch of him until there was nothing left. It would be the last lovemaking they ever did, and the best. Ultimate in every way. The climax to end all climaxes.

Something in the grin of the man beside her – the looseness of it, the ferocity – told her he was feeling the same way. He laid aside the coilgun.

"That's right," crooned a soft, luxuriant voice nearby. "Give in to it. That emotion. That impulse. Take each other. Have each other. Fuck each other. Fuck each other up and over and under."

Aphrodite stalked towards them like a catwalk model, hips leading the way.

"And leave my husband be. He has work to do, and I'm here to make sure he can do it, uninterrupted."

The loveliest woman in the world. Sam felt inadequate before her, and also gratified that so exquisite a creature was taking any notice of someone as ordinary as herself. Her ravenous hunger for Ramsay continued to sharpen under the gaze of Aphrodite's glittering, long-lashed eyes. With each step the Olympian took closer to her, Sam's arousal grew. What she would do to Ramsay, she would do to appease the goddess – and goddess this was, make no mistake about that. It was the only word that suited a being who belonged so clearly, supernally, majestically to a higher order of existence. Sam was her slave. She would do anything Aphrodite demanded, anything this living angel asked of her. It was that simple. If it was Aphrodite's will that she consume Ramsay in a frenzy of passion, and be consumed herself at the same time, so be it. What else was love, after all, but a sacrifice, a surrender, a submission to a force greater than oneself?

She was about to turn back to Ramsay and start unbuckling his battlesuit straps. He was ready to do the same for her.

Then her visor display registered a fellow Titan, Theia, coming in at a fast lick from behind Aphrodite. She flicked a glance in that direction and saw only a vague outline of a human being, a shimmer of white that mimicked the stronghold's pale stone and the mist. Aphrodite saw nothing at all. Heard nothing either. She was focused on her pair of thralls, the couple who were about to butcher each other in her name. Theia marched smartly up and placed the business end of the pistol against the back of the Olympian's head, pointed at her brain stem, execution-style. There was a burst of light, a muffled report, and one side of Aphrodite's faced distended outwards. An eye bulged. Her flawless beauty was gone in an instant, all symmetry lost. She opened her mouth and blood frothed out over those plushly perfect lips. Her long legs gave way and she crumpled, head lolling back. As she hit the ground, Theia shot her again. And then, just to be sure, once more.

"Witch," she said. She switched out of camouflage mode, materialising as her full, solid self. "Jezebel. The lake of fire for all eternity. How's *that* feel?"

All at once, everything that had boiled up inside Sam simmered down again. She was left feeling foolish and ashamed, as in the aftermath of a one night stand she knew she should never have had, that same remorse only magnified a hundredfold. She felt bereft, too, as though she'd lost something unutterably precious, a certainty she normally never had. She assumed Ramsay was experiencing a similar degree of embarrassment and ruefulness. Through their tinted visors neither of them could quite meet the other's gaze.

"Now, are you going to kill Hephaestus or what?" Theia said. "'Cause that huge walking pile of trash is coming right this way."

Talos was, indeed, stomping towards them. It moved with obvious purposefulness, not pausing to bother with any of the soldiers who got in its way. Sam glanced in Hephaestus's direction and saw that the Olympian had emerged into the open, at the top of the temple steps, and that his face was a tangle of grief. Tears coursed down his cheeks.

"My wife!" he keened. "Aphrodite! Aphrodiiiteee!"

"Hyperion," Sam said, "for fuck's sake...!"

Hyperion snapped the butt of the coilgun into the crook of his shoulder. The metal giant was mere yards away. Theia was already retreating from it. Its shadow loomed over the Titans, its faceless head hazed in the mist. One hand rose, pivoting on its wrist so that the excavator bucket was turned upside down and became an immense hatchet, a toothed guillotine.

"Shoot him!" Sam cried. "Just bloody well shoo—"

The coilgun snap-crackle-spat. Hephaestus was hit dead centre of his body mass. The bullet punched a hole through him the size of a teacup saucer. The kinetic energy of the impact was such that the Olympian was thrown ten feet through the air, flying backward as though he was as light as a scarecrow. He struck one column of his temple, rebounded off it at an angle and struck the next column along, leaving a gory splash on both. His corpse rolled floppily down the steps, fetching up not far from his late wife, near enough that his outstretched hand was almost touching hers.

At the same time Talos halted in its tracks. For a few seconds it looked as though the metal giant would stay like that, frozen in the act of bringing its hand down on the Titans. Then the static figure began to teeter. Countless sharp edges screeched against one another as its upper half canted forwards and its legs bent at the knees. Off-balance, and without Hephaestus to animate it, it could no longer support itself. It toppled, plunging straight toward Hyperion and Sam. Theia cried out in alarm, but Sam was already moving, and she had Hyperion by the scruff of the neck, one hand slotted down the top of his backplate. Servomotors churned furiously as she sprang clear of the tumbling Talos, dragging Hyperion with her. A dozen tons of scrap metal slammed into the floor, breaking asunder. All the artful structuring Hephaestus had done disintegrated. When everything stopped avalanching and subsiding, what had been the giant now resembled the places its parts had been sourced from – vast, shapeless mounds of junk.

Soldiers started cheering. Meanwhile, Sam and Hyperion picked themselves up out of the litter of debris that was scattered around them. They waded through it over to Theia.

"We owe you," Sam said.

"Just glad to have you back, Tethys," Theia replied. "I prayed to the Lord Jesus to keep you safe, and He did."

"How's the arm?" Sam remembered Theia getting hit by one of Apollo's arrows at Bleaney.

"Ain't what it used to be," Theia said, flexing her elbow gingerly. The joint would bend through only a few degrees of its full range of movement. "That's why I'm down to just a pistol. But it's still good. I'm good."

Over the comms came Iapetus's voice. "Ah, all Titans? Iapetus. Anyone hear me? Little spot of bother here, and I'd really appreciate some help."

Sam consulted her visor display to gauge his whereabouts. Then, without another word, she rushed off in that direction, Hyperion and Theia close behind.

75. AMPHITHEATRE

ARES AND IAPETUS were cat-and-mousing across the amphitheatre. The Olympian, though slowed by his damaged knee, pursued the Titan wherever he went, allowing him no quarter, no let-up. Iapetus jinked now this way, now that, but Ares stayed doggedly on his tail, battle axe swinging.

"Hold still, impudent mortal flea!" he shouted. "Hold still and fight me!"

"Can't really do that, mate," Iapetus replied, "on account of I value having my head attached to the rest of me."

"What makes you think I'll be so merciful as to lop your head off first?"

"Yeah, all the more reason not to stop moving then."

As Sam arrived on the scene, she could see Iapetus was beginning to tire. She could see, too, that Ares was as volcanically vigorous as ever, his bad leg notwithstanding. Bit by bit he was gaining ground on his quarry. Every lunge he made got him a little nearer. His axe blows were missing by an ever narrower margin. Iapetus wasn't being given a moment to stop and draw breath, let alone draw a weapon. Ares's relentless hounding would soon wear him out.

She raised her gun and blasted at Ares. Spurts of sand kicked up at his feet. A couple of rounds dinged his armour but failed to penetrate. He glanced over his shoulder long enough to sneer at her, then resumed his pursuit of Iapetus. Shots from Hyperion's coilgun blew a series of small craters in the ascending stone seats behind Ares. Again the Olympian was unscathed.

"Ain't as if he's a big target or anything," Theia admonished.

"He's also leaping around like a jackrabbit," Hyperion retorted. "You're so damn deadeye dick, *you* try hitting him."

"Closer," said Sam. "We need to get in much closer."

She loped off across the amphitheatre's oval arena, threading between the archery targets and mannequins and items of outdoor exercise equipment. "Iapetus," she said over the comms, "lead him towards us. Maybe we can pincer him."

"I'll give it a try," Iapetus said, panting. "By the way, Tethys, thank God you're back, because these past few weeks, that bastard Hyperion's been mooning around like a koala without a gum tree."

"Save your breath. Just bring him to us."

"Fair go, I'll – Holy shit! All of you! Get down!"

Sam did as Iapetus said, dropping to a crouch without even thinking twice, and at that same instant an arrow embedded itself in the face of the mannequin nearest to her. If she'd been a split second later ducking, it would have gone straight through her own face.

She scurried round behind the mannequin as a further three arrows thwacked into the sandy floor where she had been squatting a moment earlier. Another four arrows stitched themselves in a neat line up the mannequin's leg. Sam hugged her knees in tight to her chest, making herself a ball. A TITAN suit was resistant to Apollo's shafts except, as Theia's experience had shown, at the joints, and Apollo was easily accurate enough to pierce those or the other vulnerable area, the face, which the acrylic glass of the visor would do little to protect.

Apollo had her trapped in position and was also dishing out the same treatment to Hyperion and Theia, forcing them to take cover with a rain of arrows. From a vantage point high up atop the amphitheatre's encircling seats he pivoted to shoot at each of the three Titans in turn, like a compass needle veering between different norths, and the arrows came thick and fast. He was loading the next as his bowstring was still vibrating from firing off the previous one.

"He's got to run out soon," Sam said. "When he does, we rush him."

But no sooner had the words left her lips than Hermes popped into view immediately behind Apollo, with a sheaf of fresh arrows in his arms, which he dumped into the Olympian archer's quiver. From the way Hermes was standing, Sam could only assume Demeter had fixed his injured feet. He vanished again, and the arrow storm continued unabated.

Iapetus, in the meantime, was near exhaustion. So was his battlesuit battery.

"I'm red-lining," he gasped, "and this mad-axeman drongo isn't giving up. Any ideas?"

"We're trying to get to you," Sam replied, "but Apollo's not letting us."

"Ah fuck it," said Iapetus, and Sam detected a kind of weary finality in his voice, and it chilled her. "Then there's only thing left to do."

"Iapetus..."

"All Titans, I just want you to know, you're a bunch of ruddy arseholes," Iapetus said, "and it's been a privilege working with you. Same goes for the dipsticks back at base."

Then he turned to address Ares.

"All right, big boy, you want me? I'm out of puff and standing still now. Come and get me."

He was indeed standing still, and Ares didn't hesitate to take advantage of the fact, springing towards Iapetus with his axe raised above his head double-handed. He brought it down on the Titan's shoulder in a whirring arc. The *crunch* of the impact was immense, and Iapetus, grunting, was driven to his knees. Sam saw his arm droop limply and knew that even though his suit had absorbed much of the force of the blow, such was Ares's strength that he had at the very least numbed the nerves in the arm and perhaps had broken Iapetus's collarbone.

"That the best you could do?" Iapetus said tightly. "And here was I thinking you were the god of war. God of woofters is more like it."

With a bellow of annoyance Ares lofted the axe again and whirled it round in a semicircle to slam the blade into Iapetus's flank. The Titan sprawled sidelong onto the amphitheatre floor, and over the comms Sam heard him moan, the sound of someone in gruelling pain. To Ares he gasped, "No, I take it back. Even a woofter would hit harder than that."

Ares straddled his fallen opponent, chest heaving in triumph. "You would do well not to mock me. It will only prolong your ordeal."

"I'll tell you what's an ordeal, mate – having to listen to you yabber on in that stupid gruff voice of yours. Anyone ever tell you you sound like Russell Crowe with a hangover?"

Infuriated, Ares whammed the axe three times onto Iapetus's back. The Titan convulsed with each blow, and the third of them finally managed to crack the battlesuit. Splinters of polycarbonate erupted around the blade.

"Ha!" Ares exclaimed. "Your shell is broken, so-called Titan. What have you got to say for yourself now? Death is just seconds away. Any more smart remarks?"

Iapetus did mutter some words, but so softly that Ares couldn't hear.

Sam, on the other hand, could.

"Base – Myrmidon Protocol."

And in London, Jamie McCann replied, "Aw no, Iapetus. No."

"Myrmidon. Do it, you useless Scots bastard."

"But the failsafe. Myrmidon won't work while the CPU's still detecting a pulse."

"Bet Patanjali can override that, can't he?"

"He says yes."

"Then do it. I'm crocked anyway."

"Come on, speak up," said Ares. He levered his fingers under the rim of Iapetus's visor and snapped it off. "There, that's better. Now I can hear you properly. Wouldn't want your last words to be a feeble mumble, would we? Say your bit, and die like a man."

"And you," Iapetus replied, loud and clear, "die like the lame-brained boofhead you are."

He clamped an arm around Ares's leg and held on tight, and then the nanobots, having been switched to Myrmidon mode, went to work. They began to eat into Iapetus's suit, but latched onto Ares as well. Anything they came into contact with, they swarmed over swiftly and voraciously. Ares stared down at his leg as the copper greave that sheathed his shin started to disappear before his very eyes, thinning, losing solidity, crumbling to a shower of fine glittering granules. The same was happening to his axe, which was still embedded in Iapetus's backplate. The blade was falling to pieces, becoming metallic dust, and now the haft was disappearing too, but Ares was too stupefied to let go, and then the nanobots were on his hand and eating through his copper gauntlet like an army of invisible termites. He flapped the hand in the air as if this might shake off whatever was attacking him, but of course that was impossible. He tried to free his leg from Iapetus's grip but that too was unshakeable, ineluctable.

"In case you were wondering," Iapetus growled, "you've been bitten by the Barracuda."

And then he started screaming, and Ares started screaming too, as the nanobots dug through to the skins of both men, and then their flesh, gnawing away at startling speed, like acid, and burrowing deeper still, into bone, into marrow.

The combined screams rose in a ghastly crescendo, and Sam clutched the sides of her helmet in an effort to block it out, but of course she couldn't block out the signal from Iapetus's comms this way. It was sickening, almost unendurable, a man's mortal agony being fed direct into her ears, but at long last it began to fade, subsiding to a series of rasping sobs, and these suddenly cut out as a crucial piece of circuitry succumbed to the nanobots' attentions.

Ares's cries of pain carried on, though. The nanobots had made quicker work of Iapetus because there had been considerably more of them on him to begin with than on Ares. They continued to throng over the Olympian's body but their progress was slower, incremental, a more protracted torment. His hand was gone, his arm ending in a stump that seemed to fizz as the nanobots wormed further up, eroding. His leg too was gone from the thigh down, the tip of his femur protruding, sharpened to a point by the depredations of the 'bots. He was half sitting, half kneeling on the ground, and writhing helplessly, and the sand around him was dark brown with his and Iapetus's blood. Eventually shock set in, and Ares slumped forwards. The nanobots munched on, occupying the last few moments of their lives with consumption of the Olympian's spasmodically shuddering form.

In the end, by the time the nanobots' five minutes of Myrmidonhood were up, almost a third of Ares had been dissolved, vanished as though rubbed out by an eraser. The dust to which parts of him had been reduced was all but indistinguishable from the sand the remainder of him lay on.

One threat had been dealt with. But Apollo remained at large.

76. APOLLO APPALLED

DURING HIS FELLOW Olympian's slow demise, Apollo was too aghast to keep up his barrage of arrows. He, like the three Titans, could only look on with disgust and dismay as a comrade-in-arms met his end in truly grisly fashion.

No sooner had the horror run its course, though, than he resumed his attack. With a vengeance. He started down the rows of stone seats, firing at the Titans, not as rapidly now but with control and deliberation. He was conserving his arrows, using them sparingly but still with sufficient frequency to keep the Titans in their place. Each time one of them leaned from cover to take aim at him, an arrow came twanging in, forcing a reconsideration of that idea. Every step Apollo took brought him remorselessly closer. Soon, if not stopped, he'd be at point-blank range.

"Dammit, there's three of us and only one of him," Hyperion said. "How come he's keeping us at bay and not the other way round?"

"Because he's hyper-fast and he doesn't miss," Sam said. "Theia, did I see a Perseus gun strapped to your hip?"

"Yup. Heck, it clean slipped my mind. Gimme a moment."

Theia was huddled behind a vaulting horse, one side of which was now quilled with arrows. Round the edge of it she sneaked the barrel of her Perseus gun. Before she could use it, however, an arrow smacked the gun out of her grasp. A second arrow send it scooting across the arena floor, out of reach.

Theia hissed in frustration. "If I was the cussing type," she said, "I'd be cussing."

"Never mind," said Sam. "Look, we're just going to have to rush him. If we all come out at once, run flat out... well, he'll have trouble hitting all of us, and there's a chance he won't hit any of us."

"How big of a chance?" said Hyperion. "Because my guess would be: not very."

"We can't stay put and just wait for him to get here."

"I know. Fuck. OK then. Count of three, then go. Tethys, you can do the honours."

"One," said Sam.

Crouching up behind the mannequin, she planted her toes in the sand like a sprinter at the starting blocks.

"Two."

Her plan was to keep her head down, presenting as little of her face as possible to Apollo. Knee, elbow, shoulder, ankle, wrist – she could take an arrow in one of those and keep going. She was prepared for it. So long as one of the three Titans got a clear shot at him. Herself preferably, but it really didn't matter which.

"Thr–"

Abruptly, men came pouring over the amphitheatre's rim, firing rifles at Apollo. A couple of dozen of them all told, dressed in plain clothes, mostly heavy metal band T-shirts. Dark-haired, swarthy, moustachioed, and leading them was a figure Sam had no trouble recognising – Paulu Galetti.

The Resistenza.

Apollo whirled to confront this new threat, and killed four of the men in the space of as many heartbeats. Then he moved to retreat, still slotting in and sending off arrows as he darted across the arena through a whining blizzard of bullets. He was no match for Hermes when it came to speed, but he was fast enough, and even when on the hoof his bow accuracy was such that not one of his shots was wasted. Resistenza members fell in swift succession, sprouting arrows from the eye, the chest, the gizzard, the gut. By the time Apollo gained the sanctuary of a niche in the low wall that encircled the arena, he'd already halved the number of his assailants.

From the niche his arrows zinged out at regular intervals, but the Corsicans did not slacken or relent. Galetti started up a cry – "Ghjuvanna Venturini!" – which the others took up and roared in unison.

The noise rang round the amphitheatre, as though for once this place had an audience filling its seats, and it was hard to say whether or not the Olympian had learned the name of the little Corsican girl he had accidentally slain, whether or not he even remembered her, but the sheer volume and venom with which her countrymen chanted it seemed to give him pause. Briefly the volley of arrows let up. Galetti and the rest noted this and made the most of it, zeroing in on the niche.

"Come on, back them up!" Sam cried, leaping out from behind the mannequin, which now looked more like a human-shaped porcupine than anything.

Hyperion and Theia emerged from cover too, and the three Titans followed in the wake of the Resistenza members, all converging on Apollo.

The Olympian realised the trouble he was in and began to defend himself again. But his momentary hesitation had cost him the advantage. The Resistenza men, with Galetti to the fore, crowded in on him in the niche. He was subsumed, overwhelmed by numbers. Sam saw one of the Corsicans emerge holding his bow aloft. Another had his quiver. Then Apollo himself was being lugged bodily out into the arena, with a man holding each of his limbs. He twisted and struggled, but to no avail.

The Corsicans, of whom only a handful remained, tossed him onto the sand and secured his hands and feet. Galetti stepped up. He had an arrow protruding from his shoulder. It must have been the last one Apollo loosed off before he'd been swamped. It would doubtless be the last one he ever loosed off. A desperate, flailing shot. That was the only reason Galetti was still alive.

Galetti lowered his rifle to Apollo's head.

"Go on," the Olympian snarled, face pressed into the sand. "Mortal scum. Do it. Try. How can you kill me? I am a god! Immortal! Eternal! Everlasting!"

The Resistenza leader glanced over at Sam. He was in obvious discomfort from the arrow but the glory of this moment trumped that. In the heat of triumph, pain paled into insignificance.

"He is ours, do you agree, Madama Tethys?"

Sam would have liked to say no he wasn't, he was hers. Apollo needed to meet his death by her hand, in order to make up for Ade's death. There was an imbalance here that needed to be restored, an emptiness in herself that had to be filled. Blood demanded blood.

But then she thought of the face of Ghjuvanna on those photocopied posters in Corsica. A short life, ended by arrogant carelessness.

Apollo had worse crimes to pay for than what had happened to Ade. It was more fitting if justice came from the Resistenza than from her. At least she was present to see it being dished out.

She nodded to Galetti, who reciprocated with a nod of his own, having no idea of the generosity that lay behind Sam's gesture.

His rifle barked.

Apollo spasmed, as though subjected to a powerful electric shock.

Then lay still.

At almost the exact same instant, even while the cartridge shell ejected from the breech of Galetti's rifle was still spinning through the air, Hermes appeared with another armful of arrows for Apollo.

Sam responded reflexively, almost without thinking. As Hermes gaped down in astonishment at the lifeless remains of his fellow Olympian, she swung her gun up and squeezed the trigger. Bullets burped, rapidfire. Hermes fell, arrows skidding and scattering around him like jackstraws.

Sam hurried over to where he lay, ready to finish him off if need be, but Hermes was dying. One look told her that. She'd got him in the torso and neck. Blood was bubbling from his mouth and pulsing out through the crater-like gouges in his chest in time to his wheezing breaths.

He tried to teleport away but couldn't. He phased out, phased in again, phased out, in, alternating between here and elsewhere. At first the exchanges were so rapid he was almost strobing, but gradually they slowed, weakened, becoming the fizzling, arrhythmic flicker of a lightbulb that was just about to fuse. Then they ceased altogether, leaving Hermes fixed solidly where he was. He rolled his head. He squinted up at Sam. Something seemed to shift in his eyes, like a cloud clearing.

"Ginger tits..." he croaked, and it was followed by a phlegmy choking rattle that was just about recognisable as laughter. "Fuck." Now he was talking as Darren Pugh. Himself again, at the last. "I remember you."

"Good," said Sam.

"I told. About Bleaney."

"I know."

"I'm..."

There was one more word, a couple of short slurred syllables, and Sam couldn't identify it. It might have been *sorry*. It might equally have been something nonsensical like *sausage*. But it made no difference. Pugh's act of betrayal was in the past.

And so was Pugh.

77. SWIMMING-POOL JELLYFISH

"DANG," SAID HYPERION, over Hermes's body. "I get what you were saying now, about Pugh. They made a new Hermes out of him. Recycled his sorry ass."

"Couldn't have happened to a nicer guy," said Theia, and hawked up a gob of spittle and let it drop from her lips onto the corpse's blank-staring face.

"Not immortal," said Sam. "Just wanting us to think they are. Now, Cronus and Rhea. Where are they and what are they up to?"

Her visor display informed her that both the other Titans were not far from each other, a little under a kilometre to the east.

"Rhea?" she said over the comms.

"Tethys! I'm with Field Marshal Armstrong-Hall and a few of his men, and we are at what seems to be some kind of swimming pool."

"Any Olympians there?"

"Not as far as I can tell. There are a lot of bodies, though, and what's left of a monster. Judging by the scaly hide, the fins, and the number of heads – six that I can count – Scylla. You should see the shell casings. It took a lot to kill this creature. Anyway, we're going to complete our sweep of the area, then move on. What's your situation?"

"Three Olympians down."

"*Fantastique!*"

"Also one Titan."

"Ah."

"Iapetus."

"I'm sorry about that. I had no great love for him, but still."

"Likewise," said Sam. "To give him his due, he went out in style."

"Hero?"

"I'd say."

"A Christmas gift in a plain paper package. He'll be – One moment. What's that? Field Marshal, do you see –"

Sudden gunfire. Shouting. Panic.

"Rhea?" Sam said. "Rhea!"

She looked at Hyperion and Theia. "We have to –"

"You don't even need to say it," said Hyperion. "Let's roll."

"Theia?"

Sam was expecting hesitation, a wince of reluctance at the very least. What she got was a surprisingly affirmative "Yeah!," followed by: "She saved my hide from the Hydra. I save hers, then we're quits, that abomination and me, and I don't owe her nothing any more."

As rationales went, it was hardly altruistic. But it would do.

The three Titans raced towards the swimming pool, passing among soldiers who were scouring the stronghold for enemies and having trouble finding any. If Sam counted right, there were five Olympians left: Zeus, Poseidon, Hera, Dionysus and Demeter. Six if you included Argus. Whether they were scattered throughout the stronghold or concentrated in one spot, not everyone in the invading force was going to be able to engage with one of them. It was simple arithmetic. So some of the soldiers, finding themselves enemy-less, were doing what soldiers at a loose end tended to do, namely vandalising and ransacking. Temples were being shot up and defaced with mortar shells. The Olympians' living quarters were being looted, the larger furnishings smashed or burnt, smaller items pocketed as souvenirs. This destructiveness was a good sign. It spoke of the possibility of victory, a prevailing mood of optimism. If the invaders were laying waste to the place, rather than being repulsed and routed, it implied that theirs was the side with the upper hand.

On arriving at the swimming pool, Sam had cause to revise this opinion.

Here, Poseidon presided, and he was using the water from the pool – nearly a million gallons of it – as a weapon of mass destruction. At his command the water had arisen in a single bulbous globule that sprouted tentacles in every direction like some leviathanic jellyfish. The tentacles latched onto the heads of the attacking soldiers, lifting them off the ground and covering their faces with a blister of liquid. The soldiers drowned while suspended in midair, their legs kicking, their hands clawing uselessly at the transparent wet masks that were killing them.

To guard against bullets Poseidon had erected a shimmering dome of water around himself. It was some ten metres in diameter, its wall three or four metres thick. Any projectile that entered the dome was slowed to a standstill and then began sinking lazily to the turquoise tiles of the floor.

Sam spotted Field Marshal Armstrong-Hall frantically grappling one of the water tentacles, which was wound round him like a boa constrictor. Rhea was helping him fight it off, chopping through it with her fist every time its tip got within probing distance of his head. The end of the tentacle would disintegrate into a shower of droplets, but would then re-form instantly, extruding itself forwards to renew its relentless snaky progress towards his face.

Parts of the sea-beast Scylla lay scattered around the rim of the pool, along with heaps of sodden corpses. Within his impregnable dome Poseidon looked overtaxed but grimly elated. It was a strain controlling so much water so intricately, but to defend the stronghold, to slaughter wholesale these mortals who had dared lay siege to the Olympians' home, was worth any amount of effort.

"Ideas?" Hyperion asked Sam, surveying the scene. "'Cause me, I'm all out. Nothing's getting through that dome Poseidon's got around him, and he's got plenty of water to play with, and even if he runs out, he'll just set to turning people's blood to sludge or exploding it out through their ears. The motherfucker's holding all the cards and he knows it."

"You said nothing's getting through the dome," Sam said.

"Yep. I think nothing can. Not even a coilgun round."

"But not no one."

"Huh?" Then Hyperion grasped what she was getting at. "Oh, you are one crazy, psycho-ass bitch, and I mean that as a compliment."

"Direct frontal assault," Sam said. "But it has to be all of us doing it, to give us the best possible chance of success. The more of us try, the likelier it is one of us will get through. Base? These suits are watertight, right?"

"The servos are sealed units," said McCann. "The electrics and electronics are water-resistant, pretty much. I'm not promising –"

"Pretty much is good enough. Rhea?"

"Yes? Bit busy here."

"Leave the Field Marshal."

"I can't. He'll –"

"He can cope. Leave him. We're going to rush Poseidon, the four of us. Top speed. Push ourselves through that dome. The seal on the visors should allow us enough air to breathe to do the job. Whoever reaches him first..."

The sentence didn't need finishing. Hyperion loped off, head down, swiftly building up momentum. Theia followed, then Sam. Rhea rapidly explained the plan to Armstrong-Hall, who nodded consent. Then, breaking away from him, she too accelerated towards Poseidon. The four Titans battered their way through water tentacles that lashed ripplingly at them. Hyperion let out a wordless war cry that grew in volume and intensity as he neared Poseidon's protective dome, becoming an abandoned, here-goes-nothing howl as he hit the curved wall of water and plunged headlong in. Theia jumped in straight after him. Then came Rhea, and finally Sam.

The impact was weird – not like diving into water, more like entering a thick, slimy layer of silica gel. Air bubbles erupted around Sam with a measured effervescence, roiling away and popping slowly. She felt herself begin to decelerate almost immediately, inertia giving way to entropy, and she could see the same happening to the others. All at once they were moving like divers at deep-fathom pressures, fighting against the extra density and viscosity Poseidon had introduced into the water.

But they *were* moving. Making headway, too. The dome stopped bullets, but bullets did not have the power of independent locomotion. All four Titans were closing in on Poseidon, Hyperion to the fore, and the Olympian was aware of their presence, their proximity, but there was very little he could do about it at that moment other than reinforce the dome still further. Sam felt the water tighten around her, pressing in on the suit, and redoubled her efforts. The servos responded, and she continued to wade through. Water began to seep in around the edge of her visor but it oozed rather than flowed. Its own gluey consistency prevented it from rushing in and flooding her helmet.

She and the other Titans were inside the dome for less than a minute. It felt longer, as though the water retarded time as well as physical objects. Everything wavered and wobbled around Sam. Her hand batted aside a drifting bullet as she thrust herself through, using her arms as much as her legs to propel her along.

With Hyperion mere inches away from breaching the dome's inner surface, Poseidon concluded that his only practical option was to drop his defences altogether. The dome lost cohesion in an eyeblink, collapsing in a great sloshing downrush of water, which exploded back upwards as it hit the floor, like some tremendous circular sea wave crashing on the shore and breaking almost to its original height.

In the midst of this white frothing up-burst the four Titans shot forwards as the impetus they'd accumulated within the dome wall, no longer restrained, was suddenly released – an unintended consequence for both them and Poseidon. They hurtled helplessly at the Olympian from different directions, colliding with him almost as one. He could not stop them, and the quadruple impact was bone-crunching. Sam, even above the roar of water cascading all around, heard something within Poseidon's body snap as she struck him with her shoulder.

The Titans rebounded, sprawling. Poseidon simply crumpled on the spot where he'd been standing, like a marionette discarded by its puppeteer. Similarly, and simultaneously, the swimming-pool jellyfish subsided out of existence. The dozens of soldiers being marauded by it walloped down onto the gleaming dark blue tiles.

The Olympian had been fatally injured.

But he was not dead.

As Sam struggled to a kneeling position, Poseidon was already extending one quivering hand towards Theia. Divining what he was up to, Sam started scuttling towards him with a cry of "No!"

Too late.

Theia was convulsing. Her limbs twisted and contorted as though she were having an extremely violent kind of fit. Her head came up, and Sam was staring her in the face, looking straight into two bulging, uncomprehending, scarlet-tinged eyes. And then Theia's face was gone. There was only blood, a massive blurt of it splurging out from every facial orifice and painting the interior of the visor dark red.

Theia slumped flat. Poseidon turned his attention to Rhea, who was lying on her side and fumblingly trying to detach a pistol from her suit. Suddenly she went rigid. A fraction of a second later, Sam leapt on Poseidon and started punching him in the face with everything she had. It amazed even her how fast her arm was moving – up and down like a steam piston pumping at full tilt – and how much damage each servo-assisted blow inflicted. Poseidon's features seemed to dissolve under the barrage, losing everything – shape, solidity, humanity. She felt bits of him cracking and splintering under her fist. She had punched through a drystone wall once. By a comparison a man's skull, even an Olympian's, was hardly anything.

She didn't dare stop. She planned to keep battering Poseidon until there was nothing left of him. It was Hyperion, however, who delivered the coup de grâce. He bent down and grabbed the sides of the Olympian's head while Sam was still belabouring it with her fist, and he wrenched it up double-handed, detaching base of skull from topmost vertebra. Poseidon's face, such as it now was, froze as if in shock. His mouth gaped, revealing two runs of shattered teeth. His head lolled to the side. Another Olympian had been scratched off the list.

78. GODS' END

"RHEA..."

Sam rolled off Poseidon's body and crawled over to her fellow Titan.

"I'm all right," Rhea rasped. She didn't sound it, though. She wasn't moving, and through her visor Sam could see a face that was perplexed and slightly panicked. "I just can't – can't feel anything. My arms, my legs... Won't move. Nothing works. I think he might have –"

"Uh, all Titans." McCann. "It's Cronus. The old geezer's been doing pretty well for himself 'til now, but he's squaring off against Zeus, and it's just him, and I think he could do with reinforcements."

Sam looked at Hyperion, then Rhea.

"Go," Rhea said. "There's nothing you can do for me right now. Go help him."

"Hang in there. I'll be back as soon as I can."

Rhea gave a short, mirthless laugh. "I'm not going anywhere."

They didn't need transponder sensors to tell them where Cronus was. All they had to do was follow the lightning, which crackled in the air above the *agora*, darting this way and that through the mist in silvery veins. In the *agora* itself, the flashes weirdly illuminated a tableau of ruin and death. At one end, amid tumbled columns, lay Dionysus. He had been crushed by falling masonry. His eyes were wide and unseeing. All colour and jollity were gone from his face.

Not far from him Demeter sat hunched over, cradling Hera's head in her lap. Hera was as lifeless as Dionysus, Sam could tell that at a glance. Demeter, however, refused to accept it.

"I can heal you," she sobbed. "I can bring you back, O Hera Of The Height." Her hands probed the many bullet wounds that riddled Hera's body, but nothing happened. The wounds stayed open. Hera was in a state that not even Demeter's curative power could remedy.

But the main business of the scene was taking place in the centre of the *agora*, beside the wreckage of the Super Puma. There, Zeus and Cronus stood face to face, their bodies rigid and bowed, bent towards each other like two sides of an arch that didn't quite meet at the top.

Father and son reunion. For the first time in a decade and a half Regis and Xander Landesman were in each other's presence, and talking.

Or rather shouting.

"This was mine!" said Zeus. "*My* dream! *My* achievement! I did it without any help from you.

I worked hard, I struggled to make it happen, but you just couldn't let me have it, could you? You just couldn't bear the idea of your son being better than you, more powerful, more successful. So you had to come along and tear it all down."

"This isn't about me and you, Xander," Landesman retorted. He had his visor up so that he could look his son straight in the eye. "You think I'd go to all this trouble to destroy you and your Olympians out of some kind of jealousy? You're mad. You've turned into a power-crazed megalomaniac – a mass-murdering monster. Someone had to stop you. Someone had to end this tyranny of yours."

"And it simply had to be you, did it?"

"I'm your father. I brought you into the world. I bear some of the responsibility for what you've done, what you've become. The blood-guilt is mine. Therefore it's only right that I should be the one who brings you down."

The lightning flashes were coming thicker and faster overhead. Hyperion took a step towards Zeus and Cronus, levelling his coilgun, but Sam restrained him with a hand.

"This is their moment. Let them be."

"I can take out Zeus while his guard's down."

"It's a standoff. It might resolve itself peacefully."

Hyperion let out a sceptical huff of breath, but stayed where he was, coilgun not fully raised.

"You're a danger to everyone," Cronus told his son.

"No, only to anyone who opposes me," said Zeus. "Do you not understand what I've managed to do here? Do you not realise how good I've made life for billions of people?"

"Do you not realise how *bad* you've made it, Xander? So bad it makes me ashamed. That's all I've felt these past ten years, nothing but shame."

"Your feelings aren't my concern. I don't seek your approval. I never have."

"Your mother would have been ashamed too."

"Don't bring her into this! Don't you dare!" Zeus bellowed. "You never deserved her. She was worth a thousand of you."

"You barely even knew her."

"I remember enough about her to know that she loved me more than your ever did or could."

"I loved you."

"No, you tolerated me at first. Then you resented me, and finally you despised me."

"I despise what you are now."

It struck Sam how truly alike these two men were. Their faces, pressed up to each other, were mirror images, almost. The level of antipathy radiating from both of them was near identical too.

"Then here I am, *Dad*," said Zeus, making the last word a vindictive snarl, a kind of accusation. "This is your chance to finish me. Take it. You won't get a better one. Or a second one."

"I don't want to kill you, Xander. I should, given how you did your level best to kill *me*. I ought to, in the light of all your crimes against humanity. But I don't. Can't you see that it's over? Your Olympians are dead. Olympus is overrun. You've nothing left. You're beaten.

But you can still walk away from all this. Come back with me. Come home. Let's start again. I can protect you, look after you, give you a new shot at life."

"After fifteen years? After all that's happened? Hah! You must be joking."

Cronus looked saddened but not surprised. "I thought I should offer. You've refused. So I'm afraid you leave me with no choice."

Seizing Zeus's shoulder with one hand, he produced an oscillo-knife with the other.

"Let the punishment fit the crime," he said, and before Zeus could so much as blink, he plunged the buzzing blade into his son's crotch.

A sideways torque of the wrist.

A blossoming of blood across the front of Zeus's robe.

"Dad...?" Zeus said, his voice wavery, strangulated.

Cronus worked the oscillo-knife like a saw, hacking away at Zeus's genitals with a cold and remorseless efficiency. His other hand bore down, keeping Zeus planted firmly in place.

"This is the fate of kings of pantheons," he hissed. "And of fathers."

"Dad..."

The lightning began to coalesce. The brightness overhead grew as though a new sun was forming within the mist.

"Oh shit," muttered Hyperion.

Cronus was concentrating too hard on what he was doing to notice. Relishing the moment too much. "You took mine." The words were a hoarse hiss, only just audible. "Now I take yours."

"Daddy," Zeus moaned. "Please. No. Stop."

But Cronus paid no heed.

The lightning swelled into a vast, lambent sphere. Plasmic sparks wormed and veined across every surface in the *agora*. The air felt alive with power.

"We gotta get out of here," Hyperion said.

And Sam knew he was right, but she couldn't move. Couldn't turn. Couldn't tear herself away.

"Daddy!"

Something plopped wetly onto the flagstones between Zeus's feet. He was shuddering. The lower half of his robe was nothing but redness.

"DADDEEEEE!!!"

Then the lightning broke, and the world went white. Not the filmy white of the mist. A pure, bleaching, incandescent white that penetrated every crack and corner and left no room for shadows, no dark crevices, nothing unilluminated. A whiteness like the beginning of Creation, or its end. Accompanied by a *bang* that was beyond sound, beyond comprehension, loud enough that it made any other noise a whisper by comparison – and a wave of intense heat and pressure that came like a giant, sweeping hand and drove all before it. A hurricane of burning brilliance that picked up Sam and Hyperion and whirled them and tangled them and tossed them aside, and left only a howling blackness in its wake.

PART 3

THREE YEARS LATER

EPILOGUE:
THE CHICAGOANS

THE L-DAY EVENT in Lincoln Park was the usual contrasting mix of solemn memorial and joyful celebration. At noon on a baking-hot June day several thousand Chicagoans gathered, some to sing hymns, some to light candles, some to sit in quiet contemplation, some to share beers, some to play music and dance, some to march in circles and chant slogans, and some just to spectate from the sidelines. It was disorganised, rowdy in places, not sanctioned by the authorities, and with no point of focus – no special monument to rally around, no single person to conduct the proceedings, no distinguished figure to stand up and make a speech and be a mouthpiece for all. Similar improvised assemblies were occurring all over the world on this, the third anniversary of the overthrow of the Olympians.

Despite much campaigning and petitioning, not one government would overtly acknowledge Liberation

Day as a formal annual calendar occasion. There was a desire among the powers-that-be to move on from the age of Olympian rule, draw a line under it, act as if it had never happened. The people, however, disagreed. Let their elected representatives sweep that decade under the carpet and the dust of political cowardice with it. They might wish to forget, but seven billion others did not.

Furthermore, many felt that their leaders should be held to account – the ones, at least, who had bent the knee most abjectly to the Pantheon. Here at Lincoln Park voices called for ex-president Stavropoulos, whose term of office had just ended and not been renewed, to be retroactively impeached. Similarly, at Trafalgar Square in London where an L-Day event had been held some six hours earlier, there'd been renewed demands for Catesby Bartlett to face prosecution in the High Court. Bartlett had stepped down as prime minister not long after the Olympians' demise, citing health reasons, but the vilification of him in the press and online – *criminal, coward, collaborator* – continued unabated. For all that he was currently serving in an ill-defined role as some sort of goodwill ambassador for the UN, he was seldom seen in public, and had not set foot on British soil since leaving 10 Downing Street, perhaps for fear of being arrested, or lynched.

At this same hour, in New York, a big band struck up show tunes on Governors Island at the spot where the giant statue of Zeus no longer stood, and people started to dance. In Paris, where it was evening, a firework display splash-painted the sky above the recently restored Eiffel Tower. In Sydney, where day was just breaking, the Australian prime minister delved a spade into the ground, declaring building work on a new Opera House begun. In Bruges, a statue was unveiled with all due pomp and circumstance – and the imbibing of a great deal of pale lager – in the centre of the Markt. It was a memorial to the Unknown Titan, to add to the countless other similar memorials that had been erected all across the planet.

Meanwhile, a breeze off Lake Michigan kept the throng of Chicagoan L-Day celebrants cool as they milled about. Conversations returned again and again to that day three years ago when it had become apparent that the Olympians were no more, all killed at the hands of Sir Neville Armstrong-Hall's little impromptu army and the last remaining Titans. Where were you when you first heard the news? Wasn't it amazing to see those interviews with troops who had taken part and listen to their accounts of shooting monsters and combating a metal giant? And how about that footage of the JDS *Inazuma Maru* bombarding Olympus from just off the coast, razing the Pantheonic stronghold to the ground? And the helicopter shots of the smouldering ruin afterwards? The long-distance images of the mountain with smoke billowing up from its summit?

Armstrong-Hall's name received repeated mention. After the attack on Olympus the distinguished old soldier had gone home to face the music: a court martial, and even the possibility of trial at the Hague on charges of being a war criminal. A vast international public outcry, however, had soon put paid to that, and he was quietly discharged and pensioned off instead. Now in retirement at his home in the Cotswolds, Britain's erstwhile Chief of General Staff divided his time between penning his memoirs and cultivating rare strains of apple in his orchard. On L-Day it could be guaranteed that at least fifty different TV stations and newspapers from all over the globe would ring him up to ask for a comment, but all he would say was: "I did what I had to do and what was right. It isn't me you should be talking to. It's the soldiers I led. They did all the work and took far greater risks than I. They and the Titans – whoever *they* were."

And of course there was much discussion of the Titans at Lincoln Park, as at every other L-Day event, most of it favourable, some of it speculative. The Titans remained anonymous. Identities, nationalities, origins – all a mystery. Even the bodies of the ones killed in action had never been found. Ghostly, they had appeared. Ghostly, they had gone. In a way, that was preferable to knowing everything about them, every last personal detail. They were blank slates, everymen who had emerged from nowhere to fulfil a function, then melted away back into the shadows. What they'd helped bring about meant more than who they'd actually been.

So in Lincoln Park, on this summery and boisterous L-Day, it was possible to imagine that a Titan might be standing right next to you. Might be that man in the queue for the hot dog vendor. Might be that woman sipping bottled water while leaning on a lakefront lamppost. Might be that rollerblader whizzing around in a cutoff L-Day T-shirt (motto: *Waking Up From A 10-Year Nightmare*). Might be that rich-voiced gospel singer leading a chorus of "Amazing Grace."

Might even be one or other (or both) of that mixed-race couple who were pushing a baby-stroller through the crowd and observing the goings-on with a detached, wry amusement.

"Don't you just feel like standing up and telling them?" said he to her. "Shouting it out loud? 'That's me you guys are all so jazzed up about. I'm the one. Come and give me a pat on the back. Maybe the key to the city too.'"

"*You* might," said she to him. "I wouldn't."

"Pride ain't a crime."

"No, but modesty's a virtue."

"You're not even tempted? Don't tell me you're not tempted."

"Not for a moment. Besides, what makes you think they'd believe us? Dozens of people have come out of the woodwork in the past three years claiming they were a Titan. They've all been debunked and laughed at. Why would we get treated any differently?"

"Uh, because it's true?"

"Face it, Rick, we're better off this way. We have a nice, quiet life. Be a pity to ruin it."

"Quiet?" said Ramsay, casting a dubious glance at the occupant of the stroller, who was fast asleep.

Sam followed his gaze. "Well, for another few minutes, at any rate. Hey, ice-cream van. Fancy a snow cone?"

They ate the cones on a bench overlooking the brilliant expanse of the lake, where pleasure cruisers, jet-skis and water skiers leashed to speedboats all vied for space, cross-hatching one another's wakes.

"Oh, I got an email from Jamie this morning," Sam said.

"And how is yon bonnie laddie?"

"Your Scottish accent is even worse than your English."

"Did I not sound like Sean Connery?"

"Not even close. And Jamie's fine. He's got a girlfriend now, so I don't hear from him as often as I used to."

"McCann has a girlfriend?"

"Don't sound so surprised. He's cute – in a boyish way. He's also pretty wealthy, thanks to Landesman."

"Aren't we all?" said Ramsay.

Jolyon Lillicrap, as executor of Regis Landesman's will, had supervised the disbursement of funds from his late boss's estate. Channelling the money through various offshore accounts so as to render it untraceable, he had ensured that everyone involved in the Titanomachy II campaign, from techs to surviving Titans, had been duly and amply rewarded for their services, himself included. By this means Sam and Ramsay had been able to buy a handsome, serviced penthouse apartment on North Lake Shore Drive, with spectacular views of the lake. They'd also established financial security for themselves for the rest of their lives.

"And Thérèse?" Ramsay enquired. "She called lately?"

"No, but the trip to Québec to visit her is still on." Sam nodded at the stroller. "I'll take him with me so she can see how big he's getting."

"The poor woman. Any, you know, progress?"

Sam shook her head. "Every treatment in the book's been tried. If it's not made any difference by now, it's never going to."

Hamel had been left quadriplegic by Poseidon's attack. Sam's intervention had prevented him from fully coagulating the blood in Hamel's veins but he'd done enough damage to trigger a series of small ischemic strokes, the result of which was complete loss of function and sensation below the neck. Hamel could afford the best of healthcare and occupational therapy and, tough old broad that she was, she remained resolutely upbeat about her condition, arguing that it could have been worse, she could be dead, and moreover it had all been in a good cause. Sam, though, still felt an ache in the pit of her stomach every time she thought of her.

"If I'd only been a fraction quicker off the mark..."

Ramsay lodged a reassuring arm around her shoulders. "Stop it. You always beat yourself up about this, and it isn't going to change anything. Thérèse doesn't blame you, so neither should you."

Sam nestled her head against the muscled firmness of his shoulder. "Rick," she said after a few moments, "what do you think about, when you think about that day?"

He gazed out over the lake. On the grass nearby a drummer was pounding on bongos, beating out a complex polyrythym for a throng of neo-hippie L-Dayers to freak out to.

"Mostly I think how goddamn lucky you and me were to get out alive. When Zeus went all self-destructo on us... I mean, Jesus, if it hadn't been for our suits, we'd have been toast. Crispy-fried bacon. Done to a turn and carbon round the edges."

"Me, I can't forget Zeus's face as Landesman – you know."

"Castrated him."

"The sheer disbelief. His own father. After all the feuding and bad blood between them, suddenly he was just a kid again, ten years old, not understanding how his daddy could be so cruel."

"Yeah, it was a regular Greek tragedy. Bet Landesman himself regretted it, in the last few seconds. Not even a TITAN suit could save him from the shitstorm Zeus called down. The two of us just got blown off our feet. Landesman was right at the epicentre..." His voice tailed off.

Sam wasn't listening. She was back there, on Olympus, reliving it – the lightning explosion and its aftermath. Tottering to her feet, dazed, dazzled, half deafened. Her battlesuit seared all over, partially melted, no longer functioning. Useless, just so much high-tech clutter. Discarding most of it, piece by piece. Helping Ramsay upright, helping him pick off the majority of his armour too. Then surveying the *agora* – blasted and blackened on every surface, a negative print of itself. Trawling through the rubble to find scorched bits of Cronus's battlesuit, with scorched bits of Cronus inside it. Finding even less of the Olympians, just a few charred, scattered bone fragments, some held together with tar-like scraps of skin. All that remained of Zeus, Hera, Demeter and Dionysus.

Then the journey back through the stronghold to Rhea, amid grinning, triumphant soldiers who sensed now that the battle was truly won. On the way, encountering a group of men who'd unearthed Argus from his chamber. Seeing them drag him into the open with detached wires dangling from his head. Seeing them push him to his knees, his belly flopping over his thighs. Seeing them retreat to form a line, rifles raised – a firing squad. Seeing a vague smile creep onto Argus's corpulent face, as if he knew what was about to happen and it was a relief, an end to the stench and suffering of his existence. Or else the smile was just the idiot smile of a creature disconnected from all contact with the world, not realising what awaited.

The multiple report of the guns, and the slumping thud of a fleshy body falling, and her and Ramsay trudging on. To Rhea, who was still lying at the poolside, and lying so still, with Armstrong-Hall squatting solicitously beside her, doing his best to soothe her. The Field Marshal, in his water-soaked battledress, standing up as he saw the other two Titans approach. Snapping off a salute. Catching their expressions. Understanding. Saying, *Done?*

Sam confirming it. *Done.*

Armstrong-Hall relaying this into a walkie-talkie: *Stand down. I repeat, all units stand down. It's over.*

And Sam and Ramsay walking on as the mist began to lift from Olympus, thinning, the air brightening. Making for the gate, and the mountainside, and somewhere, elsewhere, anywhere that wasn't here.

On the bench, Ramsay could see Sam unreeling this vivid memory-movie in her mind.

"Come back, Sam," he said. "Come back to me. That was then. This is now. You don't have to be there any more. It's over."

"You know what's odd?" she said, finally.

"Your accent? You pronounce the 'r's in the middle of words, and your sentences go up at the end. You're becoming a local girl."

"Well, I have to, to make myself understood. Otherwise, I say something and I get looked at like I'm speaking in tongues."

"Fitting in."

"Yeah. I'm a mistress of disguise. Who needs a TITAN suit with chameleon function?"

"And the less English you come across as, the less likely it is someone might recognise you as that woman who's still wanted in the UK for murder."

"I'm not in hiding, Rick. If the British government finds me and wants to have me extradited, I'll go back and face the music. I'm innocent."

"I'd testify to that."

"And Dai Prothero would be in my corner too. The only trouble is, to clear my name I'd have to admit to being a Titan, and that'd open this huge great can of worms. Life's simpler if I just keep my head down. Anyway, as I was saying. You know what's odd? I still can't get used to the idea that, in the end, I only actually killed one of the Pantheon. Hermes – Pugh. I never got my reckoning with Apollo and Artemis, or with Aphrodite."

"That bother you?"

"Not as much as it might have. I wanted revenge badly, so badly, but maybe it was better that I didn't get it."

"Better for you," Ramsay said. "Better for your soul."

"Right. But still I'm left with this feeling of, *So what was that all about then?*"

"You did your bit, and the Olympians got what was coming to them. Guess it doesn't matter who from, long as they got it. The only one who didn't really deserve to die was Argus, but that was necessary."

"A mercy, almost."

"Yeah. And soon as he was pulled off his machinery, NORAD got back control of its nukes, and so did all the world's other missile commands – Russia, France, and so on. Big whoop all round when his firewalls suddenly went down. 'Hooray, we can blow up the planet again, if we want to.'"

"Only, we won't, will we?" Sam said. "We're grown-up enough as a race, aren't we? We can manage things for ourselves. We certainly don't need self-styled gods lording it over us, telling us how to behave and treating us like infants. We're capable of making sure humankind carries on and prospers. Aren't we?"

"Hell if I know," said Ramsay. He jerked a thumb at the L-Day celebrants. "But maybe that's what all this is in aid of, and why it should carry on year after year, even become an official event. Long as people remember what they were liberated from, they'll do their best to enjoy the freedom and make sure it continues. We've been slaves a while. Freed slaves tend to treasure what they've gained."

A soft burble from the stroller was followed by the sound of small limbs furiously shifting.

"Ah," said Sam. "Nap time's over."

She unfastened straps and hauled a pudgy, clammy eighteen-month-old out of the stroller and onto her lap.

William Dai Ramsay rolled a sleepy eye at his mother, and then at his father. His light-brown face set into a grumpy pout, and he nuzzled against Sam's breast with a sigh that sounded far too heartfelt and careworn for one so young. He'd been named after his paternal grandfather. Sam had lobbied to have Dai as his first name, but Ramsay had vetoed this. "Sounds too morbid," he'd said. So William it was, Will for short.

Ramsay stroked his son's head, with just a hint of wistfulness, briefly recollecting another small boy, another head of dark nappy curls like this one.

"You wake up in your own sweet time, kiddo," he said, and kissed Will's crown.

In response, Will just snuffled, and Sam hugged him close, feeling the heat radiating off him and inhaling the mix of milk and sweat that was his unique, heady musk.

Will.

Her Will.

Will, Will, Will.

What more fitting name to give to the future?

Acknowledgements

Profuse thanks are due to: Gary Main and Johnny Reade, for technical advice relating to, respectively, military helicopters and riot policing; the fine folks at "new" Solaris, principally Jonathan Oliver, David Moore, Jennifer-Anne Hill and Ben Smith; Marek Okon for another awesome cover; and Eric Brown, Liz de Jager, Ron Fortgang, Tim Mitchell and Andy Remic for continued support and encouragement.

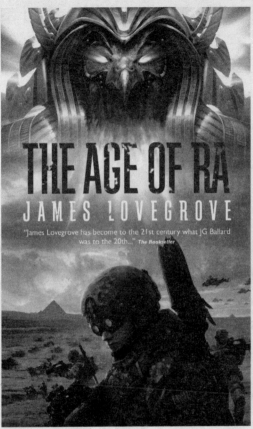

UK ISBN: 978 1 844167 46 3 • US ISBN: 978 1 844167 47 0 • £7.99/$7.99

The Ancient Egyptian gods have defeated all the other pantheons and divided the Earth into warring factions. Lt. David Westwynter, a British soldier, stumbles into Freegypt, the only place to have remained independent of the gods, and encounters the followers of a humanist freedom-fighter known as the Lightbringer. As the world heads towards an apocalyptic battle, there is far more to this leader than it seems...

 WWW.SOLARISBOOKS.COM

Follow us on Twitter! www.twitter.com/solarisbooks

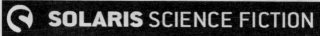

A COMBAT-K NOVEL

ANDY REMIC

The new master of rock-hard military science fiction

WAR MACHINE

ISBN: 978-1-84416-522-3

Ex-soldier Keenan, a private investigator with a bad reputation, is about to take on the biggest case of his career, To have any chance of success, however, he must head to a dangerous colony world and re-assemble his old military unit, a group who swore they'd never work together again...

 SOLARIS SCIENCE FICTION

A COMBAT-K NOVEL
ANDY REMIC
HARDCORE

UK ISBN: 978 1 844167 93 7 • US ISBN: 978 1 844167 92 0 • £7.99/$7.99

Charged with finding the evil Junk's homeland and annihilating them, Combat-K head
to Sick World, a long-abandoned hospital planet once dedicated to curing the deformed,
the insane, the dying and the dead. The Medical Staff of Sick World - the doctors, nurses,
patients and deviants, abandoned with extreme prejudice, a thousand-year gestation
of hardcore medical mutation - and their hibernation, and they can smell fresh meat...

 WWW.SOLARISBOOKS.COM

Follow us on Twitter! www.twitter.com/solarisbooks